monsoonbooks

OPERATION BLIND SI

T0169093

Lt. Col. JP Cross is a retired British officer who served with Gurkha units for nearly forty years. He has been an Indian frontier soldier, jungle fighter, policeman, military attaché, Gurkha recruitment officer and a linguist researcher, and he is the author of nineteen books. He has fought in Burma, Indo-China, Malaya and Borneo and served in India, Pakistan, Hong Kong, Laos and Nepal where he now lives. Well into his nineties, he still walks four hours daily.

Operation Blind Spot is the second book in a trilogy of historical military novels set in Southeast Asia, which may be read in any order. *Operation Blind Spot* and *Operation Janus* involve Gurkha military units, and the author draws on real events he witnessed and real people he fought alongside, or against, during the Malayan Emergency and the Borneo Confrontation. *Operation Four Rings* starts in the British Army's Jungle Warfare School in Malaysia and comes to its dramatic conclusion in Laos.

'Nobody in the world is better qualified to tell this story of the Gurkhas' deadly jungle battles against Communist insurgency in Malaya in the 1950s. Cross spins his tale with the eye of incomparable experience.'

John le Carré, on *Operation Janus*

'... a gripping adventure story ...
learn the ins and outs of jungle warfare from a true expert'

The Oldie, on *Operation Janus*

OPERATION BLIND SPOT

JP CROSS

monsoon

monsoonbooks

Published in 2018
by Monsoon Books Ltd
www.monsoonbooks.co.uk

No.1 Duke of Windsor Suite, Burrough Court,
Burrough on the Hill, Leicestershire LE14 2QS, UK

ISBN (paperback): 9781912049325
ISBN (ebook): 9781912049332

Cover design by Cover Kitchen.

A Cataloguing-in-Publication data record is available from the British
Library.

Printed and bound in Great Britain by Clays Ltd, Elcograf S.p.A.
20 19 18   1 2 3 4 5

This book is especially dedicated to those who crossed the Malay-Thai and Sarawak-Kalimantan borders with me: thank you and may your souls be resting in peace.

List of Characters

Nasution, Abdul Haris, General, Indonesian Army

Rahman, Abdul, Tenku, Prime Minister of Malaya

Sheikh Azahari, Brunei politician and rebel

Sukarno, President of Indonesia

Tek Miu, guerrilla working with Malayan aborigines

Too, Chee Chew, a.k.a. C C Too, Special Branch, Malayan Police

Yasin Effendi, Commander, North Kalimantan Liberation Army.

To protect some people's integrity, they have been given fictitious names:

Ah Fat, Chinese boy in pre-war Kuala Lumpur and later 'guerrilla'

Ali Wiranto, Indonesian nickname of Kesar Pun, q.v.

Alif, nickname of Soetidjab Alaydris, q.v.

*Chakrabahadur Rai, Sergeant, 1/12 Gurkha Rifles

Fordyce, Jim, British intelligence representative

George Ningkan, probationary police officer

Gloop, Edward, Brigadier, Commander Central Brigade, Sarawak

Hassan Soekadis, Indonesian guerrilla

*Hemraj Rai, Rifleman, 1/12 Gurkha Rifles

Hung Lo, 'Bear', nickname of Wang Ming, q.v.

Jenko, Lao-speaking Thai Isan guerrilla

Jiang Yun, Communist 'sleeper' in Kuching

Kamhaeng Thanaboon, Thai alias of Manbahadur Limbu, q.v.

Kesar Pun, aka Ali Wiranto, ex-2/1 GR soldier, escort to Aidit, q.v.

King, David, Commissioner of Police, Sarawak Constabulary

*Kulbahadur Limbu, Sergeant, 1/12 Gurkha Rifles

Lalman Limbu, Sergeant, 1/12 Gurkha Rifles

*Manbahadur Limbu, ex-1/7 GR soldier, a.k.a. Kamhaeng

Thanaboon, q.v.

*Minbahadur Gurung, Sergeant, 1/12 Gurkha Rifles

Mulia, Major General, GOC Military District XII at Pontianak, West Kalimantan

Pang Hau, 'Hare Lip'/'Broken Face', Communist agent

P'ing Yee, 'Flat Ears', nickname of Ah Fat, q.v.

Rance, Jason Percival Vere, Major, 1/12 Gurkha Rifles

Rutherford, Don, Head of Special Branch, Sarawak Constabulary, Kuching

Sim Ting Ong, Secretary General of the Sarawak United People's Party

Shandung P'aau, 'Shandung Cannon', nickname of Major Rance, q.v.

Sodimedjo, Intelligence Colonel, Indonesian Army

Soetidjab Alaydris, Indonesian guerrilla

Souk Vongvachit, Lao police officer

Sprinter, Walter, Major General, Director of Borneo Operations

Townsend, Peter, Brigadier, Commander West Brigade, Sarawak

Wang Ming, one-time guerrilla now 'mole' for Malayan Special Branch

West, Sir Lucas, General, Commander-in-Chief, Far East Land Forces

Zai, nickname of Hassan Soekadis, q.v.

Zhong Han San, leader of Killer Squad in south Thailand

*Gurkha names often use the 'é' ending instead of 'bahadur' or 'raj', especially when talking, such as Kulé for Kulbahadur and Hemé for Hemraj.

Abbreviations

2IC	Second-in-Command
ADC	aide de camp, personal staff officer to a senior officer
casevac	casualty evacuation
C-in-C	Commander-in-Chief, a 4-star appointment
CO	Commanding Officer (Lieutenant Colonel)
CQMS	Company Quarter Master Sergeant
CT	Communist Terrorist/s
DA	Defence Adviser, Commonwealth country, otherwise Defence Attaché
DCM	Distinguished Conduct Medal
DOBOPS	Director of Borneo Operations
GHQ	General Headquarters
GM	George Medal
GOC	General Officer Commanding, a 2-Star appointment
GR	Gurkha Rifles
HQ	headquarters
ID	identification, in ID card
IO	Intelligence Officer
Int	Intelligence
JCLO	Junior Civil Liaison Officer
MA	Military Assistant
MCP	Malayan Communist Party
MGBG	Major General, Brigade of Gurkhas

NCO	non-commissioned officer
NTR	nothing to report
OBE	Order of the British Empire
OC	Officer Commanding (Major)
'O' Group	Orders Group, those needed to receive tactical orders
QGO	Queen's Gurkha Officer
PKI	Partai Komunis Indonesia, Communist Party of Indonesia
RNAC	Royal Nepal Airlines Corporation
RPKAD	Regimen Pasukan Komando Angatan Darat, Indonesian Army Para-Commando Regiment
RV	rendezvous, term used for designated positions to 'close on'
sitrep	situation report
SEATO	Southeast Asian Treaty Organisation
SUPP	Sarawak United People's Party

Radio Jargon

key	using Morse code
Roger	'message received'
Sunray	senior officer
Wilco	'will comply with message'

Glossary

CHINESE

'Ch'uan jia chan'	'May your entire clan be wiped out': an ancient curse
doh mai nok gwat pai lei lun	domino (bone slab) theory ('bone slabs' are the actual pieces)
Goo K'a	Gurkha
gwai lo	foreigner, 'devil person'
ham sap kwai	salty-wet devil, randy
kongsi	a communal labourers' dwelling
maang dim	blind spot
pang hau	hair lip, literally 'broken face'
sei gok	a military blind spot, literally 'dead angle'
sinsaang	sir, literally 'elder born',
t'o yan	aborigine
yam sing	'drink to victory' (not, as often wrongly thought, 'bottoms up')

INDONESIAN

Konfrontasi	Confrontation, the name of a political and military action against the formation of Malaysia

MALAY

Enche	term of respect
gunong	mountain
jalan	road
KL	Kuala Lumpur
kongsi	logging camp
ladang	aboriginal settlement
orang asli	'original' men, aborigines
parang	chopper, cleaver
perak	silver
ringgit	Malay dollar
salamat jalan	good-bye
sungei	river
titek buta	blind spot (also 'blind drop')
Tuan	term of respect
ulu	headwaters of a river, colloquially 'jungle'
upas	poisonous tree, Antiaris toxicania.

NEPALI

Cheena	Chinese
daku	guerilla, (literally dacoit)
keta	lad
hajur	term of respect, inert conversational response (literally presence)
hunchha	is, okay
gora	'fair-skinned'

Major-ba	one way of addressing a Gurkha Sergeant Major
jyu	polite suffix
rajdut	ambassador
Sarkar	word of address to member of royalty of Nepal, government
ustad	non-commissioned officer, instructor

TEMIAR

senoi	man
tata	old, term of respect
tongoq	headman

THAI

baht	Thai currency
farang	European, lit French
isan	northeast
krab	suffix used when a man talks, no equivalent English rendering
wai	ceremonial greeting, two hands joined in front of body

Maps

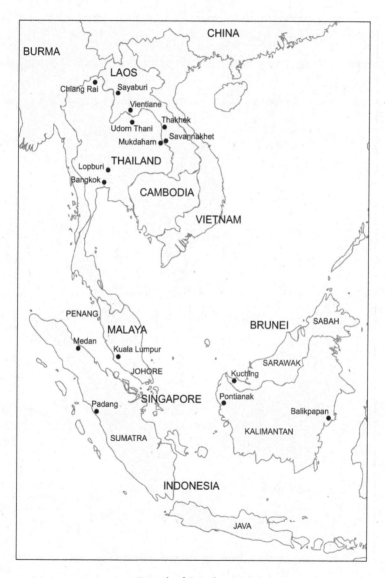

Detail of Southeast Asia

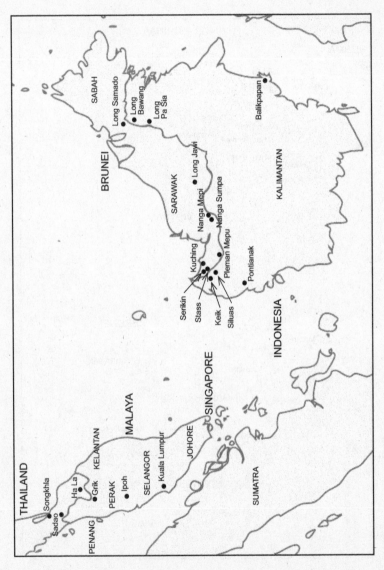

Detail of southern Thailand, Malaya, Brunei and Kalimantan

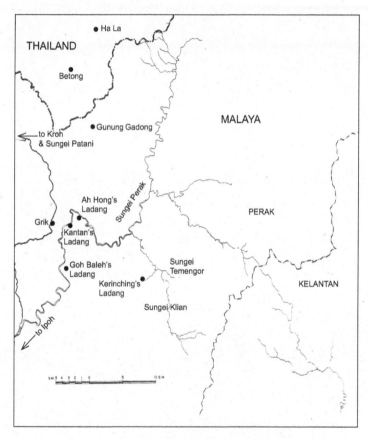

Detail of Operation Bamboo

PART ONE

1

Dawn was just breaking when the ghastly spine-chilling shriek of near-animal anguish reached the two sentries guarding the outer fringes of the jungle camp. One of the sentries, Kamhaeng Thanaboon, turned to the other, Jenko, who was lying behind a tree a few yards off, and said, 'That must be Zhong with the kid who was brought in yesterday. Sadists like Zhong shouldn't be allowed.'

'He's a pervert all right. We'll find out more when our relief comes. Can't be long now.'

A few minutes later they heard footsteps approaching from the direction of the camp and the two sentries, only temporary inmates of the camp, cowered behind their leafy cover.

Three people, a comrade escorting a young Thai girl and a young Chinese boy, both walking slowly and in obvious pain, came into view. They moved beyond the sentries to a clump of bull rushes where the escort told them that his boss would soon hear if either spoke about what had happened in the camp during the night. The comrade strode back, not bothering about the two sentries.

'Nasty,' said one of the sentries when all was quiet again.

'Since our people left us in this camp, I've been bored to tears. Still, I'm glad we don't have to witness that kind of grotesqueness too often.'

'I'm always bored here,' said the other. 'Except for those two or three times we were sent south to the border. It took us four days to get there, remember?'

How can I forget? The name of the village was Ha La, mused Kamhaeng Thanaboon. *When I was a boy I had a puppy with that name and my younger brother used to call me Hala too.* He could never have imagined that his puppy's name and his own nickname could one day instil so much fear into what remained of the MCP Politburo that it would put his life in grave jeopardy. *As a young lad my brother was an excellent tracker, any game, any spoor. I wonder where he is now. He was too young to have served in the war.* He came to with a jolt: 'Yes, of course I remember it well. Ha La. We spent nights in the camp where the leader was, um, Ah Soo Chye, I think.'

'You'd better call him "Comrade Ah Soo Chye" when you speak of him in front of the hierarchy, you know how fussy they are about protocol. He is the leader of the group that keeps an eye on those "junglies" south of the border. I forget the names of his two senior men but one was said to be moon-struck.' He giggled. 'But full moon or new moon, I forget which.'

Jenko looked round, just in case they could be overheard. 'If we hadn't both been taken ill when we last came here with our people we'd have been away long ago. We'll have to wait until our lot comes back. We'd never be allowed to try and go back alone.' A wistful look came over his face and his brow creased. 'Once our lot comes back and takes us away, let's make a real job of it and try and disappear from them once and for all. Go back and be normal people for a change.'

Jenko and Kamhaeng Thanaboon were guerillas of the Thai Communist Party.

Hidden in the jungle not all that far north of the Thai-Malay border, near a village named Sadao, was the camp that held the Politburo of the Malayan Communist Party (MCP) and the defeated remnants of its military wing, the Malayan Races Liberation Army (MRLA). It was under the auspices of Chin Peng, the Secretary General of the MCP, who had developed a nodding acquaintance with morality but preferred to keep it at arm's length. He was more of a thinker than a doer, deliberately isolating himself from any strong-arm work considered necessary by the leader of his Killer Squad, one Zhong Han San, and his ten-man group of sadists.

By 1959 the eleven-year-long Malayan Emergency, a civil war fought between the minority Chinese Communist guerrillas and the rest of the population – Malays, Chinese, Indians, Eurasians and a few British expatriates – was, to all intents and purposes, over. Only the timorous, almost stone-age, jungle inhabitants in the farthest northern reaches of the country with a culture pattern only properly known to themselves ever met the rump of the guerrillas who tried to cultivate their affection and loyalty. Farther south were Proto-Malays but the biggest group near the border were known as Temiar.

The 'Emergency' had only been a war of serious intensity –

close fought and outcome uncertain – from 1948 to 1951. Since then it had been a war of 'cat and mouse', infinite patience and relentless endeavour, stamina and cunning, craft and stealth, a monstrous game of fatal 'hide and seek' and, without instantaneous reflexes, death.

Even though Malaya was now self-governing there was still a large British and Commonwealth military presence in the country. Had it not been for massive British and Gurkha effort, supplemented by units from Australia, New Zealand, Fiji and Nigeria, the Malayan forces, military and police, would have been totally swamped with far too few troops to cope nor any intrinsic air or naval forces for support. The country would almost certainly have become a Communist state. Instead of which the MCP, with the rump of its military arm, was hiding in south Thailand, mentally licking their wounds after an ill-chosen fight, unable to keep its base on Malayan territory any longer. It was the only time in the history of Communist expansion that Communism had been beaten in a territory of its own choosing.

If anything, the struggle had been just as much, if not more, of an 'Int', Intelligence, endeavour than a fighting war, despite so much 'ulu bashing' as jungle operations were known. These had tested the military skills, stamina and patience of both sides to extreme limits and had involved many brave actions, some of which had made headlines with Security Forces being awarded medals for bravery. At the start of Emergency operations Intelligence work, which seldom, if ever, had any publicity or public rewards, was almost non-existent because Special Branch became virtually moribund during the Japanese occupation. Slowly and painstakingly it became a working entity once more, fostered by dedicated anti-Communist Straits Chinese and equally dedicated Chinese-speaking British officers. The 'hearts and minds' concept was seen as a vital ingredient and, coupled with the-carrot-and-stick philosophy of gradually making the peninsula into 'white areas' where there were no restrictions on movement and food supplies, had overwhelmingly turned the tide in the government's favour; unlike in Vietnam where some Americans had it that 'pull them along by their balls and the hearts and minds will follow' so making the situation there entirely different.

By 1961, Chin Peng had realised that armed guerrilla activity was no longer useful as it could not achieve his aim of a Communist Malaya. With fewer than a hundred men under his direct command and a handful farther south near the border at Ha La, he still resolutely refused to give up or change his philosophy. He was trying to go to China and the camp was his base until permission was granted. Fighting had come to an end ... almost. 'Almost', because a residual armed Communist guerrilla presence was still maintained, albeit fitfully, in the far north of Malaya in the area only populated by fewer than a thousand peace-loving Temiar, however forlorn the Communist hope that they would be the 'springboard' for any further activity southwards once more, such a hope existed. The military counter to eradicate the last remaining guerrillas was designated Operation Bamboo.

In mid-1959, after fighting Chinese guerrillas in Malaya since 1948, 1/12 Gurkha Rifles was posted to Hong Kong for a two-year spell where, apart from obligatory duties – Force Guards,

Border Protection, Community Relations activities and Aid to the Civil Power when the Police requested it – modern warfare could be practised from section up to brigade level. Classification on the range on the Bren light-machine gun and rifle was also an imperative as were, at long last, games and athletic competitions. It was certainly the first time since 1942 that any of the Gurkha soldiers had permanent accommodation to live in.

Major Jason Rance of that battalion, having put his company through all the necessary range practices, was in his company office catching up with routine paperwork when the CO's 'Stick Orderly' – the smartest man of the day's Quarter Guard – unexpectedly came to the door and, standing rigidly to attention with his stick under his left arm, gave a cracking salute. 'Major sahib, the Commanding sahib sends his salaams. He wants you to speak with him, now, in his office.'

Why, I wonder? Jason had a slight tinge of apprehension, rubbing the back of his wrist across his mouth. ... *but at least I have a clear military conscience ... unless ... was it that baton-changing practice?* So, with a '*Hunchha, keta*' – Right-ho, lad – the pair of them set off for Battalion HQ.

Jason Rance had an unusual background: an only child, his early boyhood years had been spent in Kuala Lumpur where his father had worked in the 'need-to-know' business. Ah Fat, the only son of his father's closest Chinese agent, became like a brother to him who, like his father, had become bilingual in Chinese as well as having a good working knowledge of Malay. He was also an excellent Nepali speaker, having served with his Gurkhas for eighteen years, initially with 1/1 GR of the Indian

Army in Burma and after the war in Cochin-China to disarm the beaten Japanese and operate against the Vietminh. It was then that he had learnt basic Vietnamese. That was some sixteen years in the past *but if I hear it again I expect it'd come back.*

In December 1947 he had transferred to 1/12 GR of the British Army, gone to Malaya and, taking part in the decade-long Malayan Emergency, had become an expert in the type of jungle operations that Counter Communist Revolutionary Warfare required, namely to be able to operate against an enemy at the level of 'active' guerrilla warfare. That entailed knowing how to live, move and operate in tropical rain forest terrain and become skilled in attacking Communist camps, tracking, ambushing, patrolling, river crossing and the other aspects of jungle movement that such work demanded – and always to be ready for that split-second contact – you or them. The greatest feather in his cap had been about eight years previously when he had managed to prevent a renegade brother officer of dubious provenance from joining the Chinese guerrillas. It was during that period that he had once more met up with his childhood friend, Ah Fat, under dramatic circumstances.

A bachelor, rising forty and still remarkably fit for his age, he radiated health and self-assurance. He was six feet tall and just over ten stone, with fair hair, a resolute face and clear blue eyes that had the ability to penetrate and probe into another's. His gaze was steady and non-committal until provoked, which was not often. The breadth of his shoulders, the long muscular neck and the convex lines of chest were evidence of a body honed to physical precision and strength. He was slender but not thin, his was the tautness that comes with discipline, training and a fully active life. Crosshatching of fine wrinkles at the corner of his eye sockets bespoke both time spent in the Asian sun and approaching middle age.

The regiment, to Jason, was his mother and father and his bit of God, even if His ways were sometimes imponderable. To his superiors, his military knowledge, although far above the average for practical, operational work, was too restricted when it came to staff matters, so essential for a 'balanced military career'. He had already sat for, and failed, the dreaded Staff College Entrance Examination so squandering any normal chance for promotion to lieutenant colonel. So 'that was that' and his soldiering seemed likely to be regimental until he was too old for it.

'Go straight in,' said the Adjutant, not bothering to look up from his paperwork, so Jason knocked on the CO's door.

'Come in.'

He stepped smartly to in front of the CO's table and gave a punctilious salute. 'Sir, you sent for me,' he said, standing to attention.

'Yes, I did,' his CO answered a touch brusquely, pinching his nose like a swimmer coming out of the water as he put the file he was working on to one side. 'I'm going to put my cards on the table, Jason, and come straight to the point, so listen to me carefully. I want to be honest with you.' He paused, as if for emphasis.

Jason flushed slightly, which was unusual for him. *As if honesty was the last thing to expect from one's Commanding Officer.*

'Although you are an "all-weather" operational soldier,' the CO continued, unconsciously crossing his legs under the table, 'you're a bit of a military maverick, don't you know. You seem to find peacetime soldiering mildly claustrophobic.' Lame laugh. 'One example: recently when on Force Guards you were invited into the Governor's box for the races at Sha Tin, the equivalent of a Royal Command. You didn't go. On the following Monday, at Guard Mounting at his residence, the Governor asked you why not; apparently your answer was because you were practising baton changing with your company for the sports. At least that's how it came back to me. Correct?' plucking earnestly at his brow with his long fingers as he did.

So that was why I had that twinge! 'Correct, sir,' eyes narrowing at the corners making incipient crows' feet slightly deeper.

'Not the best way to become popular with authority! You excel in what interests you operationally, on training and linguistically: you are excellent with the men, all of which I fully realise. What you're not all that interested in you seem to ignore.' The CO, hands palms upwards on the table, as though he was reading Jason's fortune, asked, 'Right or wrong?'

'Sir, put that way, I can't argue with you,' said flatly.

'Although you have an exceptional sense of rapport with Asians, it seems to me that your military elastic is pretty well stretched. You are meticulous and articulate, conscientious and savvy but, at times your ribald wit is misplaced. In short, you are not all that tactful with Europeans.' The CO looked down at a file on his desk, unhygienically putting his pencil in his mouth as he turned the pages. 'I'm going to say something that will sound strange, Jason. Somewhere along the line you missed the chance to be ordinary ...' The CO's pursed lips reminded Jason of the coin slot in a telephone booth.

Jason gave a little inward sigh. *Speaking languages and laughing with the men must look different to those who can do neither.*

'... and "both the army and the Royal Academy require docility in their children and originality has to be stereotyped", as I've heard it neatly put,' said the Colonel, his eyes leaving the file and looking up at Jason.

The blighter's copying what I thought I'd once said as a joke! but Jason merely looked straight into the older man's eyes without a retort. None was needed.

'So, another example of not being tactful with Europeans,' continued the Colonel. 'I remember hearing what you said to your Grade 1 Staff Officer when you were still a captain doing a staff attachment as a Grade 3. Apparently he complained, one lunchtime, to another Grade 1 officer that you had sent him a draft that he simply could not understand and your unasked-for retort was that however hard you tried you could not write words of less than one syllable. You're a hard case, Rance, insufficiently manipulative for tact, as I've heard it put. Correct again?' he gratuitously asked, uncrossing his legs as though his crotch was nipping him.

Jason frowned. *Fancy that having gone the rounds.* 'Correct again, sir.' *Don't argue. Ride it out.*

'I have been reading up what you managed to do in what

never became public but is still known as Operation Janus in limited circles. Few, if any other British officer could have done as you did. That was about nine years ago and you are still in your "military Eden" shall we call it and still munching the regimental apple but you're living on borrowed time at your age. You have missed the chance of going through the gateway to senior rank and a nice desk.' The CO had been brought up in the belief that a military career was unfulfilled unless an officer had been to the Staff College. 'Because the army does have a use for mavericks like you,' the CO continued with a twist of his lip and eyebrow raised indicating approval, 'you could still, just, qualify for promotion to lieutenant colonel. But the Brit Mil Machine only promotes beyond major if it can see three, not one, not two, but three jobs in that rank that you can be suitably judged to do by the relevant promotion board.' A delicate pause. 'So, with Staff College out of the window, from now on your options are strictly limited. A few, just a few, majors qualify for promotion by becoming "Staff Qualified – s.q." As your future is as fathomless as it ever has been or probably ever will be I'm about to give you that chance, your one and only and very last, by sending you on a six-month staff tour to Bangkok ...'

He gave Jason a swift, reproachful glance in response to an over-loud intake of breath.

'... as the British Army's Grade 2 Staff representative to SEATO, that's the South East Asia Treaty Organisation as you well know, which is planning a large-scale paper-cum-skeleton-troop exercise. Not all its eight members will be taking part: France, Pakistan, Australia and New Zealand have said that they will send observers but UK, USA, the Philippines and Thailand will be fully involved. So far so good?'

'So far, so more than good, sir,' replied Jason with a smile that widened into a broad grin. 'Have you any idea as to how I'll fit in?'

'I was coming to that: as far as I can tell you'll be the leg man to help decide where Red Land or, if people are aiming nearer, Yellow Land, will be the most active and for the logistical planning needed to counter the threat. Once you are there you will get your full orders. The reason for the exercise being planned is because the Americans have become even more fixated than ever before with what they call the Domino Theory, where one country goes Communist, then its neighbour will too and so on. I'll give you a bit of background: I was the Assistant Military Attaché in Washington and was invited to President Eisenhower's press conference on 7 April 1951 when he publicly enunciated that Laos was the most pressing foreign policy issue in the world. And now I am surmising that, as a result of the findings of this exercise, secret US training teams may well increase, if they have not started already, making Laos a buttress against it being a domino.'

'Yes, sir, I've read about the theory but hadn't realised it was about five years old.' *We in the West seem to have become so wet in not answering the call in Vietnam you could shoot snipe off us*, he said to himself.

'That is all I have for you, except to say try and understand the way the staffs of allied armies work as it will help you get a good report and, if so, you could become s.q. Enjoy yourself and make good use of your time. The Adjutant has your movement details.'

Jason saluted, made a smart right turn and marched out.

The CO could have had no idea that by detailing Jason for this temporary attachment not only Jason's future would be irrevocably changed.

The camp where the Secretary General of the MCP lived with his Defence Group and Killer Squad was well hidden on a small knoll in a narrow valley in a bowl of hills and was cunningly camouflaged. It was never really in any danger as similar camps had been in Malaya. In the early nineteenth century, the southern tip of Thailand, the Betong Salient, had been part of Malaya and the many Malays still there would have preferred not to have become part of Thailand. Unhappy under the Thai government, they were confrontational enough virtually to rule their own roost and the local Chinese kept to themselves, ruling theirs. The Thai police there were weak and only had two Chinese speakers. The Thai government's writ was shaky and ineffectual so far south. The authorities seldom interfered and, anyway, the local police were paid not to by the guerrillas. Being five hundred miles from Bangkok, out of sight was out of mind.

A few weeks before Major Rance's surprise posting order was announced, the Secretary General was given an important letter that had taken months to reach him. It was from the General Secretary of the Indonesian Communist Party (PKI), one Dipa Nusantara Aidit, who had written, in veiled speech, that he dared not correspond in depth with Chin Peng in any other way but by word of mouth so important, despite being risky, was the matter to be discussed. A date was given. He would bring three others with him. It was written in Malay: except for some different spellings basic Malay and Indonesian were almost similar. Chin Peng ordered one of his most trusted aides, Ah Fat, to go to Penang, fix hotel accommodation, meet Aidit and his men at the airport, arrange double-entry tourist visas then escort them to the camp.

During the Emergency Ah Fat had acted as the Military Consultant and non-voting member of the MCP's Central Committee. He was still highly regarded by the Secretary General although, by now, he had much less work to do in that the Emergency was over. He was a good-looking man, attractive to the ladies, well built and solid, with fluid movements. His eyes were always alert, never missing a trick, even though his peripheral gaze was not easy to follow. He looked a tad glum and not all that intelligent, a saving grace, but he was, in fact, razor-blade sharp. He had a habit of rubbing the palms of his hands together when thinking. His ears, close to his head, had, in some circles, given him the nickname of P'ing Yee, Flat Ears. Normally taciturn, he could turn on the charm when needed. Well educated, he spoke excellent English. However, for safety's sake, he kept that skill a closely guarded secret lest his other, real, role be jeopardised. Whenever he did speak English in front of other Chinese, it was only of middle-school standard. With him as escort was a grizzled, short, almost square and powerfully built man, Wang Ming, trustworthy, stolid but slow-thinking. He looked like a bear and his nickname was Hung Lo, Bear. Both men were in fact working for the Malayan Special Branch under deep cover; Ah Fat since the Japanese had occupied Malaya in 1942. Wang Ming, a one-time Military Commander of a guerrilla unit from 1942, had been persuaded by none other than Captain Jason Rance himself to change sides in 1951.

Chin Peng had no idea of Ah Fat being a long-term mole of quite exceptional ability but had used him in what he thought was a 'one-way' double agent and indeed, from time to time, Ah Fat had been able to feed the MCP with tidbits of information that the Malayan Special Branch felt would do no harm. Since 1955 there had been an agreement for some members of the Malayan Police to travel twenty miles into Thailand. Both P'ing Yee and Hung Lo had managed to procure a signed and stamped permit for this so there was no difficulty in their crossing the border at will. All others needed visas which were strictly scrutinised as the area was under the jurisdiction of the Thai Border Police as it was 'sensitive'. Weapons would be fired at any suspicious person. If not, the Killer Squad would want to know why.

A week or so before Aidit's arrival Ah Fat said he'd better leave and arrange for his reception in Penang. Once back in Malaya the two men changed their *persona* and made straight for Kuala Lumpur where they met with Mr C C Too, one of the finest men to work for the government on Chinese guerrilla mentality, and fully briefed him on what was unfolding. 'I'll have a few people to keep watch and ward, Ah Fat,' said Mr Too. 'Even if you were to recognise them they won't blink an eyelid in your direction. Likewise, Aidit will be travelling on *bone fide* documents so, unless he breaks our law, we cannot touch him.

The PKI is not banned here.'

'Indeed so,' replied Ah Fat. 'I'll play my usual role but that should present no difficulty. Once it's over, I'll come back and give you all the details. Not often we get a scoop like this.'

Mr Too opened the top drawer of his desk. 'Here, take these,' he said, giving him a mini tape recorder, several reels and spare batteries. 'Used properly they'll be a goldmine for us.' He called a clerk to bring the file with Aidit's details and Ah Fat read it. Aidit was a year older than Chin Peng, at thirty-six years of age, and his photo showed him to be taller and more handsome than most men of his country, open-faced, clean-shaven with larger than normal nostrils.

It was indeed a gamble as to whether such a high-ranking official should leave the country but Aidit's task was considered of such importance that it was decided he had to go. He took with him three bodyguards. One was a short, squat, swarthy man who had a scar on the right of his nose, a 'hatchet' man from Java, the second, with the sulky and epicene face of a pervert, was originally from Sumatra and the third who looked like an Iban from Borneo. He was, however, so unusual that nobody would believe it, a Gurkha of 2/1 GR, who, when a prisoner of war in Singapore, had been taken by the Japanese to Sumatra with a dozen more Gurkhas, as coolies. Because of poor conditions all, except this one man, had died. He had become so ill he did almost die but had been looked after by this same Aidit. As there were no chances of getting back to Nepal, he had stayed with him, pretending absolute loyalty so working his way up the ladder of 'helpers' until he was trusted enough to be taken to Thailand as

Aidit's personal bodyguard.

The Indonesians already had Malayan visas and, at the airport, Aidit told Immigration that they were in the tourist trade and wanted to scour the town for tips. 'Now that Malaya is once more peaceful and Indonesia needs to learn from people who know the trade, we see Penang as a good place to start.' Once outside Ah Fat and Wang Ming introduced themselves and escorted them to their hotel. A couple of days later the five of them travelled north and crossed the border openly, having got a month's tourist visa from the Thai consul in Penang. After that it had been simple to 'go sight-seeing' and disappearing from public view, finishing up at Chin Peng's camp.

Comrades Ah Fat and Wang Ming brought Comrade Aidit and his escort late one afternoon where Comrade Chin Peng greeted their guests at a welcoming arch, with a limply hanging red flag and a hastily stitched Indonesian one. While still under the arch he introduced his politburo to them, though Comrade Aidit did not register most of them. He was not a Chinese speaker.

Customary courtesies and refreshments were the first day's staple, serious talk only starting the next day. Ah Fat, after being extolled as the one safe link between Sadao and Malaya, was detailed to make notes of the two leaders' conversation. In essence, what it boiled down to was that Aidit wanted Chin Peng's help for some of his potential guerrillas to go to China for training as he had heard strong rumours that Chin Peng was planning to move there. 'As you will know,' Aidit explained, 'I went to China soon after the end of the civil war and contacted several high-ranking people. However, that was long enough ago for much change to have taken place. Your intended but yet-to-be sanctioned visit there makes my visit here even more of an unexpected bonus than had seemed possible at first.' He sat back in his chair and regarded Chin Peng intently.

They discussed how to set about such a project, the Secretary General of the MCP saying it would take at least two years before anything concrete could eventuate. 'No matter,' said Aidit, 'I can't see us needing to use such training and expertise until, say, 1963 at the earliest. What I really want is to leave two of my three men back here with you for training, even up to two years. In fact they can go back to Indonesia without any trouble as they have passports valid for a few years yet. The two I'd like you to train are nicknamed Alif and Zai, A and Z – come here you two,' he called out to them – 'and, if possible, I'd like them to be part of your Defence Group and Killer Squad under Comrade Zhong Han San, I think you said his name was.'

'Comrade,' countered Chin Peng, with an airy wave of his hand, 'that will be a pleasure. May I tell you sincerely that your visit here is of more use to me than you could have realised. Once I have gone to China I don't want to waste the experience of my guerrilla soldiers sitting here doing nothing. As you seem keen on provoking trouble in your part of the world, it would be good to get some of my guerrillas over to your country, Sumatra, Java, Borneo and even, possibly, to Brunei, currently British territory, to help you and it has been worrying me how best to manage it. I'd like to hurt the British where and when they won't be expecting it. And you,' with a triumphant ring to his voice, 'are my answer.' A relaxed smile of triumph spread over his face.

'Yes, I'd like that,' answered Aidit gravely and outline details were made during which Zhong was called over. 'Have you any relations anywhere in Borneo?' he was asked. 'If so, we'd like to use them in our Cause.'

'Strange that you should ask that, Comrade, a cadet branch of the family went to Borneo instead of coming here. I am their third uncle. When I last heard of them they were ardent members of the Sarawak United People's Party and that my fifth niece is a dedicated worker. Once you are back in Indonesia you could contact them and try to arrange for various members to become "sleepers" in the police or administration. That would be a *maang dim* as far as the colonialists were concerned.'

'*Maang dim?*' queried the Indonesian Communist Party Secretary General. 'Sorry, I don't speak Chinese.'

'My mistake, I should have said *bintik buta,* blind spot,' Zhong apologised.

Aidit thought that over. 'Yes, I like that idea, most satisfactory indeed,' he said and told Alif to make a note of it. The other two men of the escort also listened in. The talk went on to other matters.

Ah Fat, who had surreptitiously made sure he had captured all talk on tape, rubbed his hands together and asked if he could pose a question. 'But of course.' 'What about the military presence we have below the border. You have your three stalwarts, Ah Soo Chye, Tek Miu and Lo See, who are responsible for conducting holding operations in the north Malayan jungle and keeping the Temiar communities there "sweet" on our side, not on the Malayan government's. Your three probably won't want to go to

China or Indonesia and the *Orang Asli*' (he used the Malay term for 'primitive men', not the Chinese phrase, *t'o yan*, 'people of the soil') 'have learnt to trust them implicitly while hating and fearing the Malays. You know that the Malays look down on them. Keep these three leaders at their job of routine checking on the ladangs' – the Malay name for the collection of bamboo-made shacks where such people lived – 'and you have them as a potential spearhead for movement farther south if circumstances for such a move were suitably engendered.'

That struck both Chin Peng and Aidit as sound. Ah Fat's poker face in no way showed that he had his own ideas for dealing with a continuing guerrilla presence in the otherwise uninhabited jungle areas.

On the third day of their meeting, nearly at the end of their agenda, the camp sentry alerted them. An unexpected patrol of Thai Communist guerrillas from far-off Bangkok was asking for permission to enter and see Comrade Chin Peng as they had an important message to deliver.

'Recognise them properly and bring them in, at the same time alerting internal camp sentries' was the order. 'Comrade Aidit. You and your three men stay in the background out of sight, at least to start with.'

'Sensible precaution,' and the four of them moved to behind the nearest hut.

Friendly relations were soon established and Aidit with his three men were called into the open and introduced. Small eats and tea were produced and, after chit-chat, with a Chinese-speaking Thai guerrilla acting as interpreter, the leader said, 'Before we tell you our news I have a letter to deliver to you.' He lifted up the rifle his bodyguard was carrying, turned it over and, after prising open the small recess in the butt where the pull-through was normally kept, pulled out a tightly rolled piece of waterproof cloth and gave it to Chin Peng.

Before he had time to read it, Chin Peng was called into his makeshift radio room: he had managed to establish a direct link with a senior comrade who had lived for the past few years in Beijing. The message was that Comrade Mao himself had approved his plan to go to China although dates for and method of movement were about two years away.

He came back to the others, face wreathed in smiles, and gave them the good news. 'Now I must read my letter,' he said, rather grandly.

He unwrapped the piece of waterproof cloth carefully and, asking to be excused, retired to his office to read it.

Chin Peng returned. 'The message is that the Imperialist-inspired organisation known as SEATO is holding an exercise in Bangkok against expected external aggression. I had heard outline news of that on our radio,' he said, careful not to hurt his guests' feelings, 'but thank you all the same for your news.'

'There is one important point you may not have heard. The Imperialist running dogs have some idea called the Domino Theory and ...'

'"Domino Theory?"' someone interrupted.

'... yes, that's what I said. The idea is that once a country has seen sense and adopted our method of government, countries to its south will also fall, like a line of upright dominoes: knock the first one over and then all the others fall down.'

Everybody contemplated that, to them, novel idea. *Is there anything in it?* they asked themselves.

'I'd heard something about it but until just now I'd not thought of dominoes as anything but a game of chance so how could there be a theory,' expostulated the Secretary General. 'Domino' in Chinese translates as 'domino bone slab' which made the allusion seem more concrete than theoretical.

'Merely that as long as the struggle in Vietnam is as drastic as it is and is sure to become even more so, you have to be more than careful as to how you choose your time and method of travel to China,' answered the Thai guerrilla leader, 'as the Imperialists will be more watchful. We have news that the American President has sent Special Forces to South Vietnam because he is worried that the North Vietnamese will become too strong. There are rumours that anti-Communist guerrillas are being trained in Laos.'

That caused immense interest as, were there to be fighting, Chin Peng and his retinue could not so easily move overland to China.

'We have also heard,' continued the leader of the Thai guerrillas, 'that those on the SEATO exercise are planning to react both if the domino fall were to start with our Chinese comrades themselves attacking south or our North Vietnamese comrades either in their own uniform or wearing that of the Lao Patriotic Front, the Pathet Lao, attacking west and southwest. Our Secretary General is planning how best he could control any local Chinese feelings. He also needs to know what, if any, counter-measures Malaya will take so make our life on this, our southern flank, less tranquil than it has been to date.' He looked around and saw his audience had pensive faces. *Our three stalwarts working with the Malayan* t'o yan *couldn't be better placed to transmit news farther north,* thought Chin Peng.

'Yes, we must come to some decision as to what best to do. We can't plan for it overnight but we'll work out an agreed solution and let you know what it is.'

As discussions and deliberations continued, Aidit's three men went over to the Thai guerrillas, only to discover that there was a language barrier. However, in the curious way of coincidences making the world a smaller place than many imagine it is, Aidit's ex-2/1 GR aide spotted one of the Thai guerrilla sentries who seemed ... who seemed just that ... just that similar to ... They exchanged glances, Aidit's man tilted his head and wandered off. The Thai followed him. They met. In a low voice, Aidit's man said, in Nepali, 'I'm not wrong, am I? You're a Gurkha hillman, yes?'

Eyes popping out of his head, 'Yes, I am, but I keep quiet about it: and you?'

'Yes, I am also.'

They introduced themselves: the 2/1 GR man was Kesar Pun, known in Indonesia as Ali Wiranto, and the 'Thai' was an ex-1/7 GR man, Manbahadur Limbu, with a Thai name, Kamhaeng Thanaboon. They asked each other how it was that they found themselves so similar yet so far apart and what chance was there of escape? Manbahadur told his new friend that 'we Limbus have some folk lore that our Limbuan, country of Limbus in east Nepal, will be severely threatened and only be saved by a *gora*, a white man.'

Both men looked round to see if they were in any way being scrutinised. No one was taking any notice of them. They only noticed the scar-faced Indonesian guerrilla picking up fallen leaves and folding them in two. *Strange habit!*

'And in real life can that happen to us?' demanded Kesar, returning to the subject in hand.

'Probably not,' answered Manbahadur, sadly, 'our gods' ploys may not be strong enough but merely to talk with you is just so good it is hardly true.'

'I agree. Time to move apart now and maybe we'll have another chance to talk but that's not likely.' They shook hands and drifted back to their own group. Seeds of return to the Land of their Birth, already firmly planted, were watered by the contact.

'Thank you for your cooperation,' the Thai leader said. 'It was also a great bonus to meet Comrade Aidit. I will report it to our Politburo as a most sensitive issue, to go no further,' and, with that, the guerrillas left, taking the now fit Kamhaeng Thanaboon and Jenko back with them.

Chin Peng and Aidit wrapped up their business. They had a final toast, Aidit only nominally being a Muslim. Ah Fat and Wang Ming escorted the visitors back to the border and into Malaya. They had one night in the same hotel and the Indonesians were to continue north to Bangkok by air next morning.

Ah Fat had worked with Gurkhas when operating on secret missions during the Malayan Emergency with Captain Jason Rance and something told him that Aidit's escort was not an Indonesian but, somehow and bewilderingly, a Gurkha. He also knew a few words of Nepali so he made it his business to talk to the escort. He took him to one side, on the excuse of looking after some luggage and said, 'Namasté. I think you are a Gurkha.'

The 'Indonesian' man did a double-take, looked round, scowling, and softly said, 'What is that to you?'

'I have worked with Gurkhas on operations' – *partly true* – 'and with a British sahib who was in 1/1 GR during the war ...'

'I was in 2/1 GR and got taken away during the war as a prisoner. I can't escape,' said with a sudden intake of breath that was so loud that he automatically covered his mouth as though he had yawned. He made up his mind. *This Chinese, knowing some Nepali and a British sahib, must be trusted.* 'Did you know that one of the Thai guerrillas is also a Gurkha?' he asked quietly.

This time it was Ah Fat's turn to look amazed. 'No, no, how could I?' Too difficult to express in his limited Nepali, he continued in Malay. 'It can't concern us here but, what does concern you is that I gather that there will be big trouble over in your part of the world in a year or two. If so, is there any way of my being able to make contact with you, or, if I can't, get my friend, a British officer, to try if, and it's still only an "if", matters come to a head. If you don't try and escape now, although you are halfway home already, that is the only way I can think of.'

They looked at each other for a long, long moment. *I saw my Nepalese house in my dream last night and I did not go inside. That's always a sign of good luck.* 'I can't make my escape, only to think of it.' *Yes, I do trust this man. I'll try my luck.* 'My real name is Kesar Pun and my Indonesian name is Ali Wiranto. Yes, my people are planning trouble in British territory, Borneo and

Brunei, in a few years' time. Could it happen then?' He closed his eyes and thought, standing stock still. He mumbled a Nepali word before coming out, haltingly in English, with 'Perseverance'. As he emphasised the last syllable Ah Fat thought of his old childhood friend: *Rance, my Jason Rance … just possible? A one in a million, ten million, chance.*

Kesar Pun was called away. 'Goodbye. I was only clutching at cobwebs,' he said ruefully as he drifted off.

After the Indonesian group had gone, 'Hung Lo,' said Ah Fat, 'next stop Kuala Lumpur. We must pass on this news as soon as we can. Our friend Mr C C Too will be more than interested. It is all fully on my tape recorder, though quite what he can do with it is not up to you or me.'

'P'ing Yee,' smiled the Bear, 'you were always one for doing the right thing.'

Once in Bangkok Jason went to the British Embassy off Phloen Cit road which had a Gurkha guard composed of ex-servicemen and, as he went through the main gates, he was delighted to be hailed by the Guard Commander who had been in his company during the Burma war. They had a brief chat before Jason said he'd have to go and report to the Defence Attaché, who he found was a moustachioed Colonel from a British regiment. 'Welcome to Bangkok,' the Attaché said, during the usual small talk with a cup of coffee. 'These exercises are all very well. They sound exciting enough but, nitty-gritty, they are an awful bore. It's not a 'live exercise' as such with troops but only a paper one with a certain amount of ground movement for major unit commanders.

Only four nations are represented, we and the Americans being 'enemy' and the other two, the Thais and the Filipinos, defending Thailand against 'our' attack. As you may know, these two Asian armies are highly influenced by American military methods: they are not nearly as flexible tactically as we are and their training suffers from there being one instructor to minimum one hundred recruits and maximum two hundred. Only the Green Berets have one instructor for ten men whereas in our army that is normal. However, I don't want to get bogged down in what is one of my rather stupid hobby-horses. Your main task will be helping to keep the British representatives' staff work involved, chiefly with the Thais, up-to-date and accurate.'

'Colonel, understood. That means I won't be expected to do any travelling.'

'Sadly I can't see it happening, unless there are unusual, very unusual, circumstances. Exercise HQ is in the Royal Thai Army Supreme Headquarters complex and my Chief Clerk will give you your passes and other paperwork after we've finished talking. Give him your passport and he'll arrange for a double-entry visa: you may have to go back to Hong Kong during the exercise and, as the Boy Scouts have it, "Be Prepared". It's on the house, anyway.'

'Thank you, sir, most thoughtful,' Jason said. 'As for the work itself, it'll take a while to get to know those I'm working with but I can't see any real difficulty. At least, from what you've said so far, I can't.'

'Have you ever worked with either the Thais or the Americans, by the way?'

'No, sir, but I can't imagine there'll be any sticking point.'

'The Thais are strange people: they regard rudeness as the worst social offence. They are nearly always polite themselves but the odd one can run amok. They think the Americans are brash and tactless and they can't stand blacks though one would never guess that from their normal quiet demeanour. The Americans say that "the Thais are the nicest people money can buy who play at their work and work at their play" and that attitude does induce an underlying friction.'

'Thank you for telling me, sir. That is new to me.'

'I gather you're a bit of a linguist,' said the Colonel, changing tack, 'one way and another. For me, I can't begin to get round Thai: the oral is hard enough but, as for the written, it's utterly beyond me.'

'I don't have Thai as one of my languages, sir,' admitted Jason, 'but I'll try and pick some up while I'm here. Could come in useful.' He was told to go to the clerk's office where details of his hotel accommodation, at the New Imperial where all staff officers such as he, would be given.

Jason was amused and intrigued at Thai protocol: the Deputy Supreme Commander, the General who actually 'ran' the army, the Supreme Commander in effect being a politician, had called in the Exercise Staff Officers to welcome them before any work started. He was a short man with good English, probably helped, certainly as far as pronunciation was concerned, by his English wife. Before his actual arrival in the briefing hall, a female Captain had brought in a large portrait of the Thai King and put it at the door where the Deputy Supreme Commander entered. Just before the General arrived she knelt down by the side of the portrait, hands joined in the *wai* position in front of her body and stayed there until the General himself had entered, saluted the picture and only then did she get up and take the picture away, carefully, almost as though it were a religious icon.

Jason was further reminded about the Thai mentality to work when he went into a bookshop to get a Thai-English dictionary. He asked if there was a military vocabulary for sale. There was: it was all in the Thai script except on one page near the back in English: 'When a diplomat says *yes* he means *perhaps*, when he says *perhaps* he means *no* and when he says *no* he is no diplomat; when a lady says *no* she means *perhaps*, when she says *perhaps* she means *yes* and when she says *yes* she is no lady.' *A literal 'turn up for the books'*, he grinned to himself.

The first weekend Jason decided to stretch his legs, a poor second to the squash courts in the club he'd use when made a temporary member. As it was drizzling he took his issue green poncho cape. His footsteps took him south towards the Lumphini district down Soi Thong Lo, a side street, and he sat down at an eating place for a snack and a beer to listen in to the music of the language as the locals talked with each other. He was determined to learn Thai. Sitting under the chop-house awning, he hung his wet poncho cape over two chairs and sat in a third, contemplating the scene: pedestrians as they jostled with each other on the cracked pavements under flimsy coverings, the three-wheeled motor rickshaws competing for passengers and the flotsam and jetsam of any poor peasantry in from the countryside, squatting on the pavement with something to sell, rice, vegetables, and, in one case, a baby bear.

He was on the point of going back when, all of a sudden, a man, no longer young, dashed passed then, spotting the poncho cape hanging down, wheeled back and, lying on the ground behind it, lay stock still, breathing heavily. A split second later, two men, bearing staves, dashed past, in turn followed by a bevy of running policemen. Jason, not moving from his seat and sitting stock still, watched this melodrama. Another police group, coming from the opposite direction, tried to stop the two men some fifty yards down the road. They turned back only to be captured by the group chasing them. A police vehicle drove up and the two were loaded into it and driven away, the small crowd that had gathered dispersing as soon as it did. The clamour and the shouting died down.

Jason looked at the recumbent man who had recovered his breath by now and saw him scratch his neck and, in one flowing gesture, blow on his fingers. *I know that gesture*: it was involuntarily made by all Gurkhas to stop them from getting goitre. *I didn't know Thais also had that belief!* He looked more carefully at the man, *reminds me of my ace tracker, Sergeant Kulbahadur Limbu* ... and he thought back to the war in Burma and Gurkhas becoming lost and, according to rumour, migrating into Thailand. *Surely not? But ...?* There was not all that difference in looks between a hill Gurkha and a Thai, the latter maybe a shade darker but the one-fold epicanthic eyelid was the same. Instinctively, in a low tone of voice, he said, in Nepali, 'Brother, the men chasing you have been taken away in a police vehicle. You're safe. Get up and come and sit with me. I'll buy you a plate of rice with stewed pork shanks and a glass of beer or *tom yung kung,* hot-and-sour soup, if you'd prefer it.'

The man was almost bowled over so surprised was he at being spoken to in Nepali. He got up, wide-eyed and mouth opening and shutting without any noise issuing, sat down next to Jason. Eventually he blurted out 'Y ... you speak our hill language? How ... how can you know it? I have not heard a sahib talk it since the battle of Meiktila in 1945,' and, staying quiet, looked fixedly ahead with the 'thousand-yard stare' for some time. He drew his lips together like a turkey's bottom and shook his head in sheer disbelief and started mumbling. Jason strained his ears and heard him mention 1/7 GR – *phas seben* –and 1/5 GR - *phas phiph.* Jason knew that both those battalions had fought at Meiktila. Eventually the Gurkha came out of his reverie and, as though he were taking a mental deep breath before coming back to the present, looked at Jason in awe. *A gora sahib was mentioned down in Sadao and here is one.* The idea of there being only one had not struck him.

'Yes, know how to talk Nepali I do as I am a British officer in the Brigade.' Mutually happy, they sat and talked, much to the satisfaction of both, the Gurkha delighted with his soup and pork. And the man's story transfixed Jason's attention ... He was, he said, one of a small group of Gurkhas who lived not far from the Burmese border. Not only were there ex-servicemen, presumably still listed as 'Missing believed killed in action', Jason thought, but also some civilians who had migrated south into Burma from the Darjeeling district, living undisturbed till the war. They had fled the fighting and settled in Thailand. They were landless, document-less and 'owned' by a rapacious mine owner for whom they worked. What money they were supposed to earn was kept as payment for their food. They never had any cash themselves. 'They are really nothing but slaves and live a miserable life.' This man had managed to escape and lived from hand-to-mouth, without any proper papers, always in fear of being picked up by the police, not known for their kindness, and being put in jail – Thai jails are infamously nasty. Jason tried to show he was not shocked at that news and merely shook his head in sympathy. *Not much if anything I can do about that.*

'What is your name?' asked Jason, leaning back in his chair.

'My Nepali name is Manbahadur Limbu. I tell the police I have a Thai name, Kamhaeng Thanaboon. I'm a fluent Thai speaker. I am trying to get a job of night watchman of a factory down the road and am not due to be vetted till six o'clock.' He automatically looked at the watch Jason wore, not having one himself.

'You so much remind me of one of my company, a wonderful tracker, Kulbahadur Limbu. He'd be about thirty years old now.'

Manbahadur's face lit up. 'Kulbahadur? I have a younger brother with that name. Kulbahadur? Surely it can't be he?'

'Why not? You look alike, the bridge of your nose is the same and your hand reflexes also tally. He lives in Hangpang, less than a day's walk from Taplejung.'

'That is my village. Must be the same one,' said the Gurkha with a wonderful smile. 'In that case, give me more news of him,' and so the conversation continued, each of them nursing a cold beer.

'Sahib, it was so lucky that I saw a hiding place so could escape my pursuers.'

Jason knew enough about Gurkhas not to have asked him why he had nose-dived behind the spread-out poncho. He knew he'd get a fully and a better answer in the Gurkha's own time.

Manbahadur Limbu looked around suspiciously. There was no one near enough to eavesdrop and Jason had given the shopkeeper enough money, with a wink, for him to keep his mouth shut. 'Sahib, I'll tell you ...' and out came an amazing story of how he had been a guerrilla in the Thai Communist Party's armed forces – 'I was a soldier and the daughter I'd sired was threatened if I didn't join them' – and had been on a mission down to Sadao to the hide-out of one Chin Peng of the Malayan guerrillas when he and one other became sick, stayed there until quite recently when the Thai Secretary General sent another patrol down with a message, 'and there I met another ex-soldier from Indonesia who had been captured by the Japanese, a man in 2/1 GR.' He paused in his story as he looked at the astonished expression on Jason's face. 'Sahib, it's true, it is. Before I went back with the Thai patrol I had decided to run away and, so pleased was I to see I was not the only one stuck with a Communist gang that, on the way back, I deserted. Those two men were sent after me either to recapture me or kill me. The police must have heard about it but quite how I just don't know. Thanks to you I'm alive. You are my god: can I work for you?'

'No, I'm afraid not. I've only come here temporarily. But how can I help you?'

'Sahib, it's a question of money. I have no documents and, unless I bribe a policeman, I'll be locked up and Thai jails are terrible. I know, I've been in one when I did not have enough money for bribes.'

When it was time for both men to be on their way, Jason took some money out of his wallet and gave it to his new-found friend. 'Here, take this. It will tide you over for a few days and maybe bribe any policeman who gets too inquisitive about no paperwork.'

'Oh thank you, Hajur. How can I repay you?' asked with obvious sincerity, bordering on devotion.

'I want to meet you again and go with you to your village to see it for myself.' Then a sudden thought struck him, making him breathe rapidly. *During the Emergency how many operations did we undertake to try and find the Politburo's camp? Never able to find it. But now … Can I …? Could I during the Christmas break?* 'Manbahadur, if I could make myself into an inquisitive tourist, do you think it would be possible to take me down to Sadao, just for a weekend, for me to do a recce of the camp and see what I could find? You know the approach routes and where we could get near unobserved, don't you?'

Manbahadur jolted back in his chair at this totally unexpected request. 'Sahib,' he blurted out, 'yes, but whatever for? The guerrillas there are Chinese. They'll kill you if they find you. You can't speak Chinese, can you?'

'Yes, I can. I speak it as well as I do English and I can read and write it, but I don't let on that I can unless I have to. I don't want to meet anyone, only to give them a message,' he added elliptically.

'Sahib, if I can help you there can you help me to get back to Nepal?'

Jason pondered on that. 'On my return I promise that I'll report it to my government but what I can't promise is what they'll do about it. As for our jaunt south, let's plan to go there over the Christmas break. There will be no work between 24 December 1959 and 2 January 1960.

On Christmas Eve Jason and Manbahadur went shopping and bought some second-hand military clothes, consisting of a hat, shirt and trousers, some black canvas shoes and a touristy-type backpack for both of them and a waterproof cape for Manbahadur. Jason also bought a large net for catching butterflies, the largest tourist map of south Thailand he could find, as well as a camera. Before they boarded a bus going south, he wrote a message in Chinese on a piece of SEATO-headed notepaper. Once at Sadao, an unfriendly place, they booked into a two-bedded room in an hotel, run by a Chinese man and wife. Jason did not let them know that he was a Chinese speaker. He overheard them talking softly, wondering if such an unlikely pair need be warned about meeting any guerrillas in plain clothes. *No, best not to say anything.*

Jason immediately became alarmed and asked Manbahadur about it. 'No, sahib, when I was here parties of guerrillas in plain clothes came from the camp to buy supplies and extort money. We never expected trouble. If we do meet any in plain clothes they just might recognise me. If we meet them in the jungle, we'll have to be butterfly hunters.'

Next morning, after a light meal, Jason told Manbahadur to ask the shop owner if he could put his passport in his safe while they were away. This, rather grudgingly, the Chinese agreed to, for one hundred baht. They took a taxi south for a few miles, got out, telling the driver they were going to photograph jungle birds and try to catch some butterflies. Once in the jungle they changed into 'uniform' and hid their packs and the net.

The two men's jungle craft was superb. They both seemed to glide over the land, almost naturally neither leaving any obvious tracks nor breaking any small branches, vines or creepers. Manbahadur knew that the various journeys camp personnel made to Sadao and other villages meant a track could be followed but here Jason's experience from the war in Burma was useful: they 'herring-boned' their approach, that is to say they moved parallel to the track only jinking towards it to make sure their axis of approach was correct before veering away for fifty or so yards and then turning parallel once more. 'These men have no imagination as to track discipline as they think they're safe,' Manbahadur said in a low tone.

They crossed a stream and saw a definite track. 'The way up to the outer sentry is along this small ridge so let's move about fifty paces below it. I'll be able to tell you when we get near it,' said Manbahadur. 'I'll climb that tree and have a look around.' Jason knew that all Gurkhas had a wonderful ability to climb trees.

'Got it,' he said as he dropped to the ground. 'Fifty yards or so in that direction,' pointing with his chin, 'just beyond that thick clump of bull rushes.'

They heard footsteps and melted into the undergrowth. From the direction of the camp two Chinese girls appeared, smiling and looking satisfied. *Surely not ... but, then, why not? It happens.*

Jason had an idea. *I know the way to give my letter to the sentry.* 'Follow me to this side of that clump,' he muttered. They made their way to it and, parting his way through it so carefully that nobody would notice that a man had come that way, he went to the other side where he put the letter in a position no one could miss. He then carefully threaded his way back, a ganglion of tension running through him the while.

Lying low and completely hidden, in a shrill falsetto exactly emulating a girl's voice, he sang the first few bars of the slightly raunchy Cantonese song, *Green Plumb and a Bamboo Horse*, 'Oh guerrilla sentry. Are you on a bamboo horse? You can't see me but I can see you. I am calling from the clump of bull rushes: come near. You know what happened to those girls in the camp: something you can't have because you're only a no-rank soldier. I haven't been to the camp but I want the same. What a good chance to open our hearts together. Please hurry. I also have a letter for you to pick up and give to your Secretary General but you can have me first.'

Manbahadur froze, never expecting anything like this. No reaction so Jason tried again. 'Don't be scared, soldier man. I'm only a beautiful girl feeling *ham sap*, salty wet randy. I can't hurt you, only make you happy. It's easier here than taking me to a film in Sadao, isn't it?' It had been Jason's brainwave to use stanzas from a popular song from the early '50s to tantalise the sentry.

This time he was successful. The sentry answered in a lilting tone, 'So there's no need to take you to a movie first,' – although, as a good Communist, he should never have listened to such lascivious imperialist songs, let alone learnt how to sing them – and the two men heard him approach them. Manbahadur had no idea that one of Major Rance's attributes was ventriloquy. When the sentry called out, 'I've got the letter but I can't see you. Where are you hiding?' he was scared rigid when a soft male voice came from behind him: 'I'm not real. I'm a ghost. Take the letter away before I get hungry and eat you.' Then, in a harsh, low voice, Jason growled, '*Paan chue sek lo foo*' – Feigning to be a pig I vanquish tigers. The sentry, who, by this time Jason saw had picked up the letter, squeaked with fear and ran off, not minding what noise he made.

'Back we go, as fast as we quietly can,' said Jason and the two men slipped away. They crossed the river as before and, moving northwest, met up with the packs and net, changed back into touristy dress and made their way back to the hotel in a local bus.

Sitting outside, once more away from any eavesdroppers, they spoke in Nepali. 'Sahib, that was pure magic. I'd never have guessed anyone could talk like that. Going without a weapon was dangerous but,' and here he made a Nepali pun, 'the tongue is stronger than a bullet. What was on the piece of paper?'

'Oh, just a message to the Secretary General that he's lost the war and any regard anyone ever had for him.'

Before they left for Bangkok, Manbahadur recovered Jason's passport. He would only learn much later that it had been taken out and a copy of the page with the photograph on it had been made. *I'm bound to be asked so I'd better*, the hotel manager had reasoned.

The sentry who had picked up the letter was literate. Once he had got over his panic he paused to get his breath back and read the letter. Two parts made him especially shudder. One was: *Your rotten system could never win and has now seriously lost, putrefying in its own recycled bitterness.* The other was: *Your ineptitude has resulted in the only time Communists have failed in a military campaign at a time and in a place of their own choosing.* He wiped his forehead and read on but could not understand an allusion to a Lustful Wolf, Sik Long, not having been able to help Chin Peng and none of those he surreptitiously showed it to could either. It had a heading on it he did not understand. Pretending he had not opened it he gave it to the Guard Commander who passed it on up the chain of command. He said nothing about the girl or the ghost: *so much safer not to,* so when asked how he had found it merely said that, being white, it had caught his attention when it flickered in a gust of wind No, he had no idea how it had got there. Nor, when asked, had any other sentry on duty before the man who picked it up.

The Secretary General was nonplussed when he was given the missive and told how it was found. He unfolded it and, on seeing the SEATO heading, knew at once that only an enemy could have written it. As he digested its contents his rage and mortification increased. He did not immediately get the reference to the Lustful Wolf. But get it he did: it was the name given to a British officer who had tried to join the guerrillas in 1951 and whose planned though unsuccessful escape he himself had approved of. The letter was signed Shandung P'aau – the 'Shandung Cannon'. On the Chinese mainland Shandung people were widely known for their strength and toughness as 'cannon'. In fact it was the name given to Jason, a particularly strong child, by his boyhood friend Ah Fat.

Can it possibly be that the man who wrote that letter and signed it is that British officer I've heard of, Jason Rance, one of the few British officers who speaks Chinese and who has that most unusual gift of being a ventriloquist? Chin Peng wondered in a haze of rage. *I'll have to find out. Really there's not one chance in a million. And yet … and yet… If so, how could he have found out where my camp is? Doubtful in the extreme but, even so … I hope one of my agents has somehow managed to get a photograph of any recent visitors in Sadao.* At the first available opportunity he called for Zhong Han San. 'Spread the word around. If ever a Running Dog named Jason Rance, known as Shandung P'aau, comes your way, kill him – and it need not be all at once. And send a patrol down to the camp where Comrade Ah Soo Chye is with the same message.' It was only later that a tiny, tiny nag at the back of his mind surfaced: *wasn't there some rumoured connection between a* Shandung P'aau *and a* P'ing Yee *and wasn't his trusted Ah Fat sometimes known by that name …?* But, if so, *what proof was there?* Chin Peng knew only too well that proof for such a matter as this was never obtained voluntarily.

After the exercise staff returned from their holiday break in early January, Phase 2, the 'tactical battle', started and the Thai General, the Exercise Controller, arbitrarily ruled that the Americans would be the invaders from the Chinese province of Yunnan south and that the British would be those from the east, through the neck of the Laos Panhandle, along either, or both, of Routes Coloniales 8 and 12, where the British were the 'baddies'. Geographically the northern route was the harder, more mountainous and fewer roads for a large army but its greatest advantage was that any force could cross the Mekong while still in Laos so advance south from the most western province Sayaburi. It was strongly challenged by the senior American, a Brigadier General.

'General, I would like to challenge your choice of "invader",' he growled, glowering at the senior British representative as he did. 'We have our forces in Indo-China and the Limeys,' he rapidly tried to swallow his last word but it was too late, 'the British have done nothing to help us. They know nothing about Brother Gook and have only been playing Blind Man's Bluff against a bunch of rag-tag guerrillas in Malaya so know nothing about Gook tactics. Let us take on that eastern route and let the Brits play soldiers down from the north.'

The audience looked appalled at such an outburst. The Thai General's features showed no change but his thoughts raced. *So impolite.* He glanced at the senior British officer and was amazed to see him smiling.

'Fine by us,' the British Brigadier drawled. 'You know, General, that the roads are not a danger.'

'I beg to differ,' answered the irate American. 'How can you say that?'

'Easily, it is what moves along the road that is the danger. And our giving in to you about which route we'll take will cost you a visit to your Special Forces camp at Lopburi and we'll then compare our jungle methods with yours.'

The Brigadier General, whose temper erupted like boiling milk, had calmed down. 'No sweat. I'll arrange that for ... it's Wednesday today ... let's say next Saturday.'

The discussion resumed its normal tenor. Those in favour of the eastern route felt that the drive through the top of the Panhandle would be merely a matter of hours, the countryside flatter and the advance doubly quick because of the two lateral roads. However, crossing the River Mekong, then the world's longest unbridged river, was where SEATO forces could the most easily come to grips with the invaders. After considerable debate, it was decided that the eastern route's counter would be Plan A and the northern route's Plan B. Then the American team had to spell out their plans and tactics.

Before the visit to Lopburi the British Brigadier called Jason over to him. 'I've heard that you're a dab hand under the canopy. Come along with us.'

'Certainly, sir,' answered Jason. 'I'd just love to.' *Right up my street or should I say under my tree?*

The visit was more cordial than expected until the end when Jason was asked what he thought of a demonstration hut that had been built by an American secret adviser, a six-foot-tall Captain, who had been working in Laos. 'Look at this,' the adviser had said, 'this is made from local materials and is a model of where I lived with the Meo guerrillas for quite some months.' Then, brashly, he had gone on to say, 'That probably beats anything you did in the Malayan jungle.'

He saw Jason shaking his head. 'What's wrong with you?' he asked abruptly.

'You were living on borrowed time,' was the unexpected answer.

The American Captain bridled. 'How come? It's perfect.'

'Hardly anyone in this part of the world is as tall as you. You have built yourself a bamboo bed: too long for a local but, in any case, locals don't use beds, do they? You've woven a bamboo chair for yourself. Locals, as far as I know, don't use chairs. They sleep and sit on rush mats. Had Gooks, as you call them, come across it, they'd instantly have known it was false, not that of a local. That's why I said you were living on borrowed time.'

The Captain's self-esteem patently drooped. He turned away without saying anything, his face as grim as an undertaker's.

Back in Bangkok the Brigadier took Jason to one side. 'Well done. From what I know of matters, you're the only one who could let us regain our military prestige. The Yanks have got something going in Indo-China that they're holding close to their collective chests. I don't think that Captain should have shown us what he did. He'll face a grilling I expect – and he'll deserve it. The urge to show off one's skills is always a danger to security – a lesson to all of us.'

Jason, feeling he was in the Brigadier's good books, asked for and was granted permission to go on a recce near the Burma border. 'Just in case a "noises-off" scenario has to be painted into the main narrative,' he said, 'and I believe my Thai language ability is now good enough for me to ask around, as a tourist, without causing any excitement.' This was granted and, having collected Manbahadur, off they went. The area, to the southwest of Bangkok, was under the jurisdiction of the Thai Border Police as it, too, was 'sensitive'. Jason was told that the mine area was named Epu but, on his return to Bangkok, could not find the name on any map. He stayed a couple of days with the desolate and thoroughly demoralized Nepali community, happy to make them laugh. He found out that there were a couple more ex-soldiers there. They had married locally and seemed nonchalant about any possibility of return to Nepal. He had taken as much money for them as he could spare, which thrilled them. 'I'll try and see if I can manage to get you rescued officially,' he told them, 'but it's now fourteen years since the war ended and it is a most difficult situation to put right. I am in the British Army now, you were in the Indian Army, so we have no official jurisdiction over you.'

Before Jason and Manbahadur separated in Bangkok they sat down in a small roadside café in sight of the British Embassy, itself not far from the New Imperial Hotel. A man came in and sat down by himself at a table within hearing distance. Jason and Manbahadur continued talking in Nepali and were surprised when the solitary man perked up, gave them a swift, probing look and listened in to what they were saying. He came over and, to Jason's unreserved surprise, said to Manbahadur, 'We meet again. I heard you talking to a sahib so I must join you.'

Manbahadur introduced him to Jason as Kesar Pun and invited him to sit down. This he did, nervously, on the edge of his chair, perched like a wary bird ready to fly. 'Can't stay long as I have to go back and escort my master, a man named Aidit, but I must say that our Hindu gods send us messages.' Turning to Jason he said 'I recently met a man named Ah Fat who said he knew a *gora* major sahib who might, just might, be the key to our two's future. Can you be he?'

Jason had seldom had such extraordinarily unexpected news given to him in such an unexpected way. He said, 'Ah Fat and I have been friends since we were small boys. I must be the one he was referring to. But, at the moment, I am empty of any meaningful answer. I haven't seen Ah Fat for some years. Tell me how you met him,' offering him a beer which he declined. *Make my breath smell. I must act like a Muslim.* 'No, I'll have a soft drink instead. You must be he,' and he told them about what had happened in Sadao and Penang.

'Kesar-jyu, as I've said to Manbahadur, I'll report our meeting to my government but I can't promise what will happen after that.'

'Is there no other hope?'

Inspiration! 'You have an Indonesian passport, haven't you? Why not slip away, here and now, with Manbahadur, let your Aidit fellow leave and, after a day or so, go and buy a ticket for Nepal from the Royal Nepal Airlines Corporation, RNAC, office. Once you're there no one can touch you.'

A wistful look came over Kesar's features. 'O-ho, sahib, if only, if only. But I don't have the money to buy a ticket. Otherwise …' and his voice trailed off.

'Apart from you and I having been in the same regiment, I always want to help Gurkhas. Listen. I'll find out how much the fare costs and bring you the money, here, tomorrow. But, whatever else you do, stay hidden till then and come back here.'

Impulsively the Gurkha leant forward, knelt down and put his head on Jason's feet. 'Sahib,' he breathed, 'how can I ever repay you,' and getting to his feet said to Manbahadur, 'Take me away now. We'll come back tomorrow.'

Jason sat back contemplating the unbelievable coincidence and uniqueness of the occasion: two 'lost' Gurkha soldiers, only one being able to go back to Nepal. *I'm delighted to be able to help Kesar Pun.*

He got up, found out where the RNAC office was, asked the price of the ticket to Kathmandu and went and drew the money from the embassy pay clerk and, as promised, he gave Kesar the money, wished him well and put him out of his mind. *Now only one to worry about.*

By now Jason had managed to learn a significant amount of oral Thai and could also slowly read and write the script. The Chinese he had learnt when a small boy and still spoke as a second language, helped him master the Thai 'tone barrier', so his pronunciation was understandable from the very start. He had used his Chinese to good effect when conversing with Chinese traders and shopkeepers in Bangkok and he felt that he might be able to put it to better use if ... *If what?* An idea struck him. *Why not use Manbahadur's guerrilla provenance, despite his new-found aversion to it, to good use once more ...*

Thoughtfully he made his way to the senior British representative attending the SEATO exercise, a Brigadier. 'Sir, may I take up some of your time, please? I want to put an idea to you, to you only, to begin with ...'

2

The Brigadier, tall and of commanding aspect whose aquiline nose, severe brows and wide-open eyes gave his face the chiselled features of a Gothic saint, looked at Jason speculatively. *A novel idea and a potentially dangerous one to boot, likewise could be politically sensitive.* He cleared his throat and carefully enunciated, 'Let me see if I have read you strength five and, if so, that we are gnawing at the same bone. Despite SEATO exercise staff having already made their recces of where Plan A and Plan B might need a military counter, you still feel that there's more to be found out. You feel there are gaps to be filled and that you can probably fill them – on your own by putting a bit more meat in the stew, what?'

Jason had only met his exercise boss a couple of times. Now, sitting in a chair to one side of the Brigadier's desk, he wondered if he had been too optimistic in his original idea. He looked at the red-tabbed officer with his impressive chest full of medals, an order and three bravery awards. He was probably on his last job before going on pension after an adult lifetime in the army.

'Yes, sir,' he answered. 'I think I have a good chance of seeing where the gaps are even if I don't fill them.'

'You further say that you have contacted an ex-Gurkha soldier who became lost after the Battle of Meiktila in 1945, is now illegally in Thailand and is also a member of a guerrilla band of the Thai Communist Party because he felt he could best hide from the Thai authorities that way.' Jason nodded his agreement. 'And furthermore, while in the Betong Salient having been left behind as sick after a visit there with a patrol of the Thai guerillas, was still there when more Thai guerrillas brought a message, allegedly from the Secretary General of the Thai Communist Party, to the Secretary General of the Malayan Communist Party, Chin Peng, about our SEATO exercise's worry about the Domino Theory and, while there, heard this Chin Peng say he'd just received a radio message from China to the effect that Mao Tse-tung would welcome him there.'

'That is exactly what I did say, sir.'

'And now a fluent Thai speaker and disillusioned with Communism, just happened to see your spread-out poncho cape – coincidence – just happened to hide behind it – happenstance – and just happened to evade some guerrillas who were just happening to try and catch him and just failed – a likely tale, indeed – so he put two and two together, made five, and having seen your poncho as divine intervention, thought to hitch his wagon to your star,' said the Brigadier, heavily repetitive and with more than a trace of a sneer in his voice. 'Don't you think he might have reacted to any European *farang*, as I've learnt to say, whose poncho he had hidden behind so told him as unlikely a tale as any that I've ever heard?' He shook his head dismissively and hid a smile behind his handkerchief.

If Jason had had any idea of mentioning his unprecedented journey to Sadao, he had it no longer. He held up his arms in mock surrender. 'I can understand your doubts, Brigadier. I can see that my story must sound far-fetched to you. This is because it is incomplete in that I am guilty of not telling you the background in enough detail. I saw that that man was a Gurkha not a Thai by certain gestures he made and that, by a facial similarity, I learnt that he is the elder brother to one of my men, an ace tracker, in my old rifle company in 1/12 GR. Such a relationship makes a bond hardly anyone else could have forged. And, as far as "hitching his wagon to my star", when I told him that the Communists in Nepal were trying to take hillmen's land from them, he was so sickened he said he'd never again believe what they said, here or anywhere else. It brought the whole wretched system into a much clearer perspective. I also told him of my plans of talking with you and, if you approved, for us to go together. His price is for me to try and get him, and maybe other similarly placed ex-servicemen, repatriated.' *Anyway, almost correct. Am I convincing him it's not all smoke and mirrors?*

The Brigadier had dipped his head a couple of times as he was listening. 'Yes, put that way, I suppose it does make sense. And, as you have said you are a bilingual Chinese speaker, your idea is to take him, and one other – but who? I wonder, not that it matters as I wouldn't know him from Adam – and make for the border. You will act as a tourist, can't be anything else, can you, and while you are looking at the border from a "Domino" point of view, he will liaise with the local Thai guerrillas to find out if they know about a real "Domino" threat. Is that as far as it goes?'

'In outline yes, sir, that is as far as it need go but there is another point before I hark back to a strange operation I undertook ten years ago in Malaya. It was very serious, and I don't use the word "very" unless I mean "very".'

'Tell me more.' Interest flickered in the senior officer's face.

'Sir, from what I have intuited during my stay here to date, the threat of Communism is far from dead. In a moment I'll tell you why I have a nose for it. What I'd like to do once I'm near the border of Laos and Thailand, it to try and "feel the pulse" and see if the threat of Communism is such that only British methods, neither Yank nor French, could achieve positive results. I fully realise that that may be pure "pie in the sky" but, even so, who knows but there might just be what I might call "willing ears" somewhere? One reason for my feeling I can intuit – I don't like that word but even so I've used it again – correctly is to tell you what happened about ten years ago when one of my battalion officers tried to join the Malayan guerrillas and I was put on his trail in the jungle. I had four Gurkhas with me and the turncoat's gang was four or more times bigger than mine. I can speak Chinese as well as I can English and was instrumental in winning out. The officer was killed in a shoot-out, as was the Regional Commissar, and I inveigled the remaining guerrillas to surrender to me. I got them to volunteer to become what was known as a "Q" Patrol working for the government but the MCP still thought they were working for them. In fact, we made some successful forays together later on.'

The Brigadier gasped at him in undisguised amazement, tilting his head back as he did. 'So, one way and another, your background has made you sharper in delving into those people's minds than many another. You'll be looking at matters out of a different window, so to speak. Fine. Now where does that take us?' he asked as he tidied the pens and pencils on his desk.

'Only that, given the opportunity of mixing with Chinese and probing their feelings about the Red Menace, I might just be able to confirm or otherwise the whole theory as well as fathoming any local thoughts.'

'And then?'

Jason put his hand to his brow and thought for a few seconds. 'My findings might just help strategic planning in South-East Asia.'

'Sounds a tad trite but it's an intriguing concept. So why not?' The Brigadier grinned, wolfishly. He, too, had had his younger days when excitement had sent the adrenaline to fever point. *Why stop this fellow? He has more spunk than many others of his age.* 'Once I was like you, Bold and Fearless, full of Blood and Thunder but now I've come to the end of my time and am Old and Hairless, full of Thud and Blunder. You're still in the former category,' and both men burst out laughing, all military 'protocol ice' broken.

'How do you plan to do that, in outline only, please?

'Sir, my idea is to visit three places south of the Thai-Lao border from Chiang Rai, to take a sniff at the northern route exit, across country by bus to Udorn Thani, south of Vientiane, then east over the River Mekong at the ferry at Mukdaharn. Let me show you on the map.' That was quickly done. 'Then, on the Lao side, starting at Savannakhet, go by bus along Route Coloniale

13, finishing up at Vientiane. Then back here. I reckon I'll need a maximum of three weeks for our military cliché "time and space" factors in that, certainly on the Thai side, I'll be going against the grain of the country. That's not long but there are two types of visit, "skim" that is short and not always striking lucky, and "in depth" that takes days or longer for results. The first type is all I have time for and is only useful in discovering what some people call vibrations there are, but these too can be of use. The fickle lady, Dame Fortune, might enable me to have a "double six" of luck.'

The Brigadier, by now almost won over, listened attentively, not saying a word. Jason went on, 'I plan to have a single-entry tourist visa for Laos so that I travel without suspicion. I'm pretty sure my two men can smuggle themselves across the river. I am not looking for adventures but I'll have to be ready to react to the unexpected. I can visit places where the Chinese gather, such as brothels and opium dens, not that I'd want to be a user myself in either case, or mahjong parlours and eating places where I may best discover any straws pointing out the direction of the wind. My knowledge of Chinese as well as one of my Gurkhas getting a Lao-speaking comrade from Thai Isan, could, I feel, give as good a feeling of what is happening on the ground in greater detail than the more conventional methods used to date. I could also visit any Christian missionary and "walk the course" with him, finding out which Devil he hates the most.' He looked at his senior to see how that had gone over.

'If nothing else, you have a vivid imagination,' said the Brigadier, rubbing his chin in contemplation. 'You seem to have done a lot of homework, Rance.'

'Sir, you would not have let me get this far if I hadn't,' answered Jason.

'Right. Let me dwell on it. I do have a contact, a need-to-know contact, an Englishman, whose opinion, not only about what you're intending to do and what any Thai reaction might be if they found out, is essential. Just you three?'

'Yes, sir.'

'How long will that take to fix the third man?'

'Say a week.'

'Good. Come back in a week's time and you'll have my verdict.'

'One last point, sir. As I feel I must be back before we break up, would you somehow let me off office work for these last three weeks?'

'I repeat, come back in a week's time and you'll have my verdict.'

Jason stood up, saluted and left the Brigadier sitting still, thoughtful and torn.

A week later the answer was, 'Yes but barefoot with the last three weeks office work excused and be back here in time for the End of Exercise Party. In other words, all you do is entirely off your own bat with no, repeat no, help if you make a mess of it. Let me know when you're ready.'

'Thank you, sir, I really mean it,' said Jason with a broad smile on his face.

Jason had contacted Kamhaeng Thanaboon, as he had made himself think of Manbahadur, and told him of his plans. 'Sahib, before I forget: remember never to speak to me in Nepali if anyone at all, except for our third men, Jenko, is in hearing distance. He is a Thai Isan who speaks Lao and some Vietnamese. I fully trust him as we have worked together, even down to the Thai-Malay border, so you can also. He knows that I am not really a Thai and that I speak another language. When I find him I'll explain what you want and that you also are not yet fluent in Thai but do know my other language and Chinese. Let me know how much you'll pay him. When do you want to start, Sahib?'

'The sooner the better, Kamhaeng *krab*,' using the Thai suffix when a man talks. 'When do you think you can get him here?'

'By the day after tomorrow at the latest.'

'Good. We can't move before then as I won't have my Lao visa. We'll be away for up to three weeks. We'll need quite a bit of money. Luckily the allowances paid to those of us working here are good enough so we won't be out of pocket.' A thought struck him. 'Do you think either or both of you can get across the Mekong without any official papers?'

'Should be able to but even if we can't you'll be fine on your own,' and with that equivocal reply Jason had to be satisfied.

Jason got his visa the same day as Jenko arrived. The new addition looked tough and resourceful; Jason took to him immediately, greeting him in Thai and adding 'I'll try and speak Thai to you but, if I can't and no one else can hear, I'll have to talk to Kamhaeng in a language you won't understand.'

'No worry. I have known Kamhaeng and about him for a

long time. We trust each other, *krab*.'

They moved off north that night by train as far as it went, then by bus to Chiang Rai, one of the oldest towns in the country and only about forty miles south of the Lao border. They booked into a cheap hotel. 'Sahib, Jenko and I will be away until tomorrow evening. We know where the local cell is but we must approach it with care. We have made up our cover story: escorting a *farang* who wants to help our cause but does not know Thailand. As for you, behave like a tourist.'

Jason had to agree. Wearing slacks and an open-necked shirt, he wandered around the town, smiling at the locals and, pretending to be a tourist, practising his Thai. He was fascinated to learn that here a different script was used. The people, too, were considerably fairer and friendlier than those in Bangkok. Outside the town the jungle-covered hills called him to explore them but, no: *it's different this time.* Many of the shops were open-fronted and he found some fine-looking strips of cloth. He bought a couple, thinking that at least one could come in handy for his CO's wife.

At lunchtime he went into an eating place run by a Chinese and sat at a table by himself. He asked for tea and sat, waiting, soaking in the atmosphere. Two Thai men, both with a short-back-and-sides haircut but in plain clothes, came in and sat at the table next to him. They ordered a beer each and spoke in low tones, Jason not being able to follow much of what they said. He picked out the word 'chin', then 'better to kill them'. He had learnt that, when the Thais spoke of an enemy, they spoke of them or him as 'it' as they did now. *Who have they in their sights?* he asked himself.

He called out in Chinese for an omelette and the two Thais turned towards him, glowering suspiciously.

They left as he finished eating. Passing him, one leaned over and said something in Thai. Jason answered slowly, '*Kho thad, krab, phom phud Thai mai kho di.*' – Excuse me, I speak Thai not so well. Both smiled and he thought their answer was 'but your pronunciation is good so speak in Thai and not in Chinese.' He noticed that they did not bother to offer to pay for their drinks. *That shows they'll be Special Branch.*

He got up, went to the counter and paid for his meal. The owner waited until the two Thais were out of earshot and grimaced. Softly he said, 'I had to answer you in Chinese but these people are so proud they don't like us speaking it so they can hear it.'

On the spur of the moment, Jason leant towards the man and, in a hushed tone, asked, 'No help from over the river, from Yunnan, say?'

The Chinese stiffened perceptibly and shook his head. 'We had some Yellow Flags here when Chiang Rai was young, long, long ago and there're still some Nationalist bandits in the Golden Triangle, but anything else? No. And another warning: never talk like that when any Thais are in earshot. Too dangerous.' He was obviously uncomfortable and showed it.

Jason thanked him, went outside and continued his walking. By late afternoon, on the outskirts of the town, he came across a shop selling liquor, also run by a Chinese. He went inside and, in

Thai, ordered a beer, which he drank slowly. He seemed a curiosity to the shopkeeper who kept a wary eye on him. After finishing his drink Jason got up and went to the counter to pay. He leant over with the money in his hand and, in a low voice, asked *'Tsun po fan tzi?'* – progressive elements? – the Communist 'password' to find out if the person being addressed answered properly. If not, no, then he was not 'one of us'*:*

'Why do you ask? Who are you?' the shopkeeper asked cautiously, in an equally low voice.

'One who comes searching,' was Jason's opaque answer.

'One from the Beautiful Land or the Brave Land?' The Chinese phonetic characters rendered the USA by the first and England by the second.

'The Brave Land.'

'I trust you people much more than I trust the others. Come with me,' and the shopkeeper led him into a back room. 'Wait here, I must call some comrades.'

Jason realised that he had to have his wits ready for an extempore performance and his impromptu responses to any deep question needed to sound genuine. He had, during the Malayan Emergency, spoken to so many captured or surrendered Communist guerrillas that he felt confident he could cope.

After the shopkeeper had returned with five men he said, 'Although you can speak our language as a native, my comrades are suspicious in that they've never had to deal with anyone like you before. They want to give you a test. Ready?'

'Of course. Ask away.'

'Tell us what the Great Helmsman said about the Government's reaction to us of the Thai Communist Party?'

'He had four points: don't curse them, they have thick skins; don't fight them because when you move in they move out; don't kill them, they become heroes; and finally improve the lot of the people.'

The six Chinese smiled at each other. 'Yes, you are genuine. Give us your background. Why come here to us?'

'Before anything else, I'm thirsty. Let's have some beer,' and, pulling money out of his pocket, he gave it to the shopkeeper. 'Once we've had a drink, I'll tell you.'

They toasted each other and drank deeply.

'Now I'm ready to tell you. I am an Englishman who is on your side but, as a secret agent, must not show it in the place I work. I come from Malaya where there is a lot of talk about *doh mai nok gwat pai lei lun* – the domino bone slab theory – and there is strong government talk that our comrades-in-arms will move south from Yunnan, cross the Mekong in Sayaburi province in Laos, re-form as an attacking army and invade Thailand. Even now in Bangkok plans are being made to repel such a force and the Thai government has asked England, USA, the Philippines, France, Pakistan, Australia and New Zealand for help …'

He was interrupted by loud cries of 'Wah, wah, what nonsense' and ribald laughter. 'Worse than the butcher hanging up a sheep's head and selling dog's meat.'

'So you think it's not true? I thought not,' cried Jason, joining in the laughter. 'I knew that people living like you do would have your finger on the pulse.'

'No, it's all a *farang* trick to make us look as though we have to wait for victory elsewhere as we're too weak except, possibly, to have control over local areas up here but we're not strong enough in the middle of the country.' All loudly agreed and a 'bottoms up' call came. They drank their glasses dry and another round was called for, the shopkeeper standing it this time.

'No, no. Our mainland comrades won't come here,' one of the other Chinese said. 'They lost too many men against the Americans in Korea and anyway the geography is against it. Besides which, as long as the bandits' – by which he meant Chiang Kai-shek's remnants in the Golden Triangle – 'are their long-range target, nothing will bring them onto Thai soil proper. We, for our part, help our Thai comrades when and how we can.'

'That is good to know,' said Jason. 'When I go back, I'll tell them the reverse so that they can waste their money and their time in preparing for something that will not happen.' They guffawed in appreciation and after a refill yet another 'bottoms up' was called for.

By this time Jason's language skills had so won over his audience they were getting to sing songs and uproariously laughing at his jokes. Small eats were called for and more beer.

'I've had enough beer. How about brandy,' Jason suggested. All agreed.

Four-fingers' worth were poured into each glass and, with the obligatory toast of '*yam sing*', 'drink to victory', they downed the contents in one. As custom dictated, hands were laid over each glass as if to say 'no more' but no resistance was made when their hands were removed so that more drink could be poured in. 'And again,' said the shopkeeper and again it was.

Food was called for and while they were waiting for their meal Jason told them about the conversation he had overheard earlier on. 'What are your relations with the local people?' he asked.

'Why do you want to know?' the senior man countered.

So Jason repeated, in Thai, the *chin* and *kha man di kwa*, stressing the *man* impersonal pronoun. 'What does that signify?' he asked.

'In Thailand, if you're not a Thai, you're nobody, unless you have so much money you can't be ignored or, as some of the Royal Thai Army Generals have, a European wife but not us Chinese,' and he spat his disgust.

'Does that have any influence on my talking about the domino bone slab theory?'

'No. The reason we're Communist is that everything centres on Bangkok and that has to be altered. But as you've already been told, it's more a token movement than the real thing.'

At that moment food was brought in so saving Jason from saying something like 'I wish I could help you.' They kept quiet while they concentrated on scooping up the glutinous rice and fried pork with their chopsticks. No Chinese ever wanted to waste time talking at meals. After putting down their empty bowls they belched their satisfaction.

By now Jason was feeling he'd had more than enough so made efforts to leave them. *I've learnt enough for one day.* The others tried to stop him. 'We have only had rice and fried pork. We still need some salty wet stimulant. Are you a *ham sap kwai,* a randy devil? If so, I'll show you where,' the shopkeeper told Jason.

'Yes, take me along. I'd like some horizontal refreshment,' answered Jason, although he felt exactly the opposite, wanting only sleep. He was led away and left alone with his woman. He was not so drunk that he knew that, were he to go to sleep, she'd probably rob him so he waited until the others had gone their own way and, pleading tiredness, told the girl he'd come back next evening at the same time, slipped off and managed to find his way to his own hotel, having told the whore a different place. When he woke with a bad hangover he was still fully dressed.

He kept to himself the next day, nursing his hangover and hoping he would not be sought out by any of those he'd been wassailing with. By evening he was feeling his normal self and was delighted when his two men joined him. They were tired and travel-stained. After a wash and a meal, they told him what they had managed to do.

'We found a cell but it took us all day. It was quite far out and we had to go by timber lorry to their hide-out in the jungle. But once we got there and showed them our credentials, we were accepted. We told them what the Secretary General of the Thai Communist Party had sent to Sadao and that we were merely passing on the information to keep them in the know. We were thanked and we then asked them about any links with other country's fraternal comrades.' Kamhaeng Thanaboon spoke quietly in Nepali to Jason but repeated himself in Thai to Jenko from time to time. 'I had a hard time to sound genuine, Sahib, but we did learn that no member of the Thai Communist guerrillas would go to another country except over the border into Laos as a sanctuary to let matters cool down here if they became too hot. As for any Lao guerrillas coming over the border, it was unheard of.'

'And any thoughts of a Chinese incursion?' asked Jason.

'No, at their level, that idea had never been mooted.'

'So what did they think of it?'

'So unlikely as to be laughable.'

'How do they get on with the Chinese?'

'They find that those merchants and shopkeepers who claim to be Communists are probably not interested in anything but being treated as well by the Government as are the Thais and, of course, making money. That's in every Chinaman's blood. Now, Sahib, let's hear from you.'

Jason told them all he felt they needed to know, shaking his head about how much beer and brandy he had drunk. He did not mention his visit to the brothel nor his running away from the Thai whore. 'Did you ask them if it was worth going on to Udorn Thani to see what their comrades were doing south of Vientiane?'

'Yes, we asked about the whole gamut. They said they had no fear whatsoever of any incursion from the Chinese but were unable to give an opinion about anything on the Lao side of Thai Isan. They asked us if we'd come alone and we said yes. We told them we were going to Udorn Thani but they gave us the impression that our visit was so unusual that they wanted to check up on us. I think they'd be more than suspicious if they knew we were with you.'

'So what does that mean? What do you advise?'

'Sahib, it's up to you where we go but Jenko and I believe it is better that we don't go to Udorn Thani but move by bus directly to the ferry at Mukdaharn and talk with our various contacts on the buses and at night stops until we get there.'

So that is what they did – and they only found parochial indifference to anything beyond high prices in the market and bad weather for the rice farmers.

Engine trouble with both normal ferries meant that a large rowing boat only was available to cross over to Laos. After a prolonged wait eight oarsmen, moody and recalcitrant, assembled at the landing stage. With baggage loaded and passengers aboard, the crew got in, took their oars and started pulling out into the current. The Mekong was wide and fast-flowing, the water brown and roiling.

The boat was full to overflowing. Wearing his pack, in which was his passport, and money in his money belt, Jason sat near the gunnels. Next to him was a Lao family of father, mother, pubescent daughter dressed in a long, wide dress, with a little white dog in her arms, and a younger son. Halfway across the little white dog managed to get on to the edge of the boat and started barking. It had smelt a crocodile which was dangerously near. The crocodile sensed something to eat and, swimming towards the boat, lashed its tail violently. The dog managed to get out of the girl's arms.

'That big brute has eaten several people since before the monsoon,' shouted the senior boatman. 'We will be safe here because the boat is too heavy to overturn.'

But the little white dog was incessant in its barking and Jason saw that the girl was afraid it would jump overboard and be eaten. So she edged closer to it, reached up to the edge of the boat but could not get hold of her pet. Her father shouted out to her to be careful but she took no notice.

She stood up, reaching over to catch hold of the dog. She was about to pick it up when a particularly strong eddy made some of the rowers miss their stroke, causing the boat to shudder. She lurched forward and fell into the river with a loud scream. The dog barked even more furiously and the crocodile quickened its speed. Consternation and shouting broke out.

'Save her, save her,' shrieked the mother. The rowers momentarily stopped rowing. The boat swung round with the current taking control. Chaos. In a sharp moment of surprise, prolonged in consciousness but instantaneous in reaction, Jason saw what he had to do. Taking off his shoes, he flung his pack to his Gurkha, picked up a long piece of rope and in one leap he was where the girl had been, grabbed the dog and threw it as far as he could away from where the girl was struggling in the water on the other side of the crocodile. The crocodile turned and went after the dog. Jason dived into the river and struck out after the girl who was being carried downstream, thrashing about, only not sinking because some air had been trapped in her billowing clothes. Soon at her side, he caught hold of her just as she was about to go under. She had swallowed some water and started to choke. At the same time the crocodile's jaws clamped onto the little white dog and an agonised howl carried over the water. Supporting the girl around her waist, he managed to get her head back above water. He saw it was useless trying to return to the boat so he had to let the current take them on downstream.

'*Chab chieuk*' – catch hold of this rope – he shouted, hoping that his Thai was near enough her Lao for her to understand.

She must have as, fumbling blindly, water in her eyes and coughing, she just managed to. Jason pulled the other end of the rope over one shoulder and again shouted to the girl to catch hold of the other end. *Chab ik khrang.* To his relief this she did but only after some lacklustre groping. Clearly she was confused, terrified and weakening fast.

Jason, luckily a strong swimmer, knew he had to swim athwart the current if he were to have any chance of reaching the far shore. But the current was strong and his wet clothing, the girl's weight and the rope round one shoulder hampered him so he could not swim straight.

He was on the point of wondering if he had enough strength to rescue himself, let alone the girl, with the implications of letting go of her flashing through his mind, when he saw a low island about fifty yards distant, almost to his front. With a supreme effort he struck out towards it and just, only just, managed to clear the current into the lee of the small piece of land so miraculously to hand. His feet touched mud and he staggered forward, pulling on the rope which, by now, had badly chafed his shoulder. He turned to help the girl who, also at her last gasp, felt safe now she could feel something under her feet. She fell forward, only half conscious, into his arms. Half carrying, half lugging her onto dry land, she collapsed into a heap as he let her go, breathing stertorously. He saw what he had to do. He lifted her upright, feet first, not worrying how much of herself she revealed, and, holding her legs in one hand, punched her belly with the other. She moaned but a rush of the water she had swallowed drowned her voice. She was heartily sick, most of it over Jason's feet.

But he had saved her, albeit at the expense of her little white dog. He laid her gently down and she shuddered, started weeping softly, then said, in French, 'Come and lie beside me. I am so cold.'

He looked around and saw a small dip in the ground. He managed to say, so that she understood, 'We are alone. No one can see us. If we lie in our clothes we will be ill. We must take them off, lay them out in the sun to dry and only then will we get warm together.' It was winter time but the sky was cloudless and the dip was out of the wind so lying naked was warmer than lying in wet clothes. *Survival overrules modesty.*

She obeyed, unashamed yet quietly shy. They lay down, touching one another. She nestled up to him, his taut, muscular body throbbingly alive and, exhausted though he was, that surge of something seldom sensed once more thrilled through his thighs. Breasts like budding melons and wasp-waisted, he devoured her with his eyes.

She flashed a smile at him, golden and equivocal, milk-white teeth glinting momentarily.

He remembered the Gurkha song about the beautiful lass ready for marriage whose teeth were like cucumber seeds and whose heels, dove's eggs.

She looked lovingly at him, her fingers fetchingly feeling; it was all she could ever want but which she could never have. Her fingers faltered and she dropped off into a dead, deep sleep.

Two whole hours later, hearing a motor boat, Jason hurriedly dressed, woke the girl up and told her to put on her still-damp clothes. He stood up and waved at the approaching boat which beached shortly afterwards. In it were the girl's parents, his two men with a couple of towels and dry clothes for them both.

Both wet people changed their clothes as modestly as circumstances allowed then, still whacked with fatigue, got into the boat. Away it sped to the Lao shore.

On their way, Manbahadur told Jason that the father was an officer in the Lao police – 'probably Special Branch' – and would help Jason through customs and immigration before taking him back home where he and his two men would be guests for that night.

Back at the Lao's house Jason was made much of. Conversation was slow because of his lack of Lao and insufficient Thai, but with Manbahadur's Nepali and his own French now and then, they talked with one another. Apparently it was unusual to find crocodiles in the river around that part of the Mekong and the police were to make efforts to shoot it.

Jason decided to tell the police officer, Souk Vongvachit, that he was, in fact, a British officer and that his two friends, and here he decided to dissemble, were both ex-military. As the evening wore on, he steered the conversation towards the Vietnamese taking over the country and then moving over into Thailand.

Souk Vongvachit said, 'Sir, you have been open with me and so I will be open with you. The Vietnamese are stronger than we Lao are. As you are new to Laos you will not have heard our saying, "The day a Lao is born is the day he starts to hate a Vietnamese". However, what we do know is that all the Vietnamese really want is to control Indo-China as the French used to. Nothing else.'

Jason gently probed. 'So no Chinese or Vietnamese action

against Thailand or, farther south, Malaya?'

'Sir, who knows the future? But, if I were a betting man, I'd say "no".'

Jason thanked him. 'My eyes are heavy and my body aches. May I be excused? A mat on the floor and a sheet over me is all I want.'

'Sir, tonight you will sleep in my bed. I will sleep on the floor.'

Next morning they were given a meal before setting off. 'Last night you said you wanted to explore Savannakhet. Let me tell you that it is a big place and many Frenchmen still live here, some in business in the town as hotel owners, outside it some owning plantations. They are an arrogant lot who don't like speaking to anyone else except themselves. They only speak to people like us if they need something or we're in the way. They might speak to you as you're a European. I have one last point to make, sir. Here on this piece of paper is my name and address. Even after I leave the police, if any Englishman were to want help, I'll always be ready to give it.'

Jason thanked him profusely and the two women of the house once more shed tears of gratitude as their three guests left.

Back once more on their own, they went off to find a cheap hotel. Jason decided to try out his French and the other two to do their searching in their own way.

Savannakhet, being so large, meant that Jason had to be selective. His money belt was still damp but his money dry as he always took the precaution of wrapping it up so as to be waterproof: he went to change his to kips and entered the first book shop he found. He bought a town plan and a map of Laos. He reckoned that talking to a hotel or bar owner, a priest or a missionary or, come to that, any other interesting person he came across, might add to his store of knowledge or merely back up what he had already learnt. His French was 'low to mediocre' as he put it to himself but it might be good enough if the person with whom he talked spoke slowly and used simple words.

That evening he looked into a number of places before choosing one where the menu outside showed venison steak. He opened the door and saw a fat, black-haired Frenchman behind the bar. He went and asked for a glass of Chardonnay. 'I see you have venison steak on the menu,' he managed to say in slightly stilted French. 'May I order it here?'

'*Mais oui, Monsieur*,' the Frenchman replied, adding, in English, 'Your French is worse than my English!'

Jason grinned back. 'We will manage somehow.'

'You are an Englishman, I think. Not an American.'

'Correct.'

'We don't see many Englishmen here. What are you doing?'

'I am a schoolmaster, taking a year off, to study the situation in Indo-China now that the Communists are, how you say, "flexing their muscles" after their takeover of North Vietnam in 1954.' He was tactful enough not to mention the French defeat in Dien Bien Phu during the octave of Easter of that year. 'I have been in Thailand and Malaya and before I return to England I feel a visit to Laos, even for a few days, will be of value.'

Jason had to re-say one of two phrases, both in French and English, before the Frenchman fully understood.

'Ah so.' He looked a bit uncomfortable. 'Are you a socialist or not?'

A difficult one to answer. Say the opposite of what the other man was and lose out. *Heads or tails?* 'I sympathise with you French people who suffered so much at Dien Bien Phu in 1954. What does that make me?'

The other man relaxed. 'No matter. I was at that place and am glad to be alive. My people in France did not understand then and do not understand now. I tried to resettle back home when I left the army as a sergeant but so many spat at me for losing the war, I came back here. It is quieter here and I like it.'

'Yes, I can understand your point of view, *Monsieur*. I'd feel the same.'

He was called away to eat his dinner and, having finished, went back to the bar. 'A night cap, as we English call it, for you and me.'

The barman poured out two glasses of Chardonnay and they toasted one another.

'What are the chances of the Domino Theory taking place, do you think?' Jason asked. 'Can you see China coming as far south as Thailand or the Vietnamese winning in the south and spreading into Laos and Cambodia then on to Thailand and Malaya?'

The Frenchman's answer was deliberate and sombre. 'I doubt it for China. They know that the Americans are scared of the Communists and the Communists are scared of the Atom Bomb. If the North Vietnamese were Communists with a world view, they would be trying to swing westwards rather than driving south. No, at heart they are nationalists, pure and simple, and only once they have taken over all of Indo-China, as I fear will happen, will they rest.' He sighed heavily. 'They will make life difficult for their own people and, of course, bully the gentle Lao.'

'That is something I had not thought of,' said Jason truthfully and, having drained his glass and paid, left for the hotel, first thanking the barman who merely replied with a Gallic shrug.

The next day, a Sunday, he stretched his legs first thing then, at eleven o'clock, went to the church. It was a Roman Catholic one but, although Jason was a not-very-often-practising Protestant, he felt that he'd try for a word with the priest after the service. This he managed to do.

'Father, may I have a word with you, please?' he asked as he left the church door.

'Certainly. Wait here while I change my vestments,' the priest answered in slow, careful French, sensing that his interrogator was not all that fluent. He came back in slacks and an open-necked shirt. 'Come this way, please. I am getting on in years and I don't speak English but, even with your poor French, I'll try and help,' he said, robbing any possible offence with a smile.

Jason asked the same question as he had asked the night before. The priest looked shocked. 'The Devil has caused enough trouble already in Vietnam. *Le bon Dieu* surely won't allow it to cause any more.'

That's not the sort of answer I was expecting. 'If the Vietnamese were to make trouble in Laos would they win and, having won, go farther south?'

'Go south to Thailand? No, I doubt it very much. But in Laos? Win they would and win they will. I have heard an English expression describing the North Vietnamese. Wait.' The old priest closed his eyes and thought hard. 'Yes, I have it. "Lacquered bamboo",' then gave the French equivalent. 'But, even though they would rule the Lao, they would never win them over. The Lao have a saying, "the day a Lao is born is the day he learns to hate a Vietnamese". *Comprenez-vous, Monsieur?*'

Yes, Jason understood. *That's the second time I've heard that saying. They must mean it.*

'And, before you go, if you were to ask that question in Cambodia, your answer would be "Would we take the liver out of a Vietnamese we kill, cook and eat it if we liked them?" I must go. *Excusez-moi*,' and the old man left before Jason could thank him, not having realised just how unpopular the Vietnamese were outside Vietnam.

That afternoon Jason hired a bicycle and rode out into the countryside, concentrating on staying on the right of the road. After about ten kilometres – *they don't think in miles here* – he came across a small bungalow in a well-kept garden. He was surprised to see a middle-aged European woman, the brim of a large straw hat pulled well down over her face, picking flowers. He heard her say 'Drat it,' as she dropped her secateurs. *English!*

On the spur of the moment, he got off his bike and said, 'Let me pick them up for you.'

The woman turned round in surprise. She had a hook nose, receding chin, pursed mouth and an incipient moustache. 'No, don't bother,' she said, with a puzzled frown squinting against the sun. 'Don't you find it hot without a hat?'

'No, I'm used to the sun.'

She looked at him thoughtfully. 'May I ask what you're doing here? We don't often see any European here except the French, which you don't sound like. Come inside and I'll make some tea for you.'

Jason thanked her and, taking his shoes off before going inside, went in.

'There's no need to follow that heathen custom here,' the woman sternly reprimanded him. 'Just wipe your shoes on the mat.' She disappeared into the back and, a few minutes later, brought out a pot of tea, three cups and some biscuits. In a shrill falsetto, she called out, 'Jacques, Jacques, tea time.'

A man, older than she, came out of one of the rooms and joined them. With a little wisp of white beard resembling chicken fluff and round-shouldered, he gave the effect of having withered inside his clothes like the kernel of a nut.

'For your interest, my husband and I are missionaries. We've been here twenty-five years, doing the Lord Jesus's work. May I ask what you're doing here?' she asked.

'I'm an English PhD student researching the Domino Theory,' Jason lied glibly. 'I'm trying to find out whether the Communists will try and take over this part of the world?'

The woman looked at him with a tinge of loathing. 'You people are all the same. Nothing but talk, talk, talk of Communists and I don't know what else. I'll tell you,' she was working herself up to some denouement, Jason saw, 'that, unless and until you people can get rid of the scourge of Buddhism, the Devil's religion, nothing else matters.'

Jason, about to take his first sip of tea, jerked upright but managed not to spill any of it. 'Buddhism, Madam, did you say?'

A defiant 'Yes.' Then, 'You started drinking your tea before my husband has said grace.'

He stood while the man mumbled their combined thanks to the Almighty. Jason, wanting to retrieve matters, crossed himself. 'Don't tell me you're a Roman Catholic,' she snapped at him.

Seated once more and not answering the question of his religious denomination, Jason said, 'I apologise for my solecism but did you really say that Buddhism is the scourge in Laos, Madam, not Communism?' faint irritation discernible in his tone of voice.

'Yes, I did. Buddhists are poisonous while the Communists are merely misguided. Holy Communion has more in common with Communism than most people realise. Our job is to teach people that.' She spoke with a Spartan authority and after a pregnant pause added, 'and I sincerely thank our Lord Jesus that there are no Hindus anywhere about here: they are infinitely worse and I see them as Satan's right hand.' Her husband nodded appreciatively. *If they have any grown-up sons, just as well none is in a Gurkha regiment*, Jason said to himself.

By the end of the meal Jason had ranked them both as with other missionaries he had met: dull, dangerous, narrow-minded, wrapped up in their self-righteous irrelevance, but seemingly, in this case here, with no perceivable peccadillo but typical particularity. He finished his tea as soon as he politely could, looked at his watch and stood up. 'I thank you for your tea and your time, Madam. I must go,' and he set off back to Savannakhet. On the way he tried to think how such bigotry could be justified, how those who allowed such people into the country tolerated their continued stay, how much damage they did and, if they did feel missionary zeal, why not spend their energies in the Wapping Docks area of the River Thames or the nastier outer fringes of Paris?

His two men had nothing new to report that night, merely echoing similar sentiments.

They journeyed north by local bus to Thakhek in the neck of the Panhandle, spending the night there. More provincial than Savannakhet, Jason found it had an unfriendly ambience. Strange stares and unfriendly looks, so different from what he had found so far, gave him the same feeling as he had experienced when working 'deep' in Communist territory during the Malayan Emergency.

Jason's two aides, as he now thought of them, came across an unusual snippet, indicative to his train of thought. 'Thakhek, although a government stronghold, is on Route Coloniale 12, the shortest way across the neck of the Panhandle over to Vietnam,' said Jenko. 'By using our password I found a courier for the Pathet Lao and he took us to his safe house – and I've made a note of the address.' Jason knew that 'Pathet Lao' was how the left-wing military forces were known. 'He said that Vietnamese Communist pressure on the Pathet Lao here was strong, probably stronger than in most other places still in Government hands, as the way that any Communist dignitary who had to go to China from Thailand or Malaya, had always used and always would. But he doubted any Vietnamese incursions into Thailand. Sahib, while we were there, we were interrupted by one named Zhong Han San, who we know as the leader of Killer Squad in the camp at Sadao. He will be there for the night. I said I had a Russian communist who spoke Chinese with me. "I'd like to meet him," he said, so why not let us go along and have a look?'

Could be interesting. 'Yes, let's go along.'

They reached the safe house after dark and the Gurkha knocked on the door. It was opened only as far as a latch in a lock would allow. Quiet words were spoken. Jason was invited in with both his men and was introduced to the leader of Killer Squad, a creaky-voiced thug with a long scar on the right of his face and a twitchy right eye. 'I am Comrade Zhong Han San,' he said, with all the warmth of a cobra toward a rodent.

Jason gave himself the name of Popov, which is how he named all Russians, and said that he was on a mission for the Chinese. 'Comrade Mao has personally told me that he was worried about safe passage for Comrade Chin Peng whom he had invited to visit him. He sent me to check,' he dissembled masterfully.

'Then it's more than lucky I was here to meet you. I am responsible for getting our Secretary General safely through Thailand to Thakhek where he'll be met by comrades both from Vietnam and the Pathet Lao.'

They were interrupted by a scuffle outside and a small boy was brought in by a Vietnamese. 'I caught this boy eavesdropping outside your window. I know he is an agent of the Royal Lao Police, Comrade.'

Zhong Han San, smirking and licking his lips, looked at the boy. 'Take off your trousers,' he said, picking up a piece of flattened bamboo. 'Bend over.' The boy, frightened out of his wits, tried to escape. Zhong, pulling him back, unbuttoned then took off the boy's trouser's before making him bend over and, in front of Jason and his two men, started to beat him with the edge of the bamboo till the blood flowed from his buttocks. Jason tried to intervene and was rudely pushed away. The boy screamed but the Chinese, an obscene bulge rising in the crotch of his trousers, put his hand over the boy's mouth and thrashed him more. Jason, sickened, again tried to stop the sadistic bully but received a thwack on his back for his pains. Before he could respond his two men had forcibly pulled him outside. 'Sahib, keep your temper. Let's get away here and back to our hotel. Luckily it's on the other side of town so that Zhong man won't dare follow us.'

Mentally fretting at what he had seen and not been able to prevent, Jason acquiesced. *The last thing we want is for any public outcry*. He was still inwardly fuming when they got on the Vientiane bus early next morning.

In Vientiane, which the Americans called 'The Ten-Minute Town', Jason passed his time as in the other places, seen and unseen, listening and talking, picking up hints, gestures, inferences and silences to add meaning to spoken words. Once again he felt those French who were there were living on borrowed time but did not realise it. In a side street off rue Circulaire he found a Chinese gold and ornament seller who had 'Formosa' in the name above his shop. Jason spoke to him at length, as one non-communist to another. So overwhelmed was the shopkeeper by their talk in the back of the shop, not only because of Jason's political thoughts but also because he was neither American nor French, that he tried to give Jason a two-thousand-year-old brass ring. Jason had enough money to pay for it and took the man's details as well as giving him his, an address care of a bank in England: 'If ever you get any news about the Red Chinese wanting to take Vientiane by force and then drive south, write to me,' was his message.

Jason went on to the British embassy in rue Pundit Nehru and asked for the British Attaché, a French-speaking Colonel. They had a long talk, during which Jason told him who he was and what he was doing. He gave the Attaché details of all his contacts. 'I feel pretty sure you won't keep those little nuggets all to yourself. I'm going to write a full report on my journey once I get back to Bangkok. What I've given you are the outlines only. I'll send you a copy.'

'Thanks a lot, Jason. Your nickname should be "Major Four Ears".'

On his return to Bangkok, the Brigadier listened to what Jason had to say – 'I'll send you a copy of my main report when I get back to the battalion, sir' – and questioned him closely from time to time. At the end, he said, 'You've done well, better than I thought you would, what with so nobly rescuing that girl and getting those names and addresses. You've also brought back "what's on the other side of the hill" and not yet thought of but don't expect anyone to thank you for it and certainly don't expect the Americans to take any notice of what you've learnt. They're a stiff-necked lot of folk with their collective heads in the air. But at least Bangkok and London will be interested. I've been warned about recommending you for s.q. or not and as you've used your nous and have not blotted your staff-work copy book, I'll give you a good report. I hope it brings you luck.' There was a twinkle in the Brigadier's eye; they shook hands and Jason thanked his senior with heartfelt gratitude, saluted him smartly and left.

He took his two men out for a meal and a drink in the nearest place to the British Embassy main gates. He paid them off and Jenko left. 'Manbahadur, I have an idea. Is there a telephone anywhere near you that you can use?'

There was. 'Give me the number.' He did. 'I'll take you to the Guard Room and introduce you to the Guard Commander.' At the gates, Jason called out for the senior man to come and talk to him. 'Can you fetch my old friend the Sergeant Major in charge?'

The Guard Commander sent a man to get him. 'Major-ba, thank you for coming, please look at this man,' said Jason introducing Manbahadur to him, giving him a short resumé of his background. 'He will be helping me in the future but, as I'll either be in Hong Kong or Malaya, I'm asking you to be my contact. Here is his phone number. Please give him and me yours. It will be easier to contact him through you. Can you help me, please, with this?'

'Sahib,' the Sergeant Major smiled widely, 'if we can't do it for you who can we do it for?'

At the end of the SEATO exercise planning, a party was thrown by the Royal Thai Army. Jason was invited and wore his best tropical bib and tucker. The British Ambassador caught his eye and called him over. 'Major Rance, I'd like to introduce you to the Nepalese Ambassador,' and seemed unconcerned when Jason, breaching protocol, broke into fluent Nepali. Then realising that the British Ambassador did not understand what he was saying, Jason apologised profusely. 'No worry,' he responded. 'I'll leave you two together,' and the Ambassador sauntered off, leaving the pair of them to have a good natter.

Jason had a brainwave: '*Rajdut* sahib, I'm so glad I can talk to you in Nepali without others listening in.'

The Nepalese Ambassador looked alarmed, then puzzled.

'Oh, don't take it amiss, please, Hajur,' Jason countered, 'but I'd like to tell you something for your ears only. May I?'

'But of course,' was the answer, the Ambassador delighted to be able to speak Nepali instead of English, a language he did not find easy at any time and even harder at noisy parties. They moved off into a corner, found a couple of chairs, sat down and Jason took the conversational initiative. The Nepalese Ambassador was transfixed as he learnt about the two Nepalis Jason had met in Bangkok, the one from the west of Thailand, first going on into details of the village he had visited and the slavish conditions under which the people lived. 'But, *Rajdut* sahib, I have had success with the man from far-off Indonesia. He had an up-to-date Indonesian passport and I gave him the money for his ticket back to Kathmandu. At least that's one worry off my chest.'

'Major sahib, that was indeed kind of you. Thank you. What can we do about those others?'

'*Rajdut* sahib, I wish I knew. On the face of it not all that much but, at your level, something might be able to be done. What I will do is to report it on my return and suggest that you also report it to Kathmandu, using my name were you to so wish.'

'I'll be frank with you, Major sahib,' the Ambassador said. 'On my own, talking with the Thai government, I doubt if anything positive would happen. Oh, they'd be polite enough, of course, they always are, but unless their problems focus on Bangkok and any threat, real or imagined, to their government, I fear nothing will happen. But since you've brought the matter up, I'll refer the matter to Kathmandu.' And that meant to the King.

'*Rajdut* sahib, thank you for that. I'd hate nothing to be tried to be done for them. After all, they've suffered a lot, first for the British as soldiers and now as financial slaves.'

It was time to rejoin the party so they shook hands and wandered off separately.

Before leaving the embassy Jason went to bid farewell to his old Sergeant Major. 'Just as well you came to see me, Hajur,' the Guard Commander said. 'I have just had a phone call from Manbahadur Limbu to let you know that when Kesar Pun went to buy his ticket at the RNAC office, he was told that his name had been blacklisted so no ticket could be sold him and, if he did appear, he was straightaway to report to the Indonesian embassy.'

Jason's heart sank. There was no time for him to do anything. 'Thank you, Major-ba,' he replied. 'Just let Manbahadur know you've told me if and when he next contacts you, please, and tell him I'll do what I can for him.'

On his way back to Hong Kong, Major Rance had to stop over in Kuala Lumpur to report to the British Defence Advisor, another Brigadier, to brief him on the planning of the exercise: even though Malaya was not a member of SEATO, the military planners wanted to know what was happening. Before organising himself a hotel, he went to the embassy and asked to meet the Brigadier. 'To save you telling the same story twice,' he said, 'I'll take you along to HQ Federation Armed Forces for a detailed session and then come back home with me. I've got a guest room and it will be pleasant to have someone new to have a chinwag with.' Before they left his clerk handed him a signal. 'Major Rance, this is really for you. You'll have to be re-routed to Hong Kong via Singapore as the Jungle Warfare School wants to be briefed on the SEATO exercise as it may – quite how? – make a difference to their syllabus – Counter Domino tactics, I expect.'

They went straight back to the Brigadier's quarter after their visit to the Malayan HQ and over a cup of tea, Jason related how he had found the Gurkha remnants and did the Brigadier think that there was any mileage making a report?

'Can't see that it will do any harm but as the men belonged to the Indian Army, not the British, I doubt the War Office will take any notice.'

The telephone rang. The Brigadier's wife answered it. 'It's for you, dear,' she said.

The Brigadier went over to the phone and said 'DA speaking'. It seemed that the caller knew that Jason was with him, someone had seen him going to the HQ. 'Yes, Major Rance is here. Do you want to speak to him? Wait one,' and he beckoned to Jason. Jason took the phone from him. 'Rance speaking,' he said.

'Shandung P'aau, it's P'ing Yee here. Can't talk openly on the phone, can we? How can I meet you?'

To the veritable surprise of his host and hostess, Jason

continued the conversation in fluent Chinese. He fixed up a meeting for the morrow and, after telling Ah Fat how wonderful it was to be in contact again and that only a one-to-one meeting in person was safe, put the receiver back down on its holder.

'Jason, you were terrific,' the Brigadier's wife said as Jason regained the table. 'Tell us how you managed such a professional performance and who were you speaking to, if I may ask.'

So Jason gave them a potted version of his early childhood years and a hazy account of 'how we met' during the Emergency. 'And what other languages do you speak?' she chirruped and Jason 'came clean': some Thai, Malay and Nepali, nothing else except schoolboy French. He did not mention that he had had a smattering of Vietnamese from twenty years earlier.

When Jason met Ah Fat he gave him an outline of his recent past. 'I'm just back from six months' staff work for the SEATO exercise. I have found two Gurkhas, one who is Dipa Nusantara Aidit's escort and the other an ex-guerrilla in the Thai Communist Party who is an elder brother of my ace tracker that time on Operation Janus, I'm sure you'll remember him.' Yes, indeed Ah Fat did. Jason proceeded to give his friend 'chapter and verse' of what he had learnt in the past six months and done, including his 'visit' to Chin Peng's camp.

'Shandung P'aau, you are inimitable. I also found out about one of the Gurkhas, the one with Aidit when he visited Chin Peng. But meeting two Gurkhas who could not get back home after the war, eh? Truth is indeed stranger than fiction. Now that bit about Thakhek is of tremendous interest because I have learnt that Chin Peng will be going to China. Until now no one knew which way he'd go. How best can we use that news, I wonder. When are you leaving?'

'In two days' time.'

'Right. That means you will have time to meet Mr C C Too. I'll arrange a meeting with him tomorrow. It'll have to be private as the Malayan authorities are getting stickier and sticker about the British poking their noses into affairs, even though, on the Malay-Thai border there has always been a Gurkha battalion engaged on Operation Bamboo. The Malay military is just not properly organised to take on the continuing remnants of the MCP guerrillas – probably never will be,' he added scornfully.

After fully briefing Mr Too and Ah Fat in Mr Too's house, sipping tea as they sat talking, Ah Fat asked Jason to tell them about how he and his Gurkha had gone to Chin Peng's camp and delivered a letter. His listeners were even more amazed at learning how he had hoodwinked the sentry first that he was a young girl and then that he was a ghost.

'Shandung P'aau, can you give Mr Too a demonstration?' and such was his intake of surprise as he sipped his tea, he did the 'nose trick' and erupted in paroxysms of coughing, with his wife running over to him from another room and slapping his back to calm him down.

'Jason, wonderful, wonderful,' Mr Too gasped in awe. 'The magic wand of fluency. I never realised you were that talented when we first met in … when was it? 1951, I think.'

'Yes, at the end of Operation Janus.' Jason looked at his watch. 'Time to go. Thank you for your hospitality. I'll write a full report both about the SEATO exercise, my recce – but not of my visit to Sadao – and the two Gurkhas for my people and send you a copy. There's nothing we can do about them at the moment, if ever, P'ing Yee, but, just supposing my battalion, back from Hong Kong in a year of so, were to be engaged on Operation Bamboo, you and I might be able to operate in the guerrillas' blind spot.' He hesitated and Ah Fat broke in, 'When you wrote that sneaky little note, how did you sign yourself, or did you leave it blank at the bottom?'

'I signed it Shandung P'aau.'

'You don't think Chin Peng would know who Shandung P'aau is?' Mr Too asked.

'No, I can't see how he could know that was my childhood nickname, unless P'ing Yee ever sleep-talked when in his hearing.'

Both Chinese grinned at that. 'What do you think his reactions were, Jason?' Ah Fat asked.

'Hard to say but more than very angry, I expect.'

'And after that?'

'Try and find out who the sender was.'

'Could he be successful, do you think?'

Jason thought back to that time. 'The only way he might be is if the hotel keeper looked at my passport that I gave him for safe keeping and told him about it.'

Silence. 'Food for thought,' said Mr Too. More silence, broken when Rance said to his friend, 'We're due back here in Malaya in 1961 and by that time the target of my letter will probably have forgotten. Oh yes, can you give me a phone number I can use for you, please?'

Rance was given it and the two friends went their separate

ways.

At the Jungle Warfare School Jason was asked to give a lecture on the SEATO exercise and there was enough time for questions afterwards. A hand shot up at the back. 'Yes?'

'Sir, my name is Lieutenant Sumbi of 600 Raider Company of the Indonesian Army. You have mentioned an attack from Yellow Land. Can you ever see SEATO moving as far south as, say, my country if ever there was an outbreak of Communist Revolutionary Warfare there?'

That's a fast ball. 'On the face of it, no, I can't. Indonesia is not a signatory to the treaty and there's a lot of water between your country and the mainland so, unless, for instance, your country were to attack northwards to Borneo, say,' and he gave a deprecatory laugh at the very idea of such an improbability. 'I can see a reaction from Britain but only if it were considered to be a real threat.'

It was only much later, as Jason rehearsed that slightly odd question, that he remembered a rather smug, complacent look appearing on Sumbi's face. *I wonder why?*

On his return to Hong Kong, Jason had a session with his CO, not forgetting to give him a piece of cloth bought in Chiang Rai for his wife: he had given the other piece to his hostess in Bangkok. At the end of their talk, the CO said, 'I've had intimation that you did well. I am glad for your sake. You probably found it strange to be in a country in the American sphere of influence, Thailand, and a one-time French sphere, Laos, so it shows you are more adaptable than you like to let on. It seems that you were sufficiently manipulative to have created a good impression. Just shows you can be tactful when you want to be,' and the CO's smile robbed the remark of any recrimination.' *Almost an apology for what he said before I went to Thailand.* 'You may appear extremely regimentally minded but you have shown you can see a long way in front of your nose. Good for you. Anything more for me?'

'No, sir. I'll get cracking on my report, two copies for the War Office – one of them for the Int boys – and two copies to Bangkok and one each for Kuala Lumpur, Vientiane and our battalion records.'

Back in his office he sent for Sergeant Kulbahadur Limbu and told him, almost word for word, of the conversation he had had with Manbahadur Limbu in Bangkok. 'Does he have a mole under his left nostril?'

Jason thought back. 'Yes, he does.'

That clenched it. 'I'll write and tell his family. They'll want to know all about it and be so glad to learn that he is not dead.'

Not many people knew that once a year the King of Nepal and his Queen dined completely privately with the British Ambassador and his wife. It was a sign of the trust between the two countries and a token of the acknowledgement by Nepal's ruler that Britain never used the Gurkha connection as a 'bargaining chip' between the two nations. It is possible that recruiting, which officially started for the Honourable East India Company's army on 24 April 1815, would have been stopped long years before had that been so but the question had never arisen. The original embassy building, built and added to in large grounds during the early part of the nineteenth century, had been handed over to the Indian government on 15 August 1947 when independence was granted, embassy land being regarded as belonging to the country which occupies it, not of the country in which it is situated. The new British embassy was not nearly so resplendent but, even so, was appropriate enough to show Great Britain's strength, just having won a war which had bled her white but not having yet fully lost the peace to her former enemies.

The dinner in 1960 took place in the third week of April. The Ambassador and his wife met the royal car, driven by the King himself. The ADC in the front jumped out and opened the rear door for the royal couple who were welcomed by their host and hostess. They went into the reception room for pre-dinner drinks. The British Defence Attaché and his wife were also present. Pleasant banter and small talk broke what little tension there was. The King had a pleasing sense of humour, honed during his spell as a schoolboy at Britain's Eton College, and was nicely relaxed when the Head Butler announced dinner was ready. The senior four only went into the dining room: the others ate in the Billiard Room. Towards the end of the main course, the conversation became serious. 'Your Excellency,' said the monarch – only the Ambassador's wife was addressed by name – 'there is one point that has been on my mind for some time and this is the only place I feel I can talk about it frankly and get an answer that is not hedged in by protocol.'

The Ambassador, ever alert on such an occasion, wondered

just what could be coming; having had no previous wisps of gossip to aid him, he hoped he could field any fast ball before it became a boundary. He put his knife and fork down on his plate, looked up at the King and said, 'Your Majesty, this is the best place for us to clear the air. We are, of course, always ready and happy to be of service to you and your country.'

The King cleared his plate. 'I'll be explicit and tell you my concern and how you can help me.' He looked his host full in the face and continued, 'Many of my countrymen lost their lives during the war and more, thankfully not nearly as many, have done so in your recent struggle in Malaya against the Communists there. What I have learnt from my own personal sources is that a few citizens of my country who were soldiers of yours when you ruled India, were not killed and, against their will, somehow or other became financial slaves in another country.'

The Ambassador, who was not as well versed in the history of Indian or British Gurkhas as he might have been, looked on, a shade blankly. 'Oh, Your Majesty, that is news to me. I had not heard about it. What countries has Your Majesty in mind?'

'Thailand and Indonesia but I am glad to say the latter has been rescued so there is only the one man left to come back home.' *Well beyond British influence*, thought the Ambassador, as the King continued, carefully watching his host's expression. 'The British Army and British Intelligence have methods of exploration and investigation, such as was shown in the Malayan Emergency and in SEATO exercises that I lack.' Even if the British Ambassador had known about the Nepalese Royal Intelligence Bureau, it would have been utterly against all protocol to have mentioned it. 'I feel that it much more likely that either service will have many more opportunities, overt or covert, to find and possibly rescue my citizens who came to rescue you, in your country's time of need.' The King paused as though considering another aspect of the matter. 'Why, Your Excellency, I say that your services have such methods is that the person who discovered these facts and reported them to my Ambassador in Bangkok was a British officer.'

Eyes met. Nothing was said as the Ambassador's wife rang the bell for waiters to come and clear the plates. The sweet course was brought in. The waiters left and the door closed behind them. By then the Ambassador had his answer ready.

'Your Majesty, this is certainly a most unusual request, if only in so far as you are talking about two countries that were never in the British Empire. I will have to confirm with my Defence Attaché that all were accounted for during the Malayan Emergency and, as for the others, I feel it is hardly Britain's concern so long after hostilities came to an end as the men were in the Indian not the British army.'

The King's eyes bored straight into the Englishman's. 'The Indian government has said that those men, Gurkha soldiers, Nepali citizens, are not its responsibility as Nepal is a foreign country. Gurkhas soldiers have been helping Britain since 1815 in retrieving situations that were not of their making or concern either.' After a pause, the King added, silkily, 'and supposing that you still had British troops missing, would your reaction be similar,' and, frowning, he gave the Ambassador a ghost of a smile about as warm as a skull.

Pin-drop silence followed that penetrating remark.

'Your Majesty,' stammered the Ambassador, feeling guilty for even having the temerity to have made such a point so having to make up as much lost ground as he could, 'I accept Your Majesty's point and Your Majesty must realise that I meant nothing derogatory by my rather abrupt dismissal of your charge. I will most certainly inform London of your wishes and can only presume that, unless any special operations were to be mounted once we have positive details, any situation that can be exploited within current government parameters will thoroughly be looked into, discreetly, of course. I and my successors will keep you informed. But, if Your Majesty knows the name of the British officer, it may make matters easier.'

'Thank you. I am sure you will, even though, in the eyes of both your Foreign Office and War Office, "blind spot" is a term I have learnt for such lacunae.' The King's vocabulary was good: he had not been educated at Eton College for nothing. He put his hand in his coat pocket and took out an envelope. 'I've written down the name of the officer who knows the full details. There're in this envelope.' He stretched out his arm and gave it to the Ambassador.

'Your Majesty, I repeat, I will do what I can.'

Once outside in the main room, the King and his Queen stayed for coffee and liqueurs before saying their thanks, taking their farewells and driving back to the palace. To any outside observer, it had seemed just another pleasant and most satisfactory evening, despite the significance of the guests. In the car the King turned to the Queen, 'When we are in England on our State Visit later on this year, I won't forget to bring the subject up.'

The Queen merely nodded her head, demurely.

Back in the British Embassy the party soon broke up. As the Defence Attaché said his thanks and farewell, his Lord and Master murmured, 'The King was talking about some Gurkhas who served with the Indian Army during the last war and who are still marooned, not that he used that particular word, in Thailand. Apparently one who had been in Indonesia has been rescued but His Majesty did not give details as to how or when.'

The Attaché's eyebrows shot up.

'The King wants us, the British he means, not we here in Kathmandu, to do something about them as apparently the Indians won't.' The Ambassador shook his head. 'Devil of a situation to be in because he harped back to how much Nepal had helped us since 1815. Can't just drop it.'

'No, can't very well. How did he get this information, sir?"

'He didn't say what his channels were, but,' as he handed the envelope over, 'you'll find the details are in this.'

The Attaché took the envelope. 'In that case he'll presumably already have reported it on his own net.'

'Yes, he certainly should have done. But, belt and braces, send your report also as it will let them know who else knows.'

'I'll do that tomorrow, sir. Thank you for inviting us this evening. Good night.'

In London, the two organs of state that would have an interest in Jason's findings about the missing Gurkhas, read his report with curiosity rather than concern. 'Apart from noting it, there's not much we can do about it. The Thai government probably already knows about it and the Indonesians wouldn't have cared even if they had known about one man,' was the reaction. The report was pigeon-holed and forgotten.

The War Office, however, took notice of Major Rance's glowing staff report and arrangements were put in train for his name to be included in the next list of those 'staff qualified'.

On 21 October 1960 the Army Board gave an official dinner at the Savoy Hotel, London, to King Mahendra and his entourage because His Majesty was a British Army Field Marshal.

Major Rance had gone to England on leave and captains and above of the Brigade of Gurkhas in Britain at the time were invited. Diners had been told that before the meal His Majesty would talk with selected lieutenant colonels and above and after it with selected majors and captains.

At the end of the meal Field Marshal Lord Slim proposed a toast to the King. In his short speech he mentioned '… our abiding affection for your Majesty's Gurkha subjects, with whom it has been our inestimable privilege to serve in war and peace …' A toast was drunk.

His Majesty made a suitable reply and anther toast was drunk.

Jason had never met the King and was thrilled to be able to have the chance. When it was his turn he was directed to where the meeting was, in a small alcove in the far corner of the room. 'Your Majesty, Major Jason Rance is here to have an audience.'

Yes, he'll be the one. Let's see if he's anything like what my

Ambassador in Bangkok reported.

Protocol had it that English was to be spoken but Rance was surprised when, sitting opposite the King with a small round table between them, he was addressed in Nepali.

'Major sahib, I know your name. I admire what I have heard from my Ambassador in Thailand about your care and concern for my subjects who have not been able to return to the Land of their Birth since the last war, but one, I understand, was financed by you to return to Nepal by RNAC for which I thank you.'

'Sarkar,' Jason knew the correct word to use to a member of the royal family. 'I will always try to help any of Your Majesty's subjects as, when and how the occasion arises, however difficult that may be. Sadly, however, the Indonesian embassy blocked that one man from buying a ticket so he will still be in Bangkok. At least he will have the money I paid for the ticket to live on for a while. Your Majesty's two subjects will, I am sure, be together.'

'My Ambassador did not know about the blocking so that is new to me. I am asking your government to try and help rescue my people. Are you willing that I mention your name as the one I trust and hope will be involved?'

Jason gulped and grasped the arms of his chair. 'But of course, Sarkar. I regard that as a duty.'

'Good. In that case I trust you sufficiently to let you into what some might see as a State Secret.'

Jason winced in surprise.

'Tomorrow I am meeting some senior people in the government and am ready to tell them that if they don't let you, Major Rance, help, I may have to stop all Gurkha recruiting. How can I let my men be recruited into an army that does not fully look after its lost ones?'

Jason's only answer was that he would wait developments and asked permission to dismiss.

'If ever you go to Kathmandu, you can have direct access to me.'

Before Chin Peng departed for China in December, 1960, he was overjoyed at the return of Comrade Ah Hai who had been in China since 1949 to be cured of tuberculosis. Once he had settled in, 'You will be in charge here as Acting Secretary General after I've gone,' Chin Peng told him 'It is now time for an in depth briefing with Comrade Zhong Han San listening in. Your main danger will be ...' and 'that letter' was shown ... Ah Hai promised he'd be ready for any eventuality and that he'd monitor all letters most thoroughly. 'I have a nose for danger,' he said proudly.

On Jason's return to Hong Kong after his leave he was delighted to learn that he was now officially 's.q.' and that in 1961 1/12 GR was due to go to Ipoh in north Malaya from where rifle companies would be deployed farther north, not so far from the Malay-Thai border on Operation Bamboo.

Will Dame Fortune roll me a double six?

PART TWO

PART TWO

3

All ranks of 1/12 GR were glad to be leaving Hong Kong that February of 1961. The place did have some attractions not found in Malaya, such as sailing for the officers, a more plentiful bazaar for the soldiers and, in the winter, some cold weather to thicken blood thinned by the tropics. However, there was a language barrier. Bazaar Malay could be picked up in a week whereas, with Chinese being far harder and the colony Chinese not nearly as friendly as were the Straits Chinese, there never was much warmth between Gurkhas and the locals. Besides which, the frenzied pace of military life in the colony never seemed real – no one really expected to be able to prevent the mainland Chinese from overrunning Hong Kong if they really did make the effort to despite so many testing exercises to prevent or to delay such an eventuality. The volatile internal security situation too jangled nerves. Yes, Malaya was preferable.

After disembarking at Singapore, the battalion moved north to Ipoh by day train. Most soldiers dozed off, mesmerized as always by the sway, jolt and rumble of any railway journey, until Kuala Lumpur was reached. Jason, for the most part, looked out at the passing countryside, villages in the foreground and jungle behind, his mind turning to the years he had spent 'under the canopy'. During the Emergency he had operated mostly in the southern half of the country where the terrain was flatter than in the north and so more inclined to have swampy patches where water leaches prevailed. *How much thicker will the jungle be and how steep will the terrain be up north?* he wondered.

In Kuala Lumpur they were shunted into a siding for half the night and started off again in the small hours, reaching Ipoh shortly after dawn. They were met by members of the advance party and taken to Suvla Lines, which were new and spacious with nearby ranges and good games facilities.

Ipoh, in the state of Perak, was a large, well-spaced-out town in the middle of a once- productive silver-mining area. Silver, *perak* in Malay, had given that name to the state. Jason, a linguist at heart, remembered that *ipoh* was the poison from the *upas* tree which the ladang people put on the tips of their blowpipe darts for killing small animals and, if the dose was large enough, a person. HQ 2 Federal Brigade of the Federation Armed Forces, as the Malayan Army was known and under which they would serve for any operational tasks, was based at the opposite end of the town from the Gurkha barracks.

Only in an area of more than ten thousand square miles of almost uninhabited, rugged, jungle-covered mountainous terrain south of the Thai-Malay border were operations still continued under the rubric of Operation Bamboo.

As soon as the battalion had settled down the officers went to HQ 2 Federal Brigade for a background operational briefing. They were welcomed by the Brigadier, a tall, broad-shouldered

Malay with excellent English. 'I know you Gurkhas are workers not shirkers,' he said with a broad grin, 'toilers not spoilers.' He got his ration of titters then continued, 'So you will be a great bonus to Operation Bamboo.' He told them that its main aim was to eliminate the thirty-five Chinese guerrillas still on the police Wanted list. 'Surprisingly to those who might have thought that the aboriginal population, now known scientifically as,' a pause then, with a quirky smirk, 'Nesiot, were already content to live under the Malay government, that has yet to happen, so the secondary aim of Bamboo is to wean these people away from the Chinese guerrillas' sway. The operation has been in progress for three years and two rifle companies of the resident Gurkha battalion have always been deployed on it. My Brigade Major will give you more details.'

With that he wished the audience 'Good luck and good hunting' and departed.

Standing in front of a large map, the Brigade Major launched into his spiel: 'This large area is seen as a potential Communist bridgehead, one of influence rather than of physical occupation, from where the guerrillas could restart any nefarious activities slanted southwards, aided by those of the majority Temiar tribe (there are nine other smaller tribes, each with its separate language) providing intelligence and a screen in front of them wherever they go. The Brigade's aim, aided by Special Branch, is to bring the area back under government control. You won't be expected to have any meaningful contact with these people until you can speak some Malay. Your task will be to patrol around their settlements, known as ladangs, hoping to make the people there feel safe enough from guerrilla intimidation to give information of hostile movement or intentions to Special Branch. Then suitable counter-measures will be taken.' Jason sensed the speaker had a slight inferiority complex because, even after independence, the Malays were unable to finish off the job themselves. Apparently no guerrillas had been sighted for five years and no contacts made for ten.

There was a short 'leg stretch' when tea was brought in by a Chinese civilian belonging to the local fresh-ration contractor before it was the turn of a Chinese Special Branch officer to give details of the Temiar, a still almost stone-age flotsam of society. As Jason went to get himself a cup, he glanced at the man who had brought it in. He saw he had a hair lip – 'broken face', *pang hau* – but did not notice the way the man scrutinised him as his attention was taken by seeing his childhood friend Ah Fat enter the room. Both faces wreathed in smiles, they waved to one another.

Tea drunk and cups returned, the audience went back to their seats and the second part of the briefing began. Part of it was that 'the Temiar are timorous by nature. Any show of anger by a tribal outsider undoes months of work of trying to win them over from the guerrillas. They live in communities varying from under a score to over a hundred. They use bamboo for almost everything, houses, food, clothes and weapons. Animist superstition prevails. There are three don'ts when you meet them: don't laugh in front of butterflies, don't flash mirrors in the open, don't touch anyone's head. There is no beast of burden, no ploughing, no manure. For many the only wheel ever seen is that of a helicopter and for most their mother's the only milk ever tasted.'

At the end of Ah Fat's briefing the Malay Major asked if there were any questions.

Jason put up his arm. The Major nodded. 'How many people, military and police, engaged on Operation Bamboo can speak Temiar?'

A short awkward silence followed. 'We soldiers leave that side of the equation to Special Branch and the Department of Aborigines. For our purposes only elementary Malay, which all the headmen speak, is needed.'

Jason thanked the Brigade Major and did not ask if the guerrillas spoke Temiar. He presumed they did.

As people made to depart Jason lingered behind. 'Go on back,' he told the others of 1/12 GR, 'I'll borrow a brigade vehicle.' He turned to his old friend and they hugged one another. 'P'ing Yee, it's been a long time, hasn't it?'

'Shandung P'aau, much too long but I somehow feel we'll be able to go hunting together if the germ of an idea I have comes to fruition. I'll not tell you about it yet so if – I rather hope when – you get wind of it your expression of surprise will be so genuine that no one will think we've spoken about it already.'

'Makes good sense and why not? But before anything else tell me about yourself. Married yet? Still engaged with ...?' and he stretched his neck towards the window.

'Yes to both. I have a couple of sons who give me great pleasure. I have my own house in Kuala Lumpur. The Malays never call the place KL now. I still have my links with the opposition. And you?'

'Still single, old friend. As our Gurkhas say, "one must marry but afterwards there's nothing but trouble." I'm a long-term thinker,' and they both laughed.

'If ever you come to KL, look me up. You have my contact number, don't you?'

Yes, Jason did have it.

They said their farewells, unaware that the 'broken face' man, Pang Hau, had overheard their conversation in Chinese. He looked hard at Jason once more. *I'll have another look at the photo I was sent. I'm pretty sure he's the man. I'll also find out his name. If I'm right I'll get it sent up to Sadao by quickest means. I'll also mention his speaking Chinese and those two names, Shandung P'aau and P'ing Yee.*

The room above the general stores at the southern end of the main road through Sadao was owned by an elderly Chinese and used as a guerrilla safe house. It was where agents from Malaya brought mail, messages or any information destined for the camp.

Only a week after the 1/12 GR's briefing in Ipoh, a courier came into the shop and, using a password known only to the cognoscenti, said 'I've got a letter for the Secretary General himself. It's from Malaya and I was told it is important. It is from the Chinese contractor who delivers fresh rations for the Malayan Brigade in Ipoh.'

'If it wasn't important you wouldn't have brought it to me,' said the shopkeeper with a chuckle. 'Right, give it to me and, if you want, I'll give you a receipt for it. If it's all that important there may be an answer to take back so it's better to stay here to see if there is one. Go upstairs and I'll have a meal sent up.'

The courier handed it over, got his receipt and went upstairs to the protected part of the house. The area was considered safe nowadays but one never knew. *If it were entirely safe, those bigwigs wouldn't be hiding up in the jungle* came to his mind as he sat down to his meal.

The next man from the camp to visit the shop took the letter back to the Secretary General who opened it, intrigued to see it came from Ipoh. *Not a lot comes from Malaya these days.* He read it carefully, nodding his head thoughtfully as he did. *So a new Gurkha battalion will be thrashing about, chasing their own shadows around the ladangs, as useless as all military units have been to date. There's no reason for us to worry about it. And there's a name ...* Yes! The letter also had it that the person, a Major Jason Rance, was a Chinese-speaker who was addressed as Shandung P'aau – *Can't be the same man who wrote that filthy letter can he? But who else?* – and that he had spoken with a Special Branch man, an Ah Fat, whom he called P'ing Yee. *Same nickname as that of my Military Consultant to the Central Committee. Same man? Impossible ... but ... if it is that means he's working more deeply for 'them' than I had thought necessary.* A worm turned in the Secretary General's stomach. *There just can't be two Chinese with that nickname, surely?* he asked himself. *I'll have to find out and I will, by any means possible, when he next comes to visit me – as he surely must before I leave for China.* He shook his head in perplexity, hoping that he was wrong. His mind went back to occasions when matters had not worked out as planned. *Was that the reason?* He knew that all deceptions were based on illusions *but the here and now is reality.*

Chin Peng called for his secretary to bring him the copy of

the passport photo that belonged to that bird-photographing and butterfly-catching Running Dog who booked into that hotel in Sadao that time. 'Yes, the names are the same and now we know he is a Chinese speaker. That man is dangerous to us. *Can I get my revenge before I go to China? Will I be away before I can get my own back?* He called the leader of the Killer Squad, the man with perverted sexual tastes.

'Comrade, Zhong Han San, these are the details ...' and he showed him the offensive and humiliating letter. 'This is something we cannot allow to escalate, especially as I am planning my move out soon. What I insist on is briefing all those senior comrades who are working with the Temiar to make sure that if ever that particular Running Dog gets into their sights or even if a braver than usual *t'o yan* can get a heavily coated *ipoh* dart into him, it will be to the benefit of us all.' Chin Peng was an optimist as far as any person being hit by a blow-pipe dart was concerned. He knew that the last known person to have been shot by one was a European Director of Aborigines who had married a Temiar girl in the late 1930s and a jealous suitor had, in fact, killed him that way. *So ... why not again?* 'We must also have our own strong-arm men ready if ever there was a chance of a hand-to-hand struggle. I have two tasks for you, make a contingency plan for use against that insolent Running Dog wherever any of our comrades gets a suitable opportunity, and to read through all our files and see where we were unsuccessful then find out where my one-time Military Consultant to the Central Committee, a non-voting member, was. If you have any doubt on his integrity, let me know and then he too is to be your target.'

Zhong Han San set about his task and came to the conclusion that Ah Fat had been playing a double-handed role highly to the Party's inconvenience. His bitterness and resentment fumed and a small smiling malice shone in his dark eyes.

Chin Peng wrote two letters, grinding his teeth in rage and cursing under his breath as he did, one to the contractor in Ipoh and the other to his senior representative in the small town of Grik, near the Sungei Perak, the base of the two operational companies a hundred miles to Ipoh's north. In both letters he included the sentence 'In the name of the Party I order you to make all efforts to kill the man shown in the photograph attached' and he fastened a photocopy of the first page of Jason's passport. Both were told to try and keep a careful watch on this foreign devil named Major Jason Rance, also known as Shandung P'aau, and his activities, to eliminate him if the chance was ripe and also to let him, the Secretary General, know immediately when and where his movements were known about. Also both were told to report on the movements of Comrade Ah Fat. Both letters were received before the first two 1/12 GR rifle companies were deployed.

There was still a British Army General, once known as Director of Operations, in command of the Federation Armed Forces, the last one to have that task before a 'home-grown' incumbent took over the reins. He was an Guardsman and unlike some of the more magisterial officers found in the Brigade of Guards, he was blessed with a sense of humour, a dislike of bombast and an ability to accept the fact that 'non-whites' had their uses. He was a tall man with imposing features that, at first blush, were intimidating, yet a kindly smile soon dispelled that impression. He wore a walrus moustache and had a deep voice, in fact he was, when based in London, a stalwart in the choir of the Guard's chapel. He was tactful, as all those engaged on Household Duties back in England knew how to be, but frustrated that during his last tour of army duty no progress had been made on Operation Bamboo. During the Second World War he had fought in Europe with great distinction so, initially, the tropical forest environment of Malaya was an unknown to him. However, he had gone on three jungle patrols, one each with men from a Malay, a British and a Gurkha battalion, so now had a much better idea of local conditions. He also knew, but could not openly mention to his Malay staff, that the Temiar disliked and feared Malays, who looked down on them, and liked the guerrillas, who spoke their language and, for some of them at least, had a willing concubine if not wife, on more than one ladang. Any Malay male equivalent was openly shunned by all local women and the whole settlement would move into the vastness of the jungle to get away from such people if they started importuning their womenfolk.

Late one afternoon, sitting at his desk, wondering how he could break the deadlock before he left his post, his black, open line telephone rang. 'Yes, what is it?' the General asked, knowing that his Military Assistant answered that phone first then monitored all in-coming calls.

'Sir, there's a senior Special Branch officer whose name you know well, Mr C C Too, wanting to speak to you. Will you talk to him?'

The General knew that the Federation Armed Forces Malay staff disliked if not distrusted Chinese officers, be they army– no Chinese officer was ever promoted above the rank of Colonel however good he was – or Special Branch, so such a call to be made was highly unusual. 'Yes, put him through.'

Mr Too was a short, balding, bespectacled Malayan Chinese of forty, with quick, decisive gestures, a perfect command of English and a round face perpetually creased in smiles. His flair for understanding Communist words and activities was of the greatest use in battling the guerrillas. He and the General already had met each other. 'General, I apologise for my unexpected call. Please excuse me. Have you a couple of minutes spare?'

'Mr Too, certainly I have, more than a couple were you to want them, and you intrigue me. I'm sorry we don't know each other better. How can I help you?'

'Sir, without sounding disrespectful, your question should have been "how can you help me"?' and he laughed engagingly at his joke. 'I have got the impression that you are frustrated by Operation Bamboo not having had even a smidgen of success. Am I right even if I am not being tactful in asking you?'

The General was momentarily perplexed. *Not the sort of call I usually get but there must be a serious motive for his ringing.* 'Not at all, not at all. You must be a bit of a mind-reader, as it happens, for that is just what I was thinking about when you rang through.'

'Sir, it's like this. I have an idea that may be of use to you in implementing your aims and which needs your personal imprint before anything else can happen – before you leave us. However, you will be aware, I am sure, that there are certain stresses and strains between my side of the house and yours so any open visit I might make to you in your office would most likely be wrongly construed. Also, although I am sure my phone is not tapped, some matters are far better discussed face-to-face.'

'Sounds tantalisingly ominous, Mr Too. I understand what you mean and agree with you. Are you asking if I can come and see you or if you can visit me at Flagstaff House for a cup of tea, so to speak?'

'The latter is precisely what I was angling for. Yes please. When can I come?'

'At half-past five today?'

'Better than ever and the quicker the better.'

'Right. See you there. Thank you for calling,' and before any answer could be made, the General put the receiver down. He called his MA in. 'Toby, what do you think of that?' His MA, also a Guardsman who tried to 'look the part' wherever he found himself, had, like his master, learnt to react to the unexpected positively.

'Unusual in the extreme, sir, and obviously something unexpectedly delicate. It sounds as though he has something that needs to be handled with kid gloves and he does not want to tread on any fellow countrymen's collective toes, although one's feet wear shoes and socks not gloves. He clearly trusts you and all you need do is to say "no" if you don't want to say "yes" or even "I'll think about it" after he's had his spiel.'

'That's about as I see it. Can you come along with me, Toby? Spoil a game of squash or tennis will it, if you do? I don't want to have to relay it to you to mull over: much better to get it first-hand.'

'No sweat, sir, in both senses of the phrase,' said with a crooked grin.

'Righty ho! Call up the car and let's away. It'll drop you back at your quarter after we've had our chinwag.'

At Flagstaff House both British officers were surprised to see two Chinese come to the front door. Mr Too introduced his companion. 'Sir, this is Mr Ah Fat who is instrumental in what I have to suggest. I didn't mention his name on the phone on purpose.'

The General smiled disarmingly. 'There's no difficulty in getting another cup or cutting another sandwich! Come and meet the memsahib for a cuppa then we'll put our collective heads together.'

Tea was a social affair, the Englishmen most surprised at the fluency of both Chinese. The General looked at his watch. 'Time for business. Let's stay here. These chairs are more comfortable than in my study. Fire away, Mr Too.'

'Sir, my idea about Operation Bamboo is based on your using a certain Major Jason Rance of 1/12 GR. Before I give you his background let Mr Ah Fat speak.'

'Please carry on,' said the GOC.

'Gentlemen, Jason and I were childhood friends here in KL and are still very close to each other ...' began Ah Fat. The General and his MA listened spellbound as Ah Fat told them about his own and Jason's father being in the intelligence world, how Jason's mother's job before her marriage had been running a Punch-and-Judy show, how she had taught her son how to be a ventriloquist, what he, Ah Fat, had done during the war before telling them about Operation Janus when the-then-Captain Jason Rance was personally instrumental in preventing a British officer from permanently joining the guerrillas and how, even after that, they had run 'Q' patrols together. He also let on that he himself was a long-term mole who knew more about the guerrilla camp in south Thailand than any other person now in government service.

At the end, 'Write all that up as a novel and no one would believe you,' breathed the MA in complete admiration.

'My turn to take over now, sir,' said Mr Too, 'but, please, please take what I say in total confidence otherwise I'll be unable to tell you more about the Major.'

'Put that way I haven't much option, have I? But I do know how to keep my mouth shut,' the General responded, permitting himself a grim smile.

'To start with, as a matter of interest, he has operated more on the far side of the boundary between knowledge and ignorance almost with a sixth sense of how to cope with situations that have never previously arisen,' and Mr Too went on to tell the General what Jason Rance had told them about his visit to Chin Peng's camp with the letter – 'Monstrous cheek but, oh, how cool!' cooed the General – leading on to the report of his reconnaissance for the SEATO exercise. 'I've brought a copy of his report, sir, in case you haven't had one already.'

'Thank you, Mr Too, but I've been sent a copy. It made interesting and unusual reading then: I can now put more faith in its conclusions than I had done. With such a full background, what have you got for me?'

'Sir, you probably well know that the remaining guerrillas use the Temiar as a screen when they leave their base in Thailand and come south, three or four times a year. I believe that Major Rance and Mr Ah Fat can resurrect their old "Q" patrol and, with sufficient training in talking Temiar, working with and through them to reach and eliminate the guerrillas or acting as guides for the rest of 1/12 GR to take on that task if there were to be a larger scale operation on our side of the border. If approved, it'll mean your having to sell it to Special Branch, HQ Federation Armed Forces staff and 1/12 GR as though it were your own idea and, of course, I'll back it up wholeheartedly.'

The General yanked his long body back into his chair, lowered his craggy shoulders to relax them, breathing through his open mouth, his eyes closed, deep in thought. *I just can't believe it … but I'll have to. These two are deep. There's more to them than they've let on. That Rance fellow has obviously impressed them one hundred percent plus.*

The MA looked at his Lord and Master. *Seldom seen him like that. Not the most usual upright position for a Guards officer!*

'It's attractively unconventional,' the General came out with. 'It might even work. Have you anything else for me?'

'Sir, as I've told you, Major Rance has his Thai-speaking Gurkha and the man Jenko and both still have some mileage left for work on the far side of the border. I've another idea that you might, just but only just, like to consider,' glancing at the General who looked up at him enquiringly.

'Go ahead, Mr Too. You've given me one military heart attack so why not two of them?'

'The idea I have is that the "Q" party goes into Thailand surreptitiously – plain clothes as tourists or in uniform with a compass that shows north 45 degrees out of true so if they were caught that would be as good an excuse that they'd lost their way as any I can think of. They could cause considerable havoc once a feasible plan has been made and approved.'

'Nothing else? No more bombshells?' asked the General a tad caustically. *It's all a bit too near the bone for an unequivocal 'yes'.*

'Were you to approve that, even "bare footed", the only other point I'd like to suggest is that you get Major Rance temporarily attached to Special Branch, initially for six months, say, when he can learn Temiar, contact and bring in his Thai-speaking Gurkha in Bangkok and work out any plans for the elimination of the remaining thirty-five guerrillas on the police Wanted list, either by bullet, blade or even garrotte, or making them so ineffectual, by winning them over to government, as to be of no menace.'

'And get me court-martialled if I'm still here,' countered the General with the ghost of a smile. He called his houseboy. 'Whisky, gin, beer or soft?' he asked.

They gave him their choice and drinks were brought. After small talk the General said, 'Thank you, Mr Too and Mr Ah Fat for your unconventional ideas for an unconventional soldier. I'll have to give it all a lot of thought but,' a delicate pause, 'I like it. But first tell me, is this paragon of military skulduggery married?'

'No sir,' said Mr Too. 'By my reckoning he'd never have been able to do what he has done had he a wife, even in the background. And he has the self-confidence of never having been manipulated by a female – as far as I know, that is.'

The General blinked at that unfettered reply and inwardly sighed at the constraints of married life.

After they had left the General told MA to freshen his drink and asked, 'Toby, can we afford to let this run? Let's thrash this out.'

The MA's answer was brief: 'Sir, can we afford not to?'

'Okay then. Let's give it a name. Any ideas?'

'Let me see. It's the Communists' blind spot … Got it! How about Operation Blind Spot?'

'Yes, that's something the guerrillas would never think of.'

Jim Fordyce was the United Kingdom representative of the Secret Intelligence Service in Malaya. He was a beetle-browed, tall, rangy man, a linguist and a musician. He spoke with an Old Etonian drawl which only the cognoscenti would have recognised. The very next morning he asked for time to visit the GOC. 'Come after lunch, say at three o'clock, if it can wait until then.'

At the appointed time Jim Fordyce knocked on the GOC's office door and was called in. 'Thank you for sparing time to see me, sir. I need to show you a highly delicate message from my people in London and to talk it over with you.'

'Sit ye down, Jim, and let's hear what you have to say.' *It can hardly be more delicate than what I heard yesterday.*

'Apparently the King of Nepal has been pressing us to do something about some wartime Gurkhas still unable to return home. One in particular is an ex-Thai guerrilla, hijacked into being one, and the other was, until recently, escort of the Secretary General of the Indonesian Communist Party, Aidit. The latter was helped to disappear when in Bangkok and had hoped to go back to Nepal on an Indonesian passport but the Indonesian embassy blocked that so the hapless man has had to disappear into hiding with the ex-Thai guerrilla. A holding reply has been given to the effect that arrangements for them are being considered. Our man in Rangoon has been sent a message about some other Gurkhas stranded in Thailand and I have taken the liberty of bringing both of them up to date of the location of the one who was a member of the Thai Communist Party. Our hands are tied by the King having named one Major Jason Rance as the man he feels is the only one to be fully trusted on this task.' He looked up at the General who nearly pinched himself to see if he was dreaming. 'During any rescue do you think that Major Rance and the ex-Thai guerrilla might also try to eliminate, or at least render useless, the last thirty-five guerrillas on the Wanted list?'

'But how strange!' said the General, not answering the question. 'It was only yesterday that Special Branch Messrs Too and Ah Fat submitted the same proposal to me without any royal prompting. I acquiesced and here you are today with the same message. What do you make of it?'

'It's unusual for an outsider, so to speak, to be engaged on an operation as intricate and possibly dangerous as this. However, in this case, it seems that with Major Rance's personal knowledge of the Gurkha and his language as well as what we have already heard about his relationship with Ah Fat, we've few grounds for not giving him a green light for a go-ahead. May I ask you initially to arrange a meeting with this Rance fellow and then, if you consider it applicable, bring me into this as well?'

'Can't very well say no, can I?' countered the General. 'I'll only veto the whole project if, after having had a chat with him, I consider him unsuitable for it.'

Jim Fordyce got up. 'That's all I have for you, General,' he said as he left the office.

And that's quite enough for one day felt the General.

In April, before being sent on operations north of Grik as part of Bamboo, it was imperative lest any chance contact be thwarted by lack of know-how, to make sure that those skills of jungle work that had become rusty in Hong Kong were re-burnished and, for two intakes of recruits, to be learnt. Jason therefore took his company on a hard, ten-day training exercise.

The way he had arranged his training was working up from individual skills being practised within sections, then for sections of each platoon, with Platoon HQ also acting as a section, to patrol and set ambushes against one another and, at the end, platoon versus platoon. It was extremely well worth the effort in planning it at all three levels, tiring work though that was.

The first part was in low-lying areas not far from Ipoh itself. They were driven to a Chinese logging camp, *kongsi*, some ten miles from the barracks. He took his CQMS and told him to bring five days' rations to the same place in five days' time.

The company moved out and after five days returned to the *kongsi* to be re-rationed before moving off to the higher ground for 'more of the same'. As the re-rationing vehicle drove off, the

CQMS shouted out, in bazaar Malay, 'see you in five days' time when the company comes back,' never believing such innocent words would spark a dangerous crisis.

Inside the *kongsi* two Chinese men nodded at one another and one went back to Ipoh on the next lorry loaded with timber.

The second part took place above one thousand feet where stream water was cool and sweet, a crisper air vitalised and sometimes, through a break in the trees, a distant view delighted. By the end of those ten days, his soldiers knew what being tired and wet through with rain and sweat meant but, until real action took place, being afraid, cold, hungry, wounded and possibly lost could not be practised. But they had experienced once more what sweat and thirst, aching limbs, a heavy pack and chafing equipment even without taut nerves and a fleeting enemy were.

Jason had radioed for transport to pick them up at the *kongsi*. Waiting for the vehicles to arrive, he said to his Company 2IC, 'There's time for a brew, Sahib, if there's enough left in the men's packs.'

'*Hunchha, Hajur,*' answered his Gurkha officer with a grateful smile. 'There'll be enough to go round.'

Neither of them nor the soldiers had noticed a Chinese man squinting at Jason from the doorway of the *kongsi*. He disappeared inside and a little later came out, holding a heavy cleaver, a *parang,* behind his back. He skirted the men who were attending to their brew and made his way to where he saw the Running Dog European – *he can't escape now and I'll get that reward* – sitting on his pack with his back resting on a large tree. He crept up behind the tree, peered around it and, taking aim, raised his *parang* and swung it sharply at an angle to take Jason's head off.

At that very moment, his batman handing him a mess tin cover of tea, Jason leant forward to take it from him. The blade of the *parang* came crashing down just where Jason's head had been and stuck into the bark with a loud thud. The noise made the orderly drop the tea and, in one bound, Jason was on his feet. Turning, he saw a man trying to extract the *parang* and sprang at him, his left hand making for and clutching the Chinese man's throat, with his left heel dug into the ground to provide backward leverage. In one motion he pulled the man off his feet, arced him sideways and crashed his skull into the tree trunk, his fingers clawing the windpipe, tightening around it. With his right hand Jason took his kukri out of his scabbard and, with the back of it, brought it down smartly above the man's right ear. The man fell to the ground where he lay in a cowl of his own blood. Jason, panting hard, looked down at him, now unconscious. *That should keep him quiet enough for some time if not for ever.* A small nerve started twitching at the corner of his mouth. *They can't come nearer than that!*

The sound of the scuffle brought every man to his feet, men from the nearest section running towards their OC to help him. Men in the *kongsi* nervously peered out, shocked at what had happened.

Jason, puce in the face and breathing heavily, turned round and said, 'That was a near one, for sure. He'll be unconscious for quite a while.' He rubbed his hands, flexing his fingers and looked down at his attacker. It was the man with the 'broken face', Pang

Hau.

'Are you all right, Sahib?' queried his Company 2IC, breathlessly, as he ran up to find out what had happened.

'Yes, Sahib, I am. Luckily my orderly brought me my tea just as the blow was made. It must have missed me only by a fraction. Get someone to search his pockets, Sahib, and if there's any paper in them, let's see it.'

This a soldier did, recovering ans ID card and a folded piece of paper which he gave to his Major sahib. Jason thanked him and glanced at it. It was written in Chinese. *I'll read it later in my own time.*

'What shall we do about the man?' the Gurkha Captain asked.

'Call the chief from that *kongsi*, Sahib, and I'll talk to him.'

Jason's batman went off to the *kongsi* and a few minutes later an elderly Chinese with a scraggly beard, flushed to the roots of his thinning hair and obviously scared out of his wits, was ushered into Jason's presence. Jason looked him up and down before quietly asking him to explain what the trouble was about. The chief was overwhelmed by the Running Dog's complete and unexpected fluency in Chinese.

Hesitantly, flecks of spittle forming at the edges of his lips, Adam's apple a-throb, the hapless man stuttered out his answer. Apparently the man was a stranger who had arrived at the *kongsi* shortly before the Gurkhas had come out of the jungle. He had said he was one of the men that the contractor who supplied fresh rations to the Brigade.

By this time the transport for the company had arrived, lorries for the men and a Land Rover for the Company Commander.

'Fall in by platoons, check equipment!' called out the Company Sergeant Major.

'Sahib, take the company back and, once you've reached the lines, tell all ranks that no one must talk about what has just happened until I've got back. Leave three men with me.'

'Embuss!' The men clambered aboard and the lorries drove off. Jason continued his interrogation of the *kongsi* chief. 'The man is not dead nor will he die. He is unconscious but will recover. He will have a sore head and ear for quite a while.' He looked hard and long at the other man. 'What will you do about it?'

The man faltered. Jason, changing from talking mildly, snapped out, 'Tell me, what will you do about it?'

He shrugged despairingly. 'What can I do?' he replied hesitantly.

'I'll tell you what you will do: say nothing to anybody. If you do, *Ch'uan jia chan*' and I'll hear about it ...' He let his dreaded threat hang in the air.

The effect was almost magical. The man sagged at the knees when Jason cursed him in the most virulent curse possible – *May your entire clan be wiped out* – which was used in ancient times on the Chinese mainland as an emperor's unbreakable edict and was still highly effective.

'*Sinsaang*, I promise I won't,' he answered cravenly, infinite pathos in his voice.

'I leave you now but if ever anyone like that one comes to you, you must ignore him once more. Understand?'

The man bowed his acquiescence and, dragging his feet, departed, shoulders hunched and head down.

As they drove back Jason read the letter and saw that it was one of two copies, each telling the recipient to kill him. *That's proof enough that that damned hotel manager in Sadao showed my passport to Chin Peng, blast his eyes. Chickens come home to roost with a vengeance. I'll keep quiet about it and only tell P'ing Yee when the time is ripe.*

Once in the lines he found his Gurkha Captain and gave orders for the morrow. 'First thing clean weapons and, after sorting themselves out, the rest of the day free. Tell the men that my attacker was a junky known to be crazed without drugs probably trying to rob me. Best not to talk about it.'

Somehow the Gurkha Captain knew that, whatever else might eventuate, his Company Commander's reputation would spread.

Half a mile down the road from the *kongsi* was a hut in which the man who had nodded at Pang Hau during the re-rationing five days earlier was waiting for news of his friend's attack. He saw the lorries with the soldiers in them pass by, followed some ten or so minutes later by a smaller vehicle with the Running Dog sitting in the front. *Unsuccessful? Why, I wonder* and he quickly made his way to find out.

He found the head of the *kongsi* almost speechless, gibbering with fear and the other inmates wearing expressions of deep concern. Before he had time to ask what had happened, he was waved away in the direction of a large tree where a cloud of flies could be seen swarming. Dragging his feet, he went over to investigate. He was utterly dismayed to find his friend lying there, head and neck covered in blood, with swarms of flies and ants clustered around his wounds. As he looked on in horror, his friend stirred and the flies rose from his body, buzzing loudly. The wounded man uttered a long groan and slumped back.

He carefully carried his friend back to the *kongsi* and, protesting violently that nothing had been done to salve the wounds, asked what had happened and demanded water to bathe them and any aid there was from the limited resources available.

The venerable head told him that none of them had touched the wounded man as they were afraid of being accused of killing him if he were to die. 'He is your responsibility, not ours.'

The man, both frightened and bewildered that none of the *kongsi* inhabitants had done anything to help, took water, cloth, soap and bandages over to his still prostrate friend. He cleaned the wound in the skull, removing pieces of bark from it, and closely examined the neck. Not broken, only the ear lacerated. He spoke soothingly to the injured man who merely grunted in return. 'Try and stand up,' he urged, helping him to get on his feet.

'Oh-o, my head hurts,' the man whimpered. 'What happened? Where's my *parang*?'

It was still stuck in the tree, mute witness to a failed attempt. 'I'll take it and you back as soon as I can. You'll have to go to hospital otherwise it'll take too long to get better.'

Groggily Pang Hau put his hand in his pocket, searching for his ID card, which he would have to show before he could be registered. To his horror, it was not there. 'Did you see my ID card by the tree?' he croaked. 'I can't find it.'

'Stay here and I'll go and see.' His helper searched around feverishly near the tree but found nothing, merely bringing the cleaver back with him.

'No luck. Gone,' he told Hair Lip and asked the head of the *kongsi*, brusquely, why no one had helped the injured man and what had gone wrong.

He was told in no uncertain terms and was also cautioned '*Ch'uan jia chan*' if you talk about it.

The next day the head of the *kongsi* relented enough to let the pair of them go to Ipoh on the timber lorry, 'But be more than careful no one in authority sees you.'

A few days after that incident, Jason was working in his office when the CO's 'stick orderly' – the smartest man of the day's Quarter Guard – unexpectedly came to the door and, standing rigidly to attention with his stick under his left arm, gave a cracking salute. 'Major sahib, the Commanding sahib sends his salaams. He wants you to speak with him, now, in his office.'

Can't think what's in the wind? Nothing to take me away from my company like when I went to Thailand I hope and I also hope he hasn't heard about that fellow trying to behead me, he thought, so, with a '*Hunchha, keta*' – Right-ho, lad – the pair of them set off for Battalion HQ. There was a newish CO, someone with whom Jason had more empathy than he had had with the previous one.

'Jason, take a seat,' the CO said once formalities were done with. 'There's something in the wind that concerns you personally.' He saw Jason looked quizzical and unhappy. 'No, don't get the wrong idea. There's nothing to worry about – yet,' he added with an impish grin.

'At least I have a clear conscience, sir, and the only possible point that comes to mind is that I worked my company too hard on the exercise just finished.'

'No, no, it's nothing like that. Frankly I can't tell you anything more than you have to go to and meet the GOC. The letter I received was most unusually graded "top secret" and "eyes only" so obviously you are plum in the sights of something special.'

'Are there any restrictions I have to comply with, sir, and when am I wanted?'

'Restrictions: at the moment "silence" is your watchword and you're wanted as soon as possible to report to the General's MA directly. Remember, only you and I know about this. We'll have to make up some mundane reason for you going to KL. Any suggestions?'

'Dental inspection? Visit men in hospital? Draw maps from stores?'

'No, can't be the first two as there are dental facilities and a hospital here. And maps can be supplied from Brigade.'

'Sir, how about our putting it out I'm being interviewed as a possible replacement for the General's Military Assistant?'

'Good thinking and why not as you are to report to him?'

So that was arranged there and then. Jason listened to the phone call: he was to go down to KL on the night train that evening and to report next morning by latest 0900 hours. 'The reason we've put out that he has to go to KL is that he is to be interviewed as a possible replacement for you, Toby,' said the CO, 'but don't take it to heart.'

'No worry, Colonel. Some time or other we're all expendable.'

And how, thought Jason, as he heard the tinny-toned answer and remembered the incident near the *kongsi*.

At about the same time, up in Sadao a courier came into general stores at the southern end of the main road through the village and, using a password known only to the cognoscenti, said to the manager, 'I've got a letter for the boss. It's from Malaya and it seems it is important. It is from the Chinese contractor who delivers fresh rations for the Malayan Brigade in Ipoh.'

'If it wasn't important you wouldn't have brought it to me,' said the shopkeeper with a chuckle. 'Right, give it to me and, if you want, I'll give you a receipt for it. If it's all that important there may be an answer to take back so it's better to stay here to see if there is one. Go upstairs and I'll have a meal sent up.'

As soon as someone from the camp visited the shop he was given the letter for the General-Secretary in his jungle camp. Reading it a frown, first of worry then of rage, creased Chin Peng's brow. Pang Hau apparently had a serious head injury and a torn ear. He had failed in his task of eliminating that loathsome Running Dog and had lost his ID card. All he remembered was that he had taken careful aim at the Running Dog's neck when he was leaning against a tree not far from a *kongsi* on the edge of the jungle but, against all odds, his target had ducked forward as the blow was struck so the *parang* merely struck the tree. He then remembered nothing else until his friend came to give him succour. He couldn't even say who had beaten him up so severely. Apparently no one of the *kongsi*'s inhabitants had seen or heard any disturbance. *And how!* the Secretary General muttered under his breath. He sat back and thought, with feral malevolence, hard and long. *If it's the last thing I get done before leaving for China...*

He called his Killer Squad commander, Zhong Han San. 'Read this then we'll talk.'

The Head of the Killer Squad grunted malevolently as he read it, his eye twitching furiously. 'This needs drastic action, Comrade, and I am the one to do it for you.'

'Well spoken. I always knew I could rely on you. What do you propose?'

'Widen our net, Comrade. I'll plan an operation. Leave the details to me.'

'Yes, Comrade Zhong, as a matter of urgency. Let us imitate those proud British people and have a code name for the operation you are about to put into action. What shall it be? What's that English phrase?' He ruminated then, 'Got it. Blind spot. Let us call it Operation Blind Spot as that's something the foreign devils would never think of.'

Jason reported in to the MA as ordered and was quickly ushered into the General's office, the MA following. Before he sat down he was introduced to a Jim Fordyce, 'A civilian on my staff,' and, seated, the briefing got under way. 'Major Rance, I know you have already been briefed on Operation Bamboo and, from what I have heard of you and your exploits, I expect you wonder why there has been November, Tango, Romeo, NTR, Nothing to report – to hammer it home – in the last three years with so much effort put into everything, tactically, logistically, and, of course, psychologically with Special Branch.'

'Sir, you've hit the nail on the head. Wonder I have and disappointed I am. I am delighted to be able to take my company up to Grik and disappear into the ulu once more.'

The General nodded. 'I thought that'd be your reaction. I now want your response to something else.' Jason leant forward expectantly. 'I have been talking in the greatest detail to your childhood friend, Ah Fat, and Mr C C Too and both have brought me up to speed about your exploits, those in 1951 I think the year was, and more recently when you were working for the SEATO exercise, both "barefooted" on the Lao-Thai border and your extraordinary behaviour at Sadao.' The General's face was neutral but his voice had an unmistakable edge to it.

Jason clenched his teeth in readiness for an enormous rocket. *How did he find out? Who told him? And all this way for an imperial rollicking?* but much to his surprise, the General said, 'No, I'm not going to say anything deleterious about this last bit. I have, unofficially of course, to take my hat off to you for daring, guts and sheer doing the unexpected.' Jason let his breath out as delicately as he could. 'Mr Ah Fat has told me all about your Operation Janus as well as your overwhelmingly entrancing, if I may use that word, demonstration of your ventriloquism there and at Sadao given both to him and Mr Too.' The General looked at Jason, mischievously. 'Especially the falsetto voice! Any comments to any possible reactions that extraordinary piece of military indiscipline might have caused?' A smile robbed some of the intended severity.

Think hard. Tell a white lie if necessary. 'Nothing yet,' said with a chuckle, 'and thinking about what I did in retrospect, it was rash of me, sir, but rage accumulating over many years had to have some outlet. I had become so angry at the way those communists mucked around with ordinary, decent people. No excuses, sir, and no real military reason.' *So interesting is this new development I won't mention that* kongsi *incident as the old man might cancel everything.*

'Major, you're not one of those crackpot Christians with a mission, I hope. If you are, you're not my choice for the job I have to offer you.'

Without meaning to, Jason glared at his audience with hooded eyes. 'Sir, I'm a normal apolitical British officer. I'm not even in the rear rank for canonisation and "Kill a Communist and Christ smiles" could never be my credo and turns me right off. What I so dislike about their creed is the way it denudes its followers of any intrinsic personality or individuality. Nothing else, sir.' His words came out new-minted and ringing with sincerity.

His small audience accepted his evocative outburst. *At least he's genuine.*

The General broke the ensuing silence. 'Right you are, Rance. Point taken so we'll leave it behind. Now, what would you say to a repeat performance of your "Q" patrols and, possibly, were the occasion to arise, in one guise or another, of visiting the camp where those guerrillas who keep an eye on the "Protos", if that is a politically correct way to call those people, to see what you can do about them even if revisiting Sadao is probably too far and too risky? Ah Fat told me that he and his Bear would be willing to go with you. What it would mean is that you would be away from your battalion for, say, a six-month period. During that time

I'd want you to learn as much Temiar as possible, getting their leaders onto your side, possibly using them as a screen for your endeavours to be more successful than you might otherwise have been.'

'Sir, I'd like that. I ...' he broke off and stared to his front, as though struck by something not yet considered. The General patiently waited for him and was totally surprised by an unexpected and seemingly unrelated question, 'Sir, how much do you know about the King of Nepal's worries?'

'As it happens, Major Rance, it was yesterday that Mr Fordyce came to see me about this same matter. Apparently he has had instructions to initiate what I had already almost definitely decided on. London has been pressed by His Majesty to get a rift on trying to rescue wartime Gurkhas stranded in Thailand. It's incredible, to my mind, that the Special Branch worthies here managed to beat "our men" in London on this very project by a short head. But it seems that you are "the man of the moment". Are you?'

'Sir, I hope so. May I give you the background?'

'Go ahead. Mr Ah Fat has fully briefed me on what you briefed him so I know a lot about it but there may be odd bits and pieces I don't.'

'Sir, it started when I was detailed to be a staff officer for the SEATO exercise a year or so back ...' and he went on to explain about the two wartime Gurkhas he had met, one stuck in Thailand and the other in Indonesia and how he'd tried to get the one from Indonesia to fly back to Nepal on his current passport but was blocked ...'Sir, there are two or three more men still in the mining area near the Burmese border ...' and again he went on to explain what he had found out. 'It's a vexatious problem as they have married locally and raised a family so may be happy to stay where they are. With such a grey area I'll have to play it by ear when the time comes.'

'Have you made any similar pact with those others?'

'No sir. They have married locally and seemed nonchalant about any possibility of return to Nepal, nor did they specifically ask me if I could help them to when I met them. Mind you, the whole idea and belief of rescue were dead and gone by then.'

'It won't be easy for you personally to ask either of them again what their choice is and you may waste time by getting your other man back to ask them,' added the General, 'and there'll be the hassle of getting them to you. Likewise there'll be a problem of their womenfolk being left husbandless. Could, I wonder, that reverberate so much that the rest of your scheme be jeopardised?'

'It's a knotty one, isn't it?' said Jason lamely.

The General, eyes closed and head slightly tilted to one side, considered that for a while. 'Yes, you have the background for the job all right. How are you proposing to get the two Gurkhas over the border without, say, having to make a huge and time-consuming detour through the jungles of north Malaya? It's that or by road isn't it?'

'May I ask a question, sir?' said the MA.

'Certainly do.'

'When you have given full thought to your new job, will you have any idea how many men will be involved?'

Jason was silent while he considered the bull points. 'Sir, first thoughts are that I will have to work in two phases. Phase one will be getting the Temiar on my side and phase two my work against the guerrillas. For phase one I'll need Ah Fat, his side-kick the Bear and at least three Gurkhas, hopefully those who went with me on Operation Janus. Phase two is too early for any useful planning right now. It will only be clear after I see how phase one plays out.'

'I accept that,' said the General. 'I wonder if you knew that there was an intelligence cell formed in my GHQ during the Emergency. It is still in place with greatly reduced numbers. I think your best cover is to be posted to that cell for temporary duty so that you can work with Special Branch as Mr Too has already suggested to me. That should cover it and that's my solution. Go back to the battalion, get your men, tell Ah Fat on your own net when you want him and his mate and inform my MA. By that time you'll have decided where you'll best be based for your training period. Have you anything else for me, Jason, before you return to Ipoh?'

'No, sir. I am looking forward to the job. It is a real challenge and fingers and toes all tightly crossed, we'll be successful. I'll go back by the night train, I have a return warrant, and this afternoon I'll go and see my old friend, Ah Fat.' He stood up and saluted. The General got out of his chair and went over to Jason. 'I'll give orders that you and Special Branch will undertake a "Q"-type operation in aid of Bamboo, as far as working with ladangs was concerned, but that nothing at all will be mentioned about the plan to rescue a wartime Gurkha. You are to deny all knowledge of any such skulduggery if ever it was even hinted at,' said the General.

'Sir, I fully understand. One question: how much of this may I tell my CO?'

'He already knows that the security grading is Top Secret and I know that he's already cleared at that level. Tell him everything but only what I'll call a Phase One briefing for the others. And yes, you will have to be fully integrated with the battalion for all normal requirements, such as re-rationing, casualty evacuation and normal sitreps.'

'Again, sir, fully understood. May I later submit a budget? I'll need some money for use in Thailand if nowhere else.'

'Yes, of course. Liaise with my MA on that. So now, on your way and best of luck, Jason, you'll need it,' and they shook hands.

4

Jason rang through to Ah Fat from the MA's office. 'P'ing Yee, I'm in KL. Before I go back to Ipoh by this afternoon's train we need to meet. Drop everything and meet me in the station restaurant, where we'll have a snack and a beer.'

'Wilco, as I've heard you say many times in the past.'

They met up and, sitting at a corner table, ordered Tiger beers and *chop suey*. They clinked glasses; 'Cheers.' They talked as they ate their food.

'P'ing Yee, I'll go first, in outline only. I've just had a long session with the GOC and he has told me all about what you and Mr C C Too had already told him so there's no need to go into any background. We've got the green light to combine forces for a "Q"-type operation involving you and me which, by the way, has been christened Operation Blind Spot. I hope you can come up to Ipoh as soon as 2 Fed Brigade have been sent the General's orders.' His friend bobbed his head in compliance. 'The MA asked me how many men I wanted to take and I told him you, Hung Lo, and at least three of my Gurkhas who were with me on Janus are still serving and are not on leave. Six of us should be enough to react to most contingencies.'

Ah Fat considered what Jason had said, with his customary

but unconscious rubbing of his hands together as he concentrated. 'Yes, that should cover most normal situations. I like the idea of your Janus Gurkhas being with us as they are exceptionally well trained and imbued with the skill for split-second decisions based on instantaneous reactions.'

Jason smiled. 'Gosh, quite a mouthful but one hundred percent true.'

'What else did you get from your meeting with the General?'

'That I be temporarily attached to an intelligence cell for the first phase of the project, learning Temiar, going around with you two and my Gurkhas, talking to the *t'o yan* and trying to get them to stop acting as a screen to the guerrillas. After that we try our luck to see what we can do against those guerrillas who keep tags on ladang activities from their base in the Betong Salient area. 2 Fed Brigade will only be told about the first bit. Total and unequivocal secrecy is imperative for the second.'

'That makes a lot of sense. It's quite a challenge, isn't it? Have you any ideas about your getting the people you want onto our side?'

'Oh, besides the language I have one or two tricks,' and Jason wobbled his eyebrows and made a distorted moue. 'Both seem to amuse people. I'll only be able to use my ventriloquist dummy once I've got a mastery of the language. It's a tad bulky but it'll fit into my big pack.'

Ah Fat grinned. 'You'll be a one-man cabaret show, Jason. My only worry is that your audience will be so frightened that they'll run away from your dummy. By the way, was there any reaction from your crazy stunt with your Gurkha when you sent

Chin Peng that even crazier letter? I've often wondered.'

'Yes, and not so long ago.' He looked at his watch. *Time enough.* 'In its way it was quite frightening …' and Jason went on to describe his intended decapitation and what he had done to his attacker in reply.

'My word! That was a near miss and no doubt about it.'

'I found a copy of a letter on him sent from the Central Committee with instructions to kill me – not only while in Ipoh but also if I go to Grik.' He pulled it out of his pocket. 'Take it. Would C C Too be interested in it?'

'I'm sure he would,' replied Ah Fat, skim-reading it before putting it in his pocket.

Jason went on to tell his friend what he had said to the *kongsi* chief. 'Here, take this and find out about my attacker,' Jason added, remembering he still had his potential executioner's ID card in his wallet.

'Do you know what happened to the man after you left him lying unconscious? From what you say, you seem to have made quite a hash of your assailant. I didn't know you were as handy at unarmed combat as all that.'

'Few people know about it. Such powers, I believe, are best kept quiet but I expect the news will spread in Bad Land. I must say that my men were brimming with pride at what they saw I did.'

'Can't blame them for that,' said Ah Fat with a laugh.

'No, I did not ask and have not heard. I told my company that he was a junky who needed money for drugs and they accepted it. With his ID you'll be able to find out about him and possibly his background. But it does give our task an added dimension, doesn't it?'

'Indeed it does. How can we best manage damage limitation, I wonder. It's much too late to send a message to Sadao saying that the executioner was successful.'

'It wouldn't surprise me if a report of his not being successful hadn't somehow filtered through already. I don't think there's much any of us can do except to be more than careful all the time.'

'Wise words. I wonder how that man knew you'd be at the *kongsi*.'

Jason told him about the re-rationing arrangements being mentioned, 'So presumably overheard by one of those warned to be on the lookout.'

'That means that there are some sympathisers among the timber workforce. That's a Special Branch target. Leave it with me. I'll look into the matter personally myself.'

'Wait one, P'ing Yee. Get someone else, not you, to do it. If we're to work together you've got to stay out of any limelight.'

'More wise words, Jason.'

Jason looked at his watch again. 'Now it is time to leave you, my friend. Today is 22 April. Let's plan on our D Day in Grik by … um, um … 15 May? That should give both of us enough time to have thought out all the administrative and logistical details thoroughly as well as thinking about our actual jungle work.'

'Good. Give me a bell as soon as Special Branch gives you your clearance for the operation.'

'Roger, out.' The two men shook hands, Ah Fat going back to his office and Jason to his train.

On Jason's return to his battalion he asked for and was granted a long interview with his CO, who was, of course, more than interested in all aspects of what the GOC had ordered, including the rescue of the two wartime Gurkhas. 'Sir, I believe that only once we have brought the men back can we best present the case for their inclusion in a leave party for getting back to Nepal to the Major General, Brigade of Gurkhas, that is if the GOC hasn't nobbled him before.'

'Hardly "nobbling" but I agree with you. Officially I can't let you go into Thailand but it may turn out that you may find you have to. How does the one-and-only Rance propose to get around being caught in another's country without proper safeguards?'

'Two ways, sir. I'll get a Thai tourist visa for six months. That should cause no problem as I've already had one for my SEATO job. With a bit of luck that should see me though many hazards. However, were I to be caught red-handed, in uniform carrying a weapon, a compass with the needle pointing to 45 degrees instead of 360 should be enough of an excuse to not being shot at dawn the day following.'

'I love your optimism, Jason. I'll find out where that can be arranged and get it done. Who will you take?'

Jason told him, adding, 'As soon as my schoolboy friend Ah Fat comes to Ipoh I'll bring him to meet you.'

'Right you are. Hand your company over to your 2IC and tell him as little as he needs to know. I think you might hark back to Janus days and your Chinese language ability for being chosen for this job. You have mentioned the men you want to take. Your one-time rifleman operator is now a sergeant in the

Signal Platoon. The Adjutant will tell OC HQ Company I have authorised his attachment to you for six months. Oh yes, one more point. By the time you start on Operation Blind Spot, two rifle companies will have been deployed across the Sungei Perak close to or on some of the ladangs, so you won't be on your own to start with.'

'Fine, sir. That's what I had been banking on,' said Jason and, dismissing himself, went back to his company lines, on the way calling in at the battalion temple and saw the pundit. 'Pundit ji,' he said with joined hands. 'I want you to come into my office at half-past 12 this morning with the items that are needed for an oath of secrecy.'

'Major sahib, a seven-generation oath? That's the strongest.'

'Yes please.' Jason knew that anyone who broke a seven-generation oath would have leprosy in his family for that length of time. 'That's just what I want.'

Back in his own office he said to his Gurkha Captain, 'Sahib, please call Sergeants Chakrabahadur Rai, Kulbahadur Limbu and Lalman Limbu and ask OC HQ Company for Sergeant Minbahadur Gurung to meet me here, with you, at 1230 hours today. He should be expecting a call, having already been warned by the Commanding sahib. Also, Captain sahib, I've asked the pundit to be present.' If the 2IC was surprised, he did not show it.

At the appointed time the four Gurkhas and the pundit came to the office and Jason told them to be seated. He warned the office runner to turn away anyone who wanted to see him, with an 'another time' answer. 'First of all, for all our sakes, I need the pundit to administer an oath that will ensure one hundred plus percent secrecy in what I am about to tell you. It will be the seven-generation oath, which is the most severe I know.' He turned to his four Sergeants. 'O-hé you four sergeant ustads, in no way will I ever hold it against you if you feel you cannot say "yes" without knowing what I'm going to ask you to do, so, if you don't want to undergo the oath, tell me now and I'll have to get someone else in your stead.'

The grim look on each face was answer enough. 'Right, pundit ji, carry on, please.'

The pundit, reciting the requisite prayers, made them all, including the Gurkha officer, touch brass and betel nut before sprinkling them with holy water using a holy leaf. After the oaths were administered, Jason thanked the pundit and dismissed him. The holy man collected his accoutrements and left the office, a hundred ringgits the richer, walking away in solitary dignity with the inviolable isolation of a religious ghost, what little tension there had been evaporating after he had gone.

'Now listen to me ...' and, by the end of the briefing the four sergeants seemed almost dazed with and in awe of what was expected from them. The Captain sahib only wished he were not so senior. Jason told him that the company would be in his hands for the next six months.

'Sahib, I won't let you down. You've got four very good men with you. If you are likely to meet another *parang*-wielding ruffian, I hope you'll be as lucky as you were before. You'll certainly need the gods to smile on you.'

'Sahib, that I already know. However, I have the same team as I had when that *gora* officer tried to run away to the daku' and he turned and smiled at his four men, 'so I'll feel as safe as ever I will.'

'Sahib,' said Kulbahadur, 'will you be taking your sham krait with you?' and he grinned infectiously as he asked. He was referring to when Jason used one in his own ventriloquist show that kept his Gurkha audience in howls of laughter and how he had used it to scare the daylights out of a guerrilla who had had the bad luck to pull his pants down to defecate a couple of feet away from where Jason and his team were hiding when chasing the renegade officer. It had had an almost magical effect.

'Kulé, thank you for reminding me. I had thought of the dummy to make our new sepoys laugh but I'd forgotten the krait. It again might come in useful.'

However much the Malay staff of HQ 2 Federal Brigade might have individual and private objections to any Englishman, a 'Mat Salleh' as they were known in the idiom, from having such an unconventional role, the orders from HQ Malaya Command were explicit. Mat Salleh was a legendary Malay who always thought he knew more than he actually did, who always knew best but in fact was bit of a bumbler but a well-meaning sort of cove and not a bad chap for all that. *Would this Major Mat Salleh be typical or worse? Hardly better! Only time will tell.*

Operation Blind Spot was due to last for six months and, certainly for the first part of that time, the 'Q' patrol would be operating to the west of the main Divide, the spine of the northern part of the country. There was always the east to be looked at later if events necessitated it. The Englishman in charge of the

Department of Aborigines was miffed at being left out of the planning: unknown to him he was living on borrowed time, being one of the few Englishmen in Malaya whose shady dealings were the subject of a police investigation.

Ah Fat came to Ipoh on 1 May and Jason met him at the station. It just so happened that the miffed and jealous Englishman was also there to meet someone and he saw his fellow countryman and a Chinese. 'Excuse me, are you Major Rance and Mr Ah Fat?' he asked. Yes they were. *Only a coincidence?* he asked himself. He remembered having recently seen the two men together in the KL station restaurant. *I'll ring HQ 2 Fed Brigade and see what it's all about.* He was overheard talking by his Chief Clerk when he rang.

Jason and Ah Fat motored off to the battalion and went to meet the CO who asked the Chinese where he was going to stay. Ah Fat said he thought that the Mess in HQ Fed Brigade was as good a place as any. 'Would you like to stay in our Mess? It will be much easier for you and Jason for planning. There isn't all that time to decide what you want *and* for us to see that you can get it.'

Ah Fat thanked the CO for his offer and accepted it. As he told Jason afterwards, 'If I, too, am on any list of suspects, I could be safer in a Gurkha camp than a Malay one.'

If you are seen to be in a Gurkha camp it could work the other way also, not now but later. 'Try it out and if you find the food and the hours not suitable, you can always go back to Police HQ,' Jason tactfully answered.

Back together in the Mess, 'I have a present for you, Shandung P'aau,' and so saying Ah Fat took a book out of his bag. 'I'm sure it'll come in more than handy.'

Jason looked at it and read, on the cover, *Tengleq Kui Serok*. 'I've found out that that means "Learn to speak Inland", Inland being what the Temiar call themselves,' said Ah Fat.

'P'ing Yee, that's marvellous. I didn't know there was such a book. That's really good of you to have thought of it. I could be halfway there before we start if I apply myself. We've got a fortnight before we leave for Grik.'

Acting Secretary General Ah Hai opened yet another letter from Malaya. It told him about how the Red Haired Devil and Ah Fat had been seen together at the KL railway station and again in Ipoh. 'It may be of interest to you,' the letter read.

It is. Calling Zhong Han San to one side he said, 'Comrade Chin Peng told me that he had had his doubts about one of his closest comrades, Ah Fat, for some time before but to keep it quiet until more positive information came our way. With this letter I think it proves that he is firmly in the Colonialist camp. If ever you get your hands on him you know what to do.'

Zhong nodded, grinning lasciviously.

Their first morning, sitting looking at a map on the wall of the battalion Intelligence Section's office, Jason said to his friend, 'P'ing Yee, for the first phase of Operation Blind Spot we must work out just what our operational task really is before we decide on our nitty-gritty needs such as rations, admin, medical, logistical, code words and communication scheduling so let's examine the map and see what outline plans come to mind.'

They studied it in detail, noting the steepness of the high mountains – 'that'll make it cold at night. Do you think we can carry half of a lightweight blanket each? Our packs will already be heavy enough. To move north up the Sungei Perak and its many tributaries with their steep sides and rocky bottoms we'll have to ask Brigade what sort of boats they have and how far up what tributaries they can take us.' For such a small force it was a huge area and whilst use of a helicopter could cut down days of travelling to a half hour or so in the air, current Royal Air Force 'Sycamore' helicopters were not big enough to take more than the size of the party even with only minimum kit in one lift. They had already learnt that in another briefing.

'The main defect of our ordnance survey maps is that they do not show any of the ladangs where the Temiar live and we can't plan anything for Phase 1 until we know much more about them,' said Jason, shaking his head in frustration. 'Look, our best bet is to motor up to Grik and having a good question and answer session with the local police. It's about a hundred miles away by road. Can you contact the Special Branch fellow there?'

'That's no problem. We both know him already, he's none other than Mubarak, known as "Moby", the four-fingered crocodile breeder from Seremban, a linchpin in Operation Janus days. I'm sure he will be ready to help us all he can. He has been there a long time and knows as much as, if not more than, anyone else does about people in the Bamboo area.'

'That'll be of enormous help. It'll be great to meet up with him after so long. Do you know his number?' Yes, Ah Fat did. 'Give him a bell on our office phone. Today is Monday. If he's free on Wednesday I'll ask for a vehicle for tomorrow and we'll get off early. I'll take my four men with me and you take your Bear if you like. A day there and a day back.'

Moby was free and a vehicle was available.

That same afternoon Jason went to the telephone exchange and asked to be put through to the British Embassy in Bangkok. The Chinese operator looked familiar. Jason spoke to him in English. Within a short time a connection was made. Jason identified himself and was happy to be recognised by the embassy operator. 'Put me through to the Guard Room, please, I want to speak to my old Gurkha friend,' he said in Thai and, with a flutter in his heart, heard the phone answered by a Gurkha. He identified himself and asked if the Sergeant Major was there. Luckily he was. 'Sahib, after so long. What can I do for you?'

'Major-ba, you remember that number I gave you? Manbahadur Limbu's number?'

'Sahib, I do. Do you want me to call him?'

'Yes, exactly that. Just tell him that Rance sahib is back in Malaya and has not forgotten him and will, in a couple of months, be in contact with him.'

'*Hunchha, Hajur*,' was the answer and after a few more words of inconsequentialities, Jason rang off, pleased that contact with Bangkok had been made.

The journey up to Grik was without incident or mishap. They stopped off halfway for a meal and a leg-stretch and, on arrival, went to the military camp where both 1/12 GR's rifle companies'

HQ were and arranged to stay there for the next two nights. Jason, Ah Fat and Wang Ming then drove to the police station. Outside was an office runner whom Jason greeted in fluent Malay, asking him where Enche Mubarak's office was. A roar came from inside and, beaming broadly, Moby came onto the verandah and hugged all three of them. 'Jason, what brings you here? My, none of you looks a day older and to see you three together must mean business is not as usual,' he said, with a wonderful twinkle in his eyes. 'Sorry I can't see you just now but tomorrow morning at around 1000 hours, as you military buffs have it.'

'Tomorrow morning we'll be here at the bewitching hour of one zero zero zero,' said Jason as they got back into their vehicle and drove off.

A Chinese itinerant seller of noodles on the opposite side of the road with his hand cart stopped and eyed Jason speculatively. *That one looks like the man in that photo. I'll have to do something about him.*

'I can only give you a briefing about the *Orang Asli* in Perak not in Kelantan,' Moby began next morning after they had foregathered in his office, facing a large wall map. 'There are four or five ladangs that will be of interest to you, all to the east of the Sungei Perak which is navigable to boats to within a couple of days' hard walk to the Thai-Malay border. Let me show you on the map.' The three ladangs nearest were in easy reach of the river and the others a long way farther east, up one or other of the two main tributaries. 'My advice is that you start by visiting the three riverine settlements, not that you are likely to gain any tactical knowledge from any of the headmen, whose names I will give you, but you will see just what a problem there is in dealing with these people. They're furtive as mouse deer and timid as birds and trying to plan anything with them is harder than knitting with eels. Even so,' he carried on after a burst of laughter, 'one point I ought to make is that the headmen have learnt about money. I've learnt that any sum above three is gibberish to most Temiar but some headmen might understand up to a hundred. That means if you are going to pay for anything it is much better to pay with coins: my suggestion is for fifty-cent pieces to be taken and,' here an expansive grin, 'if you need a lot of them they'll make your baggage heavier than you ever experienced. The women like to make necklaces of them which they cannot do with notes.'

'Moby, that is a useful point to remember and I thank you for it. My aim is to learn Temiar and the time spent on these three nearest ladangs won't be wasted from that point of view.'

Moby looked quizzically at Jason. 'Learn Temiar, did you say? The headmen have learnt to speak Malay and, from what I heard outside my office, your Malay is of a higher standard than is theirs. There will be no need for you to learn Temiar.'

Moby, that coming from an ace operator such as you! Almost can't believe it. Jason had the good sense not to answer that that was probably why Operation Bamboo still had had no positive results after all the effort and time spent on it so he changed the subject; 'Moby, will there be any problem arranging boats? We will be seven passengers plus boatman so one boat should be enough for us, surely?'

'No problem there. Once you have clearance from the Brigade

Liaison Officer, having given him dates and times, he'll get the boat and crew ready for you. You can let me know through the company up in the camp when you want, for instance, to come back over the river.'

'I have another question, Moby. As the three headmen you've told us about don't seem to be likely to be of any tactical help, what about the other two headmen farther into the jungle who have their ladang up a tributary?' Jason noticed that Moby's eyes momentarily flickered. *Why?* Ah Fat also noticed. 'I believe you have been trying to, how shall I call it, cultivate one of the two headmen there, whose name is ...' and he broke off.

'Kerinching,' offered Moby. 'He is the most powerful of the headmen in the whole of Perak. He is moody and does not like outsiders so I have tried to respect that by limiting those in his vicinity. I have to admit it has not paid any dividends yet. He has a son, Sutel, and a brother, Rijed, who are used to travelling over the Divide into Kelantan where the most powerful headman there was told he was headman by the guerrillas even before the government recognised him as such.' *Shall I tell them ...? Yes, why not.* 'Kerinching has a powerful relative, Senagit, who has been cook, scout, guide and friend of Ah Soo Chye and the other two guerrilla leaders, Tek Miu and Lo See, for as long as I have known about him.'

Jason glanced at Ah Fat. 'Moby, that is most important news and something that you must have worked hard to happen. It gives us something to work on.'

'It could do. I have managed to get Kerinching down to Grik once or twice to try and win him over, so he knows me even if I have yet to be successful. But, as for Senagit, none of us have ever come across him. It's almost as if he were only a name. All I know about him is that he has peppercorn hair, is an expert with his blowpipe and is said to be dead scared of snakes, especially kraits, having nearly died from a krait bite when small,' Moby finished off, shaking his head melancholically.

'Even that little nugget might come in useful one day,' said Jason, not linking it to his sham one.

They left Moby with the promise that they would keep him fully informed of everything they found out and would also tell the ladang headmen that their one hope of getting rid of the guerrillas bothering them was to keep him informed.

They had a meal in the camp and decided there was enough time to drive back to Ipoh that same day, collected their Gurkhas, asked one of the Company HQs to radio the battalion about their return and drove off. Jason, sitting in the front, still had his side window shut when, minutes later, as the vehicle slowed down to go round a sharp bend above a stream, a large rock was hurled at the side window of the front-seat traveller. A web of cracks spread though the glass and the rock bounced back onto the road. The driver slammed on his brakes and the four Gurkhas, as one, jumped out and gave chase to the rock thrower, a Chinese noodle seller whose barrow was by the side of the road. He had reached the top of a bank of the stream when Kulbahadur, eyes reddened in anger, drew his kukri as he caught up with him and wielded it with all his strength. The Chinese saw what was about to happen out of the corner of his eye and lunged forward. The Gurkha's kukri managed neatly to slice off the edge of the stone thrower's left buttock as he fell headlong down the bank.

Jason caught up with the red-eyed Gurkha. 'Much damage, Kulé?'

'No sahib. Hardly anything. Look, there's more cloth than buttock and blood on my kukri.'

'He'll find it sore to sit down for a few days and will probably be too frightened to report it,' said Ah Fat.

'Say nothing and drive on,' commanded Major Rance.

They continued their way south, stopping off at Taiping for a snack and a leg stretch. After a while of deep thought Jason said, 'If Chin Peng can afford to be so hostile against us and can keep such close tracks on us, we'll have to be even more cautious than ever. Lots of range work and our cutting blades to be razor sharp. I alone will carry a garrotting wire for silent strangling. There may well come a time when speed and silence alone are essential for killing.'

'Jason, one thing that worries me,' said Ah Fat with a frown as they neared Ipoh, 'twice you've been a target, both times a near miss and next time you may not be so lucky without a gunman. I strongly recommend you take one more man to keep you in sight at all times. I have my Bear. Can you afford to have one of your sergeants so tied to you? What's your answer to that?'

'I see your point. Let me ask my sergeants what their view is.' He leaned back and asked them. 'Sahib, we had come to the same conclusion. You have your own batman, Hemraj Rai, take him with you. He won't come amiss and we can always do with just one extra man. Indeed, for all you know, he might save your life.' *And to that there's no answer* mused Jason.

'P'ing Yee, are you worried that our being seen together will get back to Sadao with ill consequences?'

Ah Fat made a moue. 'It hadn't struck me but, yes, it might just ...'

They planned their nitty gritty details with finical care: how and when to re-ration the team after the initial five days' worth was finished; money for any local-purchase produce; code words to be used for various places such as ladangs, headmen and rivers; opening times for radio communications – they had been given call sign 1-2 –how and when an air search would be instituted for how many days with no radio contact; any 'medevac' – medical evacuation – needed; number of rounds to be carried by each man, including grenades; and any 'goodies' to be taken to the headmen.

'We'll start work on the three riverine ladangs first and, if we find nothing definite, we'll move inland ...'

Zhong Han San, leader of Killer Squad in south Thailand, ground his teeth in rage. Creaky-voiced, sadistic bully that he was, he did not like it one little bit when he learnt once more that the latest attempt to kill or wound the Red-Haired Devil had resulted in a wounded and dispirited minion. *A pity the idiot didn't duck as he seems to have done* he thought testily, loins swelling as he thought of where the blow had struck. *It would have served him right to have had his head taken off. My Grik agent is not up to standard. Grik: that means they'll be moving off into the jungle and meeting the* t'o yan. He scowled as he thought how to counter that. Yes, it was obvious that his target should be given to the

Temiar for their blowpipes. *I suppose the answer is to alert the* t'o yan *who we know are on our side. That will mean all except those alongside the Sungei Perak.* The long scar on the right of his face reddened and is right eye twitched more than usual. He had not shown the letter he had received from Grik to Ah Hai as it would, he felt, point to his own inefficiencies. It had taken a week for it to reach him. He now needed to send two letters to Comrade Ah Soo Chye, currently on a three-monthly visit to the ladangs in deeper jungle, both for Kelantan and Perak 'post boxes'. This latter was a large dead tree with an inside split by lightning close to the junction of the Sungei Perak with the tributary, Sungei Temenggor, some five hours boat journey from Grik. It had been used in the past and was completely safe but always with the risk that the letter was insecurely lodged so had fallen to the bottom and was out of reach or heavy rain made it illegible. It was not a guaranteed method and he felt probably that the last one sent this way had somehow gone astray but, even so, standing orders were that, whenever any of Ah Soo Chye's group or his local screen were in the area, they should always peer into the bole of the tree, just in case.

Once more he put pen to paper, dating it 1 May 1961.

From the boat point on the wide, fast-flowing Sungei Perak was a vista of tree-girt mountains, cresting and ebbing across the horizon. *It's a mighty large area to look into: actually seeing it for real makes me wonder if we haven't bitten off more than we can chew,* Jason said to himself as he looked at its immensity and feeling insignificant, impotent and ineffectual as he and his group started off on Operation Blind Spot with a visit to the nearest settlement at Kantan's ladang, almost opposite the boat point. Expectantly they crossed the river.

Their collective heart dropped when they saw a collection of squalid shacks with timid, poor and dishevelled inmates. Kantan, small and wiry, smiled and joked when Jason used his *Tengleq Kui Serok* book, which also had Malay equivalent words. Day one passed in pleasantries and on day two he scowled and laughed in turns as he claimed that he had not set eyes on or heard of guerrillas for seven years – thereby showing he could count above three as he spoke in Malay – glowering at the idea of their thinking he knew more than he would say. On the third day they went on a dawn-to-dusk patrol of the area, more of an acclimatisation exercise than anything else. They paid a visit to a platoon of 1/12 GR, which was not far away, and asked the commander to arrange for their next lot of rations to be included in their indent. Jason did not feel in the mood either to use his ventriloquistic skills or his dummy.

'I can't stay here any longer, it'll make me and all of us mad,' sang out Jason, looking at his map on the fourth day, 'so on up to Ah Hong we go.' That ladang was bigger than the one before and the Ah Hong more mature than Kantan. As soon as he saw there were no Malays in the group he made his wife cook some tapioca and they sat down together at the river's edge to eat it. Jason found he could make himself understood in Temiar for easy talk, which was most encouraging. Ah Hong said that he had heard that there had been five guerrillas sometime in the past who had supposedly visited a Malay village on one of the larger tributaries of the Perak. When asked for more details he could only say that the guerrillas may have come from Thailand. It was so vague that it was worthless but at least good relations had been established.

'Jason, don't get dispirited,' said his Chinese friend. 'You English talk about needles in haystacks: here it is a pinhead in a bunch of haystacks.'

Jason grinned sheepishly. 'I know, I know but if we have as much luck with the rest of the Perak headmen so have to go to Kelantan our six months will be over before we know it. Let's ask for a boat to take us downstream to Goh Baleh's ladang. We'll pick it up opposite the boat point.'

The new ladang was bigger and cleaner than either of the other two and a small medical post had been established by a previous Gurkha platoon where the women brought their children for treatment. Happy and good relations between soldiers and civilians were obvious. Goh Baleh spoke about rumours of guerrilla movement, rumours that were again no more substantive than dandelion wisps. He also fulminated about a brother-in-law of his who had come from the north, by-passed his ladang and gone on south. Bad family etiquette ... *but is this what we're looking for?* Even so, the group stayed around the place for a few days, Jason learning his Temiar and the others moving into the jungle to practise 'immediate action' drills.

'P'ing Yee, tell you what. Let's go back to Grik for a night, get cleaned up, get more rations and boat upstream to the Sungei Temenggor and visit Kerinching. He's almost bound be a better bet than this lot. Happy with that?' and he also asked Hung Lo.

Both liked the idea 'and it'll probably suit your chaps as well.'

Their evening sitrep back to base was, as on previous days, November, Tango, Romeo, nothing to report.

Their boat arrived later than expected so, after a hot and uncomfortable five-hour journey upstream, they reached the Perak-Temenggor river junction too late to go any farther safely before dusk. The flocks of hornbills and the monitor lizards they had seen on the sandy banks were interesting to look at, otherwise it was much of the same: thick jungle either side with an occasional Malay village.

Ah Fat asked the boatman about spending the night before going on up the smaller river. No, not suitable, so he asked to go back downstream to the last Malay village where he had a distant relative and spend the night there. Ah Fat and the Bear chose to go with him. 'We'll have our morning meal before getting back up here at around ten o'clock.'

Jason collected his men around him. 'From now we're in enemy territory. We'll open fire on seeing any armed and uniformed men.' He looked at his watch. 'We've sat down all day. Let's go on a short recce patrol if only to stretch our legs. We'll wear our kit as I don't like leaving it behind with no one to guard it.'

The idea was gladly accepted. 'Shall we shoot anything for our evening meal?' Sergeant Kulbahadur asked.

'Only once we've done our circuit just in case there's anyone in earshot.'

Off they went, moving east and half an hour later decided to return. Some birds flew towards them from their north. An unseen mouse deer whickered and some monkeys above them chattered, signs of someone approaching. In front Sergeant Chakrabahadur stopped, put his hand up to make the others halt, turned round, put a finger to his lips, pointed to a tree struck by lightning, hollowed out inside, and again put his hand over his mouth, miming the need for silence. He knelt down, merging into the ground cover and took up a firing position, as did the others. Eyes and ears were strained and, to their surprise, three men, two young and a third, with peppercorn hair, considerably older, all wearing only loincloths and armed with blowpipes, came from behind the tree. They studied the ground and looked round, checking for safety. *All clear!* 'Peppercorn Hair' pulled something small and white from the quiver of darts that hung from his waist. *A piece of paper? What else?* As he put his arm up and dropped it inside the bole of the tree an owl flew out. The older man said something and Jason picked up the Temiar for 'far' and 'finished': he thought he also heard *ha la* as they turned back the way they had come. It had taken less than a minute.

Chakrabahadur looked at Jason enquiringly. Jason put his hand up. Wait. After no one had turned up to claim it within the next twenty minutes they got to their feet and went to the tree. Chakrabahadur felt around inside the hollow bole and his fingers felt the piece of paper. He pulled it out. 'Sahib, it's a letter. It looks as if the three were postmen for the daku as they wouldn't write a letter to themselves,' he said with a giggle as he gave it to Jason. Indeed it was a letter which he opened, glancing at it the minute Chinese writing. 'Well done, Chakré. That was quick of you. It could be important. I'll read it later. Before we go back search around down at the bottom and see if there's anything else.'

Chakrabahadur leant forwards. 'Catch hold of me one of you,' he said softly, 'so that I can lean farther down.'

Securely pinioned by willing hands, he swung both arms around. 'There's something else that seems like paper,' he called up. 'I'll get hold of it. Got it. Pull me up.'

He gave it to Jason. *Yes, it is another letter.*

They moved silently back to where they planned to make camp, cooked their meal and prepared for the night. Two men searched for and found large dry bamboo leaves that crunched when trodden on. These were laid around their sleeping places and would do instead of sentries. No sensible guerrilla or local moved at night if he didn't have to.

'Sergeant Minbahadur, open your set but use key. I don't like the idea of voice booming round the jungle. I'll write a short sitrep.' The Signal Sergeant quickly got his set into action and, using his torch, took the piece of paper that Jason had given him and sent: 'Three men seen putting letter into dead tree. Two letters recovered. Too dark to read now. No physical contact made.'

After their meal they sat round the embers of their fire and talked about the coincidence of coming across such an unusual occurrence. 'I'm going to ask you in turn how you would describe those men,' Jason said. The general opinion was that the two younger men, both in their twenties probably, were lighter of hue than any Temiar they had had seen yet and the older man, probably the leader, was darker. That meant that the two younger men had come from a deep jungle ladang where they was less sunlight and that they were supremely confident, lithe and deft in jungle movement and probably in using their blowpipes. But was the darker man local?

'I think it also shows that the letter was written after any southward movement from the Thai guerrilla camp was made, more as an afterthought – hey! Do you think it was the man whose backside was tickled by Sergeant Kulbahadur who reported that he failed in his attempt to put me out of action was the cause of the letter, which is a hasty sitrep for action?'

Yes, the others did as it seemed more than likely.

'That means that more daku were sent south to contact the nearest people who might meet up with us. The headman we're on our way to meet, Kerinching, is not the most northern headman even though it is thought he is the most in touch with the guerrillas, so probably the men with the letter were not his men. This to me means that our target is wiser about our operation than any of us had thought. What are your views?'

Yes, it did seem that way.

'Would you be able to recognise any of them if you saw them again?'

Doubtful the two younger ones but the elder with the peppercorn hair, probably yes.

In Ipoh and KL the message was only received after office hours but next morning both the Brigade Commander and the GOC enthused. Both sent back messages asking for the contents of the letters to be sent once they had been read.

Next morning Jason saw that he could only read the more recent letter as the older one had become so smudged with rain as to make it illegible. The new letter was, though, foreboding: he showed it to Ah Fat as soon as he got out of the boat and had sat down. 'P'ing Yee, I've read it. It is for Ah Soo Chye and signed by Zhong Han San. I am an especial target of all headmen who have been warned to use force against me. Ah Soo Chye is wanted back in Thailand before mid-August. Have a look at it yourself.'

Ah Fat read it. 'Shandung P'aau, that's just about it. Its provenance is interesting. Zhong Han San is the leader of the Killer Squad, which shows that it originated in Thailand from the main camp near Sadao. Our movements and possibly our whole operation's secrecy have somehow been blown. Have you sent a sitrep yet?'

'I did last evening and I opened my set with an overnight 'about to move, letter not yet read' at 0800 hours. Now you've come and confirmed the legible letter's content I must send another sitrep.'

The boatman came over to them. 'Tuan, if I am to get back to Grik tonight we must move upstream now.'

'Into the boats, lads, and on our way.' *The latest sitrep will have to 'wait out'.*

The journey was slower than even the boatman had thought, what with eight passengers. The river was much narrower and shallower than the Sungei Perak and Jason felt he was a sitting target for anyone wishing to ambush him. The boat grounded several times and everybody got out and helped push it forward, paddling in water halfway up to the shortest man's knees. The driver knew how far the boat could go and that happened to be where the map had 'Halting Bungalow' marked. Only a concrete base and a low wall showed that pre-war there had been a bungalow for the open-cast tin mining overseer. Jason thanked the boatman who turned round and departed.

'Cook a meal and open the set.' A sitrep was sent, showing their position and the letter's contents. At the end of the sitrep Jason, realising it would have been his unthinking foolishness at Sadao that had alerted and worried the rump of the guerrillas, felt it politic to add 'req[uest] op[erational] info[rmation] rest[ricted]'.

In Brigade and Divisional HQs the greatest interest was taken by this report. *The rump of the guerrillas is more powerful than the Int boys had thought!*

Jason knew Kerinching ladang's grid reference as a platoon of Gurkhas was there already. There was also a Chinese Junior Civil Liaison Officer, Goh Ah Hok, whom Jason had met in Ipoh, to act as interpreter for the platoon. A path led from the river and twenty minutes later Jason's party reached the ladang and a little farther off was the Gurkha camp. They saw the JCLO talking to a Temiar who seemed, from his stately bearing, to be a man of some importance. Middle-aged, he was dark-skinned, with a flattened nose, a deep frown, creased lips and a receding hair line. His large eyes were two stones of shining hard coal. He had to be headman Kerinching. He and the JCLO were sitting on a bench and some soldiers were nearby. *I've got to do a little showing off,* thought Jason.

He called out to the soldiers in Nepali and got friendly answers back, the men smiling. A Gurkha Lieutenant, the Platoon

Commander, came up and saluted him. 'So you've come to see us, Sahib,' he said. 'Yes, Lieutenant sahib, we'll have a chat later on.' Jason then approached the bench and, although he knew that Goh did not speak his brand of Chinese, Cantonese, he greeted him in it. He turned towards the Temiar and said, *'Tata Tongoq Kerinching me-ed? Eloh gah ääq? Könun yeeq öh* Rance. *Papööd ma-loh?'* Both Goh Ah Hok and the Gurkha Lieutenant seemed momentarily taken aback at Jason's fluency.

Jason's effort was rewarded. Kerinching's face unpuckered and a faint smile appeared. He answered in Temiar, most of which Rance was able to pick up. It was a welcome to him and his men to stay there. Then Ah Fat and Wang Ming, using Malay, introduced themselves. Goh glanced at Jason and hooded his eyes as a signal that said, 'We'll talk later.'

'Major sahib, what did you say?' asked the Gurkha Lieutenant.

'I said "Old man," using a term of respect, "headman, are you well? How are you? My name is Rance. Where are the children?" I said that last bit as you know I can make my dummy talk and, unless I frighten them out of their wits, it'll make them laugh. My secret weapon. Sahib, I'm going to spend a few days here, have you a space in your camp where we can have a sleeping place? There are seven of us. We have our own rations.'

'No problem, Major sahib. I'll show you where.'

Jason, Ah Fat and Goh Ah Hok held a council of war after their evening meal. Jason told Goh about the incident at the old tree and showed him the letter, which was full of interest to him. 'It looks as though you are Public Enemy Number One,' he said with a smile. 'I wonder why?' he added, shooting Rance a quick, appraising glance.

'Probably because it is known that I have mastered Temiar to an extent and can speak Chinese,' Jason dissembled glibly and Goh was wise enough not to probe and changed the subject. 'I made a sign at you' – 'yes I saw it and wondered why' – 'because I did not want you to mention or ask for Senagit.' Jason nodded. 'I thought that just might be it.'

'Senagit is, as you have already been briefed, cook, scout, guide and friend of Ah Soo Chye and Kerinching is struggling with a problem: can he get rid of his close links, not allegiance exactly but a long and quite close association with the guerrillas after maybe twenty years and come over to government without either being a target of the guerrillas' wrath or putting Senagit, a close relation of his, in a more difficult position?'

'Yes, I can see it is a problem,' Ah Fat said. 'What is your answer, Goh?'

'Is the Major sahib able to win him over? If Kerinching trusts the Major sahib, and you seem, sir, to have made an excellent start, he may possibly say where Senagit is. I believe he is hiding not so far away, possibly ill, but even I, who have known Kerinching for as long as I have, daren't press him on it. "Illness" may just be an excuse for non-appearance. If I, or anyone else come to that, press him too strongly, all the work I've managed to do, and you, Major sahib, have started to do, will come to naught.'

'Thank you for that briefing, Goh, but all is not lost.'

'How come, sir?'

Jason grinned. 'I have to admit I don't know yet but it is something for me to sleep on, which isn't far off as I'm turning in now. Good night to you both.'

Jason and Ah Fat decided to stay in the military camp and spend the days walking about Kerinching's ladang, becoming recognised, with Jason practising his language skills. 'When I am ready enough with my Temiar I'll give them a performance,' he said to Ah Fat. 'In the meanwhile, I'll add our request of seven more days' rations to be delivered, dropped or brought up by boat, whichever way the powers that be wish. I can send my sergeants on patrols, with the platoon or on their own, but I think I must stay here.'

'Makes good sense to me,' said his friend.

So, for the next few days, morning and afternoon, Jason, always with Hemraj with an eye open for any suspicious movement, sometimes with Ah Fat and the Bear and at other times with his Sergeants, walked around the ladang. He knew that nobody there was used to Europeans and he also felt that their children would be like children everywhere else he had met them: curious and eager to respond to any individual kindness. All the while he practised his language skills.

At first the children were shy but, as Jason wobbled his eyebrows individually, his hands and knees to and fro in a way that looked as though the knees were passing through each other, making bird noises with his hands – always remembering that Malayan cuckoos did not 'cuck' – and pretending to play tunes on a stick as though it were a flute, they started to follow him round the ladang, Pied-Piper fashion. When he sat down on a log, they came up to him, trying to imitate him. Although he knew not to touch anyone's head, he gently poked them in the tummy, making squeaking and grunting noises, mice and pigs. *Wonders never ceased!* The third day he sat down, the menfolk gathered around and on the fifth some of the women.

By then Jason had found the crucial differences between Temiar and his other languages: there were no words to count above three, hence the rather baffling reference by Moby, while everything talked about had to be related to the stream, actual or notional, flowing in relation to the object under discussion, speaker and listener. Time and distances were not relevant concepts: no time more than two days in the past was able to be specified, likewise any future happening more than four days ahead was too remote to be comprehended. Distances, depths and heights were all expressed by the same word, so the word for 'long' of a finger nail, *jeruq*, was the same as 'far' for a week's journey. Even the concept of an animal was too much to understand, so individual animals had their own names, likewise did trees. His book had words for over a dozen different types of bamboo *and I only recognise one!*

On the evening of the sixth day Jason and Ah Fat walked over to see Kerinching, who had not come over to the camp for a chat. *'Tata Tongoq Kerinching me-ed? Eloh gah ääq?'* called out Rance as he came to Kerinching's shack. He had learnt that 'what news?' was always asked after asking a person how he was. A grunt and a smile as an answer showed that the headman was in a good mood. Jason said that he would like to gather all the children and as many parents as possible some short time before dusk tomorrow. 'As at now,' he said, knowing that 'an hour' meant nothing to any of them.

Kerinching was suspicious. 'Why?'

'I have a visitor I want people to see.'

'What sort of visitor for people to see?'

'My young cousin for people to see. I will need a log of wood to sit on when I bring him. I will ask my soldiers to get a log for me to sit on.'

So it was arranged. 'P'ing Yee, I have a feeling Kerinching is watching out for something or someone,' Jason said. 'Let. us pretend to go back but walk once more round the ladang. I'll show Hemraj where I want the log.'

Ah Fat looked questioningly at his friend: he knew that if Jason had a hunch he needed it to be played out. So saying nothing, Jason and Ah Fat, followed a few yards behind by Hemraj, walked round the ladang. 'Hemraj, tomorrow with a couple of ustads, roll that log there', he pointed it out, 'over to there,' indicating where he wanted it. All three of them, pretending not to notice, saw that the headman did not go back to his shack but turned into the surrounding jungle, something they had not seen him do before: *on his way to meet someone?*

Back in camp they sat down for a mug of tea. Each thought that Kerinching's behaviour was unusual at best, suspicious at worst. 'Even so, I'm going ahead with my dummy show. Hemraj, I want you to hide in the jungle during it, camouflaged, behind where you put the log earlier on today, but hiding to a flank. I want you to watch your rear and, if anyone were to try and come out of the jungle to see what I am doing, do nothing until you hear me shout. Got it?'

Yes, Hemraj understood.

Jason called the Platoon Commander and told him of his plan. 'Sahib, if anyone wants to watch, welcome. You've all seen what I do before so it won't be new.'

The Platoon Commander smiled broadly. 'Yes sahib, see it we have and see it any spare member of my platoon will.'

Late next afternoon a crowd had gathered well before Jason made his way to the ladang with his team. His idea was, within the limits of his vocabulary which he had practised that morning, to bring out the dummy as his younger cousin and pretend to teach him Temiar. He had his sham krait in his pocket with which to 'frighten' his dummy. Nothing seemed untoward, everything normal, so away he went, followed by his team who would be part of the audience.

A hush greeted him. He wobbled his eyebrows, twisted his nose backwards and forwards with a yodelling whistle and laughter erupted. He put his hand up for silence, took his pack off and opened it, taking out the dummy. There was a gasp of surprise from the audience and an even louder one when Jason put it on his knee and, unseen by those in front, manipulated its head and mouth. '*Keloq, keloq,*' Jason said, meaning 'older cousin'. The dummy astounded all with a shake of its head and '*hoi keloq, pöq*', not older cousin, younger cousin.

Even so early on the audience felt bewitched, some fearful, others merely inquisitive. Jason continued with a few more 'misunderstandings' and then, by sleight of hand, threw the sham krait on the ground in front of him. Those in front of the crowd shrank back, the dummy's scream frightening them as did the snake.

Jason, of course, heavily concentrating on what he was doing, was blissfully unaware that Hemraj had heard, to one side, movement. Slowly turning his head, he saw the elder man with peppercorn hair who had been at the hollow tree. Looking intently to his front he did not see the Gurkha, who remained immobile. Reaching the edge of the jungle, 'Peppercorn Hair' took a dart from his quiver, put it in the end of his blowpipe, lowered the pipe to shoulder level and, squinting as if to aim it, puffed hard. There was no noise. Then another dart was shot. Again no noise.

Jason suddenly saw a dart in the sham krait and another in the head of his dummy. In a flash of inspiration, he shouted out, '*Tang ösh köbush. Pöq köbush*', krait dead, younger cousin dead, and got up, moving quickly away to a flank. The audience scattered. Kerinching, face a mask of rage and horror, strode up to Jason, now with Ah Fat and Goh Ah Hok flanking him with the Platoon Commander not far behind, and started berating him.

Hemraj, weapon in hand, had already taken five quick steps towards the man with the blow pipe and jumped at him but missed as the man, shrieking '*Aughhh! Aughhh! Tang ösh tung tung.*' – krait, afraid, afraid – threw away his blowpipe and darted into the jungle. Hemraj gave chase. Not being weighed down with any equipment, the attacker was the fleeter of foot. He was about to move out of sight when, looking back over his shoulder, he did not see a large wild boar wallowing in a muddy pool. He trod on it. Screaming with fright, it reared up backwards, throwing the unbalanced man head over heels onto the ground, momentarily winded. Hemraj caught up with him and pinned him down.

Jason bounded into the jungle and saw his bodyguard sitting on someone whose head was being held face down in the dirt. Joined by his three sergeants, he relieved Hemraj of trying to hold the squirming man down and, lifting him up, frog-marched him back to the edge of the ladang where Kerinching immediately told Jason to let the man go. Hemraj's eyes were red. 'He's one of those who were at the tree, Sahib. He tried to kill you.'

'*Tata Tongoq Kerinching*, we must find out what all this is about. Who is this man? I saw a day in the past at a tree with paper and two more men. I want news this now. He go no. Who is he?' demanded Jason, firmly, showing no anger but eyes probing like a scalpel.

Kerinching, feeling trapped like a mouse in a corner with two cats ready to pounce, saw that he had to give way. He bent over Senagit and softly said something that sounded like *ha la* but Jason wasn't sure. Then Kerinching stood up and, turning to the English major, said 'This man is Senagit. He is so afraid of kraits that he wants to kill them whenever he sees them. He also thought your younger cousin was a ghost. He was so frightened he wanted to kill both, not you.'

Jason saw that he was at a critical point in his journey 'to the hearts and minds' of the Temiar. He told his men to let the man go free and, as he turned to Senagit, he felt a tickle in his throat. He tried to clear it but coughed at the same time, making a snarling noise.

Senagit looked at Jason with wonder, '*aab, aab*', he cried out. He looked at Jason with a smile: '*aab me-ed*' – tiger good.

Jason, bewildered at 'tiger, tiger', said 'Senagit, you kill my enemy the krait and my ghost. You are now friend and help,' and, without a second thought, pursed his lips open and shut, desperation and improvisation his instinctive probe.

Senagit looked at Jason, initially perplexed then face brightening. '*Tata*, now snake dead. Now ghost dead, we friends. Tiger ours. *Me-ed hup, kääd ayamb*. You have a kind heart and a face like a chicken's arse when it shits,' and burst out laughing. The others joined in and it really did seem that the crisis had passed.

Jason looked inquiringly at Kerinching who nodded. '*Tata*, we'll talk tomorrow.' *Has the yeast started working in the dough?*

That evening in the camp, Jason, curiously feeling both deflated and inflated, sat round the fire with his whole team, including Goh Ah Hok and the Platoon Commander. He had to use a mixture of languages because his Gurkhas' and the Bear's English was not up to an adequate standard. He had already heartily congratulated Hemraj on his skill and dexterity, and he now told him but for his behaviour and correct instantaneous reaction the situation now to be developed could not even have been imagined. 'I wonder why Senagit said "tiger, tiger, tiger good" when I had that tickle in my throat. Goh, have you any idea?'

'Yes, Major sahib. I think that when he heard you coughing, you were making a tiger noise on purpose as you somehow knew that the tiger was his soul animal,' was Goh's unexpected reply.

'Soul animal?'

'Yes. When young, all Temiar are given a soul animal by the shaman and that means that that animal will never attack that person.'

Jason shook his head in wonderment. 'What an incredible coincidence. How can we take advantage of Senagit's seeming to be on my side is what we have to discuss. Is he the breakthrough we have all been hoping for?'

It was Goh Ah Hok who put forward the critical point. 'Maybe you're halfway there but you will never get anything from these Temiar without a price,' he said. 'Even if Senagit wanted to work with you as "eyes and ears" he won't do a thing unless he is given authority from Kerinching. So our question is "what will Kerinching's price be for that to transpire?" I happen to know that his son and brother are as skilled operators as any I've come across. With them as well you will have a screen to work in front of you just as Ah Soo Chye and his gang have used in the past.' He let his words hang while Jason translated to his men and Ah Fat to the Bear.

'Goh, I don't yet know enough about the workings of these people's minds to give you an answer. I'm sure you know what Kerinching will ask for.'

'I have as good an idea as any but fresh ideas are always welcomed. Ask around and see if anyone does have any.'

While a general chat in Nepali and Chinese ensued, Jason dug into his pocket, picked out the letter that had been pulled out of the tree and gave it to Goh. 'I should have given you this before but what with one thing and another, it slipped my mind. Please read it.'

This Goh did and looked up at Jason with a grave face. 'This alters your plan, Major sahib. It is just not worth your while searching any other ladangs, especially the way you're operating now.' He cleared his throat as if contemplating whether to say something in his mind. 'If you don't object to my suggesting something to you, and if I were in your shoes, I'd go straight up north to the border, with Kerinching's three men, get them to go to Ah Soo Chye's camp, tell them they've hoodwinked you into coming to the border and that you have no idea of the Communists' camp, bring them down to ambush you then you clobber them ...'

Jason interrupted. 'Goh, no more need be said. I like it. Thank you. Now all we need to do is to persuade Kerinching to let that happen as far as his three men are concerned. Wrap it up a bit, will you and tell the others.' *Phase 1 about to finish already? Hardly possible if so.*

By then the others had finished their discussion with nothing substantive thought of.

'Right, I'll tell you what I recommend,' said Goh. 'Tell Kerinching, who does not really like either the Security Forces in his ladang area or the guerrillas that, with his three men, yes, all three, Senagit, Sutel and Rijed as your scouts, you will almost guarantee that the guerrillas will be induced to leave this area for ever and, with that in view, the troops also, provided you don't waste time in going all over Perak and Kelantan but move straightaway up to the border and let the Temiar do the rest.' He looked around and, after suitable translations, the others nodded their acceptance. 'Then, you, Rance sahib, will tell him that if the plan does not work for any reason *no blame at all will ever be levelled at him*, emphasised and repeated. And finally, once that is settled, as I have a feeling that the old man, *Tata*, even as he calls you, sir, out of respect, a reward of money will be supplied from Special Branch's Enche Mubarak, whom he knows. Quite frankly, if he does not accept those terms, there is nothing else that he will. If he visits us tomorrow, and I think he will, let me start off the conversation, only handing it over once I'm sure enough he's thinking positively.'

Everybody understood that so there seemed nothing more to say except 'bedtime'.

Next morning Kerinching came into the camp by himself and Goh Ah Hok welcomed him, offering him a mug of tea, something no Temiar had ever met before soldiers came their way. The 'Well, are you well?' 'Well, I am well.' 'With what news?' 'With no news' routine inaugurated the proceedings. Some ten or so minutes later Goh, in basic Malay which Kerinching understood, said 'I hope, I hope strongly, hope in dream, wind bring thought, *Tata* is a good man.'

A hungry look came over the headman's face. He knew that such talk meant something more than pleasantries.

'My friend the white man would like to use Senagit, Sutel and Rijed to help him help you once you have said you agree.'

'What is it he wants?'

'He wants to use them to go and search out the Chinese men so that they never come again, leave you in peace so that the soldiers can also leave you in peace.'

Kerinching considered this for so long without answering that Goh was worried that his ploy had failed. 'And any other reward?' greed showing in those shining hard coal eyes.

'Yes, *Tata*, no blame at all if anything goes wrong and that

Enche Mubarak gives you money when the white man's work is over.'

Again silence, with Kerinching's face a mask, eyes beady and predatory. Eventually, 'I come back tomorrow. I speak with Senagit, Sutel and Rijed.'

Kerinching departed and Goh briefed Jason and his team.

On the morrow Kerinching came back with the three men.

'They will go with you but not yet ready. They need reward first. Give now.'

It was then that Goh called Jason and Ah Fat. 'This is the situation we have reached,' he told them. How much can you spare them?'

Jason was well enough off to say five hundred ringgits but that was immediately countered. 'Much too much. Say fifty at the most. Show it.'

Jason went to fetch it. There were three red ten-ringgit notes and four green five-ringgit notes for all three whose eyes glistened greedily at such riches. They put their hands out and almost snatched the money from Jason.

Jason looked into the distance, thinking hard. *I have managed to convince these three to help me much more quickly than ever envisaged. Um …* 'I will come back a day in the future. I am not ready. I will not forget,' he told Kerinching, in basic Malay so the others could understand. I will contact the Platoon Commander and give you time to get ready for me. I will come and fetch you. But first I will ask that Enche Mubarak to come here for the reward.'

This was happily accepted and Jason radioed to Grik with a

message. 'Please ask Inspector Mubarak to come up to the halting bungalow on the Sungei Temenggor as soon as convenient. We have a lot to talk about but it has to be face to face. I also need a boat for my eight men to return to Grik.'

Two days later Jason, his team, Kerinching and his three men were at the halting bungalow when Moby arrived shortly before sunset. 'I have Senagit here also!'

'Jason, that's something I never thought would happen. We must talk straightaway as I have to get back tomorrow. My boatmen will cook my food, you presumably have had yours.'

'Yes, Moby we have eaten.' They made themselves comfortable and Jason started. 'First of all I'll brief you on what has happened. After that I'd like you to talk to Kerinching and his three men. I believe I have had the breakthrough we had hoped for and much earlier than expected. Ready?' Moby nodded. 'This is what and how it happened ...'

The end of Jason's briefing coincided with Moby's meal being ready. While Moby ate, Jason had a bathe in the river, as did his Gurkhas. They were fed up with the smell of unwashed bodies that Jason likened to pencil shavings, rancid butter and manure.

When Moby was ready he called Kerinching over to him and both men spoke softly, Senagit, Sutel and Rijed listening in. Jason with Ah Hok sat in the background, saying nothing.

Eventually the mumbling of low voices came to an end and Kerinching, with the other three, moved back to where his wife had prepared somewhere to sleep. 'Tuan Major, fixed, as far as anything with these mercurial people is concerned can be fixed.

Kerinching has told me that if your venture is successful, he will tell the other headmen to cut all ties with the guerrillas and, as Senagit has a wife over the Divide in Kelantan, one of other of them will try and persuade the most powerful headman there to follow suit. Isn't that a wonderful step forward?'

'Yes, Moby, looked at in that light it does really seem as if matters were about to turn in our favour but we've got a long, long way to go yet.'

'I'm sure you will let me know when you've decided to return for your next phase.'

'Yes, of course I will. Bedtime now.'

Before Jason's team left for Grik early next morning Senagit sidled up to Jason and, grinning fiendishly, said that *Tata tongoq* had allowed him to go fishing for fish with two legs. Jason joined in the laughter and said goodbye. By the following day they were back in Ipoh. Before starting to plan for Phase 2 Jason wrote a report on Phase 1.

The GOC, the Head of Special Branch and HQ 2 Fed Brigade were excited and pleased by Jason's report. It seemed a fitting reward for the trust shown to the 'unconventional' British officer and his mixed team for the surprising speed at his success...to date. On the other hand, the mood up in Sadao was quite the opposite. It was muddled, someone was reported as killed and yet exactly who was unsubstantiated. *Was it that inquisitive and troublesome Running Dog? If not, who? If not, next time will definitely be the last* ... but last for whom was not mentioned as it was taken for granted ...

5

'The one question I didn't think of asking Senagit was who had given him that letter to put in that tree, not that we can't guess,' said Jason as he and his Chinese friend, back in their Ipoh office, were talking over their time in Kerinching's ladang.

'Probably just as well you didn't,' replied Ah Fat. 'Those people have different thought processes from the likes of us and his, what shall I call it, conversion to being on your side rather than on the letter writer's may have been too raw for a forthright answer.'

Jason frowned as he thought that one out. 'You may well be right.' He gave a small chuckle. 'It finished up so very differently from how I expected it would and probably you, also. But at least we're at the end of Phase 1 so it is now full speed ahead for Phase 2. As I see it we have two separate aims apart from confirming whether those three Temiar will work with us or not. One is to deal with Ah Soo Chye and his gang in their hide-out in Thailand if we don't come across them in Malaya first, which is most unlikely, and the other is to get the two Gurkhas down from Bangkok and across the frontier. It's a bit "chicken-and-eggish".' He relapsed into silence as he tossed the various conflicting factors around in his head.

After a while Ah Fat said, 'Needn't be either but both at the same time. I go to Bangkok and get the Gurkhas ... No Jason, listen to me,' as his friend tried to interrupt. 'You are a known target and I am not. You have already had three lucky misses, number four may well be unlucky so the less you show your face the better. You must always travel with your bodyguard and with the others where possible. I and the Bear will go to Bangkok, meet and bring both Gurkhas south via Songkhla down to Betong and on as far as a bus or taxi can take us, then hoof it to an RV we've yet to fix just over the border in Malaya. We'll only take minimum food with us to start with so it will look as though we aren't going far and buy more in Songkhla,. And don't forget, Jason, I've been around that neck of the woods a few times already. Simultaneously, you, your Gurkhas and your three Temiar will be moving north and by then you should be somewhere not all that far from us so let's work on meeting up on or near the border and move back here together. Why not?'

Why not, indeed? Jason could not fault his friend. 'Yes, it will give us a fixed target that Manbahadur knows rather than looking for our quarry in an area where nothing has happened, for what, ten years. I'll take a carrying party of a platoon with me rather than taking an airdrop with, say, fifteen days' worth of food and some clothing. The platoon can guard the dump and be a reserve if we need one in a hurry as its radio will on the battalion net. We'll have one boat convoy upriver and make our dump where the boats can go no farther. And my group will go on up to the RV. Such a plan is sound enough for me to get Kulbahadur to give his brother a bell. He'll be itching for some sort of news and to know when to stand by from. When do you think we should warn Manbahadur to be ready to leave?'

'How about a pencil-entry for 15 August although that is rather a long way ahead, isn't it?' queried Flat Ears.

'I doubt it can be much before then. Going up to Kerinching's ladang once more to get those three, Senagit, Sutel and Rijed, could well take quite a bit of time. An unknown is will they have changed their minds and if so how long will it take to be cajoled into action? Probably not at all if Kerinching has not changed his. They already know we'll provide rations and shelters for nights nor will they be out of pocket, except,' with a giggle, 'loin cloths don't have any. Tell you what: you come with me to their ladang. We'll both go back to Grik with or without any Temiar and there we'll separate till we meet up on the border.'

Ah Fat thought that one over. 'Yes, why not? Talking to Goh Ah Hok will help matters if unexpected problems crop up.'

'Then I'll make contact with the Guard Commander at the British embassy tomorrow. Poor old Manbahadur must be getting anxious.'

'Let's leave that, then, and move on to money, Jason. What's the size of your budget? Did you fix up anything when you were with the GOC?'

'I did. It's been authorised, all twenty-five thousand ringgits of it. How much do you think you'll need?'

'At least half or, better still, twenty thousand. Apart from the expense of kitting ourselves out and hiring taxis rather than going more slowly by bus, even at Betong there maybe frontier problems. Though the road doesn't go into Malaya somebody somewhere may have to be bribed if only to keep his big mouth shut. At Songkhla I'll get a message to you by phoning Ipoh to pass on to you by radio and you in turn can get a message back to me that way. Slow but should be sure ... enough.'

Jason went to the Ipoh telephone exchange and once more, in English, asked the operator for the British Bangkok embassy number. The operator, who looked at the Englishman with a quick penetrating glance, was the same man as before whose vague likeness of someone Jason couldn't place nagged at him. When the call came through he asked to be put through to the Guard Room. Luckily the one-time Sergeant Major answered the phone and Jason asked him to contact Manbahadur and tell him to be at his number at noon in two day's time, Friday, and every day at that time until contact was made. Once again the operator in Ipoh was surprised at a British officer wanting Bangkok but not, as it happened, more surprised or more suspicious than the Thai operator at the other end was. *Somebody I know will be interested* he thought as he remembered the safe house in Bangkok used for some of his friends from down in the Sadao area, *one or other of us will listen carefully to any more calls from Ipoh.*

On the Friday, Jason, with Kulbahadur, went back to the exchange and asked for the number that Manbahadur had originally given him. The operator was the same as the two previous visits and in no way looked any friendlier at Jason. *I'll ignore him.* The Gurkha had been briefed on what to say to his brother, namely to stand by for a call at noon on 15 August from the Chinese man he had met 'that time in the main camp' and their RV was to be at the same small roadside café where he and the Major sahib had last met. If no phone contact was made on 15 August to be at the phone every day after that at the same time until the call came through. The ringing tone had sounded several times before Manbahadur answered it. Kulbahadur spoke to his brother in the Limbu language, not one of Jason's, but he could almost feel the surge of hope, love and joy that came down from the other end. Kulbahadur at last put the receiver down and smiling broadly said, 'Sahib, if my brother were a dog his tail would have fallen off he'd have wagged it so much. *Was* he pleased to establish contact once more! He didn't know your Chinese friend's name and I did not use it, I merely told him that it would be the same Chinese he'd met "that time in the main camp" who would tell him how he would be rescued. I told him to expect a call on Tuesday, the 15th and, if it didn't come, to be ready every day at noon at the phone until the call came through. He also told me he had Kesar Pun with him and he'd bring him along as well.'

'Excellent, that should prevent any slip up. My mind is much happier than it was as indeed your brother's obviously is. At long, long last soon to be safe,' said Jason, delighted to learn that Kesar Pun was still in the 'Land of the Living' but not realising that the phone calls had stirred a hornets' nest. Back in camp he remembered who the operator reminded him of: the man who had tried to kill him with a cleaver. *I haven't asked Ah Fat if he ever managed to trace him* and the next time he met his friend, ask him he did.

'He was found to be a hard-core man who had spent some

years in detention. He was re-arrested and is now serving time not for attempted murder, which would most certainly have settled his hash for many a year, but for not having an ID card. The reason for being charged with the lesser crime is because the last thing we in Special Branch wanted is for your name to be plastered around by the media. It could have spoilt so much of what we've managed so far. Why ask now?'

'Because each time I've been to the exchange the same man has been there and I couldn't place who he vaguely reminded me of. I now believe that he could well be that fellow's brother.'

'I'll tell you after I've checked up on him.'

Neither Ah Fat nor Jason was to know what else was about to spoil what they thought they were about to manage without too many difficulties.

On the phone the two brothers had been overjoyed to renew contact after so long. They both let off a lot of personal steam as they started to reminisce before coming to the 'bull point' of where and when the RV in Bangkok would be. While being fully confident that no listener could have understood a word of their conversation, Manbahadur had no idea that his childhood use of calling his brother 'Ha La', which came to him automatically without thinking, had mightily intrigued the Thai telephone exchange operator, making him think that the speaker, of whose language he was completely in the dark, was referring to the village of that name at the very bottom of the Betong salient, almost next door to the Thai-Malay border. He already knew that it was a sensitive area and therefore what his duty was. It did not take long for him to trace the Bangkok phone number and set up arrangements to see who came to use it if, or more probably when, that strange language was heard again. The elderly Thai woman in charge of the safe house, a double-storey wooden 'bungalow' by chance quite near the phone that Manbahadur Limbu used, would be told to warn any temporary resident to stay put and be ready to go to the phone when warned that it had been rung again to try and find out who the caller was: the situation had to be resolved. Even talking Limbu the word 'August' was used – 'Ha La' and 'August', most suspicious!

After the phone call Jason said to his friend, 'Flat Ears, one point that is bothering me is how best to synchronise our meeting at the border. As I see it you will need a day to get to KL, a day there, another day to fly to Bangkok, a day there, say another two days to the border, that's a total of six days. It'll take me maybe nine days to get there from Grik. I, too, will always be looking over my shoulder for more rations if for any reason I'm slowed down. Neither of us wants to stay there longer than absolutely necessary. No one will know about you but I've learnt never to take anything for granted.'

Ah Fat looked at a calendar on the wall. Provided we can get back from Kerinching's ladang by, say, the 11th and you move north on the 12th that will be three days before I can talk to Manbahadur on the 15th so, unless something goes terribly wrong with either of us, the difference in days you mentioned won't happen.'

'No, nor it will,' Jason grinned. 'I hadn't looked at it that way and I was never much good at maths! Let's pencil-entry those dates before we go and brief the CO. Now, I must look at the map again. Please can you bring me the map sheet of Betong Salient? It could well pay me dividends to study it.'

'Yes, there's one here. I'll bring it over.'

A moment later, 'P'ing Yee,' Jason called out excitedly, 'Listen to this. I'm really on to something here. Twice I've heard those Temiar say something I didn't understand and which stuck in my mind: Ha La. I heard that name when Senagit put the letter in the tree and when Kerinching spoke to him after he'd shot at my dummy and the krait. Surely, surely that'll be the place where Ah Soo Chye and his men have their camp. Look here, that's the name of the Thai village nearest the border. Betong is not so far away to its north.' He got up and paced the room as if he were entangled in an unseen web.

'Bother!' countered his friend, pinching the bridge of his nose as if fighting off a headache. 'That was my blind spot. Your mentioning Ha La has only just reminded me that of course I have been there. When we had to leave Malaya I can remember moving up through the headwaters of the Sungei Perak and crossing the border – where's that map?' He scrutinised it and, with a pencil, pointed to the pass to the west of Gunong Gadong on the border. 'There's a stone border marker there and I can recall Chin Peng getting someone to scratch a hammer and sickle in the stone stem as a reminder as we made our way over into Thailand. Virtually the whole of the bottom of the Betong salient is controlled by his people, or was when I was last there, and the camp belonging to the group that oversees and cajoles the Temiar was to be built between the border and Ha La.' He studied the map as he was talking. 'Yes, here it is. Let that be our RV. We'll give it a code name, something if overheard can distract the ungodly ... How about "Sadao" to put people off the scent if they overhear us?'

'I can live with it,' said Jason with a satisfied grin. 'There's no reason for any old contact your side not to recognise you as they think you are still one of them and ...' looking at the map again in the light of his new knowledge, 'once I've left my carrying party at the dump my lot will continue north, make for the pass to the west of Gunong Gadong, look for the marker and make a temporary base there. Meanwhile you, the Bear and the Gurkhas will move south, by-passing the guerrillas' camp and meet up with us there. Then "Home James and don't spare the horses" as the old song has it.'

'I should have a clear run in the Ha La area as there's no reason for anyone in that part of the world to suspect me there so there's no reason for us not to expect a safe passage.'

After finalising their planning they asked for a meeting with the CO, who had the IO with him. 'Sir, in outline this is our plan...' and Jason gave him 'chapter and verse'. 'For that to happen, sir, I'd like to take a platoon from my company with fifteen days' rations, theirs and ours, to make a dump so there'll be no noisy airdrop and stay here,' pointing out the place on the map, 'and act as a reaction force were one wanted. From there I will continue north to meet the four from Bangkok at the RV on the border and together back home we'll come. That is what we would like you to authorise.'

The CO considered what he had been told, inwardly pondering on the pros and cons of it. 'I like it. It seems better than I had thought you'd come up with. Have you made any plans for your two groups to contact one another? Mr Ah Fat will have no radio.'

'Our solution is for him to phone the battalion here from Songkhla to tell you that they have arrived and that will be relayed to me when I next open my set. Pencil entry date is the 19th provided the Temiar are still willing to go with us and we back to Grik by the 11th. So, if I am already at the RV by then, you give Ah Fat our code word, "Sadao", otherwise say "at Sadao in ... days' time" having judged my speed from my last sitrep. Just in case any suspicious person is monitoring our calls, both from here to Bangkok and this one, saying "Sadao" rather than "Songkhla" may confuse any ungodly snooper, sir.' He smiled and added, 'that's the type of blind spot that should work in our favour.'

The CO nodded his assent before saying, 'Yes, it makes good sense. Don't forget that, as a soloist, you are sometimes in danger of drowning out the chorus even though what you're about to do is but a footnote of regimental history that many never be written.' *Damning me with faint praise or the opposite?* 'IO, confirm those details with Major Rance outside.' He opened a drawer of his desk and took out a compass. 'And, as an act of faith in your incurable optimism and unconventionality, here is your compass with its needle pointing to 45 degrees. It is a poor substitute if you're out in the boonies in someone else's country, alone as a man can be, as there won't be the helicopter lifeline back to base. You'll only be tethered to us by an invisible thread of radio energy at best.'

'Sir, I have my Gurkhas,' said Jason as he pocketed the compass and thanked the CO.

'Major Rance, you are the only one of my officers I'd let go on such a wild-goose chase.'

'Sir,' answered Jason with a grin, 'the geese will be wilder still after we've chased them.'

He then made arrangements to draw his entire budget, giving Ah Fat most of it.

Ah Hai and Zhong Han San had been both shocked and alarmed when the unexpected and unpleasant news of possible activity against the guerrilla camp at Ha La reached them, would it come from the south or the north, they wondered. Presumably the former but why had there been those phone calls from Malaya to Thailand suggesting the latter? The telephone operator in Bangkok had never before heard the language spoken although he was adamant that he had heard the name Ha La several times but had not understood anything else but he had heard the word August in a previous call. He also notified the camp what arrangements he had made for tracing the phone call and that he had alerted the safe house for possible follow-up action. *He's done us well* the guerrillas told one another. The two men went into a huddle, trying to decide if the news they had received might be bluff and that a real attack on the camp at Sadao was being planned to try and stop the Secretary General from going to China, not realising that he had already managed to escape. It was most unsettling.

There were still only the sketchiest of details as to results of the last letter that Zhong had caused to be sent to Ah Soo Chye and, disturbingly and disappointingly, nothing from those sturdy supporters, Kerinching and Senagit. A dwarf's death! Just didn't make sense. Later reports from Ipoh and Grik were that neither of their two main suspects was dead, so who was it who had been successfully hit by a blowpipe arrow? Most muddling and inconclusive. They had received no reports of any unusual troop movements or any change in normal military activity so if any reinforcements from Sadao to Ha La were wanted they would only be sent if any definite news was received – either from Grik or Bangkok. Even so, as a precaution, Comrade Zhong himself, suitably escorted by a squad of half of his hard men – the other half had to stay in Sadao, just in case – would go to Ha La camp, give a warning of possible activity and make any preparations necessary. *I really feel I'll be successful,* Zhong Han San crowed inwardly. *I'll make a killing, slowly, slowly.* He licked his lips and felt 'that' familiar urge. *My being there before them will be their blind spot* and he laughed to himself.

What else? He would also take a copy of Major Rance's passport photograph for showing their comrades and selected villagers. The description of the Englishman's companion that the hotel owner in Sadao had supplied to Comrade Zhong, as far as could be remembered, only fitted the Thai guerrilla Kamhaeng Thanaboon, an unlikely renegade but already known to everybody in camp. But his involvement certainly suggested a northern approach. One pointer to his being a traitor was that the hotel manager had heard him speaking a language he'd never heard before, just like the Bangkok operator had – but were they the same language? If either or both of those hotel visitors were seen they were to be arrested and brought back to Sadao. If an escape seemed imminent, they were to be shot, preferably not to be killed, only to maim. The Acting Secretary General was, by then, almost fully confident that the one-time, non-voting Military Consultant to the Central Committee was probably also heavily involved in anti-Party activities as reports had come in that he was living in the mercenary Gurkha camp. 'If I can get proof, he'll need ruthless treatment as will his Bear,' he told Zhong Han San. 'I'm busy for the next couple of days. Think about this strange language and its implications and we'll talk about it when I'm free. Only then will you go to Ha La'. Zhong Han San was unruffled about being ruthless: he had watched how the Japanese Imperial Army's Military Police Corps, Kempeitai, punished people during the Japanese occupation in Malaya and had learnt many of their methods. He'd just love to try them out himself. The sour subsoil of his disturbed mind was ready to work its innate horrors.

Back once more in Kerinching's ladang, Jason and Ah Fat found that the *Tongoq* had changed his mind. He was adamant he would only allow his three men's being used as guides if they were wanted to go east over the Divide into Kelantan, not north towards Thailand. They went over to the Gurkhas' camp to talk with Goh Ah Hok but found he had decided to stretch his legs with a shotgun for something for the pot and had taken Senagit with him.

Jason was greeted handsomely on the return of the hunters,

who had managed to kill a deer. Senagit went to put his blowpipe back in his hut and Goh Ah Hok said, 'Major sahib. The three men are having wife trouble. No wife wants their man to go with you as they are afraid something bad will happen.'

'But Kerinching told me that it was he who would only allow them to cross the Divide with us,' countered Jason. 'He didn't mention any wife trouble.'

'No, he wouldn't. If somehow you can coax only Senagit to go with you, I'm sure he will.' He saw Jason looking doubtful. 'Surely, Major sahib, you could use your animal spirit's voice somehow, couldn't you, to coax him?'

'Can but try, I suppose, but it will have to be as if for real to work. If I can't, all our efforts to date will have been for virtually nothing. *What* a waste of time if so.'

'Don't speak too soon, Major sahib. It's not like you to be overly pessimistic.'

Senagit came back, smiled up at Jason who wobbled his ears and eyebrows back at him. *My one-man cabaret show: all or nothing*, he thought and picked up a stick off the ground and, putting it to his lips, whistled a tune as though it were a flute. Senagit roared with laughter and repeated his description of Jason, '*Me-ed hup, kääd ayamb.*'

And then Fate, Providence, Destiny or Chance showed that Jason had spoken too soon: one of those extraordinary coincidences happened that, almost nothing in themselves, have an eventual critical effect. He was standing just behind Senagit when a krait slid out of some grass a few yards in front of them and Peppercorn Hair stopped laughing immediately and tried to edge back. Jason, remembering the tiger noise he had made that had first won him over, made it again but as though it had come from Senagit's own mouth as he was near enough to throw his voice that far. The krait stayed where it was. A sudden flash-back came to Jason: it was while still in his old Gurkha battalion in India he had been watching stacked camouflage nets for vehicles being moved when a krait had slid out from under one of them. He had been enthralled as he watched how one of the older drivers had defanged it before throwing its still live body away. *Can I do it myself now, after all these years? Go on although it's an almighty gamble, death twenty minutes after a bite. I'll defang it.* Before Senagit or anyone else could move he whipped his sweat rag off his neck and bound it round his left hand, fingers free. With the piece of wood in his right, he approached the krait with the stick at arm's length.

'Be careful, be careful,' came warnings.

Jason did not answer but continued moving towards the snake, waving the stick from side to side till it was above its head. He hit the snake hard on the end of its tail then waved the stick above its head. The snake stared at it, hissing, moving its head from side to side as though getting ready to strike: four more hits on the tail and after each the stick was waved over the snake's head, just out of striking range. Then he waved the stick up and down in front of the snake's eyes not hitting its tail, which was, by then, smashed and bloody. He took the stick in his left hand and, gradually drawing the snake's attention away from his right, suddenly gripped it hard at the base of its neck. Moving his fingers up to the snake's jaws, he prised them open and, with his left hand, still in its protective cloth, deftly plucked out the two poisonous fangs. He carefully put those to one side and dropped the snake that was by then harmless and flicked it into the undergrowth with his stick.

.Those watching Jason's masterly performance were overawed and roundly congratulated him. Senagit didn't know if, in Jason's military way of saying it, he was 'punched, bored or counter-sunk', so utterly surprised at his own ability to sound like a tiger in the face of danger without even trying to and at Jason's cool and successful performance at defanging the krait. Jason and his soul animal were bonded irrevocably, one and the same, once and for all. He looked up at the tall Englishman with complete confidence shining from his features: '*Tata,*' he almost shrilled, 'I'll go with you wherever you take me. My wife won't stop me. No one will stop me. That China will not stop me. *Hoi kadeq teeg-tuug senoi China.*' – I'm not afraid of that Chinese man.

'Kerinching seems to have turned sour,' Jason said to the JCLO. 'Can you tell me what's behind his change of mind? My gamble with the snake was to try and form a bond between me and Senagit which Kerinching cannot break. If that doesn't work with him, nothing else will.'

'Major sahib, Senagit's wife was the cause of the change of mind. She had a dream about his future being cloudy and once any of these people have had a dream there's no way they'll change their mind about its meaning. The three who would have been going with you and Kerinching have shown their hands to such an extent that, were they to go back on their word for a reason they're shy of explaining, they would lose tremendous face with their own people even at the risk of losing out financially with Special Branch. Trust you they do: but they have to live with their womenfolk and not with you. Kerinching is in a cleft stick and by playing it this way he feels he is acting in the best interests of his people. My advice is to thank him for allowing his men to go over the Divide into Kelantan if necessary and to thank him for Senagit's help, even though he has yet to say anything about it,' and he smiled disarmingly. 'After your masterly performance with the krait no one here now dares challenge you. And if I could add one point, may I advise you to leave Sutel and Rijed behind? I have a feeling Senagit will work better by himself.'

'Kind words, Goh, you have heartened me. As for Kerinching's brother and son, leaving them behind is a kind of compromise. I'll tell him that he'll need them for his own protection just in case anything unpleasant develops. I'll leave tomorrow so I must send a message to battalion to get my platoon up to Grik straight away with rations, a lightweight blanket and a poncho for one more man.'

Next morning they made their farewells and moved down to the boat point, Senagit with them. 'Now let's go hunting for those "fish with two legs",' Jason said to him. His new shadow grinned.

By then it was 9 August, six days to go for contact with Manbahadur was due.

Before the two groups separated in Grik on 11 August, Jason told Ah Fat that he had a couple of points. 'The first is do you think that you are suspected and, if so, how much? You and the Bear have been seen with me in Ipoh, Grik and in the ladangs.

How much danger do you think you'll be in when you and the two Gurkhas arrive in Betong and Ha La? You ... no wait a minute,' as his friend tried to interrupt, 'each time I've been to the Ipoh exchange the operator has looked at me in a quizzical, if not suspicious, way and, who knows, the Bangkok telephone operator might even be an agent. If that were the case, and of course it could just my overworked imagination, wouldn't it be better if you were to go down to KL, stay a night or three with your family and phone Manbahadur from there?'

'Seeing red shadows everywhere are you?' Ah Fat replied, almost without thinking.

Jason gave his friend a swift, worried look. 'Maybe I am. Red shadows may not hurt but "Reds under the bed" are a different matter, especially when they climb up from under them and start making themselves a nuisance, as you well know when you had to keep your mouth shut when the one we knew as the Lustful Wolf, Sik Long, accused you of treachery. You were tied to a tree and tortured. Surely you haven't forgotten that?'

No, forget it he hadn't. It had been ten years before when, masquerading as a loyal Communist, he was in the group going to Chin Peng's camp in north Malaya escorting the turncoat British officer who had deserted to the guerrillas. His cover had nearly been blown by the discovery of a 'bug' in the guerrillas' wireless that he, Ah Fat, had had installed so that an Auster aircraft could listen in to and fix their location. The bug had been discovered and he had been accused of putting it there. He was unconscious, lolling head down from being tied to a tree, thinking that he'd be killed at dawn, when miraculously Jason Rance had rescued him. At dawn Jason's secret group had attacked the camp and the renegade officer, along with a number of guerrillas, had been killed. It was from that day on that the Bear had joined Jason's 'Q' group.

'Jason, you're right.' *My life has so often been nerve-tautening and only eternal vigilance has kept me alive.* 'Only Westerners think lightening can never strike in the same place twice. We Chinese say that misfortune never comes singly although we also say it doesn't come in pairs,' Ah Fat answered apologetically. 'I haven't visited the camp up in Sadao since I escorted that Indonesian Aidit some time ago and it could well be that my one-time so-called boss is wondering why I've never been back since and never had an official farewell. There was nothing to go back for once the Emergency was over and he never recalled me.' *Of course he used me as a double-agent but I don't think he ever did know that the work I did was really against him and his Communism and for the Government.* 'Thank you, Jason. And your second point?'

'It's only a small one but don't forget that Malaya is half an hour ahead of Thai time.'

'Thank you, Shandung P'aau, I had quite forgotten about the time difference as I'd never had to fix anything by phone before. I could have gone badly wrong if you hadn't reminded me.'

The two Chinese travelled back to Ipoh in the empty transport that had brought Jason's platoon and the rations. Ah Fat went to Special Branch and asked the clerk in the Records Office for details of the man without an ID card. Sure enough one of his brothers was working in the Ipoh telephone exchange. He remembered what had alarmed Jason. Although there was probably nothing wrong with another call to Bangkok from Ipoh it would be safer to make the call from the main exchange in KL where direct dialling was possible.

'We'll take the afternoon flight to KL, Wang Ming. I'll make the call at noon minus thirty next Tuesday and we'll go to Bangkok the next day. That means we'll have five nights at home. Do us both good. There'll be no need to be with me when I go and have a talk with Mr C C Too.'

Ah Fat rang Bangkok on the 15th as arranged and got Manbahadur. 'I talk with Kesar,' Ah Fat said slowly.

'He is here, Sahib, tell him in Malay.'

Ah Fat told Kesar when to be at the tea shop opposite the British embassy with his friend then immediately went to the booking office and bought two tickets for the next day's flight: only first class was available but *the budget is enough for that!*

'Comrade Zhong Han San, tell me your thoughts,' the Acting Secretary General of the almost defunct Malayan Communist Party said to his Killer Squad leader a couple of days after their last talk. 'Have you fully digested the disturbing report from the telephone exchange operator in Bangkok? If ever there was a shot in the dark this is it but it could be what we've both been wondering about for a long time past. Our man there had no idea at all what language was being used. It was certainly a new one to him. Can you guess what it might be?'

Zhong was one of those men who never wanted to be lacking an answer. 'Could it be an African or a Fiji language, do you think, Comrade? Troops of both countries were used against us when we were in Malaya. I can't think what else it could be.'

'No, neither can be correct. We'd have heard about such troops if they had been sent and, in any case, now that military action is only confined to the border, large-scale operations will have to wait until our Indonesian comrades attack Peninsular Malaysia – Malaya's proposed new name if this weird idea of Malaysia ever comes off. I read once that the British used Welsh on their radio transmissions to confuse eavesdroppers. Are there, I wonder, any British troops left?'

Then Zhong had a brainwave. 'It could be a tribal language of the Gurkha troops, Comrade. I'm told that Nepali is not the only language in Nepal. If it were a tribal language then it will surely mean that Gurkha troops are probably engaged in some sort of trickery. Is it possible to find out from the Ipoh exchange who made the call? We already know that 1/12 Gurkha Rifles are there and that the Running Dog major is in that unit so it should be easy enough to find out with all international calls logged.'

Ah Hai looked at his watch. 'Good idea. It is still early enough to find out today. There's no phone in Sadao is there?' *I've never bothered to find out, having lived where there's been no phone for so many years.*

'Yes, Comrade Acting Secretary General, there is one in the police station if not in that hotel. I'll send someone down with a note from you to ensure that the request is complied with and some money to pay for a call to the main exchange in Bangkok. Get someone there to contact Ipoh and see who it was who actually talked on the phone that day. Shouldn't be too difficult to check and, if we're lucky, we'll know almost at once. It's only the 15th today so the details will be easy enough to find.'

And know they did: it was the Running Dog whose photo had been secretly circulated with a Gurkha soldier.

'Right, Comrade Zhong, I want you to be on your way to Betong and Ha La soonest, tomorrow morning if possible but before you go I want to have a last meeting with you and your team as there are some serious points to be aware of.'

They met later on that evening. 'Before Comrade Chin Peng left he gave me certain details and this last news about the origin of the telephone call from Ipoh has me worried. Let me run through the Comrade Secretary General's points and what I have learnt. If you, Comrade Zhong, have any, please give them when I have finished.' During the discussion which started from 'that letter', the meeting heard that all three efforts to 'dissuade' the Running Dog from interfering – the cleaver, the brick hurled at the vehicle window and the blowpipe attack – had been abortive. 'If he were to be in any activity in the Ha La area, obliterate him is my firm order,' seethed the Acting Secretary General. He pointed to Alif and Zai. 'I want you to go with Comrade Zhong. Comrade Aidit warned us of trouble over where you come from. The last thing he'll want is such a man over there were anything to develop. So, although the chances of that happening are infinitesimally remote, one just cannot be too careful. Comrade Zhong, you have sufficient photos of him to give to all at the village and the camp?'

'Yes, Comrade Acting Secretary General, I have,' Zhong replied. The meeting then broke up.

The five-day wait in KL for the Tuesday phone call was sufficient time for Zhong's group to easily get to Ha La by the 17th, the day the two Chinese and the two Gurkhas planned to move south from Bangkok.

Jason was delighted to meet up with one of his platoons again. That night in the Grik camp he gave his men the background of their forthcoming operation. All eyes were button bright in anticipation at an exciting and unusual task as he let them into the secret of why he had been targeted after their first jungle training exercise – 'I was reckless, I know, but somehow I wanted to avenge those Gurkhas who had been killed and wounded during the Emergency' – as well as the King of Nepal being worried about Gurkhas in Thailand left over from World War Two. They were even more excited and matters came even nearer home when the Major sahib let on that the one man, whom he already knew, was Sergeant Kulbahadur Limbu's elder brother. 'Once we've rescued him I've arranged that he be sent home on a leave party's airlift. Sergeant Kulé, when are you due leave?'

'Sahib, on the next leave party. If we're successful, I and my brother can go together. After so long away he'll need quite a lot of help in readjusting.'

'I'll ensure that happens' and Jason continued with his tactical briefing that included the journey upriver. The last point he taught his team was how to cause breathlessness by throttling: 'It could well come in useful one day.'

None of the six boats which were due to leave at eight o'clock the next morning were ready to move off on time but twenty minutes later two were so Jason's team and a half section went ahead. The rest were to follow on in tactical groups as soon as the other boats were ready. 'We'll meet up as far as the boats can go, tonight if we're lucky otherwise tomorrow.'

But Jason had been over optimistic. Within two hours one of his boats had broken down, so he radioed Grik either to send up another boat or a fitter with his tools and left it where it was. Although annoying, it was no hardship as it was self-contained with arms, ammunition and rations. Jason's boat pressed on alone. His progress was further slowed by his boat also breaking its shear pins on underwater snags several times. As the hours passed the passengers grew uncomfortably hot, as there was no awning, and cramped. The river wound around the contours, with a strong current in the main channel. Occasionally they came across rapids that needed considerable skill to navigate.

By evening, instead of being anywhere near their final destination with all six boats, Jason was barely halfway with one other. It was no use being annoyed; there was nothing that could be done to hurry things up.

Next morning the two boats continued upstream, the river becoming more and more narrow and more turbulent. At one place between large rocks not so far apart from each other the boats had to navigate over an incline of two almost vertical feet of fast-flowing water. Jason doubted whether it was safe to even try and would have preferred to get out and walk around the hazard, enabling him and his men to stretch their legs and avoid any drowned weapons. However, the boatman felt it was safer to go ahead rather than try and get back to a flat bank. Halfway up the incline the engine failed. The boat was immediately slewed sideways and caught the whole force of the current, just missing the other boat. Water poured in. There was near panic until the soldiers saw a large fish swimming around in the water at their feet and their foraging instincts prevailed. The boat only just avoided upending but was quickly swept back down into the comparative calm. 'Out you get, lads,' Jason sang out. 'It's not worth our while to risk another attempt,' so everybody got out and walked until the boat caught them up where the river was more placid. Jason's unspoken comment on the whole journey up till then was haphazard with more hazard than hap.

They reached the boat limit before dusk on the second day and could only send local patrols out before the remainder arrived. Almost immediately one patrol found recent traces of two or three guerrillas, its judgement based on the state of some dried blood from an animal carcass. Senagit looked at the tracks and recognised them as men from Ha La. A follow-up was not possible until the others arrived, which they did at midday on the third day, in a rainstorm, more than glad to step ashore. By then it was 14 August.

On 16 August, sitting at a table outside the small roadside café in sight of the British embassy in Phloen Cit road, Ah Fat and Wang Ming, both nursing a cup of coffee, anxiously awaited the arrival of the two Gurkhas. It was now ten to 1 and still no Gurkhas. *Fifty minutes overdue.*

Suddenly a voice called from an inner room. 'Hello, hello. Mister, come inside please.' The two Chinese looked round and saw the owner beckoning to them. In they went and there, to their joy, they saw the Gurkhas standing in the background. *Why?* Ah Fat asked them if they would like a beer and after an appreciative nod, both were given a large bottle. 'Why are you late and why didn't you come down the road?' he asked.

It was Kesar who answered in Malay: what had happened was when they went to the telephone as ordered, a snooper had followed them and stood outside the phone booth, menacingly. On leaving it, the man had tried to catch hold of Manbahadur. The two Gurkhas had managed to escape but had only returned to their room after dark, so afraid had they been to be seen by day. And again, this morning, as they set out to come to the RV, they were followed by two Chinese and had had a hard time to throw them off the scent to prevent them from following on behind to the tea shop. They had been forced to dodge their way around until they found the small lane Manbahadur knew of leading up to the back of the shop. Kesar was in a bad state of nerves and almost breathless by the time he came to the end of his story. 'Are men watching us?' he asked.

So Jason's worries were not unfounded, Ah Fat mused as he sat considering his best move. 'Have a cautious look outside and see if any of those trying to catch you are lurking anywhere,' he said to Kesar. The Gurkha borrowed a rain coat and a hat from the owner, put them on and went outside where he sat at a table by himself. He appeared not to move his head too obviously as he looked up and down the road.

Ten minutes later he came back inside. No, there was nobody he could recognise moving up and down the road nor were there any loiterers and the open British embassy grounds meant that no one could look down at them from any upper window from over the street.

'Hung Lo, stand outside and stop the next empty taxi that passes,' Ah Fat said as he paid the bill and told the Gurkhas to finish their beer. Ah Fat thought their best course of action would be to go to the station, buy tickets for the night then go shopping for clothes – coolie-type for the journey and uniform-type for the move south on foot – water bottles, dixies, torches, biscuits, raisins and chocolate, one rucksack each and heavy walking sticks as make-do weapons. They'd travel by rail to Songkhla, leaving tonight, the 17th …

The Bear shouted to them. 'Taxi is waiting. The driver's in a hurry. It seems he is not allowed to stop here.' They dashed out, got into it and away they went, giving instructions to go to the railway station. Once there Ah Fat told the others what he had decided upon.

As Manbahadur looked out of the carriage window, minutes before the train was due to leave, he saw the two Chinese who had tried to catch hold of him dart in from the entrance, look around, espy him, point at him then run up to the train and jump into a carriage several down from theirs. Quickly gathering up his pack, he blurted out 'Danger, danger. Enemy men come, see me. Move out now if not we finish.' He grabbed his pack and the others grabbed theirs. Running down the corridor to the door on the far side of the platform, Manbahadur threw his pack out then jumped down, quickly followed by Kesar, Ah Fat and the Bear.

It was quite a drop but they managed to jump down safely and they scuttled over the lines to the next platform where they hoisted each other up in the gloom without being seen. Keeping their heads away from the train, they were glad to see it slowly move off and, as far as they could make out, no one looking their way.

That was too close for comfort, thought Ah Fat before saying. 'Let's go and have a meal, we'd have had one in the train in any case, and work out what to do.' They did not go to the station restaurant but found a place nearby. Over their meal Ah Fat said, 'Even if we were able to get a taxi to take us to Songkhla by the morning, it is unwise, in my view, because those two men will be looking for us. Far better to leave tomorrow morning by taxi, breaking our journey halfway. That'll mean we won't get to Songkhla till the 18th and maybe not to Betong till the 19th. That should still be enough time to meet up with the others as planned.'

They reached Songkhla late on the 18th. Ah Fat paid the taxi off and they booked into the only hotel, scarcely worth the name, for the night, the four of them having to share a room. There was a phone in the hotel office and Ah Fat used it to put a call through to the main exchange in Bangkok and, giving the battalion's number, asked to be connected.

'How long do you want to talk?'

'Three minutes.'

Ah Fat was told the price. 'Do I pay for it first?'

'Yes.'

He paid it to the clerk who confirmed he had done so with Bangkok.

'Ring you back.'

While they were waiting for the call they ordered a meal. *It may be that we will be better off not brazenly showing ourselves in Ha La village before we get to the camp*, Ah Fat thought, so ordered eight portions of rice and dried fish, not four, putting the rest into their dixies. 'Before we move off, make sure your water bottles are full,' he said slowly to the Gurkhas.

Eventually the call came through and Ah Fat asked the Gurkha operator to find the CO urgently. Luckily the CO had not gone to bed. 'Sir, from Thailand, Sadao has been reached. Please pass it on.'

'Yes, I will. All okay?'

'We're managing and so far are all in one piece.'

'Well done. Good luck. Hope to see you soon.'

Ah Fat put the receiver down, happy that his call to Ipoh had been successful and that the use of the word Sadao was a wise one. Unbeknownst to him the man on duty at the Bangkok exchange immediately put a call through to the one hotel in Sadao. After identifying himself, he said to the owner, 'Tell your people to beware of an intrusion.' As previously instructed the owner went hot foot to the camp at dawn with the message and gave it to the Acting Secretary General himself who thanked him. *Lucky Comrade Zhong only took half his squad* he mused as he gave orders for the camp to be put on stand-by.

The time lost on the river was more unfortunate than Jason could ever realise as he could never know that it gave the Zhong Han San sufficient time to put the Ha La camp defences in a higher state of readiness for a probe from the south as well as alerting people in Betong about a small group, no one was quite sure how many men, from the north. One of the precautions he had made was to put a sentry in the highest tree nearest the camp with a pair of binoculars and trimmed the leaves so as to have a 360 degree all-round observation capability.

On his map, Jason showed his platoon commander his area, told him of suspected guerrilla movement and warned him to listen in on the radio for anything he might have for them three times a day. After a quick brew Jason's team and a carrying party from the platoon with rations moved north and soon came across more evidence of guerrilla activity: an overnight resting place ... the animal hunters? That evening, just as Jason was deciding it was time to make his base, the leading scout saw footprints of two men wearing hockey boots moving north., 'That means more silence and more caution than ever,' Jason said.'

Game abounded in the area: bear, elephant, rhinoceros, tiger, deer and pig, recognised by their spoor. They also found a large patch of trampled and bloody undergrowth and a pig and a python that had fought to the death. A day and a half later and about a quarter of a mile short of the border, Jason's carrying party unloaded their rations, made a waterproof cache and made ready to return to base. 'Bring another load to be here in five days' time,' Jason told the sergeant in charge as they left. They heard high-pitched animal noises and had the rewarding sight of three otters fishing in a stream as they were making their way for the pass to the west of Gunong Gadong on the border. They got there late afternoon, found the stone border marker with a scratched hammer and sickle in the stem and made as hidden a base as possible.

Early on 19 August before Senagit, armed with his blowpipe, went across the border into Thailand, Rance called him over and gave him a letter he had written for Manbahadur. It was a message of welcome and, if there was any doubt as to what might happen to the two Chinese, to make for the border with Senagit just as fast and safely as they could. Rance called over Sergeant Kulbahadur and told Senagit that his elder brother would be with the Chinese 'and he looks like him. You must give him this letter, like this,' and Rance stood with his back to the sergeant and put his hand with the letter in it behind his back, waggled it around until it was taken. Again, 'This way. Understand?' Yes, Senagit did. 'Not like this,' and Rance repeated the pantomime face to face but like this and once more showed him the behind-the-back method. 'Can do?'

Yes, Senagit said he could. He tucked the letter into his loincloth. 'I go now?'

'No. More one. That man knows way here. One day in the past he come here. That man China he knows the way here. Easy for you. Say "come", they "come".'

Senagit considered all that, practiced it twice, was told it was correct, laughed at his cleverness at remembering it properly the second time and moved off. Within twenty minutes he came back. 'Tata, we must go together,' he insisted. By the look on his face Jason saw that something he probably could not explain was troubling him. He made his mind up, *my 'wrong' compass is my passport.* 'Cook a meal, break camp and,' he looked at his watch, 'we'll all move off at 1000 hours,' he told his small group who had gathered round him. 'We can't afford not to go over the border with Senagit having come so far. We'll change into those hockey boots we've brought with us to keep the guerrillas guessing if they see our tracks. In case our new plan means we have to wait for more than three days without going back for more rations, we'll have to do with half rations. That will last us for ten days which will be plenty.'

'Sahib, if you hadn't mentioned it we would have made the point,' said Sergeant Kulbahadur.

Jason felt almost undressed as he and his group crossed the border into Thailand. He leant over to Kulbahadur and softly quoted a proverb, 'How do I know what a comet looks like till I've seen one?' and his Sergeant answered with another proverb, 'The goat is religiously got ready for the slaughter, all that can happen is for matters to go wrong.' Yes, it now really was a journey into the unknown and, as they stepped over the border, two determined pairs of eyes locked on one another.

After Ah Fat's phone call the four of them went shopping once more to top up their rations, this time rice, dried fish and matches. 'I'd rather not hang around here till tomorrow,' said the Bear, 'it smells wrong. Have we enough money to get a taxi to take us to Betong tonight?'

Ah Fat did a lightening calculation, 'Yes, even if we have to pay more than double the price.' He looked at Manbahadur, remembering that he knew the area from before. 'What do you think? Go now by taxi or go tomorrow?'

'Go now. Wait in hotel. I come back,' and, so saying, he disappeared down a side road. He had just remembered that one of his Chinese friends from the time they had been together in Sadao camp had told him where he would live if ever he got the chance to get away. The Gurkha had, in fact, been allowed to visit Songkhla on leave as a reward for some hard work in the rice fields so it did not take him long to find his old friend's house. He knocked on the door and a woman came to open it. 'I am Kamhaeng Thanaboon,' he introduced himself and asked for his friend. His luck was in and the woman, his wife, called her husband.

The two friends clasped one another. 'Friend' – never any names – 'I need help and I expect you need money. Get a taxi for me and four others to go to Betong tonight and I'll guarantee you'll be well paid.'

'I can do that and, if fact, I do need money,' said his friend with a smile, never wanting to know why there was such urgency. 'It'll take about half an hour. I have a friend who is indebted to me and I have a licence. Wait here,' and off he went. A few minutes before the half hour was up, a car, old, noisy and ramshackle, drew up. 'Get in,' the driver said softly. 'Where do you want to go to pick up the others?'

Manbahadur told him. 'No, too public. Go and bring them here, leaving the hotel from the back and crossing the main road where the light is dimmest.'

Off the Gurkha went and, at the hotel, he found the three others fretting. 'Where have you been all this time?' Ah Fat asked.

Manbahadur put his finger to his lips. 'I have taxi. Get packs. Follow me to back. I take you to taxi.'

Once at the friend's house Ah Fat asked about the price. He knew it would be steep but felt it was worth paying. Without haggling pay it he did. Manbahadur sat in front with the driver and the other three sat in the back, and, hats pulled down over eyes, they were driven away, the driver shouting out loudly to his wife that he was on his way to Bangkok.

'Do you know Betong?' Ah Fat asked Manbahadur.

'Yes.'

'Can you find way south in dark?'

'Yes.'

'Get as much sleep as you can,' said Ah Fat to the Bear. 'I can see us bypassing Betong before dawn.' All Gurkhas get rocked to sleep when children so easily fall asleep when in anything that sways, so both hill men had already been lulled to sleep by the jolting of the car. 'Driver, if we are not awake already, wake us up a few minutes before we reach Betong,' said Ah Fat before he, too, dozed off.

With Senagit in front and moving even more cautiously than normal Jason's group had reached the flat ground less than an hour's walk from Ha La by early evening. Senagit told them that there was a bamboo grove to their front and that they should camp to the mountain side of it, in thick jungle by the side of a stream. It was too late for any more forward movement so 'I go to Ha La, look and see. Come back later,' Senagit said as he disappeared after a surprisingly good night's rest. He reached Ha

La camp well within the hour and met up with the three Chinese he knew, Ah Soo Chye, Tek Miu and Lo See. 'I'm so glad to see you,' Ah Soo Chye said, 'Where are the others who normally move with you?'

Senagit grinned. 'Wife trouble. I got some youngsters to come most of the way with me but they were scared to cross the frontier,' he dissembled. 'They'll come back *nai ish hatop*' – in a few days. The Chinese knew that it was hopeless trying to pin any Temiar down to a fixed time so he merely said he understood. Senagit continued, 'I've come to tell you that I got your letter from the tree and when the one you wanted shooting at was not looking I shot at him and hit him and a krait that was near him. I then hid elsewhere.'

Ah Soo Chye took Senagit to meet Comrade Zhong, whom he had not met before, and took an instant dislike to him with his grating voice and damaged face. *Not like my new friend. This one's a danger.* Zhong gave Senagit a long look: *too old and wrinkly for me and a peppercorn* t'o yan's *pubic hair is repugnant.* Senagit was already edgy, alert and ready to disappear at a moment's notice if something bad happened – and it smelt bad before anything had happened.

Awake once more just short of Betong, the group in the taxi reckoned it would be safe to drive through it in the small hours and certainly much quicker than floundering through the backyards of houses on the edge of the town, setting every dog barking and waking people up thinking that thieves were busy. 'For an extra fifteen hundred baht go as far along the road to Ha La as you can,' said Ah Fat, handing over the money. The driver smiled and drove on. When they saw Ha La in the distance they stopped the taxi and got out. Thanking the driver, Ah Fat told Manbahadur to move off in front. 'Do not go through the village. Move into the jungle. We find water and eat food,' he told him. *Today is the 19th, we're on time*, he mused, *I wonder where Jason has got to. All seems quiet enough.* He was unconcerned as both of them knew their RV.

They cooked and ate as expeditiously as they could but it was their bad luck that none of them knew they had been seen at their meal by the sentry with binoculars from the tallest tree. It took him longer to climb down, go back to the camp, find and then alert Zhong with his five men than it did for the three men to wash and pack their dixies before moving off.

Jason opened his set and, on key, sent '1-2, NTR, over'. He was sent Ah Fat's phone message. 1-2, Roger, Out.' *Almost home and dry but ...*

Senagit heard the commotion in the camp as the alert was sounded. As the man with the binoculars led the way out of the camp followed by Zhong's men armed with rifles and one with a rope and a knife, he knew that there was big, big trouble. Like a wraith he followed on behind, moving silently with every sense alert. He smelt cooking before the others noticed the remains and, realising that his three men would have moved off south – not that 'south' as such had any meaning to him – he jinked, moving off circuitously, ahead of Zhong's men who were finding the tracking difficult as the man with the binoculars could not recognise the terrain from ground level, especially as they had to pass round a bamboo thicket on their way. But tracked they were ... successfully because their path led through some wet ground where leaving traces was unavoidable.

Senagit, now a few minutes in front of the search party, saw Ah Fat and the three others so ran to catch them up, calling out, 'Senoi China, senoi China.' They turned and saw him. Ah Fat rallied and, using simple Malay, asked him what he was doing.

Pointing behind him, obviously scared stiff, he spluttered breathlessly that bad men were coming. He looked at each man, saw the Gurkhas, hesitated before putting his hand into his loincloth, pulled out Jason's letter and gave it to Manbahadur. The Gurkha opened it, scanned it and felt he was safe at last.

Ah Fat looked over the Gurkha's shoulder and saw Jason's signature at the bottom. *Oh this language problem,* he inwardly cursed, *how can I plan without knowing details?* He began to ask the Gurkha in simple English when a hail of bullets unexpectedly crashed overhead from behind. Zhong's men, having come across their tracks, had made good time and had opened fire on espying them from about seventy paces away. As they approached, firing, shouting and crashing through the thick undergrowth, Senagit urgently took hold of Manbahadur's sleeve and tried to pull him away. The Gurkha struggled to stay there, *I must stay with my friends* was the thought that passed through his mind, forgetting what the letter had in it, but Senagit just would not let go. Tugging frantically and helped by Kesar forcibly made him move on – only just in time as the pursuers reached the other two and overpowered them easily. Glancing over his shoulder as he fled, Manbahadur saw the two men come to rescue him lying on the ground and that man with a sadist's face, Zhong Han San, kicking them hard turn by turn. There had been no time to use their heavy walking sticks.

Jason and his men heard the shooting and shouting so took up firing positions from behind the nearest trees. Something told him that the five men were in serious trouble but he was in a quandary as what to do: go forward now and deal with anything that came their way, even if heavily outnumbered, or wait until matters had seemingly quietened down. But there was no more firing and Jason presumed, wrongly, that Ah Fat's lot had managed to get away. He was sadly disillusioned when he heard frantic spine-chilling screams which turned his blood to water. *Oh no! Too late after so much planning,* he thought, angrily and sadly. They heard movement coming their way – enemy or friends? – and all minds were in a whirl when only two Gurkhas and Senagit came running hard into view. Jason signalled them towards him. They came, breathless, and sank to the ground. Before he could stop them, brother had embraced brother, almost twenty years since they had set eyes on one another. They separated and Manbahadur spluttered out, 'The Chinese have captured the other two. Can we go back and save them?'

'Is there anything to save?'

'There might just be.'

An eerie, foreboding and ominous silence had settled. Yet, less than half an hour later, taut and agonising screams were witness to something worse than horrible. The listeners' skin froze with fear.

Ah Fat and the Bear were stripped naked. The money was found and given to Zhong before they were bound and beaten with a thin bamboo stave while the Chinese sadist decided what to do with them. As he thought he taunted both of them. 'Clever, clever, lickspittle traitors, both of you,' he call out over the noise of the beating. 'Traitors, both of you. Thought you'd get away with it, didn't you? Working with one you called Shandung P'aau who called you P'ing Yee. I've a good mind to cut those flat ears off here and now.' He turned to the two men who were taking turns to beat them. 'Make them bleed,' he roared, knowing that blood coursing down flesh was the one sight that made him hard quicker than any other. His orders were obeyed. Ah Fat was barely conscious by then: the Bear, cursing under his breath, was stronger, but not by much.

It was too much for Zhong. 'Stop. Undo the smooth-skinned one,' he said pointing at Ah Fat, 'and bring him over to me. I'll give you a demonstration of how strong I am. Two of you open his legs, two of you bend him over and hold him so that he cannot move. You others guard our flanks. There were two others with them who won't be all that far away. We'll go for them after I've shown you how powerful I am. Watch me.' So saying, he took off his trousers and underpants. Rampant as to penis, he sodomised Ah Fat. Even his followers, used to his bestial methods, turned away when he withdrew, limp.

'We'll take them over to the bamboo grove,' said Zhong,

remembering one particularly nasty way the Kempeitai used to punish offenders. 'I think it best to mete out a lingering punishment to the main traitor and a quicker one to his so-called Bear. We'll get rid of him and leave this Flat Ears here overnight to consider his heinous ways. Tomorrow morning I'll come back and see how he is. But there is no hurry, slowly, slowly is the way to punish people like him.'

The two prisoners were undone and forced to walk, stumble was more how they moved, back to the bamboo grove, being hit on their Achilles tendons to make them hurry. Once there, Zhong walked round the grove searching for a clump of younger shoots. He pulled some of them towards him as though testing their resilience. He finally made up his mind when he found two clumps only a couple of feet apart. He called his men to him and divided them into four, one to pull down one length of bamboo till it was parallel with the ground, another to do the same at the other clump. The other two took the Bear, who was too shattered to give more than token resistance, stripped him and took a leg each. Holding him head down, one leg was tied to one of the pieces of bamboo, the other leg to the second. The people holding the pieces down let them up a bit, so the wretched man, gibbering with fear and eyes almost popping out of his head, was stretched taut.

'Bring me the sharpest knife you have,' ordered Zhong.

Another piercing and more frenzied scream split the air but came to a gurgling murmur when Wong Ming was punched in the stomach so all his breath was expelled.

Through his haze of pain, Ah Fat saw what was happening,

knew he could do nothing to help his friend of so many years and shut his eyes when Zhong, bulging in his crotch, took the knife and delicately cut the end of Wang Ming's penis off. Ah Fat could not shut his ears to the dreadful noise – a penetrating shriek, a horrible babbling, a gurgling murmur then silence. He trembled as fear and helplessness seeped through his body.

By the time he had been castrated, his eyes pulled out and the testicles put into the empty sockets, Wong Ming was almost dead. But not quite. In the mists of his pain, as consciousness returned once or twice, he heard Zhong say, 'Your friend's death will take longer than yours.'

The Bear managed to croak, 'Kill me, kill me,' and, on a sign from Zhong, those holding the bamboos let them go. As they sprung back to their natural position the bound man was split up to his navel and the death that he had craved came to him instantaneously.

'See that? Traitor that he was. See that?' Zhong crowed to Ah Fat. 'For you we have a slower death.' He had found a bamboo sprout. In sunny, moist surroundings, young bamboo can grow quickly, some kinds an inch overnight. Ah Fat was hauled over to a bamboo that just came to the edge of his bared rectum. As some men held him there, Zhong told the man to take the rope to the nearest water, wet it and bring it back. 'Quickly!'

The wet rope, not as wet as Zhong would have wished but wet enough to shrink when it dried, was brought back. 'Now tie this man up so tightly that he can never get away. By the time the vultures have picked clean the body of that traitorous cur up there,' and he indicated the remains of the Bear's body dripping blood and entrails and already attracting flies as he turned and faced Ah Fat, 'the bamboo will be an inch up your rectum by tomorrow morning – unless the jackals make a meal of you tonight,' and Zhong laughed hugely at his own joke.

As he was talking, men once more opened Ah Fat's legs and Zhong tied them to a branch either side and his body and arms to the nearest grown clump. A gag was forced into his mouth. It smelt vilely and the bile rose in the bound man's gorge. 'I'll have you know I've had this treated with the most delicious item that I could think of. It could not be more personal as I donated it myself, from my very bowels but I doubt if that will stop any hungry jackal,' and he guffawed again in evil joy.

'Right men, leave this fellow here. Back to the camp we go. I'll come tomorrow morning to visit this man … if there's anything left to visit!'

When Jason felt it was safe to go and see what dreadful tortures had been committed on his two friends, he and his men cautiously followed Senagit back to where he had fled from. They heard an angry buzzing and could hardly believe their eyes when they caught sight of the sordid mess that only recently had been a man, stretched out between two bamboos. In such a short time a host of flies pulsated and crawled in, around and over the tacky, viscous fluid that was still oozing from a most horrendous mess of gaping wounds. None looking at it had ever seen a human body so badly mutilated. It had to be the Bear, the stolid, hard-working, loyal Wang Ming. *But where is Ah Fat?*

As Jason turned, retching, he espied his boyhood friend tied to a tree, gagged, naked, blooded, with flies crawling over him, completely still and a bamboo sprout high up between his legs. He had never felt so outraged and disgusted although he had seen many hideous sights in Burma. His men, spitting their disgust, saw the expression on his face: a man almost drugged by ice-cold rage. He momentarily wedged a knuckle of his forefinger between his teeth to protect him against unprofessional emotions before saying, 'Hemraj, stay with me, you others take up positions facing outwards and if any daku come our way, mow them down remorselessly. They don't deserve to live.' He went over to the bound man and, in a quiet voice, said in Chinese 'P'ing Yee, it's Shandung P'aau come to save you.' After taking the vile-smelling cloth gag from out of his mouth, he poured some water from his water bottle into the palm of his right hand and dabbed the battered lips while Hemraj, gently cut the ever-hardening ropes with his kukri. Mouth open, Ah Fat spat out some of the dirt from the gag. Ropes cut, together they lifted the mutilated body up from the bamboo. Flies buzzed angrily as they did. Still clutching him, 'Try and rinse your mouth again and drink some water,' said Jason as gently put the rim of his water bottle to the mutilated man's lips and poured a few drops into his mouth which Ah Fat swallowed. Jason poured a little more in, reviving him sufficiently to be able to croak, 'Shandung P'aau, I ... I ... hurt.' He moaned and tears flowed copiously. His eyes flickered, closed ... and he fainted.

Kulbahadur's proverb was spot on ... and so was mine.

'Carry him back to our base,' Jason said to the two Limbus. 'Mané and Kesar help out. Chakré go ahead, Lalman bring up the rear and Miné keep tabs on Senagit.' The Temiar had been hovering near Jason the whole time and was clearly happy to be on his way back out of sight of such dreadful and unexpected happenings. On their way back they came across the clothes that the Bear and Ah Fat had had to take off. They were picked up and Ah Fat's were placed over his nakedness. It was then that Jason noticed how foul his crotch was, showing that something unmentionable and savage had been done to him.

At their temporary base Jason, with Hemraj, took Ah Fat, now conscious once more, down to the stream. 'This will sting but you must be cleaned up. Don't feel ashamed by my stripping and washing you. I have some medical stuff and I can only put it on if your wounds are clean.' Ah Fat hung on to Hemraj while raw wounds were gently washed. Jason had a small towel and patted his friend dry. By the time they were back in their temporary bivouac the others had made a bed of cut saplings and leaves for him. Jason gave him a jab of morphia and the mutilated man was dead to the world in less than a minute.

'Senagit,' he said, 'tell me what happened when you got to Ha La.'

The Temiar gave as full a description as his limited vocabulary allowed, mentioning that he knew the ringleader's name sounded like Zhong and that he was a bad, bad man.

I'll get the bastard if that's the last thing I do even if that means sending on my team ahead and catching them up, said Jason to himself before calling his men to gather around, one man with eyes looking out and both rifle and kukri ready. 'We can't stay here much longer. We have to get back into Malaya just as soon and as safely as we can. My friend cannot walk well: I believe the man Senagit calls Zhong used him as a woman.' His men looked horrified and fists clenched. 'However, we must also pay him and his daku a lesson: that's what we're here for, doubly so now. We can't afford to have them think they can chase us without our fighting back. We can't make firm plans until Ah Fat wakes up but I believe this is what we'll do: Hemraj and I will deal with the daku while you others gently, slowly and carefully make your way to where the carrying party will be bringing our next lot of rations where we will join you if we don't catch you up first.'

Yes, on balance that did seem to make sense.

Later that evening Ah Fat awoke and, bemused as he was, remembered hearing the man named Zhong say he'd come back in the morning.

'Can you recall if he said "I" or "we"?'

'Oh, I was hurting so much it's hazy but I think he said he'd come alone.'

'Can you tell me how many men were in his group?'

'No, but Senagit should know.'

Senagit said Zhong and five men, holding up all the fingers and thumb of his right hand not knowing how to say, or forgetting, the Malay for 'five'.

Night fell. The shrieks of the tortured men haunted every man in their restless, muttering sleep.

Back in Ha La, Zhong was gloating. He had released his urges, his loins were tense no longer: he had killed someone the way he'd only seen the Japanese do once and he had humiliated a traitor.

All that was left now was to finish that Flat Ears off.

At first light Jason's men packed up. Jason's and Hemraj's pack would be carried by the others so that the two men staying behind could move back so much the quicker. It wasn't expected that the revenge would make them all that much late.

A few minutes after six o'clock, after a brew of tea, Jason took his garrotte, made of catgut cord with wooden handles, out of his pack and put it in his pocket. He and Hemraj, weapons at the ready and kukris in their belts, moved back to the scene of the slaughter and the others moved south back to Malaya.

The two executioners – *that's what we are going to be!* – hid as near to where they had found Ah Fat tied up and within half an hour were rewarded by hearing the tread of one man that sounded hollow in the hush. Jason stiffened involuntarily when he recognised the bully he had seen in Thakhek, all that time back during the SEATO exercise, beating the Thai boy raw and so obviously enjoying it. *So it's you then and you now, you sadist,* he said to himself, remembering the three times he himself had been a target, *his target.* He tensed: fear of failure was his caution and righteousness of rage his strength.

He waited until Zhong was brought up sharply by seeing no body. He looked around in perplexity then reeled on hearing a disembodied voice in front of him saying in Chinese, 'Thought you were coming to kill me, didn't you. But I didn't die, did I? I curse you: *Ch'uan jia chan.*'

Seeing nobody Zhong spun round and again saw nobody. Being the bully he was, he was frightened. 'Where are you? How did you escape?' he asked, breath palpitating pitiably.

'Look hard at where you tied me up,' came the voice and as Zhong turned back, Jason silently jumped out and whirled the garrotte round the man's throat, encircling his neck with his right arm before hooking his hands together on the man's left shoulder. Then he squeezed Zhong's neck just below the jaw between his biceps and forearm, clamping down on the carotid arteries, preventing blood from entering and leaving the brain. Zhong immediately tried to tear it away, struggling and choking as he did, but in vain. With breathing almost impossible his eyes bulged.

'Hemraj, give me my weapon and take hold of this,' said Jason and, once his gunman had caught hold of the garrotte, relaxed the pressure enough for a few gulps of air before the garrotte was tightened again. Jason went around the man and faced him from in front. 'Remember me from Thakhek?'

Zhong shook at the knees, gibbering with fear. From the look in his eyes, yes, he did. The man floundered, strength ebbing, voice rasping, 'Popov, Popov, save me, save me.'

'No, not save you but kill you, Zhong. You don't deserve to live. You were born under a falling star. I'll pin a note on your body telling your other comrades that the men you have heard of as P'ing Yee and Shandung P'aau are all powerful.' A dramatic pause. 'Hemraj, I'll take back the cord'.

By now Zhong's face was purple and his tongue distended, jet-black snake-eyes mirroring the depravities of a lifetime. It did not need much more pressure from Jason to kill him, without regret and without remorse but clinically and capably. The dead man slumped to the ground as Jason released the garrotte. Going through his pockets he found an ID card. Copying the name on it he wrote a devastating note for the people who would come to see why Comrade Zhong had not returned for his morning bowl of gruel and laid it on the corpse's chest. The note read, '*Ch'uan jia chan*. Any more intrusions into Temiar territory will result in your being dealt with like this.'

'Sahib, let's get out of here,' implored Hemraj, mind in more of a whirl than ever before in his life, never having witnessed anything like that nor having seen his Major sahib so coldly furious.

'You're right, Hemé, on our way it is. What I did is between us two forever. Neither of us will mention it again. It's over and done with so let's get back safest and soonest.' Quickly checking they were still unseen off they went, easily following the tracks of the others.

But unbeknownst to either of them Alif and Zai had seen them. They looked at each other: 'That European is the man in the photograph. No point in staying here any longer. Once we've told Comrade Ah Hai, it's back home, Alif, back to Indonesia.'

'More than suits me,' answered Zai as the two men went back to Ha La.

'How is my friend?' Jason asked after they had caught the others up just over the border, once more safe in Malaya. He was on a rudimentary stretcher made of branches and a poncho cape. 'Let's have a halt and a brew of tea.'

'Bearing up but in great pain, passing in and out of

consciousness,' answered Sergeant Kulbahadur.

Sergeant Lalman asked Jason if anyone had come back. 'Listen, everyone, I recognised the man who came back this morning and what I did to him is only to be known to me and Hemraj. He'll stay there forever and bother nobody again. It was enormous bad luck that we had two casualties, one fatal, but we should be very proud and pleased with ourselves with what we were able to do: rescue two of our own.'

Everybody agreed wholeheartedly. 'Do you think anyone will chase us?' asked Manbahadur, by now blissfully happy but still afraid of being captured.

'No chance whatsoever,' answered Jason with confidence, 'and anyway we are now back on our own ground.'

Both Gurkhas moved to their rescuer and made obeisance, bending down and placing their forehead on his feet, expressing undying gratitude.

When Comrade Zhong Han San did not return for his morning meal his five men, as well as Comrade Ah Soo Chye, went to call him back from the bamboo grove. Before they reached the spot they saw raptors circling above the trees, smelt a bad, bad smell and heard the buzzing of many flies. And indeed something was very wrong indeed: when they saw the almost severed head, the popping eyes and thrusting tongue, to say nothing of the ants crawling and flies buzzing over what was left of their leader and the grotesque, torn, fly-covered body, two of the party retched. *Who could have done that?* was the question each man less Alif and Zai asked themselves. Then one spotted the note and read it:

somebody more powerful, more energetic and more cunning than they had been responsible. The utterly unthinkable had actually happened.

Ah Soo Chye ordered that the bodies be laid to rest according to how he remembered his parents had done. After that he and his two legmen, Tek Miu and Lo See, voted to go and live with the Acting Secretary General in Sadao: the five remaining men of Zhong's gang thankfully 'melted' into the civilian population. None of them dared say out loud that they thought the place would now be haunted forever.

At midday Jason opened his radio. 'Hello 1-2, fetch Sunray,' he said to the operator in Ipoh, who answered '1-2, wait out.'

Soon came '1-2, Sunray on set.'

Jason gave his position in code and continued, 'Am on way back. Operation Blind Spot completed. Wartime men rescued and with us. Two cas[ualties], both non-Gurkha one fatal, one critically injured and in need of speedy cas[ualty] evac[uation]. Request Auster recce area for suitable landing point nearest my position soonest. Roger so far, over.'

'1-2, Roger, over.'

'1-2, Request send grid reference when known. Suggest he is met and escorted to hospital by quote Sierra Bravo unquote. All other details on debrief. Over.'

'1-2, Wilco your casevac. Well done. Out.'

Jason turned to his Signal Sergeant. 'Sierra Bravo, Ustad, Special Branch: we can't have him talking under an anaesthetic to people who'd start asking awkward questions but we never did give any grid references in the Ha La area so we never left Malaya, did we?'

With a wonderful smile and a twinkle in his eyes, Sergeant Minbahadur Gurung answered, 'No, sahib, we never did.'

The trudge back to the heli pick-up point was slow. That night Jason said to his men, 'You have done brilliantly and your performance couldn't have been bettered although the ending is wonderfully happy and cruelly sad. In accordance with our seven-generation oath, what we did over the border must remain secret. Both you two, Mané and Kesar, must only talk of how Ah Fat brought you all the way to Ha La: you will have to keep mum about what we did as long as you are in Malaya.'

Ah Fat stirred when he heard Jason's voice. 'Shandung P'aau,' he whispered. 'Where are we and are we safe once more?'

'P'ing Yee, safe we are and safe we'll be forever. There is no need to worry about the man who treated you so vilely. He'll never bother anyone again. You can relax. I've ordered a heli for you and in no time at all you'll be in hospital where you'll get better quickly.'

A serene smile showed that his friend's message had been understood.

At noon next day they reached the place suitable for the helicopter and waited for it to come. After it had landed Jim Fordyce ducked under the rotor blades and went over to Jason who, mouth to ear, gave him a quick description of wounds and gag. 'Get him to a hospital in KL if you can where his wife can be with him.'

'Damned sorry about the other one but congratulations on

bringing both Gurkhas back,' Jim said, watching as the injured man was being strapped in. 'I'm off now. See you in KL.' He got in and the heli lifted off.

During the journey back to Grik Jason got as many details from Manbahadur and Kesar about their rescue as they could and, once in Grik, had a telephone conversation with his CO about getting both men back to Nepal, Manbahadur with his brother, Sergeant Kulbahadur, who was due leave. 'All other details when I get back, sir, but I must take Senagit back to his ladang otherwise I'll break faith with his boss. I can now recommend that the platoon there can be withdrawn, details later, but it will be a great gesture of confidence if you can take my word, sir, and let me, in front of everyone on Kerinching's ladang, order it to return to base.'

'Yes, I agree to all that. It's essential that you finish off as cleanly and irrevocably as you can.'

As transport took the carrying party back to Ipoh, Jason, Hemraj, Senagit and Moby boated upriver then walked to Kerinching's ladang where Moby paid Senagit handsomely for his work and Kerinching also for allowing Jason to take Senagit with him. Jason told Kerinching that he was sure the bad men would never return and, in front of his Temiar audience, told the Platoon Commander to get ready to return to base. Kerinching and the others were profoundly grateful.

In Ipoh Jason handed back his compass to the CO and gave him an inclusive description of everything, except how he had despatched Zhong. 'Sir, he's dead and that's all I need to say and all you need to know.' From the look in his eyes, the CO was wise enough not to ask how the deed had been done.' *It can't really matter now, can it?*

Jason had to go to KL where the GOC took him to his residence. Jim Fordyce and Mr C C Too were also present to be given a blow-to-blow briefing of the military events then the Gurkhas' version of the journey down from Bangkok. 'There will be more details that Ah Fat can provide but probably not for some time,' said Jason.

His audience digested what they had heard. 'Yes, you've done well, Rance,' said the GOC, 'better than I originally expected.' – *I've heard that before.* – 'I appreciate that you did not mention the method of despatch ...' and he left the rest of his sentence unsaid.

Jason gave the General the same answer as he had his CO and the General likewise forbore to press him further. 'Fully understood: best thing now is for you to go back to England on leave. But before you go I want you write a full report on your Operation Blind Spot as, apart from Intelligence and historical aspects, it must not be lost to sight. I don't want you to "undersell" yourself in today's army that is getting more and more sceptical of people like you.' He lifted up a warning hand. 'I say that in no way deprecatingly. You did magnificently. It is to my sorrow that no official British cognisance can be made and if you were to be recognised, it will have to be by the Malayan authorities.' He shook his head in embarrassment. 'To make up for it just a little, I will authorise you to fly via Kathmandu so you can make a personal report to His Majesty the King of Nepal.'

'General,' said his MA, 'we must now inform London, the MGBG and the Ambassador in Kathmandu that the rescue of the Gurkhas was successful and the last-named to let the King of Nepal know.'

Jim Fordyce said he'd tell in people London how matters had successfully been concluded. Both he and Mr C C Too congratulated Jason. The General saw him to the door and shook his hand, having arranged his car to take him to visit Ah Fat in hospital. Jason was delighted to see his friend recovering physically although the mental trauma would probably scar him for life even with an understanding wife to nurture him. 'Shandung P'aau,' Ah Fat managed to say through his bruised lips. 'That's twice you've saved me. I'll never forget it.'

He looked down at his friend lying in the bed. 'P'ing Yee, don't worry about anything else except getting better,' he said. 'You did wonderfully well to save two people you just happened to meet by chance years before. You've done much more than your bit for society.' He leant over and took his friend's hand to shake it before he left. The Chinese man turned his face away, tears rolling down his bruised cheeks.

As Jason left the hospital to go to the airport to fly back to his battalion he felt weary beyond belief. *At least going to Borneo is no longer an option so I'll be spared that*, he said to himself as he stared unseeingly out of the plane window. It was lucky for his peace of mind that, once again, he could not know what the future held for him.

INTERLUDE

As far as HQ 2 Fed Brigade and their superiors in Kuala Lumpur as well as the Department of Aborigines were concerned, the slightly controversial Mat Salleh's Operation Blind Spot did not seem to have had any immediate effect but over the following months the department and those it looked after suddenly realised that peace and quiet now reigned. Those in 2 Fed Brigade also wondered how it was that Major Rance's small team had been successful without any kills or captures to support their efforts, none of them realising that the key to success was his learning Temiar. Special Branch members were glad Ah Fat had been successful but were saddened at learning about a severe motor accident that he had when in Thailand. The guerrillas never did come as far south as the ladangs again although the Special Branch aspect Operation Bamboo continued until the Malay authorities felt satisfied that the thirty-five Chinese guerrillas on the Police Wanted List were now permanently in Thailand so posed no more threat. Ladang life returned to its pre-Emergency rhythm with Kerinching and Senagit's reputation indelibly enhanced. Meanwhile Chin Peng quietly hibernated in China. The Domino Theory of Communist conquests tumbling countries from north to south remained stillborn yet, even so, as prophesied by the Secretary General of the Indonesian Communist Party, Comrade Aidit, as far back as 1961, almost as soon as the Malay-Thai border was settled, a mirror image situation with its own dynamics arose over a thousand miles to the east, first in Brunei then in Borneo where the Communist virus had spread to the other end of the rapidly disappearing British Empire and even farther south to Java.

For eighteen months, until February 1963, the various pieces on the Southeast Asian chessboard moved, some with good intent and others with malice aforethought. Before Major Jason Rance, once more an unsung hero, had left the battalion on leave he had asked if he could do a refresher parachute course when in England. 'I did a course when in India so I know the basics already. I realise I'm on the old side for the physical grind of it,' he had told his CO, 'but I'm fit and healthy enough.' When asked exactly why he wanted such activity, his answer was that he had been skulking so long in dense jungle with limited vision that merely to have the rush of air on leaving the aeroplane and a distant, all-round view during descent would help wipe out the jungle ghosts before they had accumulated too heavily.

A properly worded request had been sent to the Royal Air Force Parachute School at Abingdon and, under the unusual circumstances cited, was sanctioned.

On leaving his battalion Jason had travelled on the Gurkha airlift from Singapore taking men and families on their three-yearly six months' leave back to Nepal in the same aeroplane as the Limbu brothers and Kesar Pun, the two wartime soldiers exuberantly happy at their unexpected, tortuous and almost unbelievable rescue yet, underneath, concerned that settling back into their old habits could be difficult after so long away. In Kathmandu the King, in a private ceremony, having sincerely thanked Major Rance for his successful efforts, bestowed him with the prestigious Nepalese award, The Right Arm of Gorkha, Third Class, only to be worn inside Nepal as it had not been cleared by Buckingham Palace for universal wear. He was allowed a three-month duty trek, six weeks in the east and another six in the west, tension slowly loosening. He had gone to Manbahadur Limbu's village and learnt how amazed and wonderfully delighted his family had been at his re-appearance after so long. His wife had been through the death ceremony so Manbahadur had to have a special period of being 'reborn' to remarry otherwise his living with her would have been taboo. His by-now grown-up and married children took quite a time to get used to having a father. He also managed to locate Kesar Pun who had remarried as his former wife had found another husband. He told Jason that although he was delighted to be back, he did have a bit of a conscience in having left the man who had kept him alive, Aidit, when he was so sick during the war.

Jason put a religious slant on it. 'That was the way your gods kept you alive to enjoy your life back here after so many years away. Don't let it haunt you,' was his advice. 'There's nothing he can do about it even though, at first, he may have been angry with you. At least, as far as I am concerned, he won't know I was behind your escape.'

In fact, although Aidit had no proof positive that would stand up in a law court about the part Major Rance had played in Kesar Pun's disappearance, he knew enough to vow that, if ever he had the chance, he would get even with the Englishman who was behind it.

In both the rescued men's houses he was made much of and the story of what he and his friend Ah Fat had done lost nothing in the telling. In both places, Jason was silent about Zhong's last moments on earth.

Back in England at Abingdon he had kept up with the youngsters and passed out having done the eight descents, five in 'clean fatigue', two with equipment and one at night. His uncle, who had a perverse sense of humour, told him he had to change his family motto from 'leave no stone unturned, no brick undropped' to 'may all my droppings be soft ones'.

Among the overseas students on the course Jason was surprised to meet Lieutenant Sumbi of 600 Raider Company, Indonesian Army, last seen at the Jungle Warfare School, now guardedly tight-lipped to start with yet inquisitive to a fault later. It was pure bad luck for Jason that the two who had seen him and Hemraj deal with Zhong had reported the incident to Comrade Aidit who –it was never discovered how – had found out that Jason was at Abingdon when Sumbi was: a letter to the latter asking him to glean as many details as possible of what Jason had done in Thailand was the reason for Sumbi's inquisitive attitude resulting in Jason's instinctive caution.

In Southeast Asia the Prime Minister of Malaya, Tunku Abdul Rahman, was working hard, both openly and behind the scenes, for a new country, Malaysia, originally planned to embrace Singapore, which later decided not to join, Sarawak, British

North Borneo, Brunei and Labuan, to come into being: target date 31 August 1963. In Singapore, on 2 February 1963, Operation Cold Store was most cleverly and subtly launched after a long, dreary, weary session of parliament had approved it and later that same day the operation netted over a hundred communists, a devastating blow to their organisation but a tremendous fillip for peace and security. Meanwhile in Indonesia President Sukarno was giving the impression of supporting Malaysia but was, in fact, working for a newer and bigger Indonesia by adding Malaya, the Philippines, Brunei and British Borneo to his already extensive country, to be known as Maphilindo.

In Brunei the Sultan's reservations to joining the new country were too many for happy inclusion so he decided to stay separate with a British Adviser. He tried to broaden representation without losing any of his real power by having an election in which the People's Party – Partai Ra'ayat – won the most votes. It was that party, backed by a secret North Kalimantan Liberation Army of about four thousand badly armed men under a Yasin Effendi who had been surreptitiously training for the military overthrow of the Brunei Government, that launched a rebellion on 7 December 1962 and which came as a bolt from the blue. Not only did a battalion of Gurkhas respond so making defeat a certainly but a red feather, an 'official order', was sent upriver to loyal Kelabit tribesmen in the Borneo Uplands who moved north to block any rebel movement back to Indonesia. The tribesmen were guided by loud hailer from a Twin Pioneer aircraft flying overhead with such instructions as 'Turn left at the next river junction where there's a big house.'

It was during Jason's last six months absence from the battalion that the Brunei Rebellion took place. As 1/12 GR were not engaged on it, he didn't fret too much by not being with it. His mother, overjoyed in having her one and only son about the place for so long, tried to get him interested in the girls she managed to 'find' for him. He doubted that any English girl who had never lived in Asia would take kindly to him and his life after initial passion has been assuaged and subsided. Although he knew a good wife was a harbour in a storm, he also believed the opposite, that a bad one was a storm in a harbour, was also true. He decided there wasn't time to find out which of the two the most attractive girls he'd met would turn out to be so better safe than sorry.

As the gradual withdrawal from Empire meant that fewer troops were needed, dark rumours were circulating that the Brigade of Gurkhas was to be drastically cut. However, with Gurkha involvement in putting down the rebellion so convincingly successful, sincere hopes were expressed that such cuts would be mitigated, as indeed, temporarily, they were.

In April 1963 four months after the rebellion petered out in Brunei, Sukarno determined to prevent Malaysia from happening by launching raids into Borneo by his army, calling it *Konfrontasi*, Confrontation. To counter any more rebellions and to alert the Security Forces of incursions two new units were raised; one in Sarawak, an Auxiliary Sarawak Constabulary force composed of unsophisticated and mainly illiterate people along the border to act as a 'tripwire' against Indonesian incursions, known as the Border Scouts, and the other in Malaya, the Gurkha Independent Parachute Company, whose role was to provide immediate cover on an unprotected airfield in the theatre if again threatened by hostile forces.

It was Jason's uncomfortable and nearly fatal lot to be heavily involved with both units, one after the other, not that he had any idea of his future at the time of either's inception.

PART THREE

PART THREE

6

It was mid-1963 when Major Rance returned to his battalion from his extended time away. A party was held in his honour by his old company the very evening he arrived. His reputation from saving those two wartime soldiers was now of legendary standing, amply boosted by what Sergeant Kulbahadur had recounted of their exploits. He was asked about his visit to Nepal so he told them how he had got on with the King when he was given his award and how much he had told His Majesty about the rescue. 'It's a shame you can't always wear it, Sahib,' someone said out loud when he had told them that he could only wear his award on official occasions in Nepal.

He smiled back and quoted a Nepali proverb: 'Pure gold needs no touchstone and a good man no adornment,' which caused a peal of laughter. He went on to tell them that he had been on a parachuting course but could not wear his 'butterfly' wings as he was not in a parachute unit. He was naughtily asked if he had also missed out on any other 'butterfly' during his spell away and his equally naughty reply was laughingly accepted.

Next morning, after a run to sweat out the effects of the party as well as stiffness from the aeroplane journey, Jason had gone to visit the Quartermaster when the CO's 'Stick Orderly' – the smartest man of the day's Quarter Guard – unexpectedly came to the door and, standing rigidly to attention with his stick under his left arm, gave a cracking salute. 'Major sahib, the Commanding sahib sends his salaams. He wants you to speak with him, now, in his office.'

This has happened more than once before! What can it be this time? I'll soon find out he said to himself and, with a '*Hunchha, keta*' – Right-ho, lad – the pair of them set off for Battalion HQ.

'Major Rance, sir, go straight in. The CO is waiting for you,' said the young Adjutant. In Jason went and saluted his Commanding Officer.

'Jason, sit down. You seem to have painted yourself into a corner,' the CO began abruptly. 'Matters are stirring over in Borneo – what do you know about the place?'

'Really nothing solid about it, sir, except that there are headhunters there and my great-uncle Reggie, the black sheep of the family, was the white Rajah Brookes' chief factotum. Why?'

Rance so often gives me unexpected answers! 'Well may you ask. It seems that your name and fame in dealing with unsophisticated Asian people living in undeveloped backwaters and your flair for languages have been taken note of at a higher level than you might have expected. Take a gander at this,' and he took a letter off his desk and handed it over. 'I got it yesterday, personal from the Commander-in-Chief in Singapore.'

The gist of the letter was that Major Rance's methods of achieving success with primitive people in the Malay-Thai border area had been duly noted and studied so he was needed in Sarawak where, to frustrate any Indonesian aggression, a force of auxiliary policemen recruited from border regions, so named the Border Scouts, had been hastily set up. Too hastily, it now appeared, and it was received wisdom that it was made up of the wrong type of person using wrong methods and was successfully failing in its wrongly ordained task. Major Rance was therefore needed to take over as Commandant and, basically, to realign the force, its men and its methods. It would mean he, too, would have to become a policeman. Before he went over to the HQ of the Director of Borneo Operations in Brunei for in depth briefing, the C-in-C in Singapore wanted to interview him personally and 'soonest'.

Rance silently handed the letter back to the CO. 'I'll be frank with you, Jason. You're on an army short list of one so you can't really refuse even if being a colonial policeman doesn't appeal to you. Although tasks like your last one and this one will never get you a General Officer's stars, the Borneo job looks interesting, unusual and unconventional enough to satisfy even you. I strongly advise you to take it as the job is up your street: in the battalion we'll all be sorry to lose you but, unless we go on operations there, peacetime soldiering is not really your *forte*.'

'No, sir, I have to agree with you about peacetime soldiering but that last job was hairy enough to last a lifetime, sir. Maybe this next one will last for two' and he grinned sheepishly at his weak joke.

'You'd better go just as soon as an air ticket can be got hold of. The Adjutant will alert them down there for accommodation.'

'How about I go the day after tomorrow? That's Wednesday. "Soonest" enough, I hope. It means I can unpack, get cleaned up and presentable once more.'

The CO looked at the calendar. 'So be it, the 31st. I'll put a call through to the General's MA and let you know what time the appointment is to be.'

At ten minutes to midday on the 31st Jason reported to the General's MA, a Cavalryman. 'Sit down for the nonce. I've already arranged for your Record of Service to be sent in,' he said, glancing at his watch which he wore with the face on his wrist as most Cavalry officers seemed to, with a deft outward movement of his left elbow. Exactly at twelve o'clock he went to the door of the General's office, knocked quietly, opened it and said, 'Major Rance is here to see you, sir.'

'Send him in. Don't disturb us.'

The MA stood to one side, tilted his head in the direction of the office, winked and shut the door after Jason had stepped inside. There was another man, who Jason recognised as Jim Fordyce, already sitting in one of the chairs placed for visitors. He raised a hand in greeting and Rance nodded his head in reply after first saluting the Commander-in-Chief, Fareast Land Forces, General Sir Lucas West.

'Sit down,' and Rance was directed to an easy chair where more distinguished bottoms than a lowly Major's usually sat.

The General, short, stern-looking and lean, with tension and purpose in him like a coiled spring, had a face that was hale and steeled having weathered many tempests on its way up to high rank. He was a pre-war Indian Army officer and knew all about Rance and his unusual background so he was particularly intrigued personally to meet the man himself. 'It is unusual for a Commander-in-Chief to become involved at your level but the politicos want to make certain sure you are aware of,' tapping the edge of his chair as he sought a sufficiently encapsulating phrase, 'certain tenebrous vibrations.' He eyed Major Rance circumspectly. 'To be really blunt, both colonial governments, Sarawak and British North Borneo, are almost frozen in a sleeping sickness of incompetence. Get my point?' he asked sharply, cracking his finger joints as he did.

'That means I'll probably be ploughing my furrow against the grain, sir.'

'Yes, correct. You will have seen from my letter to your CO that I need you for a special task. I have read the report you wrote for the GOC Federation Armed Forces and heartily congratulate you on your outstanding work,' he continued, eyes, wrinkled at the corners from too much squinting in bright sunlight, burning with hardened determination. 'I have another job for you, more peripatetic by far than your last one and you moved around plenty enough then. It is to be the Commandant of the Borneo Border Scouts, initially in Sarawak and probably later also in British North Borneo which, I am told, will change back to its old name of Sabah after Malaysia has taken place. Listen to what Mr Fordyce has to say before I continue.'

Jim Fordyce cleared his throat and, looking at Jason intently, started off: 'In my line of work you have a high reputation as a linguist who not only can keep his mouth shut when needed but also open it to probe others' thoughts and opinions. I need only remind you of your attachment to SEATO for this.' *So my efforts were not unappreciated! Good.* 'The administrators and colonial police in Borneo are an inward-looking bunch whose method of working is in contra-distinction of the old days of the White Rajah when no 'Native' – not a derogatory term – was stopped from approaching his British superior at any time of day or night. Now lethargy, partly because come Malaysia most British colonial policemen will be out of a job and partly because the senior ones are so near going on pension that taking no initiative is the safest way of making sure of their getting it. That has meant we have not had any real intelligence of what is happening on the border or what is drifting over from the other side of it. How much do you know about Borneo?'

'Really nothing solid about it, sir, I remember my great-uncle Reggie, the black sheep of the family, was the white Rajah Brookes' chief factotum talking about headhunters, it has lots of rivers, mountains and jungle and that the border with Indonesia is ...' and he sought the phrase he had just picked up, 'a cartographer's folly.'

Both men listening to him smiled dourly and each gave a small nod in agreement.

'As a linguist you'll be interested to learn that there are a dozen major languages and about twenty separate dialects in British Borneo alone. You won't be expected to learn more than one and we strongly advise that to be Iban. Not only will you be the "eyes and ears" on the border with the mostly illiterate peoples there but you will also do in the major towns on the coast what you did during your Thai and Lao journeys. We want you to use your Chinese to good effect. So far so good?'

So far so bad, Jason thought to himself as he looked at a map of Southeast Asia on the General's wall, pin-pointed Borneo and inwardly blenched at the enormous extent of his scope of operations. He had the good manners not to stare or gawp in disbelief.

'Finish off first, Mr Fordyce,' the General interpolated before Jason had time to think of a suitable answer.

'There is another reason why you have been chosen for this task. After reading your report on how you managed to persuade …' and he looked at a piece of paper in his hand, 'Kesar Pun to abscond, it seemed a golden opportunity to go and interview him. After your Nepal trek, the Defence Attaché in Kathmandu took me to Kesar Pun's house and we debriefed him in depth. We have learnt more about Indonesian power politics than we thought possible. It is the General's intention that I brief you in detail on the bull points of what I learnt especially as they affect the border region after he has finished with you.'

Jason's mind swirled. *I wonder how Kesar took to such treatment.*

'Did he mention anything about a Lieutenant Sumbi?'

Both the C-in-C and Jim Fordyce looked at Jason with renewed interest. 'Why do you ask about him?' the General enquired, furrowing his brow.

Jason reiterated the strange question Sumbi had asked him when he had visited the Jungle Warfare School on his way back to the battalion after the SEATO exercise, which caused both men to raise their eyebrows. 'I met him again at Abingdon. Initially he was friendly then, having had a letter with an Indonesian stamp on it – I saw the stamp when he tried to hide the envelope from me – his manner towards me changed, cooling considerably, almost as though the news he had received was anti-me.'

'Now that is of extreme interest, Rance,' said the General. 'The question of allowing him to attend both courses had to come up to this office and to my Political Adviser before allowing him to.' Jim Fordyce gave a satisfied grunt. 'Better and better,' continued the General, 'it makes your choice as Commandant even more apposite. So you're ready for the job? We are living in stirring times.'

And I'm supposed to find out whose stirring them? 'Sir, I will of course try my best. What will I be as Commandant of these Border Scouts? I understand it's a police outfit not a military one.'

'You'll be a Superintendent in the Sarawak Constabulary for starters, on loan. That organisation has never had any military officer attached to it before so you'll be as strange to its officers as they'll be to you. But don't worry. We won't lose sight of you. One snag of being in command of what are known as "Funnies" is that you won't get sufficient points for command of a battalion even though we'll ensure you are given the military rank of Lieutenant Colonel as well as the police rank of Superintendent.' Jason could see that his Record of Service was open on the General's desk. 'Sadly you won't get two lots of pay! But to be brutally frank, in a contracting army, many officers more highly qualified than you, certainly staff-wise, won't get command so you might just as well get promotion this way. Now, back to your job. You will make periodic reports of your progress on the purely functional slant of the Scouts but also I'll expect anything else of interest you might come across separately, sent through DOBOPS, the Director of Borneo Operations,' the General explained the acronym seeing Jason's perplexity.

'Is there a time limit on this, sir? Will I be wanted as a policeman till I go on pension? If this Malaysia business comes off, with Sarawak being subsumed into it, I'll be even more remote, surely?' Jason looked worried. This whole new undertaking was something he'd never contemplated and he just did not understand the implications – *but does anybody else?*

'We'll see you're a rozzer only for one year. Apart from any intelligence aspects, you have to re-slant the Scouts from the mess they're in after having been raised along the wrong lines as I put in my letter but you'll first have to undertake an initial recce in depth. I expect that you will be able to find some tempting Indonesian targets on the other side of the border but until such a policy is officially endorsed, you'll be hung, drawn and quartered if you do cross it – that is cross it, come back and are found out. If your Scouts were to go across *as civilians* of course we'll be more than interested in what any have to report.' The General leant forward. 'And not a word of what I'm going to say now is to be mentioned outside my office. When Malaya and Indonesia sent troops to the Congo they often operated together, even having companies under command of each other's battalion. It may be that they still consider themselves friends, at least at soldier level, rather than enemies.' He paused as an idea struck him: 'It's like when the British and German troops got out of their trenches on Christmas Day in 1914 and played football together, you know. Camaraderie and human nature, young men and all that.

Understandable but politically embarrassing. Anything you find out about such activities must be reported personally to DOBOPS. You see, Rance, *if* the border people cannot stand up to Sukarno's troops trying to penetrate first British then Malaysian Borneo, Sukarno will win. Of course you'll get more details once you're over there but …' and he let it hang in the air, '… it's to be your task to ensure that does not happen.'

Inwardly Jason recoiled. 'Sir, you have given me a tremendous responsibility, an enormous amount of territory to cover and a great deal to think about. I've already said I'll do what I can but quite how much you expect me to achieve is impossible for me to say.'

'Understood, understood. Neither of us are idiots,' replied the General a tad harshly. 'Maybe one of your more difficult jobs to add to the frustrations that I feel sure will come your way is pretending you know nothing about any higher matters.' He paused, letting that sink in before asking a curiously irrelevant question Jason had never before been asked. 'Rance, do you have premonitions?'

Premonitions? 'Well, sir, I have good days and bad days, gut feelings and all the rest of it as I suppose we all do but I'm no oracle out of Delphi,' said Jason, trying not to prevaricate and wishing he could have given a straighter answer. 'With the Temiar I could sometimes, how shall I put it, sniff dicey situations before they occurred and as a good marksman "aim off for wind" but successes I had could have been put down as much to luck as to judgement.'

The General nodded. 'Any before you went on that parachute

course despite your comparatively advanced age to be prancing around the countryside rather than going up in a hot-air balloon?'

'No, sir,' Jason answered a trifle wearily. 'I only asked for it as I was fed up with skulking and seeing no horizons always with something on my back so even before my Nepal trek I felt that the rush of air and a good view even for only during the inside of a minute would be a good way to, how shall I put it, correct the imbalance. And, till now, I'd never even thought of a hot-air balloon, sir,' and he smiled wanly.

The General looked at Jason more kindly than before. 'The reason I asked is because I have another surprise for you. Ready for it?'

'As ready as I will ever be, sir,' answered Jason, wondering why the change in the General's demeanour.

'After the year I have been told that you will take over command of the Gurkha Independent Parachute Company and be in a wonderful position to build on what you have been able to achieve during the previous year although of course it will mean you dropping to your substantive rank of major. Happy?'

'Happy, sir? That is the first time you've made me smile today. I'm a soldier by preference to being a policeman.'

The General, with his smile of kingmaker still evident, buzzed for his MA. 'Bring me a certificate for clearance for Top Secret for Major Rance to sign in my presence. After that I want him to be given the documentation that will take him to Brunei as a Priority One passenger. I also want you to draft a submission for him to be made a lieutenant colonel during his time as Commandant Border Scouts for me to sign and to send priority to the Military Secretary personally in the War Office, although it will be the new Ministry of Defence by the time it is acted on.'

The MA left and came back with a certificate for the necessary clearance and a message which he gave to the General. Jason read the certificate, signed it and it was counter-signed by the C-in-C and the MA. 'Rance,' said the General, 'before you leave I have one piece of sad news to tell you. This signal has been sent to you here from a Mr C C Too to tell you that your friend Ah Fat died last night. Apparently that which was smeared into his mouth was lethal. I know you'll be sorry to lose probably your oldest friend.' Jason felt the bottom of his world fall out. The General continued, 'Mr C C Too also puts that he has heard that you were not unseen when you were dealing with Zhong Han San. There were two Indonesian guerrillas with code names Alif and Zai, now back in Indonesia, who had heard that you probably visited the MCP camp at Sadao. I don't know the implications of Mr Too's information but presumably you do.'

Not yet, but I'm certain sure I will and not to my advantage, I fear.

The C-in-C took Jason's frown of worry as one of sadness, so he finished off 'Let me wish you the best of luck in your new job. I feel sure you'll come up trumps. Go with the MA and Mr Fordyce will join you presently.

'General,' said Jim Fordyce once Rance had left the room. 'What odds do you give him on being alive in a year's time?'

'As many as fifty-fifty?'

'You're an optimist, General. I'll show him my "Rogues' Gallery" and any other lowdown I think he needs now that he's been cleared for Top Secret.'

Jim and Jason had a long talk together and, just before they finished, Jim had one more look at his notes. 'Oh yes, there is one point that might, just, be of interest. Kesar Pun told me that he overheard Zhong Han San tell Aidit that he was his fifth niece's third uncle and that she was being trained to act as a "sleeper" for the Cause, as he put it, in Kuching, to be used at the right opportunity. Probably that's a load of nonsense but, in this game, one must never take anything for granted.'

Jason nodded and, more jocularly than seriously, said, 'Who knows, she might be my blind spot if I'm not hers!'

'Anyway, best of luck,' said Jim and they shook hands on it.

Jason left for Ipoh on the night train, head spinning and mind reeling at the news of Ah Fat's death. Because he needed one stepping stone between his old life and his new one, he decided to break his journey in KL and go and console his friend's widow. *That's the least I can do ... but once over there I'll make sure no one of the ilk that caused his death will be allowed to get away with it.*

Back in the battalion he said his goodbyes. He mentioned that after the Borneo job he was going to command the Gurkha Independent Parachute Company and the news spread: Sergeant Kulbahadur Limbu and Rifleman Hemraj Rai both volunteered for it and both, having passed the tests, were accepted.

Far away in the island of Java President Sukarno was angrily addressing his military brass. He was questioning their inadequacies in not having ensured that the so-called North Kalimantan

Liberation Army under Yasin Effendi would be effective when launched against the Sultan of Brunei. The Generals were effusive in their apologies and were instructed to take immediate steps so to chastise and frighten the inhabitants of Sarawak, which he called Kalimantan Utara – North Kalimantan – by military incursions from the south 'while I work on my political people to stir up trouble in the coastal towns.' He was referring to the Sarawak United People's Party, SUPP. 'That Effendi has left the country and my agents tell me he has gone to the Philippines. He will have to be taken care of if he ever returns. If I find that the Command boundaries are too stretched for quick results, I will need a strong person to be based in Kalimantan to look after operations there.' He looked up at General Abdul Haris Nasution. 'You are the man who has written about guerrilla warfare. I want you to pay special attention to this problem. Understand?'

Yes, the General did. 'I'll make sure the General Commanding Military District XII at Pontianak also understands that.'

'I hear that Sarawak at least and maybe that British North Borneo place are raising an auxiliary police force termed Border Scouts composed of half-trained locals to be the armed screen against any of our attacks,' Sukarno continued. 'If you can't better them, I'll certainly better you,' and the angry man let his threat hang in the air. 'Likewise I hear that the Gurkhas are raising parachute troops. That means the reaction time will be much quicker as there will be no need to wait for any British paratroops to come from so far away. Warn the RPKAD. Our para-commando troops are a match for anyone, anywhere, anytime.'

There was no need for any of the army brass listening to make any comment.

'Before I let you go, I hear that there is one who is well trained in British methods, Lieutenant Sumbi of 600 Raider Company. Let him be the West Kalimantan District Commander's special leg man. He has done a British Army Jungle Warfare Course and a Parachute Course in Britain and will be regarded as an ally. What is that quaint phrase the British use?' He put his hand on his chin as he thought. 'Oh yes. Got it. He will be their "blind spot". He has two assistants, one known as Alif and the other Zai. Both can recognise another of our adversaries, that Major Rance of the Gurkhas, were he ever to find himself in Borneo.'

Sycophantic appreciation rippled through the room.

'And before you go, if there is ever an outsider who is put in charge of those Border Scouts' and he almost spat the name, 'he too will need special treatment. I want one of you to contact Comrade Aidit and get him to contact the liaison person of SUPP in Kuching to find out if there is anyone who can be suggested as an additional to the office staff, say typist for instance, for the new organisation. From what I know of the Sarawak government, they have no money to spare so will have no clerical staff to spare either. It may not come to anything but it's worth trying.'

In another office in Jakarta, the Secretary General of the Indonesian Communist Party, Dipa Nusantara Aidit, was similarly fulminating. 'I saved that Gurkha's life during the war. If there were any chance of who I think was responsible for his defection, a Major Rance I remember hearing the name, being involved in military action against us, all efforts to eliminate him will have to be made.'

The telephone on his desk rang. He answered it and listened carefully. 'I'm to arrange for a SUPP member to work in the police office in Kuching? There's already a "mole" of ours there, so I've heard. She was taken on when the Commissioner of Police asked for a typist for the Border Scouts' office.'

He took the phone from his ear at the loud peal of praise. As he replaced it a satisfied smirk graced his lips. *It's time I struck lucky ...*

The Director of Borneo Operations was Major General Walter Sprinter, a dedicated anti-Communist and a brilliant military thinker who wore his authority with a bland good will and dominating resolve. At Brunei Jason was met by his ADC and was driven to Flagstaff House where the General was waiting for him. The new Commandant of the Border Scouts saw a medium-sized, barrel-chested man with close-cropped hair, ruddy-complexion who exuded confidence: *A soldier's General*, Jason thought. Over a light lunch the General told him he would be based in Kuching. 'Borneo is a new country for you so you'll feel lonely and rootless at first and a whole lot different as a policeman from the military life you've been used to but you'll be travelling so much, visiting units and Scouts, you'll probably soon get used to it. I hope so, anyway.'

After lunch, over coffee in comfortable chairs, he was given a thick folder to read before talking about his task. 'I'll be back at four o'clock,' said the General and left Jason to himself. There were many details to absorb, far too many to remember at first glance. He saw that his new parish was spread over a thousand miles, Sarawak being divided into five Divisions, with differing types of peoples and terrain, the administrative machinery in towns on the coast but his charges way away on the border and vastly different conditions between Divisions. Roads did not link the towns and there were none in the interior where travel was either by boat along the major rivers, walking or by air. The more Jason looked at the task he had to perform and at the map, the more he felt that he, one man with an inadequate staff, was being asked to do the impossible. Even so, it was a tremendous challenge, with the merit of not having a 'school solution' tailor-made by text books or postulated by pamphlets. It had the supreme virtue of being utterly unconventional, where common sense and experience could come up with the correct solutions, whatever these were to be. He saw that his parish only covered Sarawak: *if later I have to operate in British North Borneo, even only to the two Residencies that have a border with Kalimantan, I'll have to ask the Almighty for twenty-five hours a day and eight days a week*, he thought gloomily. *Let's hope another sucker gets stuck with that.*

Over a cup of tea the General told Jason to keep the file. 'All I want to emphasise at this point,' he said, 'is that despite however many troops I have or will have, none will be any use if the border people lose heart because the Scouts are unable to act as a screen, as "eyes and ears with a sting", to prevent the enemy from doing a lot of damage before troops can react quickly enough. The Scouts have been wrongly set up. It is up to you to put them right and to make sure that the border people understand what you are doing and why. I have faith that you can. In the important First and Second Divisions, Gurkha Independent Parachute Company NCOs and riflemen are acting as Scout Section Commanders. They are essential even though the Company was not raised for such a role. One of your tasks will be to train up junior leaders from among the scouts themselves but you won't be ready to start on that for a couple of months at least. After your visit to all Divisional HQs where you will liaise with the police officer in charge and carry out what the C-in-C has told you to do, I want you to visit all the scouts along the whole border and only then concentrate on the First and Second Divisions. Once you have done that, probably your best course of action will be to concentrate where they are weakest.'

What if they're weak everywhere? Jason could only say that of course he would do his best, that he was honoured to have had such trust placed in him and please could he have direct access to the General himself if matters got out of hand with the police? 'Of course.'

That settled, next morning he was put on a plane and went to Kuching where he reported to Police HQ in Badrudin Road. He met the Commissioner of Police, a Mr David King, a small, sour-apple of a man, parchment-skinned and shrivelled, well past his prime who talked to Jason as though he resented his presence and giving the impression that he, the Commissioner, and the rest of the Constabulary, were out of their depths. *Nothing dynamic here.* Jason told Mr King that as he had the whole of Sarawak to cover he would be more out than in: 'I have to do my own thing, sir, so you'll have to excuse my absences.'

Mr King, cupping his chin in his hands which were brown and fragile, like last years' leaves, grudgingly supposed that would be the case. *The less I have to do with these Scouts the more I'll like them* were his private thoughts. *These army types would never have been good police officers.*

Jason, while never having felt less prepared for any job, felt even less prepared the following day when Radio Sarawak gave details of the new Commandant on its English and Malay news broadcasts, and a plain-clothes photograph was taken of him, ordered by the Combined Services Public Relations Officer, ludicrously a naval Lieutenant Commander, who happened to be the husband of an old family friend. Hundreds of copies were produced as leaflets, with photo and blurb about the 'new Commandant of the Border Scouts' and, as well as being distributed to every Border Scout section, were taken to the hundreds of border crossings in the First and Second Divisions so that fear would strike the hearts of those on the other side. *If I'd have known why I'd never have let him: I thought the photo was just for his wife* Jason inwardly railed but that such blatant and unnecessary news would reach Comrade Aidit's ears and well as Lieutenant Sumbi's never crossed his mind. Once DOBOPS heard about both incidents, the naval man was on the next plane back to England. It was only later that the Intelligence authorities in Borneo found out that a large price had been put on the new British police superintendent's head. Sumbi and his two easily recognised Jason's face when they eventually were given a leaflet.

Radio Pontianak at Military District XII picked up Radio Sarawak's broadcast and rebroadcast it, saying that it was typical

British colonial arrogance to put an Englishman in that job and not a local. 'We did well to get that "sleeper" in place, didn't we?' Aidit said to Sumbi when next they met. Sumbi gave a gloating grin and agreed with him.

On the Sarawak side of the border the actual text on the leaflets took longer than might have been expected to be understood: not only were the two languages, Jagoi for the First Division and Iban for the Second, only understood locally but in their haste to announce the new boss the leaflets in Jagoi were placed at the frontier crossing places of the Ibans and *vice versa*.

Jason was given an office in the Police HQ where he met one of his two staff officers, a pensioned Dyak news reader from Radio Sarawak. The third member of his staff was a Chinese girl typist, named Jiang Yun. In her late twenties she was good-looking enough to make any bachelor's heart beat a wee bit faster than before with the pearly delicacy of flower-like skin, lustrous black eyes, slender little nose, cherry mouth, tiny even teeth, all in a perfect oval face. Jason looked at her and his heart did beat a wee bit faster. She looked at him and was instantly reminded of an American film star she had had a crush on in her youth. Her heart fluttered. Three days later she was called by her handler and told that the new police officer was a target of the Indonesians who wanted to kill him. 'Any time he goes near the border you are to let me know,' he told her, 'and I'll tell them.'

She nodded dutifully but felt sad and glad at the same time: sad because he looked such a good man and glad that she had made no advances and that her orders were explicit. *A pity he's not on our side.*

Jason liked the look of her – so different from that hungry-mouthed, peroxide brunette with a braying laugh who had cocked her dish at him in Aldershot – and felt that were other circumstances pertinent and she not his typist, she'd be a pleasing diversion but *a stiff upper lip and stiff nowhere else will have to be my motto.* She spoke good English and Malay, gave an impression of competence and had a winsome but reserved manner. Something told him never to speak to her in Chinese, quite why he never could explain to himself. Later that week he was delighted when a friend of his, Captain Tommy Watts, was seconded from his Gurkha unit in Malaya to be his other and senior staff officer – 'I'll stay and help you, Colonel, but leave when you do.'

Before the new Commandant left on his first set of visits to the four Divisional police chiefs and the British Residents his typist seemed unusually conscientious on all details. *Maybe because she's new.* He went unarmed and unescorted. What struck him was in each place each person he spoke to sniped at the last person he had met, gave him opposing views about the job, the country and its inmates and offered such ludicrous suggestions for Scout enhancement he was left gasping. He spent a night in each place in the Government Rest House. After dark he visited the Chinese quarter, listening to what was being said where he could. Again he never let on he spoke Chinese so, once his presence had been 'registered', he was ignored. The snippets he picked up were that the benign British colonial rule allowed them to carry on with their business unbothered but after the British had left there would be trouble. Jason could see that there was no love lost between the islanders and the mainlanders.

That was on the way from Kuching to Brunei where he gave his gloomy views to DOBOPS, both about the administration and the police – 'I'm not surprised you found them like that at your level as I have found them like that at mine' – and that the tone of the Chinese was pro-SUPP, anti-Malaysia and in all cases with an eye to the main chance. 'Atmosphere only, sir, nothing tangible.' 'And anti-Brit?' 'No, merely apathetic.'

On his way back, by a series of helicopter visits to the army units in the border areas he spoke to as many Scout sections, who recognised him from the leaflets, as he could, in Malay, telling them how he hoped to change matters, to have patience and that he understood their frustrations. He wondered if anyone anywhere understood his.

My next task is an in-depth visit along the border. I'll need a weapon. He asked Mr King if he could have a rifle and an escort for his journey. He was underwhelmed to be told that there were no spare weapons for him and that the police were neither trained for, nor available even if they had been trained, for escort work – period.

'As one of your staff, sir, you're putting me in an unenviable position,' he replied.

The Commissioner picked up a paper-knife and held it poised as delicately as a scalpel. Jason's future also seemed as finely balanced. 'Colonel Rance. You are not really one of us yet as you have not been gazetted,' he said with marked distaste.

'In other words, my Border Scouts, auxiliary policemen all,

have the judicial power to put me under arrest as I am not a police officer?'

'Correct.'

'And I have no jurisdiction over them?'

'Correct again.'

'In that case you'll have to find someone else to be the Commandant of the Border Scouts unless you gazette me before I go out on my next lot of visits.'

And there and then Lieutenant Colonel Jason Rance was gazetted as an Auxiliary Superintendent of the Sarawak Constabulary.

'How well do you know this country, Miss Jiang Yun?' Jason asked his typist, using English to her.

'Oh, sir, I have travelled quite a bit to the border and back during school holidays but don't know it all that well. Why, sir, do you have anywhere particular in mind?' she asked, simpering a little. *That simper. Acting or natural?*

'Nowhere in particular but a typical border village. Can you recommend anywhere?' he asked more as a conversational ploy than anything else.

With no hesitation, 'Yes, sir, Keik is a good place to go to. It is beyond Stass, a major village at the end of the only road going south from here and then less than an hour's walk on south. In Keik there is a Border Scout section commanded by a Gurkha. I have their nominal roll,' and she searched in a file and showed it him.

Jason read it and recognised one of his old company of 1/12 GR.

'Right! Tommy, let's go together next Monday. Stass for a couple of nights to see the Border Scouts with their Gurkha Section Commander attached to the Marines then on to Keik.'

'Colonel, my walking days are over! Better you go by yourself.'

That night Miss Jiang Yun contacted her handler and told him the details. 'There are four days to prepare matters,' she said and her handler thought that was time enough. He went to where he had a secret radio, unknown to the authorities, and made a call to HQ Military District XII in Pontianak, West Kalimantan. Its northern border was contiguous with Sarawak's First and Second Divisions. The call was acknowledged.

Stass was entirely different from villages Jason had been to in Malaya. He sensed it was one of the places that lie dormant for a thousand years and, through the perverse fortunes of fate, famine, earthquake or war, suddenly spring into world headlines. None of 'romantic Borneo' was to be found here. No invigorating upland climate, no absurd straw hats or complicated tattoos pricked out over strong, brown bodies. Here dwelt a gentler, more ordinary person, in a climate that was hot and sticky. But they were nice, kind, inoffensive folk and, once shown how, would become capable leaders and scouts. Like so much of the rest of Borneo, deep knowledge was at a premium, individual personalities held tremendous sway over others and hearsay was endemic.

On Sunday, the day before Jason was due in Keik, a man from the other side of the border reached the village late in the evening. He had a relative there, ex-police corporal Jihed, and told him that a platoon of Indonesian military had unexpectedly came up from the nearest military base to the south and was planning to cross the border the next day. He had been shown a copy of a leaflet with a photograph of the new Commandant of the Border Scouts and been told that he was to go to Keik and make sure that the man was entertained 'until we arrive' as the Indonesian's 'wanted' him. Jihed was puzzled and suspicious as no one had been told about such a visit; the Border Scouts had no radio. He told the headman and suggested to the Gurkha Section Commander that he go to Stass with his scouts, ask the Royal Marines stationed there urgently to reinforce the village and to guide them back. 'I'll go with you.' They left Keik early the next day before any Indonesians had been seen and reached Stass.

Jason's one-time rifleman saluted him. 'Sahib, the Indonesians from over the border told us you were due in Keik but we didn't know about it. How could they know about it when we didn't? It is too dangerous to go to the village without a proper escort. I see you don't even have a weapon. Why not?'

'*O-hé keta*, you've no idea what working for the police is like. They say they don't have any spare.'

'Sahib, that's nonsense. Look, there are always a few spare weapons in our Para Company armoury. Why not borrow one?'

'Good idea. Yes, that's something I must do. I have seldom felt as naked as I do now. Like a Brahman walking around without his sacred thread.'

That made the soldier laugh. 'Sahib, when you left our company none of us could believe you had really gone. It's a pity you can't come and command us.'

'If I did and we were allowed to cross the border I could talk to the villagers and find out a good target.'

'We'd go with you anywhere, Sahib. With you we know no fear.'

Jason thanked the Gurkha for his kind words. They went to see the Marine Troop Commander who decided it was better to stay and defend Stass rather than go to Keik.

On the Monday an Indonesian platoon reached Keik and surrounded the village. The leader, with one other man, went in search of the village headman. He showed him the photograph. 'Is this man in the village?' he asked brusquely. As there was no attack as such, warning gongs were not struck.

'No, he isn't,' the headman answered fearfully but truthfully.

'I don't believe you,' came the uncompromising reply and he ordered his men to make a house-to-house search. No European nor any traces of one were found.

Disgustedly the Indon commander said, 'If we find you were telling a lie, we'll come back and kill you. One day this man will come and you must immediately send someone over the border to let us know.' He asked for a piece of paper and wrote a message. 'Give this warning to the man when he comes,' and with that uncompromising message, the platoon went back the way they'd come and re-crossed the border.

Come Tuesday it was decided that Jihed, the Gurkha and his scouts would go back to Keik. Jason would go with them. Once there they learnt that the Indons had gone back over the border and the headman, shakingly surprised to see Major Rance of the photo, told him what the Indon commander had said. 'My men are angry,' he said, 'they want revenge. Oh yes, this is a message the enemy commander left for you.' Jason put it in his pocket then tried to make light of the photo, under his breath cursing the land-locked sailor's unthinking flash of unwanted Public Relations stupidity.

Back in Kuching Jason wrote a report about the incident, including the bit about the photo. Jiang Yun dutifully typed it with much interest. *I can see what went wrong. It'll have to be more effective next time,* she thought.

'Miss Jiang Yun, it is time I went to visit the Ibans in the Second Division. I have been trying to learn Iban and it now time to put my knowledge to the test.' He turned to his Dyak Staff Officer. 'Where do you advise?'

'Sir, the best place to set up a training camp for Scouts in the Second Division is at Jambu. Let me show you on the map. My idea is that you and I go and have a look at somewhere there suitable for a camp then you go on down the Nanga Sumpa by boat and meet the one-time chief of all headmen, Jimbuan, now on pension. He was awarded a Police Gallantry Medal after the last war. He is the most influential man in the whole area and you'll learn a lot from him. The longhouses on the approach to his are all SUPP-inclined.' Jason had learnt that the Iban villages were all under one roof so one 'long house' contained many people. 'Government wants to relocate that longhouse farther north as they fear Indonesian probes and incursions will prevent any planting and harvesting and so induce famine. This is vastly unpopular.'

Neither of them noticed their typist's instant, albeit subdued, reaction. She knew about the man and the place. *Is there time?* she asked herself.

Jason, with two Iban Border Scout escorts, went by boat to Jimbuan's house at Nanga Sumpa which lay between two strongly flowing rivers. It was twenty doors long, meaning that twenty discrete families lived there. The house, built on posts, was entered by a notched pole from the ground. Running lengthways in front of the rooms was a long verandah. Outside each room was a fighting cockerel, tied by a piece of string. Curs, used for hunting, cowered and slunk, scavenged and yapped. With a motley crowd of all ages, talking, singing, laughing and arguing, ever arguing, Jason found it noisy in the extreme and smelly. He was shown some floor space and took off his jungle boots, exchanging them for 'thongs'. His two scouts took his rifle and disappeared. He was invited into Jimbuan's room and taken to the small part that served as an eating place. They sat down on the bamboo-slatted floor. Rice beer was offered in two glasses, one small and one big. The smaller glass was lifted first and, having been brought up to the mouth as though to be drunk, its contents was poured through the slats onto the ground below. Jason presumed that was for Jimbuan's gods.

After their meal the two of them went and sat with backs to the outer wall and gradually the men of the longhouse came and sat, in serried rows, facing them. A strong-looking bunch, in the dim light of the open-wicked lamps, the flickering shadows made their unsmiling faces relentlessly stern and satanic. Young and old there were about forty-five of them. They sat, silent and staring, their eyes boring into Jason's whenever he looked at them. When Jason told Jimbuan that he could in no way influence the unpleasant and unpopular decision already made to relocate the longhouse farther north, the Iban started to pick a quarrel with his guest.

Jimbuan launched into a litany of frustration, anger and menace: rights and wrongs, imagined or real, out they came. In twenty minutes he had worked himself into a towering rage. In brief Jason understood enough Iban to understand that the enemy were not those who lived on the other side of the border. Those were Ibans and friends. The enemy lived in Kuching and their name was Government. 'You are from Kuching', he spat out, 'you are part of the Government, you are the enemy. You should be killed as I, Jimbuan, have killed nineteen enemy during the war …' Even if Jason had not understood every word of the diatribe in Iban, he had no doubt as to the meaning, especially when Jimbuan showed him nineteen tattoos between the knuckles and on the back of his left hand, one for each head, '… with this,' and, so saying, the angry man, with surprising agility, jumped to his feet and, from behind the open door, produced a Japanese sword. Unsheathing it and branding it over Jason's head, he continued, voice quavering with rage, 'I will do to you what I did to my enemies … look up above you.'

Roll with the punch. Play it cool. So insistent was Jimbuan and so little choice had Jason that look up he did, fully conscious of the stares, unblinking in their intensity, of the men in front of him. They, to a man, all firmly agreed with Jimbuan. And there, previously unnoticed, was a large bunch of sightless, grinning skulls, Jimbuan's nineteen, dumb witnesses to former acts of violence, hanging over his head, ready to act as witnesses again.

Jason, horror-struck, hoping he did not look as terrified as he felt, looked up at Jimbuan standing over him, then to the men still staring unwaveringly at him. Their expressions were set, without regard, without remorse, without regret. The one-time headman still had his sword above him, poised, ready.

'What have you to say? Why shouldn't your head be there? Why should I treat you differently from them?' he queried, gesticulating up at the squalid bunch of skulls.

Jason found the atmosphere unbearably tense. His throat was dry and the sweat of raw, animal fear had yet to break. Escape was out of the question. *Play it cool.* The adrenalin coursing through his veins thankfully also acted on his Iban fluency. He knew enough to answer slowly and clearly without any embellishment that might have angered his tormentor. 'No reason at all, old man,' he said, realising that argument was the last thing needed – the very last, probably. 'I am your guest but tonight I am tired and you too are from working all day. Also the light is dim. Put away your sword and use it tomorrow morning when it is light, after you have had a good night's rest. Your aim will be better then.'

Will that be enough? There was an endless pause of a few seconds while Jimbuan considered Jason's answer. It must have turned away his wrath for he sheathed his sword, put it away behind the door and, in Jason's view, ludicrously and unnecessarily sat down again beside him. *Yes, it had been enough!*

An uneasy quiet ensued, broken by a bard at the end of the room, who started singing. Jimbuan got up and moved over to him as did, gradually, those men sitting in front of Jason. Long verses recounting glories of past deeds, now embellished with the present hapless situation were being intoned. Jason sat on alone and it was then that the sweat of fear broke and, as he sat cross-legged on the floor, he heard the drops of sweat as they ran down his nose onto the straw mat he was sitting on.

After a few minutes of lonely introspection, a woman came over to him and directed him to an empty room. Creakingly he rose and followed her across the open space. She opened the door for him. In he went: there was a sleeping mat and nothing else. She locked the door behind her and he lay down. It was hard. *At least I am still alive. Tomorrow will come soon enough.* Completely worn out, he fell into a troubled sleep.

Next morning Jason rolled up his sleeping mat and, to his chagrin, found he'd been sleeping on a leaflet with his photo on it. Any fear now turned into anger. After he was let out he met up with his two escorts, took his rifle and went to upbraid Jimbuan who, he later thought, had only responded with such little alacrity because of suffering from a mammoth hang-over. The three men left the long house and, at the end of the day, reached a platoon of Gurkhas at a place called Mepi. The two scouts went their own way and Jason was allowed to stay there for the night by the Platoon Commander, who recognised him. The hot tea he was given was probably the best he had ever tasted, or would ever taste, in his life.

An Indonesian patrol reached Nanga Sumpa midday on the day that Jason's small group left. 'You didn't kill him?' the patrol leader asked Jimbuan.

'No.'

'Why not?'

No answer.

'You didn't even capture him for us?'

No answer.

On leaving, the leader said, menacingly, 'I expect you'll be next on our list.'

Why didn't I kill him? Will there be another time …?

'Time to go to the Third Division,' said Jason after his return to Kuching when he again wrote a report which his typist typed out with great interest and not a little concern. He looked at the map on the wall which showed every Border Scout post. 'I want to go to the one nearest the Indonesian border, Long Jawi. I'll plan to stay a couple of nights there. As it'll take some organising I'll arrange to visit it in ten days' time,' and he wrote out the details for Jiang Yun. *Make no mistakes this time*, she said to herself.

It just so happened that Jason decided to visit the remaining Border Scout posts in the Second Division before he moved to the Third Division. He told his staff officers he'd 'wander around' for a few days. This he did, met those he wanted to meet, felt much happier as no enemy were anywhere about. There had been no typed programme.

Long Jawi was remote. It had a Border Scout post of twenty-one locals and a few Gurkhas who were more than three hundred river, not road, miles from Battalion HQ and fifty from their Company HQ. The terrain was sparsely populated, jungle-covered, mountainous, unmapped and intersected with innumerable wide and fast-flowing rivers. Jason went there by Royal Naval helicopter, a journey of minutes compared with one of days had he walked. He was told that another heli could not pick him up when planned in three days' time so he'd have to fly back on the morrow, early.

He inspected the area, made a change in some of the dispositions against any attack then asked everyone – villagers, scouts and Gurkhas – to assemble to hear his plans. Sitting at the back in the gloom, unbeknownst to him, was a small Indonesian recce group. The leader looked critically at Jason, took a piece of paper out of his pocket and looked at the photo on it. 'That's the one,' he said to his mate, 'but with the main force half a day's walk away we don't do anything now. The day after tomorrow morning is quite early enough.'

If the villagers knew about them they kept quiet.

Jason's heli picked him up as planned and at dawn on the following day a large attack killed all but three of the Gurkhas and those Border Scouts who hadn't managed to run away. That was an act of anger in frustration at having missed their main target. The Indonesian victory and Border Scout massacre reverberated all over Sarawak. The Gurkhas would avenge themselves later.

'He's had the luck of Saitan,' Sumbi spat out at his weekly meeting. The Military Command opposite the Fourth and Fifth Divisions of Sarawak, and all of British North Borneo, was Number VI, with its HQ in East Kalimantan so did not come directly under Sumbi's jurisdiction, something so far overlooked.

After an uninterrupted in-depth visit to the Border Scouts in the Fourth and Fifth Divisions, Jason was ordered by the Brigade Commander to go to a place called Pleman Mepu in the First Division where the scouts' performance was reported not to be up to standard by the Royal Malay Regiment battalion there. Resignedly he gave the details to his typist, saying that he planned to go after he had caught up with some office work. 'It is Tuesday today, Miss Jiang Yun,' as he politely called her. 'I'll go next Monday, after the weekend.'

Jiang Yun looked at him for longer than usual before demurely noting down the details. *That's time enough, he's got away with it till now,* she thought.

Jason and a Cadet Police Inspector, George Ningkan, learning the ropes, reached Pleman Mapu around noon. They were just on their way to a shop to buy some tinned fish for George when an agitated headman arrived. With scant ceremony he hustled both of them inside and upstairs into the loft.

'I have reports of enemy coming. You must hide,' he told them breathlessly. 'I know who you are,' he said, 'I have your photo and I have had news that the enemy also believes you will be here today or tomorrow.' Not for the first, nor probably the last time, did Jason curse those wretched photos ... yet there was a nag at the back of his mind. *Can such forewarning always be coincidental or is there a leak?*

The loft was airless and musty. They sat on the floor and

asked for details; after all, rumours were many, but there was a Malay platoon in the village, surely?

It was explained that a man flashing a torch had been seen prowling about in the village the previous night, that the Malay platoon had denied it was theirs, that the light must have been flashed by the Indonesians and that the Malay platoon had left for the border that morning.

After sundown Jason and George were called down and offered some rice and vegetables. Neither of them had much of an appetite. Dogs started barking at half-past seven, not just baying at the moon but the kind that is set off by humans not being recognised.

Their kit had been hidden in a safe place and they only had their rifle with them. Jason had taken the precaution of bringing a towel to use as a pillow-cum-head binder to keep as many nasties as possible from going down his ears. The two men had just lain down on the bamboo-slatted floor when the house dogs started barking. 'You must hide,' they were told.

Part of the floor bamboo slats was rolled back and they were told to jump down and hide in a narrow trench that had been dug for the headman if the longhouse were to be shelled. This they did, with urgent whispers, imploring them to hurry. Once they were under the floor, a man rolled the bamboo slats back in position and unrolled his sleeping mat, placing it over the 'trap door'. It was hoped he would act as a decoy if the Indons were to enter the house.

Under the house, in the narrow pit, it was pitch dark and fetid, stinking of stale rubbish, pigs, curs and chickens. The two men squirmed themselves as comfortably as they could, arms pinioned to their sides. Jason managed to put the towel over his head and draped it over his face, as they soon found themselves beset with rats. George wriggled and moaned, bringing whispered curses and pleas for silence from above.

Jason dozed off but was awakened by a loud altercation above him. Someone was asking the headman where he had hidden that European and if the answer was not forthcoming he'd have the house searched. 'There is no stranger here,' said the headman. 'Search the place for all you want but do not harm the women and children.'

'I'll bring my men to do just that. You are not my enemy, the colonialist Europeans are and I've been sent to look for one man.' Jason heard a rustling as of paper being unfolded. 'Here, look at his photo. His name is Mr Rance, a Superintendent of the Sarawak Constabulary.'

Again the headman denied it. The two men left and Jason breathed a sigh of relief. He whispered to George, 'Stay absolutely still.'

Some time later Jason heard voices outside the house getting fainter. *They've gone, heaven be praised!*

Dogs barked again at ten o'clock. The rats continued to run over them and George's struggles to keep his face clear caused the earthen walls of the trench to start crumbling. More agonised whispers demanding quiet came from above. 'They may come back.'

Partly as a result of being nudged by George, partly because of the rats running over the draped towel and partly because he must have been moving his head from side to side, the towel slipped off Jason's face. He was awoken by a large rat sitting on his nose. Instinctively, knowing that he could not get his hands to brush it off, he blew up, violently, through his mouth and it scuttled off. He managed to drape the towel more firmly and continued his sleep, albeit intermittently.

Next morning, apart from the adverse situation even were it known about, the wet weather was not conducive to helicopter flying, so the heli they had tasked for themselves that day seemed unlikely to arrive. There was nothing to do but to sit tight.

By mid-morning the rain had stopped. At two o'clock in the afternoon, twenty-six hours after they had arrived at the longhouse, they heard the sound of a helicopter. They hardly dared believe their ears. As soon as they were sure it was coming their way, they ran the two hundred yards to where it would land and thankfully boarded it.

Both men were delighted to get back to Kuching, tired out but safe and sound. News of the incursion had quickly made the rounds but the two men's narrow escape had only been confirmed after office hours as both men had gone straight back to their lodgings. Next morning in the office, Jiang Yung gave her boss a protracted glance, as though taken by surprise. *I thought they'd got him this time.* Jason noticed her surprise and took it at face value because of his escape. The Pleman Mepu incident severely nagged him. In three Divisions he had been close to the scene of an Indonesian attack twice, a near-death Iban unprovoked show of force once and constant rumours of his being looked for. *All because of that unnecessary broadcast and those unfortunate leaflets?* When he had not told Jiang Yun where he was going nothing untoward had happened, when he had, they had. *Unlikely coincidences or ... or ... what? I'll probe.* He went to the Central Registry and asked the Chief Clerk, a Jagoi-speaking Land Dyak, if he could see his typist's documents.

'Why, sir? She can't be causing you any trouble. She is an extremely hard-working, conscientious and efficient typist. If you are recommending a rise in pay, sir, I have to say that the procedures do not allow a temporary worker to be recompensed for efficiency.'

Jason grinned back at the Chief Clerk. 'No, no, Chief, nothing like that. She's always hesitant when I ask her about her family, where she lives and her educational qualifications. I am new and I don't want to offend her so I thought a private peek at her documents would tell me what I wanted without going against protocol.'

It was the Chief Clerk's turn to smile. 'Tuan, let me get her file. Wait here a moment please. I wish all our officers were as circumspect as you are.'

He came back with it. 'I'll sit down and have a look at it if I may,' Jason said, taking it from the Chief's outstretched hand. He read her signature written in the Roman script and in characters: and it struck him like a kick in the face by an angry mule that her family name, Cheong, was the Cantonese rendering of the Amoy family name pronounced Zhong in Amoynese. *That rotter Zhong Han San's Cantonese pronunciation had been tinged by an Amoynese accent.* Had Jiang Yun's family somehow been subsumed into a Cantonese-speaking one or did she put Cheong rather than Zhong on purpose? He had heard her speak Cantonese on the phone, not Amoynese. And then it hit him: *Kesar Pun's enigmatic message delivered by Jim Fordyce. Jiang Yun must be the third uncle's fifth niece! Can't be anyone else, can she?* Sweat broke out on his brow as he remembered that macabre scene in the jungle near the village of Ha La. He took out his handkerchief and dabbed his forehead. He had learnt Zhong Han San's name from the card he carried in his pocket after he had throttled him. He had learnt that the Zhong clan was a small one but had branches overseas. Was there a connection in Zhong's death and he himself being a target of Indonesian attacks? *Was I looking for a deer in the jungle when there was one below the longhouse?* he asked himself, quoting an Iban proverb he had recently learnt. He knew that there had been other incursions when he had not been present but, *what was that old saw? If you want to hide a leaf was it, or a stone, go to the forest or the quarry.* He wasn't quite sure which, not that it mattered. It made sense either way.

He made a note of her home address, phone number and parents' names. 'Thank you, Chief,' he said, giving him back the file. The Chief Clerk took it. 'Any comments, sir?' he asked.

'No, Chief Clerk. All as it should be,' Jason answered and left the Registry. *All as it should be for them but not for me.*

Back in his office he sent a signal to DOBOPS asking when he could come and see him. The answer came back before the office shut, 'Tomorrow at 1300 hours, prompt'. He told Jiang Yung to book him to Brunei on tomorrow's first flight. He told his two staff officers that it was time for a routine report to DOBOPS and that, as business was slack, he'd feel happy if both of them took the afternoon off. 'Just in case there's a phone call, I'd like you to guard the phone till closing time,' he told his typist. 'Once I'm back I'll arrange for you to have a few days off as you have been so busy with all the typing I've given you.' In no way did his demeanour change when he spoke to her as these were early days yet but ... Jason once more recalled how he had often learnt more about people by hint, allusion, intonation, facial expression, inference, gesture and sometimes silence than by spoken words. He played back in his mind the times he and his typist had been together in the office, with or without the two staff officers.

She thanked him demurely, wondering why his sudden concern for her. *Despite what I have heard he is a nice man, kind and easy to get on with.*

He left an hour early for his flight to Brunei to go and to see the Head of Special Branch and, making sure no one could eavesdrop, asked him for a briefing on the SUPP. 'Have you a nominal roll of those you know about that I can have a look at, please?' he asked.

He was shown one. No Cheong Jian Yun was shown on it.

'How many sleepers do you think there are serving in government or police offices?'

'If I knew I'd be a happier man than I am. Why do you ask?'

'Just feeling my way,' Jason answered enigmatically and, thanking him, left for his plane.

He met General Sprinter as planned. 'Sir, I have two points for you, both important. The first is that I now know how to put the Border Scouts on an even keel, so to speak, briefly these are my ideas ...' The General listened intently.

'Good news, Rance. And the second point?'

Jason looked intently at the General. 'Sir, I am living on borrowed time because of those wretched leaflets. Not only have I found them at the three places where I was a target of the Indonesians but I have to beg or borrow a weapon and between Border Scout posts often have to move unescorted through jungle, at times where Gurkha troops won't move with less than a platoon. Something has to break before I do.'

The General shifted uneasily in his chair. 'It's as bad as that, is it?'

'Worse, sir. I have a strong feeling that my Chinese typist is a "plant", there to watch me. Each time I've given her details of where I'm going I've been attacked, each time I haven't told her where, I haven't been. I want to prove or disprove the latter by trying to eradicate the former. I think I have a way of doing so and, in all fairness to you, I must tell you how. This afternoon I am planning to make a phone call,' and he went into details.

The General looked stupefied at the end. 'While what you are planning might constitute an indiscretion it doesn't violate military law or contravene military tenets. After all, although the Army does encourage initiatives, it views novel instigation with suspicion. However, as you're a policeman I can't stop you,' he said after a long pause, 'but this is something I'd never have considered feasible or even the slightest bit safe. Can't you think of any other way?'

'Sir, surprise is paramount. If I didn't think I could pull it off I wouldn't have told you about it. I am telling myself that this is another Operation Blind Spot and I can't think of any blinder.'

'You're probably right there,' the General said with a smile. 'Does your typist know you speak Chinese?'

'No, sir, although I grew up bilingual in Chinese and English I've never given her any reason to. Mostly I speak to her in English and she knows that I speak fluent Malay as it is spoken on the mainland.'

'Keep me informed how events develop but "eyes only" correspondence. If you can't type yourself, send me reports hand-written. You're skating on very thin ice.'

'Thin it may be, sir, but the others' may be thinner still,' said Jason, 'They won't expect anything like this.'

Neither did I, thought the General, inwardly marvelling at the younger man's resourcefulness.

Jason left the General's HQ and made his way to the main Post and Telegraph Office in Brunei Town. He dialled his office in Kuching. His typist answered.

In Cantonese he growled at her, 'Are you alone? Is there a Running Dog to hear you talk?'

She was taken aback. 'Who...who are you? I don't recognise your voice.'

'I am your third uncle and you are my fifth niece. I was in south Thailand until recently and am now in Brunei under another name that is no concern of yours.'

He heard a gasp. 'Third uncle ... fifth niece? What branch of the family are you from?' Somehow the voice sounded familiar.

Jason had done his homework and gave a convincing answer,

then 'I can't, no daren't, stay long on the phone but listen to me. The man who is your boss is not who he seems to be. I have known him from a long time past. His real name is Popov and he is as dedicated as you are. He is working under deep cover and is our *maang dim* and you have been quite wrong to let the SUPP' – he used its full Chinese name, *Sa Lai Yuet Yan Num Luen Hup Dong*, thankful he had bothered to find out what it was – 'tell our friends in Kalimantan where he is going. You have nearly had him killed three or four times. That is the opposite of the *sei gok* we are planning.'

These were terms the hapless woman had not heard before. 'I … I don't fully understand what you mean, Third Uncle. Can you please explain?'

'Cursed dimwit. You are no more clever than I was given to understand, listen carefully,' and he gave her an explanation of 'blind spot' and 'dead angle', the military equivalent, letting those meanings sink in before sharply saying, 'Fifth niece, do you understand me or not? If you get this wrong I, despite our family ties, may not be able to defend you.'

Hesitantly she told him she understood. 'Who shall I say told me?' she asked in a quavering voice, 'otherwise my people in Kuching won't believe me.'

Jason inwardly cursed himself for not having an instant answer. 'What's that you're asking on a clear line?' came to him.

Jian Yung tentatively repeated her question.

'As it is an order from the Centre, say "Reach Comrade Aidit and say 'Remember Sadao'".'

'Remember where, Third Uncle?'

'Sadao. Say it back, twice, slowly.'

This she did. 'Third Uncle, confirmation from the Secretary General will take time. Is there any other method of getting my people to accept your credentials?'

'Yes, Fifth Niece. You are wise.' *Got it!* 'Tell them to say "*Mi kham klaw wa khon haw*" and if Popov answers "*Lan mai mi wan chan*" then he is the man. If not, no. You can't be more secure than that.'

As he expected he had to repeat it several times before he was sure that she had written it down correctly. 'Third Uncle, what language is that. I can't understand it and I'm sure the others won't either.'

'It is Thai. You say "There is a saying that" and he answers "bald men are never poor".'

'Again please.'

Jason repeated it, then abruptly, 'One final point. In Brunei I will meet Popov and tell him what I have told you. I speak English and Russian. I will further tell him that you will secretly introduce him to the Kuching branch of our party and, in turn, the branches in the main Divisional towns. This is an edict. Instantly obey,' and Jason abruptly rang off, wiping his sweat-covered forehead and breathing hard as he did.

Jiang Yung contacted her handler that evening and told him everything. Initially he was totally flabbergasted then rallied manfully. *Our agents are deep and clever.* 'I'll fix a meeting and get you to explain everything. This could play into our hands,' he said.

'And I?' she asked.

'You are known as a "sleeper". Act that way. Sleep with him.'

It's what happens before one goes to sleep, she said to herself, with a lascivious look spreading over her gorgeous face.

7

It so happened that General Nasution, Chief of Staff of the Indonesian Army, was visiting Military District XII, under command of Major General Mulia, when a message came in from the secret radio set belonging to the SUPP in Kuching. It contained information the like of which had never previously been conceived: their sleeper in the Border Scout office had been contacted by her third uncle who called her his fifth niece with the news that the Superintendent of Police in charge of the Border Scouts was really a Russian by the name of Popov and only disguised as an Englishman, named Jason Rance; and, if proof of identity of the so-far-unnamed fifth uncle were needed, they were to ask Comrade Aidit and remind him of Sadao. Not only that: there was a Thai password 'there is a saying that' and counter sign 'bald men are never poor' to be said in Thai, not English and not Russian! To say that such unexpected information caused almost electrical interest would be putting it mildly. Surely no one could hoodwink the British Army to that extent and for so long, could they? The Indonesians had been trying to kill the one man on the other side who could really help them. Disastrous!

Silence reigned supreme for more than a whole minute as each tried to digest such singular news. A second reading was ordered after which something along the lines of what advantage can we make of it if it is true? came to everyone's mind, followed by but how can it not be true with such an unassailable source?

'We have to take all that on trust until or if proved otherwise but the point about Comrade Aidit is one we can clear up,' General Nasution told the Military District Commander. 'Send him a coded message asking for comments.' Major General Mulia wrote one, showed it to his superior who told him to grade it with the highest priority and get it sent off straightaway.

Sumbi, still only a lieutenant, looked at his two friends, Alif and Zai, also lieutenants, and broke the ensuing silence by saying, loudly enough for all to hear, 'You have already identified the man whose photograph is shown in this leaflet,' and he took it out a drawer and showed it to them, 'as the man you saw kill Comrade Zhong Han San at Ha La without any shadow of doubt whatsoever, haven't you?'

'Yes, indeed and just as surely as you told both of us that you first met him in the British Jungle Warfare School in Malaya and again when you were both on the same parachute course in England,' Zai said. 'There can be no doubt whatever that the man notified as – it puts Lieutenant Colonel here – is the same as the Commandant of the Border Scouts. He was known as a fluent Chinese speaker, reader and writer.'

The two Generals showed intense interest and considerable perplexity. 'There is no doubt in my mind either,' added Alif, 'he is the one we both,' and he cocked his head towards Zai, 'saw kill Comrade Zhong Han San most brutally. We saw the Comrade turn round as if he heard a voice but couldn't see anyone and then this man jumped on him from behind. They had some words with each other then the Englishman strangled him with a garrote after talking to him. There was another man there. We think he was Gurkha soldier.'

'Did you hear anything that was said between them?' General Nasution asked.

'No sir, we were too far away,' one of them offered, 'and neither of us speaks Chinese.'

Sodimedjo, the District Intelligence Colonel, asked, 'As a matter of background interest why do you think he killed him? As far as either of you are aware had they ever met previously?'

Again heads shook. 'Comrade Zhong never spoke to us about him but ... wait a bit,' Zai stared at the wall as if trying to recall something. 'Yes, we hadn't been at Sadao long when Comrade Chin Peng became most upset at a derogatory and insulting letter that was delivered to the Secretary General written by a man who signed himself as Shandung P'aau and that, apparently, was the name written on a note placed on the dead man's chest. We saw the killer search Zhong's pockets, take out a piece of paper, looked like his ID card, and, having written on his own piece, place it on the corpse. It was written in Chinese. There can be no mistaking him for anyone else.'

'Let me recap,' said the Intelligence Colonel. 'You say that Comrade Chin Peng was most upset about a letter, correct?'

'Yes.'

'Did he or anyone else ever see the person who actually wrote it or, as I have heard it said, "you are putting two and two together and making five"?'

Alif answered. 'Colonel, we did not give you the full story. I should have told you that the letter was found by the camp sentry on the outer perimeter. Someone, nobody ever saw who, had placed it in some bull rushes and when the wind moved them the letter fluttered. It was then that the sentry saw it and went over to pick it up. At the end of his tour of duty he handed it over. It could never be established whether the writer or someone else actually delivered it.' He looked at the Colonel who stared back at him.

'Nothing else at all? Think hard.'

Alif looked embarrassed. 'Well, sir, it just may have been brought by one of the village girls who used to visit the camp for social services, shall I say?...who could have put it on the bull rushes.' He coughed delicately. 'Even the camp sentries availed themselves of the girls' services if circumstances were propitious.'

The Colonel pursed his lips. Such behaviour wouldn't happen in our army! 'Think harder. Bring it out from the back of your mind. Absolutely nothing else, is there?'

'Colonel, now I come to think of it, yes there is. The only foreigner who booked into any hotel at all in Sadao on the day the letter was found was a man whose passport photo was copied and the name on it was Jason Rance, the same name as the new Border Scouts' boss.'

Colonel Sodimedjo considered that. 'Fine, as far as it goes but it still does not go as far as it might. There is no proof, only strong inference, that Shandung P'aau and Jason Rance are one of the same.' He paused for effect, unaware that one of the agents of the Secretary General of the Malayan Communist Party had heard Rance and Ah Fat talking to each other in Chinese at their meeting at the briefing by HQ 2 Federal Brigade in Ipoh. He went on, 'So it is entirely possible that the man you saw killing Comrade Zhong was not the letter writer and it was someone else who wanted to remain anonymous who used the Chinese name on the letter.'

Yes, they had to agree that it was, indeed, entirely possible that the letter writer was someone else, although most of them considered that the coincidence of two people being involved was highly unlikely.

As they thought out the conundrum one of them asked if the new Superintendent of the Border Scouts had been heard speaking Chinese. 'That's a good question to ask,' said the Intelligence Colonel, 'but still that in itself is not proof that he was the original letter writer.' He asked his GOC for permission to send another message, this time to Kuching, asking about the new police officer's ability in various languages.

Lieutenant Sumbi then added, 'There's much more to this than we here can fathom. None of us can know what went on between any of them before our two guerrillas here went to Sadao. Those leaders kept most of that stuff to themselves, so I've been told.'

The two lieutenants concurred.

'The two men you captured as you chased their group south from Ha La, didn't you say one was killed by being split when tied to two curved bamboos and the other, mouth smeared with shit, was left, tightly bound, all night to be interrogated on the morrow then to be killed, if not dead already?' That was Major General Mulia's question.

'Yes, that was the plan.'

'Tell me again, who were those two?' General Nasution, now totally intrigued as to how to make this situation redound in his favour, had not fully absorbed the details of those few years back. After all, as Army Chief of Staff he had many other more important matters to look after.

'They were both Chinese,' explained Alif. 'After the first killing and the torture of the second man we went back to camp and Comrade Zhong told us that the man killed was known as Hung Lo, the Bear, his real name being Wang Ming, and the other, the man who disappeared before Zhong Han San got back in the morning, was an Ah Fat, a favourite of Comrade Chin Peng, known as P'ing Yee, Flat Ears, and who had been his Military Consultant to the Central Committee, a non-voting member. The rumour was that he and the Englishman were firm friends from childhood days in Kuala Lumpur.'

'That certainly puts a different slant on the killing. Do you think that the Englishman killed Zhong because he was angry that his friend had been so hurt and this other man had been killed?'

'Could be,' said Alif, 'the man was a notorious sadist with, how shall I put it? "masculine thoughts" but who knows?' and relapsed into moody silence.

'All most interesting, I'm sure,' said the Chief of Staff. 'There's nothing we can do until we get answers to our messages. I must make a move as I'm behind schedule. I'll call in tomorrow before I fly back to Jakarta,' and he and the District Commander went off.

By next morning there was an answer to the signal from Kuching and, instead of sending a signal, Comrade Aidit phoned. He told them that he had only stayed a day or so at Sadao, had been introduced to the politburo members but, not speaking Chinese, could not remember any of their names except that one was a Zhong Han San but could not put a face to him. 'As for the third uncle you mention, he could be any of the others. These Chinese have extended relationships only they can fathom so there is no telling who he is.'

'Do you think he's genuine?' queried General Nasution.

'Why not? He knows Thai and lived in Thailand. Sadao is in Thailand,' he added lamely.

'So what do you want us to do?'

'In your signal you said you sent a message to Kuching to the sleeper about the new Superintendent speaking Chinese. Have you had an answer?'

'Yes, wait while I retrieve it.' A pause. 'Here is its. In essence it says that the sleeper was asked about her superior's language ability and she says she has never heard him speak Chinese nor shown any reaction when she had spoken Cantonese in his hearing. They normally speak in English but he is fluent in Malay. He is learning Iban and used it to good effect one time when threatened with being beheaded. The sleeper has been told that as she was a "sleeper" to put that into practice and to see what could be learnt from any pillow-talk.'

'That's it, Aidit.'

Aidit thanked General Nasution, said he'd consider the whole issue and come back to him on an 'as-and-how' basis and rang off.

The Intelligence Colonel asked for permission to speak. It was given. 'It would certainly be a great pity not to take advantage of this new situation if it really is a help to our Konfrontasi being successful. I suggest we continue as we have been doing up to now but not make where the Commandant of the Border Scouts is going a priority target, in fact not to make it a target at all. We can't afford to lose him, can we? We can tell our cell with the SUPP in Kuching where our next raids will be and if there are obvious reactions from the Security Forces in Sarawak to try and cut us off or ambush us, we'll know that Popov isn't the help we hoped he was going to be. If he knows in advance and we see no different reaction from normal or even no military intervention when some was expected, then Popov will be proved genuine. But just to make completely sure, signal to the Secretary General of SUPP, Mr Sim Ting Ong, to test Mr Popov out by talking to him as if he were a Chinese linguist.'

That was considered a wise move. None wanted to endure the wrath of Sukarno by getting this wrong.

General Nasution looked at his watch. 'I must be off in half an hour. Get my helicopter ready then drive me to the heli pad,' he told Sumbi. 'I accept what Colonel Sodimedjo advises and unless matters work out differently I will tell the President that that is how we are reacting to the news we have just received which, of course, he knows nothing about yet.'

And that became the 'school solution' for Military Command XII.

'How did you get on with the General?' Jason was asked by his friend Tommy Watts when he met him at the airport on his arrival back from Brunei on the midday Borneo Airways flight.

'Well enough, Tommy. I told him that I now knew what was needed to be done to get the Border Scouts trained up as Section Leaders, where I wanted the training camps and how many army officers to help me run the training. For his part he wants me to lecture all the Gurkha NCOs who will be in charge of my new guidelines of operating using the Border Scouts when any battalion comes to Borneo on roulement. I told him I was well satisfied with how you are helping me and that we both planned to leave our jobs after one year. And anything new your side of the house?'

'No. Thank you for telling the General what you did. The only other thing ... No it's not worth my mentioning it.'

'Don't be a tease, Tommy. There must be something on your mind. What is it?'

'Well, nothing really but our typist seems somehow to be different from when you left to go to Brunei.'

'Different? How come?'

'Nothing really but she is behaving just a bit strangely, one minute not paying attention to her work so making many typing errors she never made before and one minute looking as though she had had something new unconnected with her work. I asked her if all was well at home and she looked at me I thought a bit skittishly, which struck me as odd, and then said, no there was no trouble at home and why was I asking? I didn't answer.'

Jason smoothed his friend's worries with an anodyne remark and the vehicle dropped him off at his bungalow at the police annex, not all that far from the HQ, his temporarily until a modest flat could be arranged. His friend Tommy Watts' room was in the annex itself. 'Tommy, take the vehicle back to the office. I'll change and walk back. The leg-stretch will do me good.'

Tommy drove off and Jason went into his room. He had travelled in plain clothes and now had to dress in uniform. This was almost the same as the army wore, jungle green shirt and slacks, and black shoes but a blue beret with the Sarawak Constabulary badge and shoulder titles that read 'Border Scouts'. A hornbill emblem was stitched below his right shoulder title. So she's reacting outwardly, even to austere Tommy, he thought. Third uncle's words must have had quite an effect as she seemed almost overwhelmed when I spoke to her. I'll let her make the first move.

He walked over to his office and smiled at all three of his staff. 'I expect my staff officers have been keeping you busy, Miss Jiang Yun,' he said to her, smilingly.

'Oh no, I mean yes, sir, I mean not more than usual, sir,' she answered tripping over her tongue in unusual confusion.

'Let me see what's new. Bring me over what has come in while I've been away.'

She collected the files and took them over to his table. She brushed against his shoulder and, as she laid the files in front of him, she let her hand touch his. Now this is a new development, thought Jason, not reacting in the slightest.

Came closing time. 'Off you go,' he said to his two staff officers, 'I've a couple of things I have to write up, one is notes for new Gurkha NCO Border Scout Section Leaders and the other is to work out a training syllabus for the potential Border

Scouts NCOs.'

They said their farewells and left. His typist did not go but waited till they had shut the door.

'Aren't you going home?' Jason asked her.

She came over to him and stood behind his chair. She leant forward and, breathing into his ear, said, 'Popov, Popov, Mi kham klaw wa khon haw.'

Jason turned towards her. 'Lan mai mi wan chan.'

She gave a shrill squeak of delight and nuzzled his ear. 'Now we are on the same side I can tell you that I fell in love with you the first day I saw you. I thought you were a colonial enemy but I have learnt that I thought wrong' and she kissed him on the cheek.

In for a penny in for a pound and Jason turned round and answered in kind on the mouth. After breaking off he said, 'Missee, we must be careful in the office. That's enough.' The office is most certainly not the best place to decide on the best of three pin-falls!

'Popov, I can now tell you all. Last night I went to the SUPP and asked my handler – oh, yes, I'm a plant here, a "sleeper" but it's what happens before we sleep that matters,' and she giggled lecherously. 'I told him I had learnt how you were working deep undercover, what my informant called a maang dim ...'

'A what?'

'Oh, sorry, of course you don't speak Chinese. Maang dim is a Chinese phrase that means 'blind spot'. This is our Operation Blind Spot against the imperialists.'

'Oh, thank you for telling me. You must be extra, extra, extra careful Missee Jiang Yun now that you know my ultra-tight secret. If one tiny little bit were ever to get out, the rest of my life will be in a British jail and we won't be able to do anything together.'

'Oh Popov, that would be too bad, wouldn't it? No, my handler wants to meet you and have a plenum to work out the best way to carry out our work.'

Not so fast, not so fast. 'Missee, that is something I don't like. There are far too many people in a plenum. People gossip. People talk too much. I am only alive today because of the strictest secrecy. I will meet only your handler and your Secretary General to begin with. Of course you can be there too, if they agree. That will be four of us. Easy to hide from prying eyes. Do you know when the Secretary General will be ready for a meeting?'

'I don't know, Popov. I only talk with the handler, not to anyone else. In fact I doubt I'd be allowed to be in any meeting you attend.'

'You'll either have to take me to a meeting place or so describe your handler so that I can recognise him without any difficulty.'

She pondered on that. 'Yes, Popov that makes sense. If I have to approach you secretly, how best can I do it?'

Jason thought of his bungalow. 'Look. It's still light. Let me work till it's dark and I'll take you and show you where.'

She looked at her watch. 'It's only a quarter past five now.'

'Leave me. Meet me at the corner of Badrudin Road at 6.30.'

They met up as agreed and, using the entrance at the back, he took her to his room and, after delicious foreplay, laid her. The frustrations and fear of the last few months had to have an outlet – and what more convenient and auspicious inlet? She turned out to be mysteriously graceful and endowed with a blend of delicate sensitivity and passionate abandon.

Neither staff officer seemed to notice the expectant flush on the typist's cheeks when they got to the office the next morning. She brought Jason the mail and the accompanying files with the earlier correspondence. 'Sir, this one is important,' she said quietly as she put the bundle on his desk. He opened it and there was a note: 'Tomorrow Saturday evening seven o'clock outside the Fata Hotel.'

He knew the hotel; it was on one of the busier streets. He initialed it and put it back in the file.

At 7 p.m. next day Jason sauntered past the entrance of the Fata Hotel. A man, wearing flip-flops lighting a cigarette whispered 'Sinsaang daang yat tsan' – Sir, wait a moment. Reflexes duck's-arse tight, Jason walked on without giving the whisperer a glance. Bastards are checking on me, he thought, I'll walk to the next corner and come back. If it's the same again I'll go back to my bungalow.

It was about a quarter past seven when he approached the hotel door. The same man was there and just as Jason was about to pass him he edged close to Jason and whispered the same thing, 'Sir, wait a moment,' in Cantonese. Jason, skilfully as though by accident, firmly trod on his foot. The man yelped and jumped back, nursing a bruised foot. Jason turned. In perfect Malay, 'Oh, I am so sorry if I have hurt you. Quite unintentional, I assure you. You came so close to me I had no time to get out of your way,' he dissembled as he moved off.

He had some letters to write so was happy enough to get back early to his quarter.

On Monday morning he was in the office early. 'I did not see anyone outside the Fata Hotel at the appointed time,' he said, 'except an unfortunate who spoke to me in Chinese, which I don't understand and, sadly, I managed to tread on his foot. I hope I didn't give him more than a slight bruise.'

'Popov,' she said, there was still no one in the office. 'He was my handler and made a mistake in talking to you in Chinese. He told me to tell you next Saturday,' and she gave him the rest of the message. She had met him on the Sunday and he had told her that he had indeed spoken to the new Border Scout boss in Chinese and, correct, he had not understood. 'I'll apologise when we meet,' he had said. 'Make it next Saturday, same place, same time, different language. It'll take me at least a week before I can walk without limping.'

Jason nodded. 'That wasn't very clever was it? I wonder what gave him that idea. Right you are: tell him I agree to meeting him next Saturday same place, same time, but to introduce himself by saying "Mi kham klaw wa khon haw"' and only to carry on if the answer is "Lan mai mi wan chan".'

The other staff officers came into the office. 'Sir, I understand,' she said demurely.

Round one to me, Jason smiled to himself.

Jason, nursing a cup of tea, sat on the flat roof of his quarter watching the sun go down, thinking about his impending meeting with his typist's handler. He looked at the sky, happy not to be surrounded by dense trees, and, as the sun went down, admired the colours change from madder red to indigo blue, to shellfish purple and finally black. A myriad stars shone, twinklingly bright. Such beauty we never saw when in the jungle: would that the next part of the evening be as clear, he thought as he went to change into a bush shirt and grey slacks. In his pocket he put a piece of paper on which he had written a grid reference where he hoped to meet an officer from the Indonesian Army over the border. Not only had he spied out the country when on a normal Border Scout visit and felt it could come in useful but had looked at an aerial photograph of the area. He had seen a small area of jungle that had a faint track leading up to it. It looked like a one-time logging area. The vicinity around it was without any habitation. The RV was where the track entered the jungle: hard to miss! Tonight? Why not? Underneath his shirt he tied a pistol he had borrowed from the Gurkha Para Company earlier on in the day. He knew the OC and, having signed for the weapon and six rounds, promised to bring it back on the morrow. Now he looked at his watch, time to go, and moved off. He saw a man standing in front of the Fata Hotel, his limp, flaccid skin looking like a worn-out dishcloth. What's he like in the light? I wonder.

A couple of yards away from the man Jason bent down to tie up one of his 'loose' shoelaces. The man moved over and quietly said 'Mi kham klaw wa khon haw'. Jason stood up, looked the man straight between the eyes and answered 'Lan mai mi wan chan.'

They shook hands. 'I am Jiang Yun's handler. You trod on my foot last week. Was it intentional?' the man asked in passable

English, laughing mirthlessly, like the croaking of a thirsty vulture.

Jason answered, in Malay, 'I am Popov. Was it you? If so your po vsem pravilam iskusstva need to be ever vigilant.'

'I don't understand that. What language is it?'

'Russian and it means "the rules of the art"; in English, "trade craft".' I won't be Popov for nothing!

'We must talk,' said the man who had not introduced himself. Jason thought he looked chastened.

'Where?'

'Not far from here. I have arranged that you and our SUPP Secretary General meet one another. Follow on behind me by about fifty yards. It's not far,' and so saying he led the way towards a poorer part of the town. Jason followed him and later caught sight of the name of the road into which his guide had circuitously taken him, Jalan Tan Sri Ong Kee. He had already found out that was the SUPP office's address. The guide jinked down a small gully and, making sure Jason could see him, beckoned him to catch up.

'We will enter our office from the back. We are expected,' he said, going to the back door and rapping on it with three short, three long and three short raps.

After an eye appeared at the Judas window the door was opened. The two men entered and went upstairs. The guide-cum-handler knocked on a door and, on a gruff command, they went inside where an elderly Chinese man, unusual in that his eyes were like extinct craters, grey, inaccessible and hard as volcanic rock, was seated on an upright chair. He looked gnarled and desiccated, reminding the new police officer, who had expected someone younger and more vibrant-looking, of a garden gnome. Pity he's not in a circus as a crowd-drawing sideshow. He'd make a fortune! Jason deliberately kept his eyes from all Chinese characters he saw on charts, maps and propaganda material.

'This is Popov, we have established our identities with that foolish Thai password and counter-sign,' the handler said in Chinese.

Foolish?

'Does he speak Chinese? He looks the type of Soviet operator who despises anyone not of his colour.' The voice was like gravel on a chalkboard, the result of throat cancer surgery which had left him with a profoundly unnerving intonation and a repulsive neck scar to match. An eel of unease squirmed in Jason's bowel: it's going to be harder than I thought, but he hid any expression of disquiet that might have come over his face by pretending to stifle a yawn. Trying to bait me or for real? Bloody man!

'No, but you try him out suddenly. I did but he didn't answer.' The handler turned to Jason and said, in Malay, 'This is Mr Sim Ting Ong, Secretary General of the Sarawak United People's Party.'

Jason moved over and proffered his hand. 'Please call me Popov while we are doing business.'

'Sit down,' said Mr Sim. Then, to the handler whose name Jason still had not found out, 'Go and get some beer,' in Chinese and without breaking his speech rhythm, Mr Sim asked Jason, 'Or would you prefer brandy?' still in Chinese.

Jason smiled back and in Malay said, 'Tuan, the only Chinese I know is "yam sing".'

Mr Sim did not look at all abashed at his 'mistake'. 'I was asking you if you preferred brandy.'

'No, thank you. A glass of beer will do fine.'

As they drank, having toasted each other unusually decorously, the conversation turned to how Popov could help the SUPP cause. Jason said that his disguised job did not enable him to help SUPP directly but what he felt he could do was somehow to keep the Commonwealth and Gurkha troops away from any Indonesian incursions so they could be even more successful.'

'What our friends over the border want to know is not only the military intentions of the British but also if you can manage to keep them away from any foreknowledge they might have of intended incursions.'

'I can only do that if I myself know what and when those intentions are,' he countered.

'Yes, you need to know a lot' and without a break said '*Yan saang yau ngai, kok mo chi king.*'

Jason looked at Mr Sim, showing mild exasperation. 'Tuan, please believe me when I tell you that you are wasting your breath in talking Chinese at me as I would be wasting mine by talking in Russian to you,' although he had fully understood Sim to have said 'Man's life is limited; learning is unbounded.' 'Why don't you believe me?' and, feigning grave displeasure, stood up as if to leave there and then.

That did disconcert the Secretary General whose grey and inaccessible eyes half closed as he pursed his lips. Again, in Chinese, he said to the handler, 'He seems genuine. I'll tell him why I spoke to him in our language.' Turning to Jason he said,

'Tuan Popov, I owe you an apology. It seems that two people in Indonesia, Lieutenants Soetidjab Alaydris and Hassan Soekadis, as well as a Lieutenant Sumbi, were highly suspicious of your being able to, so, when told about the mysterious third uncle's call to his fifth niece, he had to make sure.'

'I beg your pardon, what was that you said? Third uncle's call to his fifth niece? You've lost me,' Jason hedged, greatly relieved at being thought not to be a Chinese speaker but inwardly linking Mr Sim's explanation with the two men mentioned in the warning Mr C C Too had put in his message that time when in the C-in-C's office. *I have to be so careful eggs won't break if I tread on them*, he thought.

Mr Sim looked nonplussed. 'You haven't heard? Our sleeper's third uncle telephoned her from Brunei and told her that he'd come across from Thailand to help us out and gave her the message that you were who you actually are, only disguised as Superintendent Jason Rance. You are to be congratulated in fooling the British Army for so long.'

'Learning that makes me happy. Thank you. But, Tuan, being mistaken for being Jason Rance has happened before. Who my *doppelganger*, sorry, my look-alike, is I have no idea but there is someone somewhere who has a strong resemblance to me. I will have to admit that my handler, now in Moscow, has been of immense use to me all my service and went to great pains to influence my appointment here. Now, let's leave that and get back to business. Can you put me into direct contact with someone knowledgeable and of sufficiently high rank to know about future plans in the Indonesian military, preferably on or just over the border, who I can meet with in perfect safety on his side of it, to work out relevant details? I can imagine somewhere between Serikin and Siluas.' They were two villages not far from each other, the Sarawak one being in the First Division. 'I have already been there on Border Scout business,' chuckling as he said it, 'and about a quarter to half a mile to the northeast of the track where it meets the border is a clump of thick jungle ideal for a talk. I've even made a note of the grid reference. Here it is,' and he slid the piece of paper with it on over to Mr Sim. 'I'd pretend to be escorted as far as the border and, unnoticed, slip across by myself. The person I meet can keep his escort to the south of the jungly clump so that what we talk about will be in the strictest privacy. I'd rather talk there than, say, in Keik to the northwest or farther east.'

'Mr Popov. It will take a week or even longer to arrange such an unusual visit but fix a meeting up I will most certainly try. Whether whoever comes to talk to you will agree with where you have chosen is something I cannot say. If he suggests somewhere different I'll let you know when we next meet.'

'I have another point, Mr Sim. Apart from the military side of affairs, I want to talk to any anti-Malaysia, pro-Maphilindo person. I have been around the Chinese part of most of the major towns …'

'… yes, we have been told about it. We wondered what you were trying to do,' the Secretary General interrupted.

'I was trying to find someone who'd pick me up and lead me to the senior SUPP representative but I was unsuccessful,' Jason explained.

'I can help you, Tuan Popov, there. I'll get a list made out and give it to your sleeper's handler for passing on to you.'

Jason smiled his gratitude. 'Oh thank you, Mr Sim. That will save me much time and means that I don't arouse any suspicion.'

After another glass of beer the meeting broke up and Jason went back to his quarter. He had a lot to think about.

Although the next day was a Sunday, he went round to the Gurkha Para Company lines to give his pistol and the six rounds back. 'I want the best two men you have in "shadowing" to help me out not so far in the future.'

'Why so?' the OC asked.

'Only between me and you – and the "shadowers" nearer the time – I'm planning to make a solo visit over the border to meet one of the Indon opposition.'

'Rather you than me! You really mean it?'

'Yes, but please, please tell no one else.'

'Don't worry. I know how to keep my mouth shut. Will DOBOPS allow it?

'He can't stop me, I'm a policeman.'

'Will the Chief of Police allow you?'

'I can't say as he won't know!'

A day after the meeting in the SUPP office, Colonel Sodimedjo of Command XII was called to the radio. A gravelly voice said that contact had been made with Popov who wanted a face-to-face meeting with someone of sufficient seniority to be able to discuss matters of tactical importance in enough detail to influence operations. 'The suggested meeting place is on the northern side of a certain area of jungle between Serikin and Siluas just over the border on the Indonesian side, at a specified grid reference. Only he and one of you are to meet. He'll be dressed in civilian clothes and will approach from a place where no police in Serikin can see him. I told him it would take a week or so to arrange. What are your reactions?'

The Colonel looked at a map on the wall. *On the face of it it seems safe enough.* 'I will have to take this up to the highest level before being able to give a definite answer. I will give you a call as soon as I can. If Popov asks before then tell him what I have told you and that I like what he suggests.'

The call over, Colonel Sodimedjo went back to his office, sat down at his desk and almost fell into a reverie, so deep were his thoughts. After a while he told the office runner to call Lieutenant Sumbi and his two subordinates for a meeting. Protocol forbade him to use their nicknames. They would be of the greatest use.

Jason did not like the idea of his 'Popov' gambit coming adrift because of fears of his Chinese-knowledge background overriding it. *I'll have to make a couple of phone calls*, he decided and well before any clearance of an Indonesian visit came through he made them from outside Kuching. His first was to SUPP's main office. A gravelly voice answered. In Chinese he asked for Mr Sim. The phone was handed over to him and Jason announced himself as 'Your sleeper's third uncle. I have come to know that you are doubting Mr Popov's lack of Chinese knowledge. Why?'

'Because of what I have heard from elsewhere.'

'You realise, don't you, the incredible strains he is working under already? By your doubting him you are putting him under more and you are hindering our work. Unless you want a serious negative reaction, you must change your approach.'

'Did Mr Popov tell you himself?'

'No, of course not. I have other sources. Beware,' and Jason put the phone down.

Later that day he rang Jiang Yun at her home. She answered the phone. 'Fifth niece, this is your third uncle calling you,' he began using his sternest voice. 'Your efforts at convincing your handler that Mr Popov is not a Chinese speaker are not good enough. SUPP are being told by people over the border that he is under suspicion of being a Chinese speaker. I am seriously alarmed with your negligence. Be warned, seriously warned and put matters right.'

She answered breathlessly. 'Third Uncle. I am worried by your words. Did Mr Popov contact you himself? He made no mention of doing to me.'

She heard a smirk. 'He was probably too busy ramming you and you too busy enjoying it. He doesn't know where I am so how could he have told me? Tell your handler to be more vigilant otherwise he will suffer for his indolence,' and once more the line was cut and Jiang Yun was left looking dismally at the earpiece in her hand.

The meeting between Jason and an Indonesian Army officer took three weeks to arrange. The protocols were that they would meet at the given grid reference and that Colonel Sodimedjo himself would meet Popov, there would be no Indonesian troops in the area and that his personal escort would be clear of it by 1000 hours after which time it would wait in the open ground to the north. Popov would be as near to ten o'clock as he could be, approaching the specified area from the north, by himself, in plain clothes and unarmed. The Colonel would be able to see him coming.

It was time to bring General Sprinter up to date with how matters were proceeding and it so happened that he was due in Kuching on a routine visit. Jason was sent a message telling him to meet him in the office of the Brigadier commanding West Brigade. Jason was relieved that he did not have to go to Brunei once more – too many times might just be noticed as 'suspicious' – and mail timings were not reliable.

Once there, the General said, 'Rance, I want to hear how successful you have been so far in deflecting the negative effect of those dratted leaflets and I want to include the Brigadier in your plans on what you have been able to do so far . Have you any reason for my not briefing Head of Special Branch?'

'Sir, the fewer people who know what's happening, the better. I wouldn't trust a laundry list to the police switchboard. I have already spoken to him about my "sleeper" and, yes, he ought to be brought up to date. But please do not mention this to any uniformed police officer as their security is virtually non-existent.'

That was completely understood and the Brigadier told his Brigade Major to ask Head of Special Branch, Mr Don Rutherford whose office was quite near, please to step over and apologise for no previous warning.

He knocked on the Brigadier's door and entered the office in less than ten minutes.

'Mr Rutherford, sit you down please. I hope you won't think I'm wasting your time in what I want you to listen to. I fancy it will interest you more than normal.'

The four Britons accepted each other because they belonged to the same nameless and exclusive club. Any member of this club could, by some subtle social alchemy, always recognise a fellow member at a glance.

Head of Special Branch looked at Superintendent Rance. *Yes, a deep thinker*, remembering the question about the Border Scout's typist. 'I'm all ears, General.'

The General began with, 'Listen to me first and Rance will let us know what has happened since then afterwards.'

Both the Head of Special Branch and the Brigadier's face were a picture of disbelief and incredulity as the story unfolded. 'What has happened since my briefing in Brunei?' asked the General at the end of his briefing.

'Sir, quite a lot and I was not wrong in my prognosis about my typist being a plant, a sleeper ...' and Jason brought them up to date.

'Hardly credible,' said the General.

'Scarcely true,' added the Brigadier in a hushed tone of voice.

'Saddens me but doesn't surprise me all that much,' was Don Rutherford's knowledgeable comment.

Jason looked on while his narrative was being digested.

'So what do you plan to do now?' asked Brigadier Townsend.

'Yes,' said DOBOPS, 'you can't very well stop and do nothing.'

'My plan is to go over the border, solo, as Popov and meet Colonel Sodimedjo, the Intelligence Colonel of Military District XII. What I need is for the Brigadier to please suspend any planned or on-going operations in that area for a couple of days before I go and while I'm there.'

A hush descended over the small gathering, each toiling in his mind the appallingly complicated political shenanigans that would ensue if this were found out about and even worse if anything untoward were to happen to the Commandant of the Border Scouts.

All three listeners tried to speak at once. They all stopped at the same time. DOBOPS broke the silence. 'I forbid it, flatly. The politics of this are at prime-minister level, two Prime Ministers, one of UK and the other of Malaya. I don't have the authority to allow you to go even if I felt I'd like to.' He cleared his throat and swallowed, 'which I don't,' he added belatedly.

'Jason,' the Brigadier asked anxiously. 'You're not out of your mind, are you? Is there no other way you can carry out your plan of meeting Colonel Sodimedjo? Can't you meet him on the border?'

Before he could answer, Don Rutherford interjected: 'It's a chance in a million. Let's discuss it in detail before we condemn it entirely.'

'Back to you, Rance,' said DOBOPS.

'Gentlemen, I have thought a lot about this. The meetings I have had with the sleeper's handler and with the SUPP Secretary General have given them enough of my supposed background to trust me as Popov and clever enough to have hoodwinked the

British Army as to my true credentials all my service, all with my Moscow handler directing me. That they are so naïve is because they themselves are ultra devious so they accept my nonsense, believe it or not.'

From the look on Jason's audience's faces it did seem that, yes, everybody sensible knew just how devious those people were.

'I have to tell you that initially they, the SUPP and the Indon army, were suspicious that I was hiding my Chinese language ability. They tried to trap me but failed. In the end I said I'd walk out on them if they kept on prevaricating. I doubt very much that I'll be able to run this for any length of time but at least I might be able to give you some planning data that will be of use, not only militarily but also relevant details of who in the SUPP are wanting or not wanting Malaysia that Special Branch might yet not know.'

Inwardly the three British officers were full of praise for Jason's obvious courage but outwardly felt he was overly optimistic about it. 'It's not a case of trying to dissuade you, it is totally unacceptable that you carry out your plan as presented,' said General Sprinter.

'Sir, I'd never be able to live with myself if I didn't carry out such an undertaking just the once and, as you may know about my next appointment, as OC of the Gurkha Paras, I'll be glad to have exact details of a good target,' and he smiled encouragingly at the others. *Got it!* 'May I offer you a promise if you don't ask me how I'll keep it?'

Three heads nodded, three mouths pursed, three minds churned.

'I promise you that neither Superintendent nor Lieutenant

Colonel Jason Rance will cross the border. Leave it to me how I actually make contact with Colonel Sodimedjo.'

'What the eye does not see ...' said Head of Special Branch. 'I have enough confidence in our Border Scouts' leader to approve his plan. I can arrange that any dealings I have on or near the border will be suspended. I'm sure the Brigadier can manage military matters likewise.'

Reluctantly the two army officers agreed with Don Rutherford. DOBOPS gave a final warning: 'If there's any backlash, Rance, you'll have to be on your own.'

'Sir, I accept that fully. You could not have said otherwise.' Jason stood up and said, 'I'll be off now if you've nothing else for me,' saluted and departed. Outside he told his driver to drive him to the Gurkha Para Company. *I'll have to sound convincingly truthful*, he thought to himself entering the OC's office. 'You look as though you want something from me,' the OC said. 'Confirmation of your last visit?'

'Yes, it is. I want somebody, two bodies in fact, rather than something, yes,' Jason answered. 'Who have you got I can borrow for a short-term but top-secret operation, preferably from my old company, and, if possible, from any of my special squad that helped me rescue those two wartime men from Thailand?'

The OC called the Sergeant Major in from the outer office and asked the same question. He knew without having to check his nominal roll, 'Sahib, Sergeant Kulbahadur Limbu and Rifleman Hemraj Rai are in the company and are on a few days' leave.'

Now that is propitious and a good omen.

'Thank you Major-ba, I'll let you know details after the

Colonel sahib has fully briefed me.' The Sergeant Major saluted smartly and went back to his own office.

'It's like this …' began Jason, and went on to say that he was to go up to the border to meet someone from the Indonesian Army and that he'd like those two men to be his escort-cum-gunmen before the meeting. 'It's higher than top secret in fact and it's only for fewer than twenty-four hours.'

The OC nodded as he smiled. 'Jason, you're up to your old tricks. I'll lend those two men for that period of time for "training purposes only".'

'Done – and mega thanks. "Training in shadowing civilians without being found out." Please, please tell no one about it. I have just come from meeting DOBOPS, Commander West Brigade and Head of Special Branch. You are only the fourth person to know what I'm planning.'

'Jason, don't worry. Mum's the word.'

'Thank you. Tell them to bring pistols, six rounds each, light kit, haversack rations, canvas shoes and camouflage veils.' He gave some money to the OC. 'There's enough here for two torches for my two men. Can you arrange for them to buy one each? I'll fix up farmer-type clothes in the bazaar.'

'For disguise purposes?'

'Disguise and safety.'

The afternoon before the meeting with the Indonesian Colonel, Jason found the note he had been given in Keik. He decided to take it with him. He dressed, packing two sets of plain clothes, also remembering to take with him a small pocket compass and a knife. *Shall I take a razor?* he debated. *Yes, I'll need to look fresh as though I have just come from over the border. The whole world seems to know the British fetish on officers shaving,* so he put it in his pack. In his Border Scout Land Rover he drove over to the Gurkha Para Company lines to collect Kulbahadur and Hemraj. 'All ready?'

Yes, they were.

'In you get.'

They got in and Jason told the driver to go to the market. 'I want you to look for and each buy a set of clothes that any farmer would normally wear. Here's the money,' and he handed some over. Like his two men were, Jason was also dressed in jungle green and had two sets of nondescript civilian clothes in his haversack.

While they were searching for their clothes, Jason went and bought two thermoses which he filled with tea and bought some potato-filled *parathas* from an Indian food stall. *We'll need something to keep the wolf from the door.*

Clothes and food in their packs, they drove off to Serikin where Jason dismissed the driver, telling him that he and the two men were on a training exercise – 'tracking locals in bushy country without them knowing they were being followed' – and to come back at 1 p.m. the next day and wait if no one had turned up already. The driver left for Kuching and Jason took his two men to a Chinese eating shop where he ordered a meal, which they ate in a cubicle to themselves. After it, in a low voice, Jason told them that he was secretly meeting a Colonel from the Indonesian Army in some jungle over the border: 'Here is our intended RV on my map and only if you feel you can come with me, I want us three to search the area from dawn to finish by 0930 hours. I don't expect anyone to be there even though I have been told that the area will be clear of soldiers but trusting the Indons is foolish.'

'Sahib, of course we'll go with you. We always have and always will. This will be nothing compared what we did up on the Thai border.'

That was the sign of true regimental camaraderie, not the bemedalled rituals of a battalion march past.

Kulbahadur asked, 'Why do you drive yourself so hard, Sahib. The other sahibs we have don't.'

Jason's answer was not what either Gurkha expected. 'One's dead for such a long time so it's better to burn out than rust out. Now, just in case there is someone and we have to immobilize him – or even them – let me remind you of what I taught you when we were with Senagit before moving north up the Sungei Perak,' and in simple terms with slow-motion demonstrations he showed them how to stiffen their fingers and jab just inside the lower edge of the jaw if the other method was not possible. This was an elbow to the heart followed by a side of the hand to the upper lip where the nose cartilage joins the top half of the jaw. Unseen by the hotel staff the two soldiers went through the motions on each other.

Before nightfall they had found a place they could recognise in a hurry, where they could hide their packs and could make out the best way to reach the jungle edge without bumping into any hazard. The countryside was not cultivated but overgrown with clumps of trees and bushes and some open spaces where cattle could graze. The crickets in the surrounds began their shrill chorus and frogs in a nearby pool harrumphed their welcome to the dusk. They had a scratch meal from Jason's pack and made themselves as comfortable as possible till in the small hours when they changed into civilian clothes and carefully hid the packs before crossing the border. It was the same strange feeling, almost of being undressed, that again overtook Jason as he moved into Indonesia, as it had done that time he had crossed into Thailand – but this time no back up, no rescue if anything went wrong, no redress for adverse contingences. Jason thought back to his training of so many years ago: *never make a promise you can't keep; never break a promise once made.* It wasn't quite the same but it was the epitome of mutual trustworthiness. He said nothing because there was already an unspoken and unbreakable bond. Luckily there was a full moon so their move forward was not difficult. They were in the northern corner of the jungly area, the one nearest British Borneo, before dawn where they lay up till they could see properly. Each man defecated and hid the result before moving round the edge of the jungle towards the south, keeping well hidden and leaving hardly any tracks at all. There were no recent signs of anyone. At half past eight they heard a vehicle approaching. They moved to the edge of the trees and saw a middle-aged man and two younger men, all in uniform, get out. The older man's shoulder bars were just visible, three golden blobs, a Colonel. *So he's come!* He gesticulated towards the jungle, looked at his watch, said something and got back into the vehicle. The two younger men saluted the vehicle as the other man drove off and moved towards the jungle, to a flank from Jason and his two men.

'Listen,' Jason said quietly. 'This is what I feared. It is bad news. We'll shadow them and when I give the sign I'll call to them like I did that time in Ha La, throwing my voice to a flank. You'll be out of sight, so will I. As they turn round to see who is calling them and move towards my voice, your job is to overpower them make them lose consciousness, if possible without them seeing you. I'll tell you what to do with the bodies after you've done it.'

'*Hunchha Hajur*, no problem.'

As the two Indonesians were not expecting anyone they moved noisily and carelessly, talking to each other. It was all a bit of a lark and rather exciting. They were easy to follow. Jason saw that both wore the Indonesian Army rank badges of lieutenant, two golden shoulder bars. They came across some swampy ground just after a particularly bosky part and Jason signalled to his men: hide! He himself stood behind a thick bush and called out to them in Malay, imitating a young girl in a shrill and believable falsetto, making them look away from where he was. 'Oh, come you here. I want one of you to do me. I didn't get any last night.'

Both men abruptly stopped in their tracks, looking almost like wax-work models.

The voice continued, smirkingly, 'Both can have me but the one with the bigger member to come first. I won't ask you to show me first for me to judge.'

The two men, bewilderment on each face yet 'hungry for it', turned but saw no one.

'Alif, can you see anyone?' As Zai asked his question he leant over – *has be seen me?* Jason wondered – and pulled a leaf from a bush – *No!* – and bent it in two, then picked one up from the ground and did the same. *Strange habit,* thought Jason ... then it hit him: *he's doing just the same as that renegade did ten years ago in Operation Janus. Uncanny!*

'Zai, no one at all.' He looked around. 'Where are you?' he called out. 'Can't see you. Come out and let us see you. Who will have you first? There are two of us.'

'Folded leaf, straight prick,' and the voice tittered before Jason changed direction and said 'the good little girl asked the bad little girl is it hard to be good and the bad little girl said "it's got to be hard to be good".' Jason's Malay version meant many fewer words than the English rendition.

Both men again looked around then blindly surged. Kulbahadur and Hemraj jumped on them from either flank and silently made both of them unconscious. They slumped to the ground, one hitting his head on a stone. Jason looked at him and saw he had an ugly scar that ran from the top of his left ear to the corner of his mouth. *Easy to recognise again, that one.*

'Good work. Here's my knife. Cut some vines, bind them tight. How long do you think they'll be unconscious for?'

'Sahib, we hit them like you taught us. Minimum a couple of hours, possibly longer.'

'Then cut a bit off their shirts and gag them but not all that tightly.' They also removed their shoulder rank badges. 'You can keep a pair each as souvenirs. I'll look in their pockets for any identity cards.' He found them: the one with the scar on his face was Hassan Soekadis and the other Soetidjab Alaydris. He put them in his own pocket and quickly wrote two one-word notes, one for each of them, in Malay: Shame. *One more thing before we go*, he thought, remembering the note he'd put in his trouser pocket. *I'll leave it here* and dropped it by the bodies.

On their way back Jason said, 'You saw the one with the scar face pick up leaves and fold them?'

'Yes, Sahib, we did,' both answered.

'Who did it remind you of?'

As one man, 'the officer who was not a sahib who we tracked that way ten years ago,' they both said.

'Yes, it struck me also. Uncanny that two people act like that.'

There was a sudden rainstorm. 'Fine by us,' Jason observed. 'It will wash out any tracks we didn't cover properly in the jungle and now keep any prying eyes from seeing us.'

They reached their packs, finished off what was left of the rations and, the Gurkhas once more in uniform, Jason said 'Go to Serikin and wait for me. I doubt I'll be all that long.' Off they went and by nine o'clock they were back at their border crossing, again unseen by anyone. Meanwhile Jason took his clean civil clothes out of his pack and put them on. Thankfully they were dry. Neatly shaved from using the water in his water bottle, he made his way towards the path that led from Serikin south before moving off it towards the jungle and the RV, keeping a sharp lookout lest anyone see him, Europeans wandering about by themselves never being the flavour of any month, but saw nobody. The Indonesian Colonel emerged. Jason waved at him and he waved back, smiling broadly. *If he's worried about not meeting up with his two men, he's not showing it.*

'Colonel Sodimedjo, I am Popov and am delighted to see you,' Jason said in Malay which he felt would be easily understood, probably much more easily than English.

'Yes, Tuan Popov, I am Colonel Sodimedjo,' and the two men shook hands, the Colonel noticing that Jason had shaved. *Yes, he has just come from the other side.* 'We must talk in detail and cover all aspects because a visit like this is not easy for me to arrange nor easy for you, I expect.' The Colonel's Malay was only slightly accented so easy to understand.

'I agree with you. Let's get it over quickly. I have a time-limit only that people don't get worried at my disappearing. Where shall we talk?'

'Here! Let's sit on that log.'

Both men sat down. 'I see you are unescorted, Tuan Popov. That is brave of you.'

'No, Colonel. Sensible. I feel perfectly safe as I am sure you do.'

I'd feel safer if I had seen my two men before coming back in the vehicle. 'So do I. What shall we discuss?'

'Colonel. You know my background. I have managed to hoodwink the British Army for many, many years but there is always a danger of being found out. Sadly my plan of letting you know that I wanted to make contact with you, by arranging that a radio broadcast of my arrival, in my English name, bolstered by those leaflets, worked against me. Whoever it was, and I am not blaming him or them, didn't take the hint and each time I felt I could make contact at the border villages, your men had copies of my photograph leaflet and wanted to eliminate me.' He paused and let that sink in.

'Yes, I am sorry for that. It was so unexpected, you see. Such a situation had never happened before so we were not expecting it. What do you propose to eliminate that worry?'

'First of all, you need information, which initially I will get passed to you through the SUPP radio link, of where I'll be on the border. I say initially because quite soon I will have my own private radio link for all Border Scout sections in the five divisions as well as my own set which I can use surreptitiously to you on a one-to-one basis once I have your wave length details and call-signs. You'll allot me mine now, please, it will be quicker and safer that way. If you can't remember your wave length, I'll get it from HQ SUPP once you have told them to let me have it. I will also pass on as many details as possible of British and Commonwealth forces' numbers, dispositions and movements.' Jason then took an imaginative leap, 'I am only forecasting, but if they cross the border in retaliatory raids, to try and let you know all about them.'

Jason could see that what he said about impending cross-border raids had startled the Colonel. 'Tuan Popov, are you sure of our enemy's cross-border activities?'

'Yes, but I don't know when they will start, of what conditions will be laid down, that is to say how far penetration will be allowed, or how long they will last. For instance, will there be aerial bombing as well as artillery fire over the border, especially in retaliation to any cruelty to Border Scouts, villagers or captured troops? Will sanctions be levied against your country? I am not near enough the top planners to know but, and here I can be of help, my Border Scouts – who, you will be glad to hear, are not nearly as efficient as the British and Malay senior officers believe – will have to know when cross-border troops move through their area. Once I have managed to get radios to each Scout section and told you the wave lengths to listen in to, you should have a good idea of what is likely to happen.'

The Intelligence Colonel obviously liked what he had heard. 'That is better than I had expected, Tuan Popov. I can say, here and now, that I will ask Major General Mulia, Commanding Military District XII, as I am sure you already know, to issue orders both for his area of responsibility, which does not cover Sarawak's Fourth and Fifth Divisions nor anywhere in British North Borneo, and will also get him to tell Military District VI over in the east at Balikpapan which does look after the eastern part of British Borneo, to act likewise. Consider it done, Tuan Popov,' and Colonel Sodimedjo beamed expansively. 'I know my radio details off by heart. I'll make a note of call signs and frequencies,' and he rummaged in his pocket for a pen and a piece of paper. He wrote out all the details and gave them to Rance.

'Tuan Colonel, I must shake your hand for that. I feel that a great weight has been taken off my back. I have only one other request and that is, if at all possible, can you tell your link in the SUPP HQ in Kuching or me once we're on net where you are considering to attack? I can then, I think, get the enemy security forces away from that area and, myself, keep away from it.'

'That is more difficult but try I will. You know, don't you, that the SUPP keeps close tabs on the Clandestine Communist Organisation, but you only need to deal with the SUPP. Now, I'll tell you what we are planning to do. We want as many troops to be brought to Borneo from Malaya so that, once the force level on the mainland is low, we make a successful parachute assault somewhere in the south of the country, probably in the Johor area but that's yet to be fixed. Likewise we also plan several attacks, the main one being by what we are calling the "Kelabang Team", commanded by Lieutenant Sumbi and maybe up to fifty men, through Sarawak, into Brunei, to sabotage the oil storage tanks – the wells are out at sea – radio stations, try and gather volunteers and setting up bases for training against Brunei once more after the British have left. That means we will concentrate our incursions to the west of the country so that enemy troops are fewer on the ground in the east.'

'That is a good programme, Tuan Colonel, and deserves to be fruitful. You can trust me to back you up in as many ways as I can.'

'I'm so glad we've made contact.' The Colonel looked at his wristwatch. 'Time I started on my way back. It has been a most pleasant, useful and constructive meeting, Tuan Popov and we now have a good mode of identity. I think it will be too difficult to arrange another one but, with radio contact, it won't matter so much. It is indeed a pity that there are not more people like you we can rely on.'

Both men stood up and shook hands. 'Goodbye, Colonel. Thank you for your time. You are a busy man and I appreciate what you are doing for me. So too will my handler in Moscow.'

'Yes, I'd forgotten that there must be someone way back there. *Salamat jalan*, Tuan Popov.'

'*Salamat jalan*, Tuan Colonel Sodimedjo,' Jason answered the Colonel's "Goodbye", turned and left.

Colonel Sodimedjo went back to his vehicle, feeling pleased at what he had managed to fix up but fuming about not having met up with his two officers. He had especially sent them into the jungle area early both to ensure that there was no hanky-panky by using Popov as a front – one can never be too careful – and also to see if they could recognise him as being the man they saw in that strangely named place Ha La. The Secretary General of SUPP had mentioned that Tuan Popov had mentioned a 'look alike' but eyeball-to-eyeball contact was of the essence.

The Colonel was not as fit as he might have been, his work being mainly sedentary, and was sweatily tired when he got back to his vehicle. Only the driver was there, no one else. 'Where are the other two?' he was asked. 'Tuan Colonel, I have not seen them.' The Colonel cursed. The driver had cooked a meal, four meals in fact, one for himself as well as for the other three. 'Get my food ready,' Sodimedjo ordered, getting into the vehicle, wiping his brow. He looked at his watch. *I'll wait till noon and, if no one turns up, go to the nearest unit and see if they have gone there, somehow. If not, I'll order a search party.*

The driver brought him his meal and had his own. As he was eating it there was a tropical downpour.

At ten to noon the Colonel looked up and saw his two men wearily coming his way, soaking wet and ... without their badges of rank. *Scandalous!* The way they moved looked as if they had hurt themselves, one had a bump on his forehead, both had swollen lips. He let them come up to him, let them salute him and then gave them the biggest rocket they had ever had, splutteringly finishing off with, 'Tell me why you are only now coming back. Tell me why you did not meet me as arranged. Tell me why you do not have your rank badges, tell me why you have a bump on the side of your head and both have swollen lips.'

The two men, swaying a bit as they tried to stand stiffly to attention, glanced at each other guiltily but said nothing.

The Colonel, with mounting apoplexy, said, 'One more chance or both of you consider yourselves under arrest.'

Zai said, sheepishly, 'We heard someone calling us. We went to see who it was but we only heard a voice. It must have been a ghost. No one could have hidden where the voice came from. Then someone clobbered us and neither of us can remember anything more till we woke up, faces aching, bound by vines and with a gag in our mouths, the gag made from our shirts,' and he pulled out his shirt and showed the Colonel the cut tail. 'And no rank badges.'

'Liar. That's not the truth. Tell me the truth. You said you heard a ghost talking. If you don't tell me the whole truth it'll be a court-martial and cashiering for you.' *It might still be once I've learnt the truth.*

'Tuan Colonel, we were in the jungle, searching. There were no tracks and, even if there had been, the rainstorm would have obliterated them by now. Suddenly we heard a woman's voice asking us to, asking for, asking …'

'… so you gave her your badges of rank as souvenirs because you had no money with you? Wretched lechers. Don't prevaricate, give me the whole story,' the Colonel interrupted, so angry and so worried, he could hardly speak clearly.

'... asking us to ... f... fu..., I-can't-say-the-word her,' and out it came with a rush although the two had told each other never to mention it, 'one at a time, I first to be the one because she said I had the ... a ... the ... bigger prick.'

'Im-possible,' the Colonel almost yelled. 'And she bashed you both as you were on the job, did she, one by one, or did you run out of strength before that happened or was needed?' he added sneeringly.

'No, we never saw her. As I said, we went to see who and where she was and something hit us so hard we lost consciousness, both at the same time. We have no idea who or what it was. When we came to we were on the ground, like we have already told you. That is why we could not meet you on your return to pick us up and hear our report. After we woke up and unbound ourselves we searched around for footprints. We saw none. There weren't any from where we heard the taunting woman's voice. What else but a ghost?' Alif asked lamely.

'Have you got your ID cards?'

'Sir, we haven't checked.'

'Then check now,' the Colonel said, trying to quench his overwhelming wrath.

He saw the two men look in their pockets and heard two sudden gasps of disbelief. 'Well, what's wrong now?'

'Nothing in my pocket where I normally keep it,' stuttered Zai. 'Same with me,' murmured Alif.

Normally eloquent under most circumstances, the Colonel

found himself dumbstruck with dismay. *Were Popov and I also spied on?* was a dark fear at the back of his mind. 'I'll give you one more chance. I cannot believe that two normal people with good hearing and good eyesight should be overcome in the way you have described to me. Do you, as officers of the Indonesian Army, understand the word "truth"?'

Both men were too abashed to answer and hung their heads in shame.

'Get out of my sight. Eat your meal although it is cold. I'll settle your hash later, once we're back in the lines,' said with a sigh of disbelief that matters should have turned out so badly having started so well.

The two men, given full plates of rice and vegetables by the driver, only picked at their food. They were still so shaken they had lost their appetite.

Jason made his way carefully back towards the border, mulling over what he and his men had done. It then hit him: *those two men. The names they called one another, Alif and Zai. Those are the names sent to me by Mr C C Too. Those were the two men who saw what I did to Zhong.* He stumbled. *Pay attention, dolt!* He saw two girls coming towards him, probably searching for kindling or fodder for tethered cattle. Hoping against hope that he had not been seen he slipped behind a tree and, as they passed, threw his voice away from him and, as gruffly as he could, threatened with rape and death if they didn't run away now, now, now as fast as they could. Blessing his art of ventriloquy still being vibrantly successful, he too managed to slip away in the other direction and reached the border. He found his pack, changed back into uniform and made for Serikin, where he met up with his two men. Smiles not words showed relief that all three men were back safely. Nobody took the slightest notice of them. 'Sahib, we knew you'd come back about now so we have ordered a meal for the three of us. The driver will come having fed.'

Jason smiled appreciatively. Few other people had such flawless manners in not eating before their senior officer ate his meal. 'Let's have a beer first,' he suggested as they moved over to the eating place. Jason could see that his two men were agog for news.

They toasted each other first and then Jason told them about his meeting. 'It went even better than I had hoped it would, the Indonesian Colonel never mentioned the two men you helped to keep quiet nor did he seem worried, at least not on the surface. I told him a lot of lies that made him think that I was much more powerful than I am and he told me about his future plans. The meeting went happily and sincerely, actual details don't matter because, as you well know, it is not a question of trust but the less you know the less you can give away by mistake.'

'Sahib, we understand,' both answered, using the collective 'we' not the individual 'I' in answer.

'Just as in Ha La you have kept all details to yourself, please also this time. None of us is allowed to cross the border. Your OC sahib only allowed me to take you "as far as the border" which, dressed as a soldier, is only as far as you went.'

'Sahib, did you get permission from the General sahib to cross the border?'

'No, like you, only to the border itself. I said I promised that Lieutenant Colonel, Superintendent Rance would not go but that I'd make other arrangements to meet the Colonel.'

'And that was accepted?'

'Of course.'

Both men's brow wrinkled as they tried to work that one out. 'But, Sahib, how did you manage it?'

Jason laughed. 'Again, mouths closed. Yes?' Yes. 'For ever?' Yes. 'You have a nickname for me in the battalion, don't you?'

'We have one for all the sahibs.'

'I also have a Chinese nickname that translates as Shandung Cannon,' a legitimate sidestep away from the truth. 'I didn't tell the General sahibs that I had said to myself that "Shandung Cannon" was going over the border. I knew myself by that name all the time I was there and am only now Rance sahib back here this side of the border.'

Smiles crinkled their faces and they broke out laughing. *There's no one quite like our Rance sahib* both of them thought.

Their vehicle arrived and back they went. At the Gurkha Para Company lines Rance thanked his two men as well as the OC. 'All fine?' he was asked. 'Better than fine,' he answered.

Meanwhile Colonel Sodimedjo, still sitting in his vehicle, was deep in thought. He knew that the Indonesian Army was not popular in the north of Kalimantan. The people who had attacked his men, had to be more than one person. The voice, ghost or not, counted as one, and both men hit at the same time, meant two. Three men? If that was correct, any three villagers looking for firewood could not have been involved as the sophistication of the knock-out technique was more than one could reasonably expect.

His reverie was interrupted by Zai. 'Tuan Colonel. I forgot to mention this. We found this bit of paper,' and he handed it over. Colonel Sodimedjo examined it closely. The rain had smudged the writing, making it illegible but ... and he looked closely at the signature which he could just read and, under it, the unit of the writer. *That's the unit that I got to attack Keik that time! Now, how did that get there?* It was a disturbing puzzle to an already disturbing puzzle.

The small group drove back to HQ Military District XII, each one nursing his private thoughts, the only one unconcerned being the driver. The Colonel's worry about the piece of paper was a personal one. He knew that neither of the other two would worry nor wonder about it, being too worried about their own future. If he were to talk about it, it would spread alarm and despondency, probably to his detriment. *Keep quiet about it.* As for the other two, now that the Colonel had established impeccable relations with Popov, it was of paramount importance not to let them be hindered by any outside influence. In fact Popov never need know that he had a problem of this size, need he? *But what to do about Alif and Zai?* They were now of no further use. *Get rid of them. Court-martial and dismiss the service is the best solution but I'll give them the option of resigning. In any case loss of ID cards was regarded as a most serious offence.* The Colonel smiled to himself at his solution, his granite visage relaxing visibly.

Next morning, back at the Military District HQ, he called both of them to his office. 'I've decided what to do with you.

Bluntly, you've let the service down badly. You are careless, liars and, trying to do what that 'ghost woman' wanted you to do, rotten to the core. You can either face a court-martial, be dismissed the service and possibly be jailed for a few years, covered in shame or you can volunteer for retirement with nothing said about the incident. You're from Minangkabau in Sumatra, Comrade Aidit's home base, aren't you?'

'Sir, may I have your permission to ask something?' Alif said, stiffly standing to attention. 'Something has just struck me. I haven't even had time to tell my friend – I hope he'll agree.'

Permission was given.

'Sir, we two are experienced fighters. We both agree that yesterday was a fiasco that has no easy explanation. However, it has just occurred to me that the ghost was not speaking in Indonesian but pure Malay and its voice was not treble but falsetto.'

'So what?'

'So, if we sign a pledge not to say anything about yesterday we will continue to serve you faithfully: also, if "that voice" is ever heard again, we guarantee to track it down, have our revenge and let our army know who is trying to defame its officers,' said with utter conviction that surprised himself as well as his friend and the Colonel. 'As for new ID cards, we're ready to take what punishment we're given.'

It's as good a way to settle the business as any and no one outside us three never need be any the wiser. The driver, luckless fellow, the only other person who had overheard the heated row between the three others, never knew why he was so suddenly posted away.

Jason, delighted to be back safe and sound once more in Kuching, popped into his office before going to his quarter. He greeted his two staff officers as he always did. They were so used to his peripatetic way of life that they never asked him where he'd been. 'Anything new?' he asked. His 'Missee' looked at him longingly and nodded slightly before bringing some files over to his desk for him to see. As she did the two staff officers bid Jason farewell, 'It's closing time, sir, and we're off.' Alone, she said, 'Oh Popov, I have been told to report to my handler after I leave the office as he wants to give me a list with the names that you asked for.'

SUPP anti-Malaysia people? 'When will you have it?'

'By half-past eight.'

'Would you like to give it to me quietly in the office tomorrow morning or bring it to my room tonight?'

She gave a small squeal of anticipation. "Popov, why ask? Let it be tonight. I'll do better than last time,' and she pouted a kiss at him.

So will I. 'Good. Quietly, quietly, please.'

Around ten o'clock she slipped away after giving Jason the list followed by a frenzied bout. *One-pin-fall is enough for tonight!* as by then he was much too tired to do anything but sleep. Next morning he saw the list was extensive. He knew that Brigadier Peter Townsend, an open-faced, burly, ex-Army rugger XV, would want a full report so he gave his Brigade Major a ring and fixed up a meeting for 1500 hours that day. He also gave Don

Rutherford a bell and asked if he was free at three o'clock that afternoon. 'Meet you in the Brigadier's office for a joint briefing.'

Sitting in a chair in the Brigadier's office, he jokingly started by asking 'You're not wired, are you, Don?'

'No, the Sarawak Constabulary hasn't got round to that yet. What have you to tell us? I'm sure the Brigadier is as full of interest as I am and wants to hear it all,' Head of Special Branch answered gravely.

'Before I start on my main briefing, I have an important list for you. It is a full one of all anti-Malaysia people of SUPP in the main towns,' and, taking it out of his pocket, handed it over.

Head of Special Branch took it, looked at it long and hard then whistled through his teeth. 'Jeepers creepers, Jason, this is gold dust. I knew the list was extensive but never thought it would be as long as this. A whole number of prominent men's names are here contrary to all our expectations. The Commissioner will have to know about it. I can't use you name can I?'

'No, no, no, Don. For heaven's sake triple no. He doesn't like the army, has his reservations about an army officer dressed as a policeman, albeit a humble auxiliary model, is suspicious of arming Ibans, so I've been told and would consider it as gross interference.'

The Brigadier nodded agreement. 'Don, I hope you're not biased.'

'No, sir. Okay, Jason. I've got your message. "My own sources" will have to do.'

'Now give us all that happened yesterday, with as many details as possible, please,' said the Brigadier.

You'll hear as much as I give you. 'Gentlemen, Colonel Sodimedjo and I had a long chat. I could not take any notes but I remember all the bull points.' His audience was spellbound as he gave them the details. When Jason came to the bit about radio contact, he stood up and placed a piece of paper on the Brigadier's desk. 'He also gave me this, sir, details of his network so that I can have one-to-one contact with him.'

After the Brigadier had studied it he gave it to Head of Special Branch who again whistled through his teeth, rather to the Brigadier's annoyance, Jason thought. 'Now this really is something. More gold dust. Tell us more.'

'I told the Colonel that I was just about to get my own private set and that I would contact him on a one-to-one basis. Now you can do that yourself or use sources I know nothing about.'

The Brigadier quickly made a copy, gave it to Don Rutherford and, opening a draw in his desk, put the piece of paper inside and locked it. 'I'll do the same, Brigadier,' said Rutherford. 'We can discuss best how to use this information once DOBOPS has been appraised.'

The Brigadier agreed.

When Jason told them about plans for a parachute assault on mainland Malaya and plans to sabotage Brunei oil storage tanks, both listeners were almost overwhelmed with excitement.

At the end the Brigadier said, 'How did you actually find the Colonel, Jason?'

'My Plan B was sufficient to get him where I wanted him, sir,' was Jason's evasive answer.

'Exceedingly well done, anyway. I won't press you,' said the

Brigadier, but just as soon as the vote on Malaysia takes place on 16 September, I want you to go to Brunei to brief General Sprinter.'

'It will be a pleasure, sir,' answered Jason as he excused himself and walked back with Don Rutherford to his office in Police HQ. 'Sit you down for a moment, while I get you a cup of coffee,' he was told. When both of them had a cup in their hands, Don asked 'Jason, did you, in the strictest confidence, go over the border?'

'Don, as I promised you all, neither Superintendent nor Lieutenant Colonel Jason Rance would cross the border, nor did either of them.'

'So you kept your promise?'

'But of course.'

'None of my men in Serikin gave me that impression,' said with the ghost of a smile twitching his lips.

Blast you. 'Tell you what, Don, when you meet Popov in Soviet uniform, ask him.'

Don Rutherford winked as he said, 'I won't forget but,' with another wink, 'I may not recognise him unless he is your *doppelganger*!'

Back in his own office Jason received a phone call from the Commissioner of Police, asking him to go and see him. 'I have some important news for you.' *Anything to do with my escapade? I hope not.*

No, it wasn't. Jason was told that the Inspector General of Malaysian Police (still designate till 16 September) wanted him to be Commandant of the Border Scouts in Sabah as soon as Malaysia became a fact. As Sabah was not in Sarawak's jurisdiction it was of no interest to Mr David King. Jason put up a silent prayer, *Dear God, please give me twenty-six hours in a day and nine days in a week,* but, apart from saying that he understood, he merely saluted and left the office.

Malaysia became a fact and Rance flew to Brunei where he briefed DOBOPS and the Brigadier under whose command troops in East Sarawak and Sabah came. At the end the General said, 'Rance, I would never have dared hope you'd be so successful. You have given Special Branch and my people enough data to work on without worrying you further or risking your life any more. You've been in deep water.'

'Yes, sir, and at times nearly drowned in it.'

'How do you read the future?'

Jason considered that for a short while before answering. 'Sir, I have a current concern of ensuring that the Border Scouts have their own NCOs and one for the future.'

'And that is?' prompted the General.

'To use my new knowledge to find out some juicy targets to use when I'm OC of the Gurkha Paras, sir.'

'And how long will the former take?'

'Maximum two months, sir.'

'And the latter?'

'It will run concurrently.'

'Then consider yourself relieved from the job of Commandant Border Scouts the day after you report to me that all sections have their own NCOs, even though that means you won't finish your one year's initial posting. You've risked your life enough: in this game you're more of a bishop than a pawn.'

'Sir, thank you. You couldn't have made me happier.'

Before Jason flew back to Kuching he had yet another phone call to make. Jiang Yun answered it. Jason began as he did before, 'Fifth niece this is your third uncle calling you. Listen well.'

'Third uncle, your fifth niece is listening well.'

'Mr Popov has failed in his secret mission. Maphilindo has not come about but Malaysia has. My handler is annoyed that your SUPP people did not trust him in time and, to preserve Popov's future, he has to leave quite soon.'

'Oh, Third Uncle. I'm so sorry if I failed him. I will indeed miss him.'

'Will you? When you next go into your next huddle with him do not act like the girl in the song "Green Plum and a Bamboo Horse",' and with that enigmatic remark, he rang off, not before humming the tune to his fifth niece, who listened in agonised bewilderment.

8

Jason's time as Commandant of the Border Scouts came to an end. He would be sorry to lose his 'Missee' but he realised that however pleasant such encounters were they were extremely rash. From his last 'third-uncle' telephone call she knew he would not be there much longer. From her demeanour in the office he was still her 'Popov', not the Englishman Rance. He waited until his very last night before saying anything about it to her. He was feeling unusually light-hearted at his release from being a policeman and had arranged that she come and see him. To his surprise she seemed unwilling to do anything more than talk. He looked at her and said, 'My heart is full of hope and wish that we could do more than just talk as a couple. It would be a chance to open our hearts together and maybe go to see a film.'

She stared at him, open-mouthed in confusion. 'What are you talking about Popov?' she demanded.

'You are meant waspishly to answer, "Yes, I know your type. As a matter of fact I can't stand you and I know what you're after".'

Her gaze never faltered as, eyes transfixed in amazement, she stammered out, 'Popov, you've never talked like this before. What are you trying to tell me?'

'Oh, Missee, nothing much. Those are the words of a song "Green Plum and a Bamboo Horse", very popular in Malaya and Singapore some years ago. The boy is on a bamboo horse and is trying to entice the girl with an unripe, so green, plum,' and he hummed the tune.

She swallowed noisily in disbelief, eyes still locked with his. After several long moments she broke eye contact and, with a vinegary smirk, said, '*That* explains it. Now I know why people thought you might be a Chinese speaker. And all the time ...'

'No, no, no, Missee,' Jason hurriedly broke in, cursing himself for his unthinking impetuosity. *Not like me at all, blast it.* 'Your third uncle taught me the words and the tune when I met him on my last visit to Brunei.' Even to him that didn't sound convincing.

'Was that the time he rang to tell me that you had failed in your undertaking?'

'Yes, it must have been,' said Jason, a little too quickly, 'Somehow he knew where I was and contacted me. I have to tell you that I'm leaving Sarawak tomorrow and I won't be coming back so I won't see you again ...' he began but had to jump back as she tore into him like a wild cat defending her kittens, leaning forward and trying to scratch his face. She had at last recognised the voice on the telephone. *The lying, blustering, fornicating cad* she thought bitterly as she made her way sadly back home, wiping her tears.

As for Jason, words he'd learnt many years before came back to haunt him ... *and I learnt about women from her ...*

Jason bade farewell to the Commissioner. Normal, kind, end-of-term, candyfloss words were spoken and he was given a small ashtray with the Sarawak Constabulary badge engraved in the centre of it. *Knowing I'm a non-smoker he is either most unobservant or has a more subtle sense of humour than I gave him credit for,* Jason thought as he thanked him for it.

He changed planes at Singapore then flew on to Ipoh where his battalion was. He reported in to the Adjutant who welcomed him back and gave him a letter from the C-in-C. 'This came in yesterday,' he said. 'Read it before you go in and touch your hat to the CO. He knows about it.' PERSONAL AND CONFIDENTIAL on the envelope presaged something more than routine.

Hesitantly Jason opened it, his mind going back to 'that' interview … how long ago? It seemed ages yet it was not far short of a year. Its gist was that the C-in-C satisfyingly thanked him for the reports he had submitted, the uncannily excellent work he had done despite the unprecedented dangers inherent in such a task. 'With death being your daily companion, you have done more than any of us could have imagined, with possibly a little magic added in some situations.' *Was that a hint at knowledge of my meeting the Colonel in Indonesia? If so, it's too late now to worry about.* The letter finished up saying that such bravery shown, efforts achieved and endeavour accomplished would normally have resulted in a high gallantry award being made 'but sadly you were not in the army but the police so I had no say in the matter. Likewise, to expect anything from a new country in the throes of setting itself up has made any reward, I fear, a non-existent event.' The letter closed with the normal courtesies.

The CO's door opened. 'Jason! Welcome back, still all in one piece. Come and have a chat.' One of the points the CO made was how sorry he was to learn about the absence of any recognition, 'but I expect you'll get your chance in the Para Company before Confrontation folds up. But first you are to go on two months' leave in England.'

'Yes, sir, that will suit me well. Living as I have been these past few months was taxing and only now is it catching up with me.' He grinned and mirthfully added, 'I am not a vain man but the only time that I can say that I was soft and attractive was as a military target in the border area,' and the CO joined in the laughter. 'Jason, you really are a one for the apt *bon mot*.'

Even before Jason's plane had taken off from Kuching, Jiang Yun had contacted her handler and told him that there were, in fact, strong reasons to believe that the whole of the Popov ploy was nothing but a giant hoax and she thought that her mysterious third uncle was none other than Popov himself and that Popov, as such, never existed. *I recognised the voice. I loved who I thought he was not who he really was* she told herself, tears coursing down her cheeks. Her handler had quickly passed her message on one stage higher.

Sim Ting Ong, Secretary General of the Sarawak United People's Party, fretting that he had somehow let himself be hoodwinked to great loss of face, knew that 'damage limitation', by whatever name, was in vogue, was important and the unnerving news had to be sent to Pontianak just as soon as it could be.

When Colonel Sodimedjo was told he was worse than saddened:

maddened would better describe his feelings. He had been led to believe that it had been an extraordinary coup in his favour and he had been promised advanced promotion for how he had helped *Konfrontasi*. He had accepted a British Army officer being a Soviet agent as news had just broken how the British Secret Service had been so successfully penetrated by Soviet spies recruited at Cambridge University, so why not the army also? Before the message had come from SUPP he had told Lieutenant Sumbi and the other two about Popov's recall by Moscow. Now, however, matters took on a different and, sadly, humiliating aspect if the news were to spread.

The four people concerned, Sodimedjo, Sumbi, Alif and Zai, therefore held a secret meeting. So as not to discredit the Colonel, the recall story would be submitted up the Chain of Command and not a word about third uncle being Popov being Jason ever to be mentioned. Loose talk among the Border Scouts about Lieutenant Colonel/Superintendent Rance coming back to Borneo as OC of the Gurkha Independent Parachute Company would be monitored most thoroughly and, if true, each, all and every effort would be made to get their own back. 'We must have our revenge,' was a constant in all four minds.

Before the meeting broke up Sumbi made a final point: 'Tuan Colonel, our foray into Brunei to sabotage those oil installations will need good men and much practice. I believe it is time we three moved over to Military District VI in Balikpapan where we can practice before taking up positions at Long Bawang, near the border,' and he took a pointer and showed where he meant on the large wall map. 'The better to recce our route I plan to send some of my men dressed as Border Scouts and try to listen in to what the British units are doing. It may, who can tell? be our good luck to come across that confounded "Popov",' and he spat the word, 'as he really is. We won't make any mistakes this time round. I know he recognises me but his "blind spot", as the English have it, is that he cannot recognise Alif or Zai.'

He would never know that that was his own one fatal 'blind spot'.

'I'll be sad to see you go,' said Colonel Sodimedjo, 'despite our disagreements. I'll arrange for that to happen.'

And happen it did.

A new batch of thirty Gurkha volunteers was about to begin initial basic parachute training in Singapore when Jason's leave was over and so he joined in both as a refresher and to learn about his new men. *I can't wait to take over as OC and get back to Borneo*, he felt after the final descent as he helped the Parachute School staff give out 'wings' to the newly qualified men. They motored to their permanent base in Kluang, on the mainland, to wait for the company to return from a 16-week tour in Borneo. In the four months before their next operational stint, his new men had to be taught how to operate in five-man patrols and the older men's knowledge and ability enhanced by all he had learnt during Operation Bamboo and as Commandant Border Scouts. He even had some special maps printed without contours to get his men used to the maps of Borneo which did not show them. He knew that soldiers everywhere talked about who their new boss was going to be: he was unaware the Border Scouts with Gurkhas had also heard and that is how Sumbi, Alif and Zai knew about his new job.

Back in Borneo on operational duty, the Gurkha Para Company was based in Brunei, in the 'Haunted House' on the edge of the Sultan's extensive palace grounds, over a hundred miles away from the border. That meant flying to near their targets either by helicopter or, if there was an airstrip nearby, fixed-wing craft, then walking. Occasionally a patrol was based with a forward infantry unit. Jason's task was to stay back in the Haunted House and coordinate his patrols, taking their twice-daily sitreps, using 'key', never voice. Without his presence back in base, guiding affairs, morale of the men would not be high as they relied on him to save them from any situation that might overwhelm them from undue Indonesian pressure, their always being in danger, or sickness.

Sumbi's training team crossed over the border to a company base of the 1st Rutland Regiment at Long Pa Sia when Sergeant Kulbahadur Limbu patrol was under their command. The Company Commander, drilled in the 'Hearts and Minds' philosophy so, thinking it the correct thing to do, invited some elders from the nearest village to his HQ to tell them how he was reacting to the Indonesian threat. He spoke in English and the neighbourhood headmaster did the translating into Tagal Murut, the local language. At the back of the group, wearing plain clothes, sat Alif and Zai, understanding enough English, avidly lapped up the briefing. Sergeant Kulbahadur Limbu's patrol was not present.

Two days later an incursion came in just where the Rutlands were not expecting it and after some confused fighting took place the Indons withdrew. The Company Commander did not understand why the Indons had come the way they had until the headmaster told him that he had found out that a couple of local Indon supporters were responsible for taking two Indonesians, dressed as Border Scouts, to the briefing. *So that is why the incursion came in that way! Blast them!* he thought furiously. By that time, Sergeant Kulbahadur's patrol had been re-rationed, found out that the Indons had crossed the border back into their own territory and returned to the Rutlands' camp. However, the Company Commander, a stupid man, felt that he needed to punish the two supporters. He told Sergeant Kulbahadur to bring his patrol and follow him to the village with a section of his own soldiers 'to learn British methods'. He had forced the headmaster to tell them where the two supporters lived and, with his soldiers, pulled the two men out of their house and tied each to a post to be there all night in an uncomfortable position made even more so every time they moved. 'I'll come back tomorrow morning after you've learnt your lesson and untie you,' he jeered at them as he left.

The Gurkha patrol had stayed behind in hiding. 'Let's see what'll happen,' Sergeant Kulbahadur said. Nothing did for a while and the Gurkhas were just about to move back when they saw two men approach the bound men, untie them and massage their sore limbs. As the rescuers spoke in Malay, not in Tagal Murut, the Gurkha sergeant was intrigued as it meant that they were not local men so he and his four men stayed listening to what was being said. He distinctly heard 'RPKAD', 'Kelabang' and 'General Mung' mentioned. They meant nothing to him but he felt they were important so he repeated them to himself to remember them. *Our Rance sahib will be interested, I'm sure.*

Clouds that had obscured the moon drifted away and the Gurkha sergeant saw that one of the men had an ugly scar that ran from the top of his left ear to the corner of his mouth. *He's the one Hemé and I clobbered.* He then saw a second. *And that's the other one. What can they be doing here?* He whispered to his men, 'Say nothing. Be ready with your kukri.'

The man with a scar on his face bent down to pick up a leaf and saw them. *That leaf! Proof you're the same one. No doubt whatsoever. You're a long way from home!*

In Malay he asked, 'Hist, are you Gurkhas?'

The Gurkha Sergeant decided to pretend he did not recognise him. 'Yes, we are. Why? Who are you and what is it to do with you?' Then, with a flash of inspiration, 'We were with the British major.'

The next question surprised them. 'Have you a new OC whose name is Major Rance?'

'Yes, we have.'

'Is he here?'

'No, he'll be back in Brunei. Why do you ask?'

'We are Border Scouts and he was in charge of us. He was kind to us and gave us good training,' the speaker dissembled. 'We'd like to meet him again. How can we do that?'

No, no, no. Why is this man lying and why is he so far from where we last saw him?

'Why do you want to meet him?'

'Because the OC of the British company wrongly tortured our

two friends here and we feel that if we could explain to Tuan Rance how wrong it was, he might talk to the OC and tell him that that is not the correct way of dealing with people.'

'Can't you report it to the new Commandant of the Border Scouts?' asked Kulbahadur, sensibly.

'He won't listen. He is a new man and not an Englishman. He doesn't seem to like us the way Tuan Rance did. It is much better if we could meet Tuan Rance ourselves. What do you recommend?'

They were startled when one of the Gurkhas slapped himself on the cheek to kill a mosquito.

'There is one way but I don't know if he'll manage it in time.'

'What's that?'

'We are due to fly out the day after tomorrow from Long Pa Sia by Twin Pioneer. If the extra weight is not too much he could fly in and speak to you and the OC here.'

The man pretending to be a Border Scout plucked a leaf from a low-hanging branch and folded it in two. The two men who had been tied up joined them.

'Tell him we were with him in Keik and our names are,' he hesitated, 'Jimbuan and … Jihed'. *More proof that he's lying but it shows he knows names from the west of the country.* 'He should remember them even if he can't remember other Border Scouts' names. But by using those two names others will know us and guide him to us. Please tell him to come. We'll stay here till he does,' and, so saying, the four men melted into the undergrowth. Kulbahadur's sharp ears picked up something like 'Long Bawang,' before they passed out of earshot.

'Back to our base we go,' said the Sergeant and off they went, trying to fathom the astonishing meeting. *He's up to no good at all.* Next morning the radio operator sent a message 'Personal for OC: bent leaf man and other one are here. Want to meet you.'

When Jason read the message his mind raced. *Let's get them out of the way.* He sent a message back: 'Tell *gora* sunray to take action against them,' and thought back to that conversation he had had with the Indonesian Colonel at the edge of the jungle that time. And the bent leaves: *Back to twice coincidence, three times happenstance. Looks like they're warming up. They can't just be after my blood, can they? Can't be worth all that effort. I'll debrief Sergeant Kulé first.*

The Gurkha Sergeant did tell the Rutland Major but was soundly rebuffed for not having returned to base with his own escort.

Back in Brunei, Sergeant Kulbahadur Limbu gave a full version of his short message, including the strange leaf-folding habit they had already seen, before going on to mention the key words, RPKAD, Kelabang and General Mung. 'Oh yes, the liar said their names were Jimbuan and Jihed. They meant nothing to me, Sahib, but I expect they do to you.'

'They do indeed. Jihed lives at Keik and Jimbuan lives a hundred miles or more to the east.' *More proof of those leaflets being used against me.*

Jason thanked his Sergeant, called for his Land Rover and drove to Central Brigade HQ and asked to see the Brigade Commander. 'Sir, may I have a few words with you, please?' As an independent unit commander he had direct access.

'Important, is it? I'm fairly busy at the moment. I'm expecting the Brigadier from West Brigade in Kuching to visit me.'

Jason smiled. 'One of your rank, sir, is almost "always busy at the moment" but, if it is not an impertinence, may I have your permission to brief you both on something I think you and he will be extremely interested in. It is what I have just been told by my patrol that was in Long Pa Sia, Rutlands' territory.'

Brigadier Edward Gloop, 'Eddy' to his friends and 'Gloop the Snoop' to some others, was newly promoted and had never served out of Europe before. Of medium height and dark features, he had a ferrety look about his small yet sinister face, with cruel blue eyes with their drooping, cynical lids. Commissioned at the end of 1939, he had been taken prisoner by the Germans in the spring of 1940, being released only in 1945. He had an inferiority complex fostered by his enforced captivity. He was not sympathetic to Asians and while he knew that 'Wogs' didn't actually start South of the Serpentine he did know that they definitely did East of Suez. He found Jason's military virtues a perpetual reproach to his own forced inactivity and regarded such officers as 'colonial relics' so was antipathetic towards them. Trying to emulate military protocol as it was when he was taken prisoner, he was not used to mere majors corralling him in his office rather than waiting for the routine daily 'prayers' at 0900 hours but there was something sincere and insistent about the OC Gurkha Paras so he didn't send his away. Instead, he said, 'You were commanding the Border Scouts till fairly recently, weren't you? One of the "Funnies". I don't like "Funnies" so don't bring any "funny" ideas to the Gurkha Paras, if they haven't got any already.' 'Funnies' to him were the first step towards military heresy.

Jason studiously ignored the rudeness. He had learnt that if a middle-piece officer had attributes his seniors did not have or were misunderstood, he was labelled 'unconventional', 'eccentric' or, most derogatorily, 'gone native'.

'You are correct, sir. Apparently I was on an Army short list of one so had no option but to take the job and do the best I could. I made certain most unusual contacts. Commander West Brigade has the background of all, or rather most of, what I did. Briefing you two together will mean you won't have to check my credentials, if I can put it that way, with General Sprinter before you listen to me.'

'Very well then and,' he looked out of his office window, 'here he is in person.'

After greeting his opposite number rather huffily Brigadier Gloop said to him, 'We have an intruder who wants to brief us both together. I've let him stay. Shall we hear him before we get on with more important business?'

Brigadier Peter Townsend turned to Jason and said, 'Rance, I'd never call you anything but the opposite of a "bad penny" but you turn up with the surprise of one all the same,' and the two shook hands. 'I'm sure you've got something of special interest for us. You always used to.'

'He wouldn't talk to me before you came, Peter,' Brigadier Gloop interjected acidly, 'so let's get him over with, shall we, rather than telling him to wait?'

Brigadier Townsend, smiling quietly to himself with a faintly mocking twinkle in his brown eyes and a flicker of a secret grin, said, 'Yes, let's first listen to what our Maverick Major has to say.

Over to you, Rance,' and the two Brigadiers sat down leaving Jason standing. He moved over to the wall map.

'Gentlemen, I'll be as succinct as I can. For Brigadier Gloop's background information I'll rehearse what Colonel Sodimedjo, Indonesian Army Intelligence Colonel, personally told me about their future plans. They want as many of our troops to be brought from Peninsular Malaysia to Borneo so that, once the force level on the mainland is low, they can make a successful parachute assault somewhere in the south of the country, probably in the Johor area. They also plan several attacks, the main one being by what they are calling the "Kelabang Team", commanded by Lieutenant Sumbi and maybe up to fifty men, through Sarawak, into Brunei, to sabotage the oil storage facilities and radio stations, also to try to gather volunteers and set up bases for training against Brunei once more after the British have left. That means they will concentrate their incursions to the west of the country so that our own troops are fewer on the ground in the east.'

The new Brigadier gawped as Jason's briefing unfolded. 'Peter, is this true? I mean to say, without any disrespect intended, such news is not what some low-level officer like Major Rance would be expected to accumulate,' he stuttered in his puzzlement.

'Yes, you have to believe him and true it is. The C-in-C, Major General Sprinter, I myself and Head of Special Branch, Sarawak, are the only people who know about this. You, Eddy, are now the fifth.' Brigadier Gloop shook his head but this time looked at Jason with a tinge of respect. 'Carry on Rance,' he said, more pleasantly than before but with a wintery chill in his voice.

The next part of the briefing was a retelling of what Sergeant

Kulbahadur and his patrol had overheard and been told. 'The key words here, Gentlemen, are RPKAD, Kelabang, General Mung and Long Bawang. I don't know who General Mung is. It would seem to me that preparations are in force for the main thrust into Brunei under Sumbi are in preparation. However, your sources may have other inferences,' he added tactfully.

'You have yet to tell us how it was that your Gurkha patrol commander was able to discuss affairs with the enemy without taking any offensive action,' huffed the new Brigadier, thinking he saw an opening to deflate the 'Maverick Major'. 'Most lamentable and unusual behaviour in a Gurkha. I thought they were more loyal than that. Are you planning to punish him, to bring up before me?' he asked vindictively, eyeing Jason with wintry disapproval. As a practising Catholic punishment for the lowering of standards was the norm for him.

Loyal service with Gurkhas had been drilled into Jason like a bead into an oyster: knowledge of them and good officer-to-man relations were keys in the dynamics of the chain of command. Any unjust slur on his men roused his anger. He gave a short, barking laugh and his intended answer would have been barbed but he merely shrugged and grinned disarmingly. 'Sir, it would be a grave impertinence to say that you have drawn erroneous conclusions without hearing full details of the episode so I will merely continue with my briefing. Your wrong reading of my Sergeant's action now compels me, though I don't like it, to tell tales out of school about the British company at Long Pa Sia,' and out came details of the treatment meted out to the two supporters after it came to light that two Indonesian spies had attended a briefing for the villagers. 'The Company Commander went to the house of the two people he blamed for bringing the Indons in, took the Gurkha patrol as escort and, with help from his own squaddies, to punish the two men he tied up each to a stake in the ground in a position where it hurt to move with the intention of leaving them there all night. The Gurkha patrol stayed behind, hidden, and saw two men dressed as Border Scouts come out of the jungle and untie the bound men. It was during their conversation that these words were heard. One of the men who untied the two bound men saw the patrol, asked them if they were Gurkhas and went on to tell them they were Border Scouts who wanted to see me to complain about the treatment meted out to the two villagers. Under those circumstances, sir, I think your condemnation of my patrol's behaviour unjust, unworthy ...'

'All right, no need to bang on,' Brigadier Gloop interrupted. 'I've got the message,' he snapped.

Brigadier Townsend tried to lower the temperature. 'Rance, Major General Mung is in charge of the eastern border area. What I want to know is how did those two Indons know about you? You have yet to explain that.'

Jason realised he had to be careful in what he said. 'Sir, they could well have been the Indon Colonel's escort whom I didn't see but could have seen me. What I have yet to mention to Brigadier Gloop is that when I started as Commandant Border Scouts pictures of me were put along the border so my face is probably known to as many Indonesians as it is to Borneans. I have been a target thereafter and have nearly lost my life a number of times under suspicious circumstances. To counter that

I made special plans that were accepted by DOBOPS and Special Branch. Like everything everywhere, leaks happen and it now seems that besides knowing I, now as OC Gurkha Para Company, was the late "disguised" person talking to the Indon Colonel, his two bodyguards want revenge at their Commander having been tricked into telling me so much.'

Too much, too little or just right?

'Eddy, it is a remarkable story and one I have already fully accepted. What Major Rance did was almost foolhardily brave but gave us a head start in many counter moves against the Indons. By good chance, his patrol has confirmed much of what, till now, has only been unconfirmed rumour. I should also add that Major Rance is a remarkable linguist and has ears where most of us others don't.'

The new Brigadier had the grace to apologise to Jason, in a back-handed way, finishing up with, 'normally one cannot believe such stories but there are exceptions, aren't there, to every rule.' Jason made to leave. 'Wait. I want to tell you I'm sending you on a cross-border operation: take two patrols and move south over the border from Long Semado, maximum three thousand yards and apart from picking up any signs of recent movement, your major task will be to recce a track running parallel to and south of the border in the first valley which we think the Indons use as a base line to mount attacks across the border. You will also assess if it is used sufficiently for a battalion ambush to be mounted after you withdraw and, if so, you will lead the battalion into its ambush positions. On the map the nearest Indon base is Wailaya but that'll be a step or three below you so I doubt they'll worry you.

However, we think that there are a few hundred Indon soldiers in the nearer Long Bawang those men talked about and they could be on the look-out for cross-border patrols so go carefully. You'll be heavily outnumbered, by more than a hundred to one, I expect, so take a couple of Claymore mines with you. Only set them off if you're attacked otherwise no, don't. Reconnaissance only, nothing in the "cowboy" line. Anyway, it's only for two nights,' this last said in a 'throw-away' tone of voice. 'But I have to clear it first and will give you the green light in due course.'

Jason's assessment was that the Brigadier's briefing lacked the gravamen such an occasion warranted and he wondered if there was any reason for it. *Not worth worrying about.*

'I have no questions, sir. Have I your permission to leave?'

Permission was granted. He saluted, shot a glance at Brigadier Townsend whose left eyelid moved fractionally, drove back to his lines and had a wonderful game of basketball to relieve himself of his many frustrations.

Although it was only a small reconnaissance patrol it was a 'first' for the Gurkha Para Company so planning and preparations were even more meticulous than usual. Jason decided that they would cross the border, make their way over the mountain ridge line and get to the valley below together before separating. Sergeant Kulbahadur Limbu's patrol would move northeast along the track to be recced and Jason, with the other, would move southwest.

They prepared their mines: the Claymore was a deadly weapon that held a cluster of metal fragments in a small, brown, concave-shaped, square, plastic container, tied to a tree or mounted on 'scissor legs'. The eastwards-moving patrol would carry it. Jason's men had yet to learn how to set it up to be set off by a tripwire attached to the firing device so they asked the Armourer Sergeant in Brigade HQ how to fix it – as a late-evening 'special request'. They were given the correct kit and took the two mines back to their camp.

They flew up from Brunei to Long Semado the next day in a Twin Pioneer aircraft, spent the night with the Gurkha battalion there and left at dawn. As he crossed the border into Indonesian territory Jason again had the same feeling of almost being undressed as he had experienced both crossing into Thailand and more recently before meeting Colonel Sodimedjo but now he and his men were properly armed and that was a great comfort, almost enough to offset their miniscule strength compared with the opposition's.

Moving down a narrow ridge well into enemy territory, they saw a small rocky outcrop, a feature not uncommon in those high hills, where the jungle floor was unusually bare of foliage and flatter than normal. Jason signalled a stop for a breather in the thicker jungle at the edge of this curiously bare patch. It was time for a meal and to send a sitrep. Thankfully the men took off their packs and, facing outwards, relaxed. There was clear water not far below where they were. 'The Major sahib will tell you when to start cooking,' was the message passed round.

Jason crept ultra-cautiously to the edge of the outcrop, not exposing himself and, slowly raising his head, had a good look around. All was peaceful, nothing was amiss. And yet, although he couldn't put his finger on it, almost as a dog will 'sense a presence', he sensed danger. There was nothing untoward between him and where the ridge dipped again except four saplings in the middle. There was something 'wrong' with them. *Natural?* He stood up and moved a few yards. *No? They formed a rectangle.* He went over to them and, on an impulse, tugged at each sapling in turn. Each lifted easily out of the ground, despite having short roots. They could only be bivouac poles for an Indon ambush facing uphill whose men had wanted to sleep on the flatter ground. At night, when the ambush was lifted, they could have a covering draped between them and, by day, they constituted no impediment to the field of fire or vision. He had first seen them from an angle so had not realised, as they looked fresh and natural, that they were in a rectangle; not nature's pattern. It was a lucky discovery, confirming that the area was 'alive'.

He went back to his men. 'No one here since this morning, early, at the latest. Start cooking. Operator, open your set. I'll write you a message.' As he spoke, in the middle distance there was an enormous rumbling and creaking followed by a thunderous crash that reverberated widely. Everyone looked startled. Jason recognised the noise from his days with the Temiar: when clearing the forest they would 'half-cut' the trees to be felled on their upper side and fully cut the top line in unison. As the top line trees collapsed it took the half-cut ones with them in one gigantic surge. *Civilians or army?*

He went to the radio set and, looking at his map, tried to work out his position. He made 'best-guest' grid reference, the map being inaccurate, and adding 'area active' sent his sitrep.

Set packed and men fed, they moved on downhill, following

a river and arrived in their target area a little later than planned. It was hard to determine their position as, by then, Jason had realised that the map was plain wrong. He was not sure that the track they had reached was the one he was meant to look at. He had to come to a decision: move up and down this track, at the limit of their three thousand yards and find it the wrong one or recce south, over the limit – a heinous military and political offence if found out – and find the right one. He was debating which option to take when a middle-aged civilian walked round a bend in the track – the men were hidden in all-round fire positions – coming from the direction of where the few hundred Indonesian soldiers were thought to be, to the southwest. He was obviously most upset by a European's solitary presence and peered around closely to see where strange soldiers had to be hiding. Jason spoke to him in Malay which he seemed not fully to understand so it was probably not his first language: the man grinned foolishly when asked where the nearest Indons were. He mentioned that a nearby longhouse was sometimes used by them.

'Are they there now?'

A crafty look come into the man's eyes as he leant forward and said that he thought they would not be there now but quite possibly they would visit it on the morrow.

'Where is the longhouse?'

It was not far away but to the north so, if there were Indons there, the patrols had hostile troops above and below them.

'And if they don't come? If they are not there? Where can we meet them?'

'Down this track, Tuan, the way I've come, about two hours'

walk away. If you can be there tomorrow afternoon I expect they'll be patrolling the area.'

Strange that he knows so much about it. I don't trust him as far as I can piss into a following wind. Abort Plan A, adopt Plan B – but there is no Plan B. Jason's two patrol commanders had joined him.

'Sahib, it's getting late and now with this man we're known about,' one of them said.

'I know. We can't recce the track as we had planned. Let this man go and we'll shadow him.'

The civilian, clearly worried, was fretting to go.

'Enche. Where are you off to now?' Jason asked him. The man pointed northeast. 'Away from Long Bawang? Away from the soldiers?'

'Yes.'

'Fine by us. We are going down the other way, to the southwest. We will stay at the longhouse for tonight and move down the track tomorrow morning after our meal.'

The man had a gleam in his eyes. 'May I go, please?'

'Yes. On your way and I am sorry to have delayed you.'

He moved off and as soon as he was out of sight Jason quietly said, 'I don't trust him one bit. We can't do what we had planned. We will shadow him and see what happens. We are no longer two patrols but one. There probably won't be an ambush the way the man's going but be ready for anything.' He looked at Sergeant Kulbahadur. 'Shadow him. I and two men will be behind you. Try not to let him see you. Leave our packs here and come back for them.'

The man's tracks, to a normal person, would not have been easy to follow but Sergeant Kulbahadur was the best tracker 1/12 GR had, probably the best it had ever had, and he could read the an almost invisible track like other people read a newspaper. A quarter of an hour later the civilian looked round and, just in time, Kulbahahadur 'froze' by a conveniently leafy bush. Satisfied he was by himself, the civilian disappeared south down a small track that, had it not been known about, would have been ignored as leading nowhere. The rest of the patrol saw Kulbahadur indicate the turning and Jason hurried up to him.

'Sahib, this track looks like one that could lead onto another parallel track. On?'

'Yes, on.'

After moving about a quarter of a mile due south, indeed they saw another, larger track, obviously the main one. Gingerly inching forward, Sergeant Kulbahadur saw the civilian, only about 20 yards away, once more look round and give a piercing whistle, to the amazement of the Gurkhas. Jason had ultra cautiously joined his Sergeant and waited anxiously. The civilian once more looked round at the way he had come and, seeing nobody, gave another whistle. It was answered by a similar noise and from the other side of the track two Indonesian officers, wearing two golden bars of lieutenant's rank on their shoulders, emerged from the undergrowth. Jason recognised the both immediately, as did Sergeant Kulbahadur Limbu: this was the second time Jason had seen them and the third time for the Gurkha Sergeant.

'Back so soon?' one of them asked in elementary Malay which Jason heard and understood.

'Tuan, I have good news for you. I have located the target you have told me about. The tall foreigner is the one you showed me the photo of.'

'That's wonderful news. You will definitely be rewarded. Did he say which route he had come by?'

'No, I didn't ask him.'

'Where will he be now and how many men will be with him?'

'Oh, I only saw two so the others must have been hiding.'

'I'll gather a squad and you will lead us to the group now. Which is the quickest way? The way you've just come?'

'No, Tuan, no. After I met them I moved northeast and they said they would move southwest. I think they will only look a little way down the track today and move the whole way down it tomorrow after their meal. They also said that they would stay at or near the longhouse tonight and move southwest tomorrow morning. It is much easier to go along this path to where you were in ambush until yesterday. Go there first thing tomorrow and be sure of getting them.'

'Yes, it is the perfect place, the jungle overlooks a blanket of thick, matted fern, so thick you could almost walk on it rather better than through it. Tell me what you said to them once more.'

'Tuan, this is what I told those people ...'

'And what was the answer?'

'As I've told you. Moving off after their morning meal to where I said you could be ambushed. That will give you time to set up another ambush and do away with them entirely.'

'You've done us well. We'll move out at first light tomorrow morning. That'll be plenty of time,' said Alif. 'Were you by yourself?'

'Yes, there was no one behind me.'

'Nor any of us,' and so saying, the two of them disappeared into the undergrowth the other side of the track, the civilian following on behind.

Whew! What now? Jason looked at his watch. It was half-past 2 which meant only another three and a half hours of daylight. He put his index finger to his lips and motioned with his head to move back the way they had come. They moved off silently and, before they emerged onto the track where they had met the man, they joined the others and the trackers put on their packs. By then Jason had decided what to do. 'Gather round me,' he said in a low voice. 'I'll tell you what I heard and what I plan to do.'

They were agog to learn. 'I didn't trust that civilian from the very start,' Jason began. 'I saw a glint in his eyes when I told him that we would have a look at a longhouse nearby then move off southwest tomorrow after our meal. This excited him. When he said he was going on northeast I felt he was lying and that is why we tracked him. He jinked down southwards and alerted the nearest Indonesian forces. I overheard their conversation and at dawn tomorrow the enemy will move to an ambush position using the lower track thinking they will ambush us as we move along this top one. So, what we will do is to move to the area now at best speed on this track and when we see where the other track joins ours we will set up our own Claymore ambush, arrange the tripwires and move back north. Hot and hard work but that's our task.'

'On the track, Sahib, not to one side?' Sergeant Kulbahadur asked.

'Yes. I heard them say there were neither civilians nor troops in the area. I know it's a risk but we should be safe. If anyone were to see our tracks, it will merely confirm what I told the civilian.'

They moved off southwest leaving the longhouse unvisited.

Lieutenant Sumbi received the report about the Gurkha patrol led by the one-time Commandant of the Border Scouts and gave his orders to a platoon of his 600 Raider Company. 'You know where you took up ambush positions only a couple of days ago, don't you?'

Yes, of course they did.

'Well, at dawn tomorrow you will return there and take up the same positions and by, say half-past eleven, some enemy will walk into it. Kill them all except the tall English officer. I need him. As soon as I hear the firing I'll come and tell you what to do with the bodies. Any questions or queries?'

No, there never were with Sumbi: it was worth nobody's while to ask.

Ninety sweaty minutes later the Gurkhas met up with the other track. Orders were given: a quick area recce to see if all was clear then assemble the Claymore mines facing towards the enemy's direction. It took only a few minutes to fix up one Claymore on each side of the track with a trip wire cunningly hidden attached to both mines. 'Before you put the primers in, I'll go ahead and view where you've put them,' said Jason. He made a shallow deviation so as to keep the area track-free and viewed where the Claymores had been sited. One needed to be hidden better so a small bush was uprooted and planted in front of it as living camouflage. Only then were the weapons primed and the safety catches removed. Finally any obvious man-made signs were obliterated. Jason took his compass out and ordered them to move north. Off they went. *We should be successful unless an animal sets the Claymores off before the Indons get there*, most of the Gurkhas thought.

By then it was later than he had hoped and Jason was in two minds about stopping and sending the obligatory sitrep or going on out of the reach of any Indon patrol before nightfall. *On for another twenty minutes and we'll stop at the next running water after that* he decided but, suddenly, they found themselves in a belt of country completely different from that which they had encountered so far. It was a vast expanse of long grass with hundreds of water buffaloes grazing on it with just one clump of trees about half a mile on. Dumbstruck, Jason and his men gawped at it: there could be no clean water amidst innumerable buffaloes and only one place to hide so too obvious for safety.

'This is what we must do,' Jason said to his men. 'Back a short way is a stream. Drink all your water then go and refill your water bottles. We'll use that for cooking. No one would ever think we'd hide in that clump of trees so that's where we'll go. Quickly now, there're only a few minutes of daylight left. Here, take the radio operator's and my water bottle. We'll go ahead and send our sitrep.'

Back in base the Company 2IC told the duty radio operator to continue tapping first the one patrol's call sign then the other's as both sitreps were overdue. There was an air of unease: the first cross-border venture with the OC, the area 'alive' and no communication with either patrol. What had happened?

A phone call came from the Brigade Duty Officer. 'The Brigadier wants to know why you have not sent any sitrep of your Sunray's efforts this first full day of his operation.'

The Company 2IC answered by saying 'So far we have not had anything from either patrol.'

'Any idea what's wrong?'

'How can I have? No.'

In the short dusk the signaller put the aerial up and tuned the radio. By the light of the dial Jason made a stab at their position and wrote the grid reference on a message pad. 'Send "All well. NTR",' he said. 'It's too dark to make out a coded message even though we are in enemy territory.'

The men returned with all water bottles full and, making sure that as little light as possible from the fires could be seen, cooked and ate their meal. Before bedding down for the night, Jason told his men to gather around. 'You've done well and we've reacted properly to the unexpected. Sentries will do duty only for forty-five minutes each. Reveille tomorrow morning will be at 0430 hours. At dawn we will pack up and move back north as fast as we can into cover. There is nowhere to hide here and the enemy has aircraft. Once we have reached the jungle at the bottom of the high ground, we'll have our morning brew. Any points, anyone?'

Sergeant Kulbahadur answered for them. 'Sahib, without

your language knowledge our position would have been far worse than it is.'

Some time after the Gurkha Para patrols had set off they heard an explosion to their south. *Can only be the Claymore mines. Men or animals?* they asked themselves. The answer had to be 'men' as by midday, when they were halfway up the high ground on their way towards the border, they heard the rumbling, grinding noise of a large helicopter approaching and the lighter noise of its fighter escort. The fighter circled around at the base of the high ground where they had skirted a heli pad and the noise of the heli itself changed as it settled on the ground. Half a minute later it rose and flew south before settling down once more. *Picking up casualties?* The fighter plane circled above it before it took off again.

Jason reckoned that even if the troops, probably not more than a platoon, came up behind them at full speed, an unlikely contingency, it would take them a minimum of two hours by which time, throwing caution to the winds, they themselves would probably be over the border.

In the event they saw neither hide nor hair of any Indons following them and they crossed the border in safety by mid-afternoon. At the Gurkha battalion they relaxed with a meal and a wash. Jason sent his sitrep and asked for air evacuation on the morrow.

Sumbi and his two officers heard the explosion. They themselves had no similar weapon so the noise had to come from the enemy. Fretting about casualties they ordered an escort to go with them and, making all speed along the track in the direction of the noise they had heard, were devastated to see bleeding, limping men coming towards them. *Outwitted again, blast that Saitan. He has eyes and ears but no body.*

'What happened?' Sumbi asked.

'There was an explosion and half of our men are dead. There are wounded men lying there and only a few of us are walking wounded,' the senior man said. 'We saw no traces of any enemy.'

Sumbi swore out loud. He ordered Alif and Zai to go forward, render what aid they could while he returned to send a medical team back to help and 'I will ask HQ on a follow-up party and get the heli to evacuate our own wounded at the same time. Those Gurkhas can't be all that far away. We'll get them before they cross the border.'

Next morning a message awaited Major Rance from Commander Central Brigade: 'Major Rance to report to him immediately on his return.'

Before he went to Brigade HQ, Jason had a haircut and put on his No 3 Dress that he had brought with him in case he had to meet the Sultan. There was no point in going badly turned out to one's own funeral. It was a tight-lipped and angry Brigadier who upbraided the OC Gurkha Para Company after being given a full version of events. 'I told you not to be a "cowboy" and that is what you were. Not only that I understand that one of your sitreps was late, it was also in clear, not in code. You have disobeyed our most stringent orders. I don't care why you did it, but do it you did,' he fumed, not in the best English, glaring balefully at his subordinate miscreant, as though he were trying not to fart but, in fact, looking for nails to put into Jason's military coffin. 'You behaved like an over-age subaltern suffering from an "it-can't-happen-to-me" complex,' and the angry man gave a snarl of a self-satisfied smirk. There is no one as stubborn as a Catholic at odds with his conscience. *If he'd been a priest of mine I'd have had him delated.*

Jason, gritting his teeth, jaw muscles a-throb and mentally counting to ten, stood to attention in front of him, a blank look on his face and said nothing. *When I joined the army this would have been 'dumb insolence'* he thought but he also knew that suspension of empathy was part of a leader's training and task. 'On meeting that civilian, your job was to have returned without risking the lives of your men. I'd have sent you over the border a few days later.' He paused, slightly surprised at himself and at Jason's silence. 'Have you anything to say, to defend your actions?'

'No sir, nothing,' *especially to a rabbit in a leopard skin.*

'Then you are dismissed with a warning. There'll be no next time as I am forbidding you from going on any more cross-border operations.'

Dear God! Save me from over-promoted military misfits, Jason saluted and left the Brigadier's office with a show of military dignity his superior did not deserve. Fuming as he went back to his company lines, even an hour's hard basketball didn't make him feel any better. The aphorism *fair-weather soldiers make gloomy regimental histories* was one he had always stood by.

Thinking about the Brigadier's tirade, Jason felt it was probably because where he, Jason, had learnt to think outside himself, to keep death and injury from his soldiers whenever possible, 'to stand up and be counted', to react to the unexpected; those like the ex-prisoner-of-war Brigadier could not do this with people from other countries, found themselves ill-attuned to be amongst them so somehow had to 'let off steam' to compensate for this inadequacy. Jason tried to shrug the unfairness of his tongue-lashing but he was still simmeringly angry about it when, a couple of months later, more action drove the nag out of his mind.

It so happened that the Gurkha Para Company patrol with 1/12 GR at Ba Kelalan was Sergeant Kulbahadur's and the CO sent it out to see if it could get any definite news of the strong rumour that Sumbi had, at last, crossed border into Sarawak. They patrolled up to the border, hoping to pick up any signs. The Sergeant saw something on the jungle floor glint but took no notice of it – many things with a speck of dew on them glint in the early morning sun. On their way back, approaching from the other direction, he spotted it again. Curious, because had it been dew it would have dried out long before, he examined it. It turned out to be a small piece of foil, smelling of coffee. Coffee was not a feature of Gurkha rations; British troops might, for all he knew, have coffee in theirs, but there were no British troops within miles. It therefore had to be Indonesians.

The patrol cast around a while and did discover tracks for two or three men – but the tracks were of British Army jungle boots. There followed an extraordinarily patient and expert piece of tracking: from midday on a Tuesday through to the Thursday, these five men slowly and inexorably tracked the footprints. For two nights they did not make camp or cook anything, fearing that the noise and the smell might give them away. It is cold at night in the Borneo uplands.

On the third day their patience was rewarded – they found not only the three pairs of jungle boots but sacking – to tie round the footwear so as not to leave any distinguishable marks – for over forty-five people. How right they were not to have relaxed their precautions. Having established that their quarry had indeed continued northwards only a short time before, they opened their set and gave a full report, confirmation of the incursion at long last, to their tactical commander, the CO of 1/12 GR and to Para Company HQ.

Initially the report was scarcely believed by 1/12 GR so, to make doubly certain, the patrol was ordered to backtrack: they led to where the fifty Indons had crossed the border over a lonely, high and cold, jungle-covered ridge between Ba Kelalan and Long Semado.

Major General Walter Sprinter and his staff came into their own, bringing in more units as the operation expanded from an augmented brigade operation to a fully-fledged divisional affair so the recalcitrant Brigadier Gloop was virtually sidestepped tactically. Tracks of Sumbi and his gang were found, followed up, lost and found again – numerous times. The country was exceptionally rugged and radio communications became difficult to maintain, so control was never easy.

Towards the end of the chase the country was viler than it had been; after two weeks of cliff hanging, river crossing and slow tracking, twenty-four enemy were eliminated. By dint of tight planning, clever debriefing and flexible deployment, success was achieved after more than a month with some of the raiders surrendering while the corpses of others who had died of starvation were discovered. Eventually only four men were unaccounted for. Threats to Brunei's oil supplies were thought to be no more, nor were any of the other planned activities Jason had pre-warned about.

During the operation Indonesia and Malaysia started once more to talk about peace and, before the last four of Sumbi's men were accounted for, signed some sort of peace deal so Confrontation was officially over and everyone in Eastern Malaysia – Sarawak and Sabah – had to return to and stay in their base camps, waiting for orders for the peacetime pullout. As the Gurkha Para Company was not in Malaysia but in Brunei these ceasefire orders did not apply, so the company was still operational. The Brunei Government wanted to know if the last four of Sumbi's gang had, in fact, infiltrated into Brunei or had died in the Sarawak jungle. In an area of wild country that could have been anything up to two thousand five hundred square miles, the odds against finding four men were infinitely remote. Nevertheless a patrol commander by Sergeant Kulbahadur Limbu was sent to the border of Brunei and Sarawak, a ridge of hilly jungle, to see what it could pick up. One of the soldiers needed evacuating and, pressure of other duties off, Jason flew in to take his place. He still had the ID cards of the two Indons in his pocket and he knew that both Sergeant Kulbahadur Limbu and Rifleman Hemraj Rai carried their erstwhile badges.

Jason was put as number 4 in the patrol and off they went

along the border ridge. The jungle was dark and damp. It had been raining. As always they travelled slowly, keeping eyes skinned. And then Hemé saw it – one single leaf caught his eye in that it had an unnatural crease making its outline straight. He called the patrol commander's attention: it surely could only mean one thing. Unbelievably, one chance in how many zillions, seemed to indicate that they would meet up again. Foot prints for four men were found.

The patrol pushed on, passed the night as quietly as possible, and, the following day, espied four weary men sitting round a fire cooking a meal.

'Sahib, do your magic just once more,' urged Kulbahadur.

'Yes, sahib, otherwise it will be wasted,' softly said someone else.

Jason wondered, *yes or no? Yes, why not?* 'Kulé and Hemé come behind me. I'm going to make a detour. You other two move over there,' and he indicated where with his chin, 'ready to give us covering fire.'

So intent were the four Indons – Jason only recognised 'his' two – with their cooking that they heard nothing until that taunting, flaunting voice was heard once more in the bushes, at times to one side, at times to the other. 'Lieutenants Hassan and Soetidjab, hungry for food now are you, eh, not for me?'

The four tired, hungry and dejected Indons were utterly flabbergasted to say the least of it, one dropping the cooking pot he was holding. Zai staggered to his feet, all fight gone, staring into the bushes. *That voice again, falsetto not treble, Malay not Indonesian.* 'Can't see you, you Saitan bitch,' he croaked.

'Do you want to surrender to a voice or to a person?'

'After all we've done? Surrender? Are you mad?'

'No, you are. Drop you rifle. All of you lay down your arms,' came the proper voice of Jason and, calling the two flank men of his patrol to cover him, he and his two men stepped out into the open, weapons aimed at the Indons. They stood up. 'You two, you are incorrectly dressed. Where are you badges of rank?' and, turning to his two men, 'Show them,' he ordered.

The effect was almost electrical in its intensity.

'Do you want them back? Or shall we keep them as souvenirs?'

Mixed oaths and imprecations followed.

'Quiet. Look at this,' Jason ordered and, deliberately, he opened his top pocket and took out two Indonesian Army ID cards. 'Recognise these do you?' he taunted. 'Do you want them back or is it too late?'

Alif and Zai threw themselves at Jason but his two men were ready and tripped them as they passed so they fell headlong and breathless, the fight wiped out of them. As though bewitched, seeing their two comrades lying dormant on the ground, the other two surrendered.

Jason told the radio operator to open his set and send a message to Company HQ to send a vehicle to the nearest road head with an escort, take them directly to Brigade HQ and to let the Commander know that the last four men had been captured.

Konfrontasi had come to an end, 'not with a bang but a whimper'.

Jason wrote a report about the incident, glossing over his

individual actions. He also put Sergeant Kulbahadur Limbu in for the award of the DCM when names were called for. The Brigadier wondered if Major Rance's name should be included but decided against it: *he didn't play much part in the actual fighting did he?* he confided to himself, *and anyway, medals aren't for cowboys.*

At the investiture ceremony at the British High Commission in Singapore, Major General Sprinter, the erstwhile DOBOPS, met Jason who had gone there as one of the two people each recipient was allowed to take, Sergeant Kulbahadur Limbu's wife being the other person. 'I never asked you how on earth did you manage to do it?' he asked.

Jason considered his answer for a long moment. 'Sir, we had fewer blind spots than did they.'

The General then bent over and said, 'Rance, I'm really sorry your name didn't come up for any award. You've got nothing for all your efforts.'

Jason looked the General fully in the face. 'Sir, I have everything: self-esteem and the respect, loyalty and confidence of my soldiers. There are no blind spots with my Gurkhas!'

REFERENCES AND HISTORICAL NOTES

For those with an interest in the historical background for the **first part** of this book (for instance details of Comrade Aidit's Thailand visit) their attention is drawn to:

Chin Peng, *MY SIDE OF HISTORY*, Media Masters, Singapore, 2003, ISBN: 981-04-8693-6; and

Leon Comber, *MALAYA'S SECRET POLICE 1945-60*, Monash University Press, Australia, 2008, ISBN: 9781876924522 and Institute of Southeast Asian Studies (ISEAS), Singapore, 2008, ISBN: 978-981-230-815-3 (Paperback) and 978-981-230-829-0 (Hardback).

A number of Gurkha soldiers were stranded in foreign countries after the war, Thailand, Burma, Malaya, Dutch East Indies (taken there by the Japanese as labourers) and even Japan. An article, *Nepalese Community on the Thai/Burma Border*, written by Captain W P Davis 7 GR, was published in the Brigade of Gurkhas journal, *KUKRI*, 1969 edition.

The esoteric belief that Limbus will be saved by a 'white man' is not widely promulgated, seldom talked about or specific in context but has deep roots.

Christian missionaries in Southeast Asia were a mixed bunch. In Laos certainly in one area Buddhism was feared more than Communism: in Borneo various shades of Christianity divided the country up between themselves and virtually took over from the government in running affairs.

The village of Ha La, in map square VE 2126, was no longer traceable when this book was written.

The Indonesian Army did in real life make a parachute assault in Peninsular Malaysia, in Johor State.

The Chinese song 'Green Plum and a Bamboo Horse' was an extremely popular number at one time, sung between a boy and a girl with lascivious glances, winks and smiles to the greatest acclaim by all audiences. It was based on a poem by the revered Li Po, a T'ang Dynasty bard of great fame. (The author is grateful to his friend, Mr A J V ('Gus') Fletcher, OBE, GM for this esoteric gem, made more famous by being sung publicly by him to a rapturous audience.)

For the **second part** there is a wealth of publications for Commonwealth troops. From the Indonesian side the following two only are mentioned:

General Abdul Haris Nasution, *FUNDAMENTALS OF GUERRILLA WARFARE*, Praeger, New York, 1965; and

Dipa Nusantara Aidit, *THE SELECTED WORKS OF D N AIDIT (2 VOLS), WASHINGTON, US JOINT PUBLICATIONS RESEARCH SERVICE, 1961.*

Lieutenant Sumbi of 600 Raider Company, Indonesian Army, obtained a B grading on a Jungle Warfare course at the British Army's Jungle Warfare School at Kota Tinggi, Johor State, Malaya, and his British Army's parachute 'wings' after his basic course at the Parachute School at Abingdon, UK. It is not know if the Gurkha Captain, Phatbahadur Sunwar of 1/7 GR, nearest but one to him at his capture, who only got a C grading, was contemporaneously at the Jungle Warfare School with Sumbi. If not, how did he know, which he did, about Sumbi's B grading?

The first and only Commandant of the Border Scouts did have his photograph taken on arrival and put on leaflets to be placed on border crossings in the First and Second Divisions: there was also a radio announcement. Shortly after he left Borneo Radio Pontianak broadcast his death on its English language news programme and the *Sarawak Gazette* published it – prematurely – as he saw for himself when he read it!

At the end of British colonial rule when turbulence could be expected, paratroops from England could not be brought in quickly enough to prevent hostile forces from occupying an airhead if such an action was needed so the Gurkha Independent Parachute Company was raised as an 'in-theatre' resource. Because of *Konfrontasi*, the company was organised as a Patrol Company, comprising up to fourteen 5-man patrols to operate ahead of main forces to gather intelligence. It was also constantly ready for its parachuting role. Its lowest priority was to act as an infantry company but without any weapon heavier than a sub-machine gun. Its deployment as leading Border Scout sections was one that was never originally envisaged but, under the special circumstances pertaining at the time, it was the only unit capable of being so deployed. Without it *Konfrontasi* could well have made a greater disturbance than it did.

'Claret' was the 'top secret' code word for cross-border operations. These were strictly controlled at the very highest level and planned only against specific targets and always with a deniable cover plan. No unit was allowed to go on such operations during their first tour. Malaysia was due to come into being on 31 August 1966 but because of marked hostility against the project, a United Nations Organisation team was sent to assess the situation before certifying the new nation, arriving after 31 August. Before the team arrived many malcontents were put behind bars. For two weeks until 16 September there was no government as the colonial Governors of Sarawak and British North Borneo had left on 30 August and new functionaries were not in existence until 16 September. There was never a better time for Sukarno to take advantage of such a situation yet take it he did not. And who, illegally, incarcerated those malcontents? If they had known that their arrest was illegal, there being no extant Authority to incarcerate them, how would the situation have developed? An intriguing 'what if'.

The last of Sumbi's group was only found, traced and caught by one folded leaf dropped on the ground. The perpetrator admitted that that and snapping twigs were ingrained habits.

On 7 December 1966, *The Times* published an account of the Sumbi incursion, it was headlined 'Courage of the Gurkhas Foiled Saboteurs' and it continued 'Details of one of the most brilliant actions in the history of Gurkhas have just been released

...' and went on to describe the meticulous attention to detail of 21149993 Rifleman Dharmalal Rai, 10 GR, Gurkha Independent Parachute Company, when he sniffed the tinfoil that smelt of coffee ...

The 1st Rutland Regiment never existed. The unit who actually did behave in the manner described has long been amalgamated into a larger regiment.

Your author was both at the Savoy Hotel, London on 21 October 1960 when the Army Board gave an official dinner to King Mahendra and also with the patrol that found 'that' leaf. He was told that the Army's computer did not have Temiar as a language when he passed the Malayan Government's examination.

And finally, your author also witnessed the defanging of a krait. During the monsoon of 1946, at Kamthi, Nagpur, Central Provinces, India, Naik Gambhir Ghale, the Motor Platoon storeman of 1/1 Gurkha Rifles, defanged a krait in the same way as has been described in the narrative.